# WELCOME
## TO THE

**ALSO BY FRANK NAPPI**

*The Legend of Mickey Tussler*

*Sophomore Campaign*

# WELCOME

## TO THE

## A MICKEY TUSSLER NOVEL

# FRANK NAPPI

Sky Pony Press
New York

Sky Pony Press books may be purchased in bulk at special discounts for sales promotion, corporate gifts, fund-raising, or educational purposes. Special editions can also be created to specifications. For details, contact the Special Sales Department, Sky Pony Press, 307 West 36th Street, 11th Floor, New York, NY 10018 or info@skyhorsepublishing.com.

Sky Pony® is a registered trademark of Skyhorse Publishing, Inc.®, a Delaware corporation.

Visit our website at www.skyponypress.com.

10 9 8 7 6 5 4 3 2 1

Library of Congress Cataloging-in-Publication Data is available on file.

Cover design by Sarah Brody
Cover photo credit iStock

Print ISBN: 978-1-63450-829-2
Ebook ISBN: 978-1-63450-834-6

Printed in the United States of America

*For Julia, Nick, and Anthony*

*And for my father, Francis Nappi, whose undaunted spirit and love of the game continue to inspire me*

# AUTHOR'S NOTE

Note to baseball historians: certain artistic liberties have been taken with regard to names, timelines, and the chronology of other baseball occurrences in order to facilitate the telling of this story.

"Baseball is an allegorical play about America, a poetic, complex, and subtle play of courage, fear, good luck, mistakes, patience about fate, and sober self-esteem."

—SAUL STEINBERG

# WELCOME

## TO THE

# THE BEE HIVE—OCTOBER 1949

The massive ballpark that stood on Commonwealth Avenue in Boston was a far cry from the quaint, intimate confines of Milwaukee's Borchert Field. Braves Field, or "the Bee Hive" as some still liked to call it, was a cavernous playground, a forty-thousand-seat venue with a rolling expanse of fresh green grass and fences that stretched out some four hundred feet away from home plate, where prospective suitors clad in decorative flannel would sidle up to the pentagon-shaped dish to take their hacks, carrying with them only a carefully treated hunk of Louisville lumber and lofty visions of clearing the impossibly distant barrier. It was most certainly a pitcher's paradise, the place where many a fly ball went to die, and in the organization's estimation, the perfect place for a young man like Mickey Tussler to shine. Mickey had dominated for two years with the minor league affiliate Brewers, and despite his idiosyncrasies and slowness of mind—two things that engendered much talk about the quizzical farm boy turned baseball prodigy—he was ready for the next step.

"Well, what do you think of your new home, Mick?" Murph asked, staring hypnotically at a thick ribbon of black smoke unfolding above the row of fir trees just beyond the center field fence.

"Sure is big, Mr. Murphy," the young man said, his heart racing. He was mesmerized by the sizable numbers on the sixty-eight-foot scoreboard towering over left field. Lester, who was standing next to Mickey with his hand on the boy's shoulder, was equally impressed. "Mickey never saw such a big place. When do we move in?" Murph laughed. His heart was aflutter as well. It had taken the baseball lifer too many years to get back to the bigs. He had endured so much disappointment. A playing career cut short due to a freakish injury. A dozen consecutive seasons at the helm of the Brew Crew, all of which had resulted in the hapless band of baseball misfits finishing in the bowels of the standings. And most recently, two very productive seasons with the new-look Brewers, both which ended with unforgivable losses to the Rangers and their manager, Chip McNally, Murph's nemesis. It looked as though he would never get back. But the Braves owner, James Gaffney, liked what Murph was doing. There was a fire in Murph's eyes, an insatiable yearning for excellence and victory that few others possessed. Gaffney also knew that it was Murph, and only Murph, who could get the most out of their quirky sensation, Mickey, as well as his battery mate, the recently acquired Negro League standout, Lester Sledge.

"Yes, it's big, Mick," Murph replied. "That's the idea, kiddo— ain't a player been born yet that's gonna hurt you in this ballpark."

Lester nodded, marginally considering the implications that the new layout would have on his own game. "You ain't just whistling 'Dixie,' Murph," he said. "And with them stiff winds whipping in off the Charles River, it'd be nothing short of a miracle if anything got anywhere near our boys out there."

It was quite a place. All three men meandered deliberately about the park, mouths agape, in awe—as if treading on hallowed ground. They walked the base paths in dramatic pantomime, attaching each step to some fantastic moment that had already unfurled with breathless wonder in their minds' eyes.

The outfield was also vast and awesome, and each man dragged his feet across the lush green carpet that stretched from one foul pole to the other, savoring every step as if somehow it was to be his last. After listening to the sacred voices of the past that continued to whisper excitement and endless possibilities from every corner, they finally came together on the meticulously manicured bump that stood sixty feet, six inches from home plate and sighed in unison.

"Is there anything closer to heaven, fellas, than a ballpark?" Murph asked.

Having satisfied their hunger for the diamond aesthetics, the trio made their way from the pitcher's mound to the home dugout. They descended the steps, taking one final look at the cavernous park from their new vantage point before finally finding their way into the locker room. Once inside, Murph felt himself leaving his feet, as though buoyed by some mystical force. It was certainly surreal. His entire life had been a quest for this very moment—the chance to manage a big league club. After all these years, his chance had arrived.

"Welcome to the show, fellas," he beamed, arms outstretched in a most public display of effusive rapture. "It don't get any better than this."

Mickey was equally captivated. Sure, he was wondering what was happening back home—where his mom was and what she was doing. He calculated to the best of his ability how many carrots remained for Duncan and Daphney, his beloved rabbits. He also tried to determine, based on the harvest moon that had shone so brightly, the degree of life that remained in the leaves of the trees just outside his window—brilliant bursts of burnt orange clinging desperately to the branches of the towering sycamores along the gravel drive as the car pulled away just days before. There was so much to think about, most which eventually faded as he perused the nameplates on the gray metal doors in the October afternoon light that faintly lit the concrete walls of the moribund locker room.

MARSHALL—BICKFORD—ELLIOT—HOLMES

He ran his hand across each nameplate, tracing the letters with the tip of his finger.

CHIPMAN—OZMORE—SPAHN—SAIN

As he continued to outline each letter in almost surgical fashion, he couldn't help but think of Boxcar, and how the burly catcher—the team's leader and his mentor—would have loved to have seen it

3

all. He had told Mickey on so many occasions that all he wanted to do was get some Boston dirt on his cleats before he hung them up for good.

"That's why we're all still here, Mick," he explained one afternoon after practice. They were both sitting in front of Boxcar's locker, Mickey prattling on about how he just could not understand how old some of the guys on the team were. He scratched his head and peppered the fiery backstop with all sorts of questions while Boxcar sat relatively quiet, staring blankly into the cold metal box as if it were some sort of a magical window to the future.

"It'll happen, Mick," he whispered with clear determination. "Yup. You'll see. One day, old number fifteen will be sitting in the bean town locker room, with all those other important muckity mucks."

Mickey moved from locker to locker, frowning as he recalled Boxcar's proclamation. His mood worsened as he considered that his good friend had never realized his dream. It had been cancer, whatever that was. That's what they told him. Mickey still could not understand how something could destroy such a strong body—and why doctors could not "fix" him.

"But why can't the doctor make Boxcar better with some medicine?" he had kept asking Molly and Murph after the secret was out. He must have asked them that same question a thousand times during Boxcar's silent battle before surrendering briefly to the devastating reality of what he was told. But when it was all over, and the Brewer icon had finally been laid to rest, Mickey resumed his incessant barrage of questions, as if somehow asking would eventually bring back his beloved friend.

Boxcar's death had been the darkest hour of Mickey's life. It was the first time he had ever experienced such a loss and it really threw him for a loop. He couldn't eat, was restless at night, and even lost his desire to be with his animals. Mickey struggled on the mound as well, as did the entire team. Both the loss of Boxcar and Mickey's subsequent tailspin seemed to infect them all.

It was only after Lester Sledge began to make his mark on a league that did not want him that the young phenom regained his old form. The chiseled African American came to the Brew Crew under a firestorm of controversy, spawned by Murph's unpopular decision to replace Boxcar, who was a Milwaukee icon, with a player from the Negro Leagues.

Despite Lester's success on the field, the catcher's early days with the Brewers was marred by many incidents of violence and hatred, some of which threatened to destroy the entire season. Mickey struggled to understand. Why did some people hate Lester so much and want to hurt him — just because his skin was a little darker than theirs? It made Mickey sick and he had trouble getting past it. Murph and Molly spent many nights explaining prejudice to Mickey and had actually made some headway. But when Mickey made the horrifying discovery that one of their own — pitcher Gabby Hooper — was involved in a planned attack on Lester, Murph and Molly were at a loss for words.

Despite all the threats, Lester persevered and eventually won over most of his early critics. He managed to make believers out of even the most staunch cynics and was rewarded for his outstanding efforts with a major league contract with the Boston Braves. The same was true for Mickey, whose spirit was instantly buoyed by his new battery mate's personal resolve and on-field exploits; he soon began to dominate the pitcher's mound again, and turned in a most magical season, one that saw the young fireballer shatter all sorts of minor league records en route to his call up to the big club.

That was all just months before, although now it seemed like a lifetime ago. As Mickey continued to peruse the row of lockers, he couldn't help but feel a little off, as if he were somehow betraying Boxcar. It made him sad — so sad that the swell of tears that had begun to form behind his eyes would have rushed to the surface, revealing themselves to his new world with explosive clatter had he not noticed something truly incredible — something so indescribable that he could scarcely contain his enthusiasm. In between the gray metal doors that read JETHROE and SLEDGE were the familiar letters that until now had always spelled nothing but trouble. It was certainly not easy being him. He could still hear his father's caustic words as if the surly farmer was standing right next to him.

"Ain't nothin' right about you, boy," his father always ranted. "I'll be damned if I can figger out where such a numbskull like you come from. I gots a reputation to hold here boy. And yer babbling and stupid shenanigans are pinching me. Damn sin that yer walking 'round with the name Tussler, that's for shit sure. Hell if I can figger it." He was free from Clarence now—thanks to Molly—who, with the help of Murph, managed to muster the strength to leave her husband and start a new life for her and Mickey. Yes, Mickey was free, but the memories lingered and were brought into focus again each time he met somebody new; there were always the same stares, the side commentary, and of course, the laughter. There was always laughter.

It used to upset him more when he was younger, but with time, he had come to accept the fact that he was "different" or "special," as Molly always told him, and that he would be treated as such. That's why the nameplate that bore his identity was such a wonderful sight; it was just like everyone else's. He was mesmerized by the letters, using both hands now to touch them as if doubting their existence— like if he did not press his fingers against each letter and hold them there, they would just disappear.

He marveled at how white they were and was pleased that they were arranged so neatly and in capitals: TUSSLER. He always liked capitals—the way they looked like blocks, each one occupying equal space. When Molly first taught him to write, she carefully explained the difference between upper- and lowercase letters. She even used his favorite poem, "Silver," as a model. He understood what she was saying and tried to use both lower- and uppercase whenever he practiced. He accomplished this for a while, but he found that his thoughts flowed much more freely when he blocked out each line with all capitals—exactly the way his name read now on his locker. He was smiling at the fabulous letters when Murph walked up behind him.

"Whatcha doing there, Mick?" he asked.

The young man turned his head slightly and looked over his shoulder, but his hands remained affixed to the awesome sight.

"Mickey is just looking around," he answered. "Looking around."

Murph laughed. "That's quite a locker there, huh? It sure is," he continued. "It's *all* pretty incredible. The whole place. Far cry from what we've been living with at Borchert Field, right?"

Mickey nodded. He felt all funny inside, like little fish were swimming inside his stomach. Murph placed his hand on Mickey's shoulder and patted gently.

"Listen, while Lester is busy with all of his stuff, why don't you take a walk with me and check out my new office, Mick?" Murph said, guiding the young man away from his present fixation. "Sure could use a hand getting things set up before the other guys start rolling in."

Mickey, still spellbound, was wondering now about the faces that would soon be attached to all the names he had read. The thought turned his mood a little; he felt a bit uneasy, like he had to wait right where he was—right there—for the others. But Murph convinced him with words and gentle prodding, and soon enough—with Mickey looking over his shoulder once or twice—the two of them were walking side by side down the runway to Murph's new digs.

Murph and Mickey spent the better part of the next hour cleaning up, moving things around, and organizing the big mahogany desk that now bore the name ARTHUR MURPHY—MANAGER. Mickey was only too glad to help, delighting in the orderly arrangement of all the implements germane to Murph's new venture. Mickey looked at the desktop as though it were a jigsaw puzzle—and began arranging everything Murph could possibly need with that same surgical precision. Rolodex and stapler were placed on the left, along with a tiny penknife and a neat row of rubber erasers. On the right rested two caramel-colored wooden rulers, a stack of lineup cards, and three rolls of transparent tape. And directly in the center, placed equidistant from the crystal paperweight Molly had given him for good luck and a decorative tin filled with paper clips, was a Milwaukee Brewers beer stein equipped with an arsenal of freshly sharpened pencils. When it was all finished, Mickey looked at his masterpiece and smiled.

There were other things to tend to as well, of far less importance, and Mickey helped with those too. The floor needed sweeping, the shelves were dusty and disordered, and the three chairs placed before the desk were in no shape for visitors. The two worked dutifully on all three tasks.

Once everything was in its appointed place, Murph addressed the entire team for the first time. He had been preparing this speech for days but still was not confident that he had found just the right words. His fragmented thoughts and tremulous voice were indicative of the strain under which he now operated. The room appeared a lot smaller now.

"Uh, I know it's not baseball season yet, and that we all just finished for the year, but I called you all here today just so we could, uh, meet each other and perhaps talk about the upcoming season. I'm sure some of you have a few questions. You know, on my way here today, I was thinking about—"

As he prattled on, he recognized that many of the faces looking back at him were incredulous at best. He could see several of his new charges, most of whom he had never met formally before, yawning and rolling their eyes. A couple were even snickering. He did his best to ignore what was painfully obvious and managed to trudge on, but his foremost thought was fear over the dire necessity of immediately gaining respect and control.

"Look, I know that most of you have grown accustomed to the way Billy Southworth does things, and I can understand that. I'm not trying to make any of you forget about him. He's a great baseball guy. But he's not here right now, and we are, and we need to figure out how we're going to get this thing done."

The strained silence was fast becoming a sort of initiation into a world where even Murph's most passionate, compelling arguments would likely be rendered moot.

"What happened to Billy anyway?" asked one of the players who was standing in the shadows in the back of the room. His arms were folded and he had his head propped up against the wall behind him. Only the lower half of his face was visible in the dim light. "None of us heard anything about any of this until a few days ago."

"I'm afraid Mr. Southworth is ill at the present time," Murph responded. "I'm sorry, but that's all I know."

A low, unremitting murmur ignited and rose steadily to a disquieting level, culminating with another question from a different part of the room.

"So that's it?" the gravelly voice announced in a peremptory tone. "Billy is sick, and you show up? Just like that. Who the hell are you anyway? And what makes you think that you can come in here and—"

Murph was just about to fire back when a tremulous yet determined voice beat him to it.

"Mr. Murphy is . . . is the best, the best coach . . . um . . . baseball coach, there is," Mickey said with significant alarm. His face was hot and flushed and appeared distorted from the dim illumination thrown from the frosted lamps; the faint light lingered on the beads of sweat that had begun their descent down both sides of his face.

"You oughtn't say mean things about Mr. Murphy," Mickey continued. "He taught Mickey how to play baseball. Taught me real good."

The entire room grew still. Then, out of this silence that immediately followed Mickey's impassioned defense came more derision.

"That's right, Coops," Buddy Ozmore announced. "You is a bad boy. Now you listen to Lennie over there, and stop bothering that nice Mr. Murphy. After all, he is the best baseball coach you know."

Laughter erupted among the others.

Mickey's eyes drooped. His lower lip sagged as well. "My name is not Lennie," he said once the snickering waned. "It's Mickey. Mickey Tussler."

The laughter grew louder.

"Naw, I'm pretty sure that your name is Lennie," Ozmore continued. "And since you are Lennie, that means that either your coach over there or that colored fellow you came in with would have to be George."

9

Mickey folded his arms and began to rock uneasily. He looked to the left, then to the right as some of the other players joined the assault, peppering the tense air with derisive comments like *"It's only a mouse, George"* and *"That's good, George. You take a good big drink."* The room erupted once again in riotous laughter.

Mickey was beginning to crumble. His rocking escalated considerably and he had already begun the catatonic recitation of some lines from his favorite poem. The rising panic was reflected in the misery in Murph's face.

"Well, this is exactly the sort of start I was hoping for," Murph said with waves of self-deprecation. "Yes, sir. Absolutely perfect. You know, maybe you guys should—"

"Maybe *you* should just go back where you came from, mister," another player said. "Ain't no use for you here. And you can take your retard and his chocolate friend with you."

The attack hit Murph hard, like a sudden wave of seasickness. He swallowed hard and locked his knees for fear they might give way at any moment. Then, like a true sailor adrift in turbulent waters, he ignored the queasiness with the belief that in doing so, he would rid himself of the malady. He walked deliberately toward his attacker, hands firm at his sides, as if he were trying to steady his gait. His eyes were narrow, his breath hot.

"Your, uh, name is Marshall, right?" Murph asked.

The surly man nodded.

"Well, Mr. Marshall. Let me tell you something." Murph spoke louder now, turning to face the entire room. "Let me tell *all* of you something. This so called 'retard' here is hotter than a fox in a forest fire. He has one of the best, if not *the* best, arms baseball has ever seen." Murph made a point to find the eyes of the one they simply called the *Invincible One* before continuing. "No offense intended, Mr. Spahn," he went on. "You are some pitcher."

Murph licked his lips and drew a deep breath before continuing. "But Mickey here has obliterated just about every minor league record there is. He was virtually unhittable last season. He's a big boy and throws mighty hard. And I'm gonna bet ya, as sure as I'm standing here, that he could make each and every one of you hotshots swing and miss as well."

He paused and raised his eyebrows before removing the baseball from his jacket pocket. "Yup, I'm certain of it. Anyone wanna give it a go right now?"

No one responded.

Each man in the room remained fixed in his place—still and silent, frozen collectively like a row of birds perched on a telephone wire. The quiet made Murph smile and buoyed his resolve even further.

"That's what I thought," he continued. "And just so we are clear here about everything, this 'chocolate friend' of Mickey's here is also a good friend of *mine*. And he just might be the most talented damn baseball player I have ever seen. And with Sam Jethroe . . . uh, the Jet . . . we've got ourselves *two* of these so-called chocolate dandies. Now I don't know about you guys, but I'm pretty stoked about that. So before you go and get your jock straps all twisted about newbies and changes, consider that these two men you just met—Mickey and Lester—have just made your ball club—our ball club—that much better."

Murph was feeling better all of a sudden, like perhaps he had squelched an impromptu insurrection. He was never too adept at that sort of thing. In fact, he still blamed himself for the whole Lefty Rogers disaster. The fact that his carelessness had allowed Lefty to hurt Mickey—first that night at The Bucket and then again after Lefty had been traded to the Rangers—still stuck in his craw. He should have seen it coming. Now, standing in front of his new team, he felt good, like maybe he had grown some—like maybe he was ready for this.

That feeling, however, slipped away from him—like sand through his fingers—when a few rays of sunlight glinting through the top two slats of the metal blinds fell across a sea of silent faces—faces that were now stone-like and vacant—like souls in purgatory waiting for the culmination of their passage. The fever of discontent made Murph shiver, as did the afternoon shadows that began unspooling across the room.

Both unnerved the new manager, something that grew significantly worse once the insidious whispering became audible. Biting his lip, he faltered momentarily before regaining his composure.

"Well then," he said, shrugging his shoulders while offering his open palms to the group. "If there's nothing else—if nobody has anything else to say, then I guess we can assume that we are all in agreement."

The room was silent, save for the barely audible sound of some restless shoes scraping the cold floor. Murph forced a smile and tipped his cap. "So, enjoy the off-season, fellas. See you all this spring in Sanford."

# BEAN TOWN BLUES

Molly found herself thinking a lot about Diamond Drive and about the old house that stood modestly amid the wooded acres just a few miles from Borchert Field. When Murph first welcomed her and Mickey to the modest gray dwelling that looked as though it had been dropped indiscriminately in the middle of a pale grass field flanked by towering dead trees and restless tumbleweeds, she felt awkward and exposed. She was even embarrassed. It wasn't just because the place was a wreck and needed attention; it was that the place was *his* place and she and her son were merely guests.

"I don't know, Arthur," she struggled. "It's very kind of you. Really, it is. I'm just not sure it's right."

Murph respected her feelings from the very beginning, but he was persistent. She still was guarded and uncertain, but Murph's warmth and attention did much to alter that. His affection was soothing, and soon Molly's trepidation began to wane, particularly after her domestic touches—which included flower beds, tablecloths, and some fresh paint—altered the face of things dramatically.

"Wow, Molly," Murph gushed. "Will you just look at this place? This is incredible. Really, it is. And it's all you. Nobody's gonna recognize it."

Murph's genuine appreciation for her was like a tonic. Her heart was still on the mend and she needed some love and affection. As the weeks unfolded, Molly and Murph's relationship took off and blossomed into what was now a most wonderful union; Mickey benefited as well, thriving in the light of Murph's patience and guidance. It all happened so fast.

That modest place became their home, a haven from all that had plagued both of them for years. She had come a long way in such a short time. She was whole for the first time in her life and had only just begun getting accustomed to the feeling.

Now, in the flat moments after the move, when the stars from her sky seemed to be falling once again, she was unable to find any solace in unpacking crates and hanging curtains in their new place. She was left with nothing but time to think about the whirlwind that had swept her from the abusive hands of Clarence and the farm in Indiana to Murph's place in Milwaukee and now to the unfamiliar, bristling streets of Boston. It gave her the discomfort of one out of breath.

"Come on, Molly," Murph encouraged each time he caught a glimpse of her broken smile. "This is Boston. The big time. There is a whole world out there for us to grab."

She could not see it. Perhaps he was right, but her inability to embrace her new surroundings prevented any act of compliance. She was out of place for sure, and Arthur's flippancy, intentional or not, only exacerbated her despondency.

He had always been so intuitive, so attentive. He was her sunshine that followed the rain. No matter where he went or what he did, he could hear her heartbeat, smell her thoughts. These were his guides, his windows to her world. They had served him well. Until now.

"But what if this is just not right for me, Arthur?" she asked. "Or Mickey?" She shook her head as desperate tears formed behind her eyes. "What then?"

He stared at her blankly. A palpable awkwardness settled before them. He groped for something to say, something soothing and reassuring, while she lapsed into painful reminiscence, thinking of her first few days in Boston.

"This has not been an easy few weeks, Arthur," she said, dabbing the corners of her eyes. She had gotten lost on the wintry city streets on her way to the local hardware store. All she wanted to do was purchase some curtain rods and a few flowerpots for their new place, but the city seemed so vast and maze-like. Worse than her disorientation was the cold indifference with which she was greeted when she asked some locals on the street for help.

"Sorry," each person responded as the aloof mass of city dwellers stampeded right past her as if she were a ghost. "Can't help you."

She had never felt more alone. She retreated deeply into herself for days afterward. It was a loneliness she had no desire to revisit.

"I do not like the way I feel, Arthur," she said, struggling for breath. "Not at all."

He was trying to hear her over the locker room voices still echoing in his head.

"Come on, Molly," he responded. "Give it some time. We just got here. It's an adjustment, for sure. This is new for both of us. But you can do it. We can both do it. You need to just give it time."

Time was not something she cared to relinquish. She had already wasted enough. She knew herself like never before, and all the time in the world would not soften her angst. Her heart raced with breathless worry; her concern for herself only faded some when she thought of Mickey and recalled with painful clarity the difficulty her son encountered the *last* time he was asked to make such a difficult adjustment. It was a while ago but she could recall the scene as if it had just happened. The pain and shock were still all so real.

"Why, Arthur?" she had asked him. She kept on asking him. He had just sat down to break the disturbing news to her. "Why Mickey?"

He was fearful on how to answer; he was still getting to know her at that point. "I don't know what to say, Molly. The guys all love him—truly. They had this idea that they wanted to take him out—to a bar—and it just didn't work out." He lowered his head, wading through the unfortunate circumstances while nervously picking away at the skin around his thumb. "We all figured that—"

"You knew about this? Before it happened?"

She stood up and turned her back to him. He could no longer see her face but imagined, based on the rigidness of her posture, that it had hardened considerably. "I'm sorry, Molly. Really. I know it was stupid. I just wanted so badly for all the guys—especially Mickey—to spend some time together so that they felt like they were part of something." His mouth was dry. He stopped for a moment, unable to complete his thought without moistening his lips. "I don't know. It's hard to explain. Baseball is funny. You can have all the talent in the world, but if you're not a team, it's all for naught."

Standing with him now, many months removed from that awful scene, she remembered all of it. And felt it too. She recalled painfully how his words had pierced her like a blade. And she remembered crying softly. Her head had drooped and he could see the spasmodic rising and falling of her shoulders.

"So my baby was in a bar, drinking, when all of this happened?" she gasped through suffocating lungs. "Nobody was watching out for him?"

She touched her mouth, perspiration breaking out all over her face and across the nape of her neck. She turned and stared at him—in a catatonic stupor, through eyes both distant and glazed.

She wore those same eyes now. And her knees were just as weak.

"So you see, Arthur, it's not just that *I* do not fit in here," she said, gripping the arm of a chair for support until the strength returned to her legs. "It's Mickey, too. Especially Mickey. We are country folk, Arthur. Simple. Honest. And Mickey? Well, Mickey is Mickey. Have you forgotten so fast? You know that. The life of a big league ballplayer in a big league city is not something that I think he can handle."

Murph, sensing the seriousness of the predicament as reflected in the panic implied in her every word and pained expression, took her hands in his and brought her fingers to his lips. He kissed each finger tip gently.

"I really am worried, Arthur," she went on, pulling her hands back from him. "*Really* worried. This is not at all like last time."

Murph, conscious that his heartbeat was suddenly timorous and erratic, sighed heavily and folded his arms.

"Look, Molly, you have to trust me on this," he began. "Sure, the location has changed. So have most of the faces. But it's baseball. Cripes, it's still just baseball. Understand? There's beauty and comfort and safety in the game. The game is home. That's the answer when all else fails. For all of us, sweetheart—especially Mickey. This game of baseball is his lifeline—it's his sanctuary from all that has threatened to destroy him his whole life. Don't you see?"

She tried to turn her head away but he would not let her.

"Look at me, Molly. When he steps onto that field and stands on that mound of dirt in the center of it all, he is no longer a charity case, someone who people ridicule or pity. He is special. I mean *really* special. It's the one place he has a chance to not only be normal but great. You just don't turn your back on greatness like that. And the bigger the stage, the greater he becomes. That's all I'm saying. I think that you are worrying for—"

"And what about when he steps off the field, Arthur? Huh? What then? Baseball is just one part of all this. And what about me and—"

"Come on, Molly, you know what I'm—"

"Can you guarantee me that he will not be swallowed up by all of the lights and fast cars and smooth-talking city slickers who would love nothing more than to take advantage of this slow-witted country boy? Huh? Can you?"

"Molly, I told you that—"

"No, you cannot, Arthur. Can you make sure that he won't get hurt? Or taken advantage of? Or that he will be as happy here as he was back in Milwaukee? That any of us will? No, you cannot. As much as you would like to, you cannot make that promise to me. And I would not ask you to because I know that it is impossible. So here's the real question then."

She took a deep breath. She was struggling with the constellation of tears that hung on her lashes. "Where does that leave us now, huh?" she asked.

Those words troubled him now. They stood for a while, as stiff and inanimate as the new candlesticks Molly had purchased, each measuring the other's gaze with silent purpose. Murph was remembering Molly as she was when they had first met. She was soft and lovely but timid and guarded, like a beautiful flower in early spring—only partially opened in the chill of the morning air. He could see her beauty instantly—but also saw the veil of sadness that hung behind her eyes. He was drawn to her instantly. It was only later that he learned of Clarence and how the man she had married for all the wrong reasons had expunged even the slightest hint of happiness from her life. He was awful to her, made her wince and cringe and wish with every breath she had for anything except another day with him.

"Molly, I love you," he began. "You know that. I never want to make you upset. You mean everything to me. I can't imagine my life without you. Or Mickey. But please . . . please listen. Baseball is in my blood. I need this. We need this. You know that too." His eyes widened and his breath became forced. There was a discernible impression that he was now fighting for his life.

"This opportunity for me—managing a major league team—is something I have dreamed about since I was a boy. I don't know. Maybe it's foolish and immature . . . and not right for all of us. Not yet anyway. I don't know. But it's who I am, Molly. And Mickey—Mickey is a big part of this. You know that, Molly. He's changed everything. You *both* have changed everything for me." He sighed and shook his head, as though trying to free a thought lodged deep within the most remote chamber of his mind.

"Can I tell you something, something I am ashamed to admit? I was nothing before I met both of you. I was a nobody going nowhere. Dennison was right. I was a loser. But not anymore. Don't you see? Now I have a chance to do something great. Just like that boy of yours. But it's only great *with* you and Mickey. I need him, Molly. I do. I need both of you. I'm nothing if you guys are not here with me."

Outside the window, night was beginning to drop its veil. The moon, peeking through a shroud of thin, gauzy clouds floating intermittently across the steel gray sky, stirred a palpable sense of distant, divine observation. Murph breathed deeply, steadied himself, slipped his hands around her waist, and pulled her close to him so that her breath was soft against his face. Her eyes were wide and soft. She sighed and tilted her head slightly, as if to see him more clearly. All the angst and anxiety melted out of him suddenly as he saw in her a sense of softening, a heartfelt understanding that seemed to welcome him, and all he desired, once again.

"Please, Molly," he whispered softly. "Believe in me. Believe in this. It's going to be fine. Really." She placed her hands on his face, closed her eyes, and let her forehead fall gently against his. For a while nothing was audible but their breathing, gentle and rhythmic.

"Okay, Arthur. I will give this a chance. For you and for Mickey. But please—please don't lose yourself in this dream of yours. I'm begging you. There are other things to consider here. You understand? Please, hear me. Don't get lost. I don't think I could handle that."

Murph nodded. He knew her words were genuine and that there was no undertone or innuendo in what she had said. He was thankful for that—so thankful that he thought about answering her, of promising her that things between them would remain as they always had been, and that all of her concern was for naught. She deserved that. But before he could form the words, he heard once again the distant cheers that he had always longed for, and all at once he was transported to someplace magical—where he was right and whole—suspended between two pristine lines of wet, unslacked lime.

# SANFORD STADIUM

An early morning sun bathed the manicured diamond in warm, luminous hues of golden honey. The players, like restless caterpillars who had finally sprouted wings after a long winter's transformation, sat restlessly in the home dugout, fidgeting uncontrollably. They chewed their nails and the insides of their cheeks, tapped their spikes on the concrete floor, and kept their eyes on the sprawling green lawn that lay just a stone's throw away, all while Murph delivered his vision for the upcoming season. It was only a few weeks away.

The new manager was intoxicated by the moment. He hemmed and hawed, careful to mention everything he had been ruminating over since he was appointed skipper. There was so much more he wanted to say but so little time. So he suppressed the impulse and abbreviated his address. It began with "Today, fellas, we stand on the brink of a new opportunity" and concluded with "Now let's go accomplish something really special." There were other things he wanted to say, but he swallowed the last few thoughts, and once that final word had been spoken and he waved them onto the field, the group exhaled with a palpable zeal, laughing and slapping backs before flitting onto and across the diamond in a display of unbridled rejuvenation.

Murph observed with considerable excitement the alacrity with which his new team bounded into the start of spring training, but his enthusiasm waned when he observed the dynamics that emerged almost instantly. On one side of the field, stretched from the first base bag all the way down the right field line, were many of the Braves' regulars, including Sid Gordon, Earl Torgeson, Buddy Ozmore, and Warren Spahn. They had formed an impromptu circle, a neatly crafted barrier in which they proceeded to banter in relative privacy about this and that while stretching out their stiffened muscles. Murph frowned at the somewhat obvious stratagem, particularly when he saw another group of players, including Mickey, Lester, and Jethroe setting up on the third base side. He sighed. There they were—his team, his very first big league club, nothing more than a splintered group consisting of rival factions that could barely share a field just ten minutes into the new season. So much for Shangri-la.

"Ozzy!" Murph yelled, his right arm waving in the morning air. "Hey Ozzy! Can I see you here a minute?"

Murph anxiously watched as the cagey veteran loped with purposeful strides down the right field line toward home plate. Buddy Ozmore was the undisputed leader of the Braves team. While his on-field production as one of the league's premier hitters certainly qualified him for the moniker, it was his unmatched brand of square-jaw commentary and unflagging commitment to the "good old boys" that anointed him as such. He expressed his thoughts with deliberate purpose and pride, and dispatched his idea of justice with attention not only for his self-satisfaction but for the approval of those he led as well.

"Yeah," he said, adjusting his cap with both hands. "You wanted to see me, Mr. Murphy?"

"Uh, yeah . . . yeah I did." Murph knew it was a bad idea to go right after him, but he could not arrest his increasing concern. "Listen, Ozzy. It seems as though—"

"The name's Ozmore," the man said; his restless hands coming to rest on his hips. Murph's brain fogged up, and he stared now at the surly outfielder as though looking at him through a gauzy curtain.

"Okay then, Mr. Ozmore. It seems as though we have a bit of a problem here," Murph began.

"How's that?" Ozmore answered.

"Well, where I come from," Murph explained, "baseball players who play on the same team do everything together. You know—practice, shower, dress, socialize. You understand?"

"So?"

"So I don't particularly care for what I'm seeing here. You and most of the others on one side of the field and the new guys on the other. I was sort of hoping that you would help bridge that gap a little."

There was a brief awkward pause. Then Ozmore turned his head and released a thin stream of tobacco juice out of the side of his mouth. It landed just before Murph's feet. When he turned back to face Murph, both men just stared at each other. After a few long seconds, Ozmore pushed the tension to its inevitable conclusion. "I signed a contract to play ball, Mr. Murphy. Baseball. And that's what I do. Ain't nothing in ink that says anything about babysitting or any other bullshit you're talking about. So you can take your whole mom and apple pie routine and try selling it somewhere else."

After practice, Murph sat in his office in silence, his mind a ship of memories that tossed violently across a vast, turbulent sea. He thought of the friendly confines of Borchert Field and of the success he had enjoyed the last two seasons. Losing to McNally was a bitter pill, but, in retrospect, it was the most rewarding time of his career, despite Dennison's abject criticisms and the disappointment of finishing behind the Rangers in back-to-back campaigns. He had really found a home in Milwaukee—the elusive niche he had sought his entire life. His days there were certainly rough at first, but out of the cloud of struggle and disappointment emerged an excitement and wonder ushered in by the improbable rise of young Mickey Tussler and his newly inspired teammates. It was the sort of experience that every coach dreams of—the proverbial aligning of the stars.

"You sure you wanna leave all of this, Murph?" Farley Matheson asked him when he had shared his news at the end of last season. "Now? I mean, I know the grass in Boston seems greener, but I've been across the bridge and back enough times to know that all that glitters ain't always gold. Ya hear?"

As he had done so many times before when Matheson began philosophizing, Murph turned a deaf ear. In that moment, all he could hear were cheers from a big league park and the distinct sound of a dream finally fulfilled. Now what resonated most powerfully were Matheson's clichéd admonitions—and Molly's misgivings as well.

"Arthur, why is this so important to you?" she had asked shortly after he learned of his promotion. "Especially now, when everything is right in our world. Isn't all this enough?"

Her eyes welled with fear. The prospect of leaving burned her stomach. He wanted to express the same uncertainty, but the call to glory was seductive.

"Come on, Molly. You know I love you and what we have here. I do. And the guys—the guys have just rallied and responded time and again. Played their hearts out for me and for this town. I couldn't be more pleased. But you know that I—"

"Yes, yes," she said. "I know. You always had the dream of being a part of a big league team—of getting back there. I get it, Arthur. I do. We all have those dreams in some form. But sometimes dreams change, Arthur. Because life does. Think about this. Not as the old Arthur Murphy, but as the man I know now."

The corners of his mouth sagged, and his entire face dulled to an anxious, shadowy mask. "It's not that simple, Molly," he explained. "This is not some foolhardy, wish-upon-a-star fantasy we're talking about here. This is baseball. This is my life. It's what I do. It's who I am, Molly. Do you know how long I've waited for this? What this means? Why would I even *think* about saying no? It's my time."

Sitting there, with only echoing voices and a montage of strange photographs on the wall for company, he began to doubt himself again. What had he done? Maybe Molly and Old Man Matheson were right. Maybe he was not cut out to be part of the major league scene. It seemed plausible now. He had barely gotten his cleats dirty and already he was in over his head. Buddy Ozmore was a thorn in his side and not going anywhere. He was a real badass, baptized in dirty water, as Matheson would say.

Murph had heard the story of how Ozmore was elevated to the distinction of the meanest SOB around. The bilious outfielder had only been in Toledo a couple of years at the time of the incident. Despite his brief tenure, he had already become one of the more vocal players on the team. The way Murph had heard it, the Mud Hens had just finished a rather uneventful road trip, one that saw them drop five of six games, and were summoned by manager Eddie Mayo for early batting practice the next morning. Buddy Ozmore had a very fastidious practice routine, one that included stretching, extensive tee work, soft toss, and then live swings. He was most certainly a creature of habit.

He also always hit sixth in the group. That July morning, however, he found himself at the cage waiting behind Clint Barnaby, an eighteen-year-old lanky kid from Fanshawe, Oklahoma. Barnaby had just joined the club the day before amid all sorts of talk about how talented he was.

"Pardon me, shit-kicker," Ozmore said, tapping Barnaby on the shoulder. The other guys laughed the way they always did when Ozmore got rolling. "This ain't no barnyard hoedown, son. Round here we have an order to things. And you ain't following it, clodhopper."

There was more laughter, along with a steady murmur that signaled the furor of what was to come next. The guys had all seen Ozmore in action before. Once he got going, he was relentless. But Barnaby was unfazed. He simply tapped his spikes with the barrel of his bat and turned his head ever so slightly—so that only part of his face was visible to Ozmore and the other guys behind him.

"I ain't no shit-kicker, jackass" he replied. "And I was also here a half hour before you. So I have an idea, boss. Why don't you dummy up back there, step off, and just worry about yourself."

Later that day, under a starless sky, Ozmore and three of his boys slipped out sometime after midnight and took Barnaby's red '41 Chevy AK pickup and rolled it onto the field, letting it come to rest just behind the pitcher's mound. It sat there all night and was still there the next morning when, at the request of Ozmore, half the team arrived early for extra batting practice.

"Ozzy, you are something else man," they all said, trying to speak through fits of uproarious laughter. They were all staring at the dew-laden truck, which in the early morning sunlight looked like it was adorned with hundreds of tiny diamonds.

"Now we've seen everything. Only you, Ozzy."

The surly outfielder just shrugged and shook his head. "I don't know what you guys are talking about," he said. "I just called some extra batting practice this morning because we ain't hitting a lick. Not sure why the chawbacon parked his truck on the field, but, heck, the show must go on."

Some forty-five minutes later, when the rest of the team filed in, the response to the unusual situation was notably different.

"What the hell is going on here?" Mayo thundered, looking at the truck that was now riddled with round dents and busted glass. "Who's the asshole who did this?"

Barnaby's reaction was equally noticeable. He walked over to the vehicle and traced a couple of the deeper dimples with one finger. His shoulders sagged and his face became a ruddy mosaic of anger and defeat.

"Hell if we know, Skip," Ozmore yelled to Mayo. "I was just as shocked as you are. Tried to move it, but couldn't. Sorry about the mess, but we had no choice. We gotta take BP, right?"

A faint swell of laughter could be heard as Mayo walked over to the truck and kicked aside some errant baseballs, each which bore the red tinge of calamity.

"Bullshit!" he hollered. "Absolute bullshit. I won't stand for this. Ya hear? I want to know who did this. And when I find out—and make no mistake about it, I *will* find out—there will be hell to pay." Nobody said a word.

Murph knew how influential Ozmore was. It was only a matter of time before his polluted attitude infected the others. This realization, which had already begun to slip its tentacles around Murph's neck, would have all but suffocated him had Lester and Mickey not wandered in.

"So, how we looking so far, Mr. Murphy?" Lester asked. He still had not shed his shin guards and chest protector. Only his mask, which Mickey held dutifully in both hands, had been removed. "Planning on another practice session I don't know about?" Murph said, acknowledging the catcher's present state. "You know we have a locker room, Les."

Mickey's eyes lit up. "Yes, Lester," he said. "The locker room is on the other side of the dugout, down a ways from the big equipment closet. Mickey's locker is third from the end, against the wall. If you turn around and—"

"It's okay, it's okay, Mick," Murph said, winking at Lester. "I think he knows where it is."

Lester laughed, then flopped into the chair directly across from Murph. "So why the long face, Murph?" he asked. "What's eating away at you?"

Murph sighed as his shoulders fell. "Aw, I don't know, Les," he replied. "I don't know *anything* anymore. Cripes, I thought this was exactly what I wanted, you know? The call to the show. The big time. What every little boy dreams of while he's pitching rubber balls against the side of the house. You know? It should all be good, no? Like sitting atop the world. Instead, all I feel is this hammering at the back of my head. This steady beat that seems to be whispering all sorts of bad things to me."

The defeated nature of Murph's expression tested Lester's patience.

"Ain't it a bit early for the white flag, Murph? Shit, what's so bad, huh? A couple of big mouths jawing at you? That's what's got you down?"

"It's that, and then there's—"

"Forget all of that, Murph. It's baseball, man. Baseball. After all is said and done, we take the field. And the field has a way of making everything seem right. Ain't that what you told me once?"

Murph remained dejected, but Lester's words had conjured thoughts of something ethereal, almost mythological, deep within the recesses of his troubled soul. He recalled the exploits of Mickey the past two seasons and the way the forlorn boy had managed to bridge the expanse between ignominy and success with just a few steps to the pitcher's mound. Then there was Lester and his remarkable resiliency despite all of the racial epithets hurled his way. He, too, had beaten the odds and was now standing on the threshold of baseball greatness as well. It buoyed Murph's resolve. He breathed a little easier now. Maybe he was overreacting. Maybe what he needed was to take a lesson from the two unlikely characters who had gotten him here. They each had a world of trouble yet somehow prevailed. Now maybe it was his turn. Maybe he just wasn't seeing it. So he decided that he owed himself, if not both of them, to at least try. If they could do it, why not him?

# URBAN BLIGHT

Molly's daily headache seemed worse in the stillness of the early morning air. From atop the narrow terrace just outside their temporary apartment, she sipped her coffee and watched as the streets below pulsed with the callous detachment of the morning rush to duty. People pushed their way through crowded sidewalks, bound to the unforgiving call of schedules, and a line of automobiles, all with pressing purposes, snaked their way through the daunting maze of concrete buildings, protesting with intermittent horn blasts—courtesy of impatient hands.

She frowned as she recalled with some difficulty the sights and sounds that adorned her former sunrise routine. Where was the bevy of prairie warblers, buzzing and whistling as they foraged in the brush, poking in and out of the lower branches of her favorite row of pitch pines with playful determination? What about the distant dance of bottlebrush grass, the distinctive inflorescence of spikelets swaying softly, rhythmically, to the gentle breath of the awakening meadow just across the way? Or the kiss of the welcoming sun, its warming rays slanting through the giant oaks that lined the modest dwelling she had come to love so dearly? It was all so foreign now.

Maybe it was worse because Arthur had been gone for so long. She had lived through spring training last year with relative ease, never once entertaining the sort of angst and malaise that presently plagued her. As she sipped from her ceramic mug, she could only conclude that *everything* was different—completely and all at once, and *that* was the problem.

Even Mickey, who had not really occupied her chambers of worry for quite some time, was on her mind. The boy continued to find solace in the guiding hands of both Murph and Lester, and he was genuinely excited about playing in the Bee Hive in front of thousands of New England's most ardent baseball worshippers. He had come a long way from tossing apples into a barrel on the farm in Indiana, and even Mickey, with his limited scope and sensibility, could recognize the extraordinary circumstances that defined his present position.

Still, Molly worried. She worried what people were saying, what they were thinking, and how they would treat her special boy. She also worried each time either Mickey or Arthur shared with her another incident that, in her opinion, placed her boy in peril.

The most recent of these moments occurred right after they returned from spring training. A few of the Braves' veterans, including catcher Walker Cooper, outfield corners Tommy Holmes and Sid Gordon, and first baseman Earl Torgeson, invited Lester and Mickey to join them one night for their ritualistic bar crawl through the heart of historic downtown Boston, where they would spend hours eating, drinking, and shooting the shit in some of the most historic pubs and taverns in the area. Lester was a little more than surprised by the invitation, especially since Cooper, his main competition all spring, was the one who extended the overture.

"Hey, country boy," the catcher said shortly after they arrived back in Bean Town. "Why don't you and your special friend join us tonight for a little R & R? A little something we like to call the Dead Man's Walk."

Cooper had not been so welcoming of Lester from the beginning, but after a spring that saw Lester outplay the aging backstop in every facet of the game, it was clear that he was feeling the pinch and had resigned himself to the fact that he had probably lost his job to the younger, much heralded Lester Sledge.

"That's mighty kind a ya, Coops," Lester said. "But I ain't so sure you really mean it now. After all the stuff that gone down all spring. I may be a colored boy from the sticks, but I ain't stupid."

Cooper laughed and put his hand on Lester's shoulder. "Listen, son. I've been around the game a long time. And I can read the writing on the wall. What it says is that you are just a little bit better than old Coops here. So I'm done holding out, Lester. Get it? It's cool. No more. I'm just happy to still be here. When you get to be my age, you don't hold out. No, sir. Holding out's a young man's game. When you get to be my age, you just hold on." He paused, put out his hand, and the agreement was sealed. "That's not to say I ain't gonna try my best to delay you a bit."

Mickey was there too. He had mildly protested when Lester asked him to join the others, but after several minutes of trying to explain all of the reasons why it would not work, he found it easier to simply acquiesce. Now he was sitting by himself, hands folded, his mind a polluted pool of anxiety. He was never so out of place as he was in these types of situations. All he could do was sit and wait. Lester had told him that he'd be right back, but he had been gone a good twenty minutes and there was no sign of him anywhere.

So he sat and looked around. Through a hazy veil of smoke, he noticed with tepid curiosity a girl sitting on a stool not far from his, coat on her lap, hands busy with her keys. Her back was resting up against the lip of the bar. He instantly became entranced with her hair—soft, sandy-brown ringlets that cascaded down both sides of her face and across both shoulders. He tried not to smile. It reminded him of the water in Williston's Creek back home—the way it would swirl in neat, tight circles, spinning like a series of tops as it slid effortlessly across the large, jutting stones that protruded here and there.

Although she remained seated, her eyes wandering from face to face through the smoky, dimly lit air, he could tell that she was taller than most girls he had seen before. This time he did smile. He hated how his own size always presented yet another barrier to cross when talking to the fairer sex. He hated leaning down all the time to hear what was being said.

He sat and continued to stare, his heart an instrument of unsteady beats, studying the pattern of her pale blue dress. He liked the tiny yellow flowers that were stitched in symmetrical rows across the front and struggled with the burgeoning impulse to get up and run his fingers over the fabric. He was sure it would be soft. But in all the excitement, images of the last time he saw someone this beautiful began littering his brain, all but destroying the rapture. It was an awful recollection. He had been sitting all by himself that night at The Bucket when she approached him. It was the first time he had ever really spoken to a girl. It was all too much. A beautiful young thing, caressing his back, kissing his face with soft, full lips, whispering wonderful things in his ear.

"You are just the cutest ballplayer I have ever seen, Mickey," she'd said. "Just adorable. Do you want to see how cute I am? Hmmm? Or maybe you'd rather just feel for yourself." It all happened so fast. She had told him that she wanted to take a walk with him in the cool night air. He was enthralled that she had any interest at all. They strolled for a while, hand in hand, eyes fastened to the full, glowing moon and the glinting constellations all around.

"Ever just sit, Mickey, and look up at the stars?"

He shook his head, too busy with the joy of her presence to answer.

"My mama, she and I would sit outside on an old blanket sometimes and just stare at the stars for hours," she said, her voice cracking. "I used to be able to spot 'em all. Andromeda, Orion, the Big Dipper. I knew them all."

"Why?"

"Why? What do you mean why, silly? Because they're there."

"I never spent no time watching stars," he said absently. "I don't suppose my pa would like it very much."

Her body gave a nervous jerk. Through the chilly summer air, she heard a faint, faraway sound that quickly died.

"That's a shame, Mickey. My mama used to say that God's promises were like the stars—the darker the night, the brighter they shine. I think about that sometimes."

A mild buzzing, nervous and uncontrolled, was in his ears. He turned his head and swallowed hard. She looked as if she was going to cry. Face-to-face with an unannounced emotion, she had no words. She breathed in the night air and shook her head as if to rattle the troubled thoughts from her mind. Then she grabbed his arm and pulled him behind a service station.

"Enough with the stars. I think we would have more fun back here."

He remembered Murph explaining how the girl had lured him outside so that three of Lefty's boys could jump him—that it was all just a ruse and that she had no genuine interest in him. He still couldn't decide what hurt more—the beating he took or the sting attached to the realization that he did not matter to the girl.

He was still wrestling with the two scenarios when the new girl, the one with the sandy curls, got up suddenly from her seat. In her haste, she did not realize that something had detached from her key ring and fallen to the floor. It was soft and white and oddly familiar except for the silver loop and chain affixed to the top.

The bar was bristling with activity. Off in the shadows, a couple kissed softly. There was a group in the opposite corner arguing over a faded dartboard while others struggled to engage in conversation as the waves of juke box music collided with frivolous banter and peals of laughter. But Mickey was undeterred. He was off his stool the second the girl's object hit the floor. He bent down to retrieve the wayward item and held it in between the index finger and the thumb on his right hand for several seconds, caressing the soft white fur with thoughtful deliberation. He liked the way it felt but it made him sad. The comfort and familiarity of the texture continued to wane as he considered the process by which such an item could be fashioned; he shuddered at what was most certainly the gory details. Who would do such a thing? And why? His mind had just begun to apply the possibility of that same horror touching Duncan and Daphney when he was roused from his nightmarish stupor by a voice, soft yet firm.

"Um, I think that belongs to me."

His whole body jerked suddenly, as if he had just been awakened unexpectedly from a dream. She was looking at him through a few sandy wisps of shiny silk with her hand extended in his direction. He could not move.

"Excuse me," the girl said, pointing to his right hand. She was smiling but seemed as though she was in a hurry. "I think that belongs to me. I dropped it by accident."

He was still frozen. She was even taller than he originally thought, and she smelled like the lilac bush he used to hide beneath as a boy when Clarence was in the midst of one of his tirades.

"Uh, do you think I could have that back now?" she continued. "I'm leaving in a few minutes and I need to have my good luck charm. Not that it's doing all that much for me and all but, hey, you never know." She laughed uncomfortably.

Mickey continued to manipulate the white fur between his fingers as she spoke but relinquished the talisman with a notable degree of concern when the girl extended her hand even further. "Don't know why folks is always saying that a rabbit's foot is lucky," he said just as the girl was about to walk away. "I reckon that it's a whole lot luckier when you have a whole rabbit attached to it."

The girl turned her head to the side in quizzical fashion and smiled. "Yeah, I guess you might be on to something there," she said. "Four feet has got to be luckier than just one."

Mickey frowned. "No. Rabbit's feet are not lucky, miss. That's not what Mickey was saying. Rabbits are lucky, or what I mean to say is that people who have rabbits are lucky. Like me. I have two rabbits. Duncan and Daphney. Duncan is a boy and Daphney is a girl. Duncan is tan but has a little patch of white on his chest and belly and Daphney is all white. They are my friends. Sometimes when I—"

"Rabbits?" she asked.

"Yes, miss. Duncan is a boy and—"

"Well, uh, okay—Mickey, is it? Okay, Mickey. I understand. You're probably right. I get it. I did not want to—"

"What's *your* name, miss?" he asked.

She abandoned the former path of her thoughts for a moment. "Jolene," she said. "My name is Jolene."

Mickey's furrowed brow announced his sudden confusion. "I don't reckon Mickey has even heard that name before. I know Joanna Dugan and Joanie Mitchell and my mom has a friend who is Leanne Bronson and she has a friend Leena something. Don't reckon I know her other name. Mickey only met her one time. I even knew a farmer who had a cow he called Jolinda. She were real skinny for a cow. And had a funny lookin' tail. Too short for a cow. Jolinda was her name. But I never ever heard of someone with a name like—"

"Okay, okay, Mickey," she said, drumming her fingers against her cheek. "Yeah, I get it." She was all at once distant and maudlin as she slipped seamlessly into one of those awful reminiscences. It was the summer of her twelfth year. Her family was spending their typical two weeks on the Jersey Shore at her father's friend's home, something she had grown to loathe. Despite the beauty and liberating call of the ocean, her visits to their summer getaway were tinged with moments of merciless ridicule and judgment, all at the hands of the girls with whom she was forced to "live" with for the duration of those fourteen days. Her plaintive cries were uncompromising and painfully real but never heard.

"Please, Mama, I don't want to go back there again," she had pleaded, tears streaming down both sides of her face. "Everyone there is so mean."

Her mother was staring out at the ocean, her eyes fixed on a pair of seagulls floating on some driftwood just beyond the breakers.

"Stop it, Jolene," she admonished. "That's nonsense. Mr. and Mrs. Carey open their home to us every summer, and this is how you act?"

"But the girls tease me and make me feel bad, Mama," she continued. "I feel so bad."

"What are you talking about?" she asked, turning her head to face her daughter. "What do you mean they tease you?"

The waves pounding the rocky shore sounded like the roll of distant guns. Suddenly Jolene's head seemed too heavy for her shoulders. Her whole body slumped.

"They call me names, Mama," she said.

"What names?"

"Jo Jo Hippo," she whispered softly. It was even more horrifying coming from her own lips.

"What? What did you say? Pick your head up when you speak. That's part of your problem, girl. I can't ever hear a damn word you say."

"They call me Jo Jo Hippo," she repeated. "They say I'm ugly and fat and they make fun of me. All the time. And they laugh. They say you had to make up a name for me because I'm too ugly for a normal one. And that I belong pulling a plow or something. Please, Mama. I don't want to be here anymore."

Her mother's eyes returned to the ocean. She frowned when she saw that the seagulls were no longer there. "Look, Jolene, we've been through this before. You're different from the other girls. You're bigger and maybe not as 'girly' and frilly as the others. But it's okay. You have to learn to live with it. It's life. Not every girl is cut out to be prom queen." Jolene's eyes flooded as her mother continued to pour her own fears and dissatisfaction over the young girl. "I have told you a thousand times life ain't fair. It just ain't. And I am sorry about all of this, including that name of yours. I don't like it anymore than you do but it was the only way for me and your father to agree."

Years later her mother's words still stung.

"I guess my name sums up my life," she explained to Mickey. "My mama wanted to call me Josephine but my daddy's mom's name was Eileen. He had his heart set on that. Story has it they fought about it for more than a while. Couldn't decide. So they came up with Jolene. Near as I can figure it's not even really a name. And neither one of them is really happy with it. So now I'm just this girl with the name that nobody really likes or understands."

Mickey's face softened. He leaned toward the girl and placed his hand on her shoulder.

"I like it, Miss. And I like your hair. But killing rabbits for their feet is not nice, Miss Jolene. Animals is just like people, only animals—they're always nice. Like in my favorite poem, 'Silver.' It's all about dogs and mice and fish. I love that poem. I don't reckon Mickey ever had a fight with an animal. And I've had a lot of animals, Miss. I had me some pigs, chicks, a horse, two roosters, a lamb, a cat, and rabbits. I told you about them. All of my animals are my friends. They can understand things and they have feelings just like other folks. One time, not too long ago, my pig Oscar—"

"Look, I'm sorry, Mickey," she said, slipping one hand into the arm of her coat. "I didn't mean to offend you. I'm not a big fan of these crazy things either. Not really anyway. My brother gave it to me. He's superstitious. All baseball guys are. Said it always helps him and that I need all the help I can get." She paused a minute when she caught a glimpse of herself in the glass of one of the picture frames just behind Mickey. Her shoulders sagged.

"I suppose he's right."

A palpable awkwardness settled between them.

"Okay then," she finally said. "Well, it was nice talking to you, Mickey. Maybe I will—"

"Mickey's a baseball guy too and I ain't superstitious one lick," he said. "My mama and Mr. Murphy and some of the guys, sometimes they say that I act a little crazy and all—you know, all weird and stuff, especially when I am preparing before a ball game and all. But I ain't ever had no good luck charms before."

She raised her eyebrows.

"So you're a baseball guy, huh?" she asked, pulling the lapels of her coat closed. "Well, maybe I'll see you around sometime. I have to go right now, but we can talk some more. Sometime—you know, about animals and things." She smiled and nodded. "I kinda like the way you see things, Mickey."

It was the girl's comment—"I kinda like the way you see things, Mickey"—that set Molly off after Mickey told her all about the meeting.

"This is what I'm talking about, Arthur," she said. Her ability to speak calmly collapsed under the weight of her anger and concern. "I cannot have people, especially girls, suggesting things to Mickey and placing him in situations which he is unable to handle. He comes home and tells me all about this girl, excited and all, but he has no idea what he is getting into. He has the mind of a little boy, Arthur. A little boy. This whole thing can only be trouble for him."

"Molly, I know what you mean when you say—"

"He never should have been at that place, Arthur, and he certainly should not have been allowed to talk to some bar floozy who is just out to make a quick score."

Murph's palms, damp with perspiration, came to rest on Molly's shoulders. He looked into her eyes and began the crucial search for just the right words to say. Her emotional storm settled somewhat, but the flood of anxiety that followed continued to rise.

"Look, Molly, I understand what you are saying here, I do. But I have to tell you, I don't feel it's as bad as you're thinking," Murph said. "The girl was just talking to him. That's it. Nothing happened, right?"

"That's not the point, Arthur," she answered. "And you know it. It's *never* only about what happens. It's also about what *could* happen. And I am very worried about that—especially now that we are in this city that is filled with all sorts of dangers for folks like us—especially Mickey." Her senses were reeling. She could feel her blood bubbling beneath her skin.

"Please, Molly, I'm sorry. Really. I don't want to upset you. And I do understand what you are saying. I do. I promise you. I will be more careful with Mickey this time. I will. But you need to give Mickey a little room to be a man. To grow up some. And you need to trust that Boston is the right place for us—for all of us."

"A man?" she fired back. "Really, Arthur? You didn't just say that, did you?"

"You know what I mean, Molly. Sure, Mickey's special. I get it. And I know this is hard. But if we are going to try and help him live a life that is as close to normal as we can, then you have to bend a little. And that means that you have to believe that we are in the right situation here in Boston and that he will be fine."

"I don't know, Arthur," she said, folding her arms tightly around her middle. "It all seems different this time. It just doesn't feel right anymore."

A nameless but primitive rebellion raged inside of him. He loved her more than he ever could have imagined but he had traveled too far, sacrificed way too much, to just let his dream wither away.

"You're going to have to trust me, Molly," he said, his mind now engaged in a frenetic series of calculations. "You do. Stop punishing me for that incident two years ago at The Bucket back in Milwaukee. That wasn't my fault. You know that. And nothing has happened to Mickey since then. Right?"

She said nothing. That brief hesitation filled him with a burning wrath that heated his body instantly.

"So that's all?" he said. "No comment. You're just going to stare at me and say nothing? Come on, Molly, be fair. I need to know that you are with me here. I need to—"

"I know what you need, Arthur," she finally said. "But it's not that easy. And other people have needs too. It's not like before. Things here are different. Feelings are different. That's what *I* need *you* to understand."

He did understand—or at least he thought he did. But honestly it made no difference if he did or he didn't. *He* still felt the same way. So when the conversation ended, he walked away, anxious and discouraged, seeking a dark, remote place where he could sit and be alone, even if it was just for a brief moment, with his roiling fears.

# POLO GROUNDS—APRIL 18, 1950

The earth continued its processional thaw as spring carried on in its usual fashion. The air, now decidedly warmer than the chilly gusts that blew through March, was filled with the robin's song and the unmistakable redolence of dogwood blossoms and forsythia. And despite the frosty rumblings that had threatened to derail Murph's managerial debut before it had even begun, there was only a remote murmur of dissension left when the Braves headed north and took the field for real in April.

One by one, each player settled in and turned his focus to the new season and the quest that all of them shared—capturing the National League pennant. It had been a long road for Murph. As he stood at home plate across from Burt Shotton, lineup card in hand, he filled his lungs and looked around at the magnificent double-decked grandstand that arched around the batter's box and down the baselines, all the while entertaining the steady montage of painful reminiscences filtering through his brain. It was good to know he had finally arrived.

"Hey there, Skip," Shotton said, his eyebrows dancing playfully beneath the peak of his cap. "You're a long way from Borchert Field."

"Yes, I suppose so," Murph replied, eyeing with a twinge of envy the two blue stripes on Shotton's sleeve—artful stitching that served to commemorate the two National League pennants he had won. "But if it's all the same to you, I think I'll stick around for a while."

Not another word was exchanged between the two men as the umpire completed his discussion of the ground rules. Then both managers shook hands and returned unceremoniously to their respective dugouts.

Connie Ryan led things off for the visiting Braves. Mickey and Lester watched from the far part of the dugout as Ryan banged his spikes furiously with the knob of his bat before digging in for good. Then just like that, the cry of "Play ball" split the air and the game was underway.

The first pitch of the season was an outside fastball that popped the catcher's glove like a firecracker. The crowd roared its approval.

"Strike one."

Ryan shook his head and stepped out of the box. Murph, now positioned on the top step of the dugout just behind the on-deck circle, took the opportunity to buoy his leadoff man's resolve.

"Come on now, Connie," he barked loudly. "Come on now. Get your hacks, kid."

Mickey remained with Lester, talking in hushed tones as Ryan fouled off the next three offerings. Lester commented about how the Giants starter had missed his spot on each of the last two attempts, but something in the crowd commandeered Mickey's eye, diverting the boy's attention while ushering in a deluge of random thoughts that temporarily sealed the young hurler from Lester's intent.

"You listening, Mick?" Lester asked. "You hear what I said?"

Mickey nodded, but his gaze was still fixed on one particular New York fan—the one dressed in a cardboard crown and burlap tunic with brown leather belt that matched the makeshift club he was brandishing in his right hand.

"Mick, come on now," Lester persisted, shaking Mickey's shoulder. "You paying attention?"

Mickey turned to Lester, then extended his forefinger in the direction of his fixation. "Over there. Just behind the other dugout. He looks like a character in a book my mama used to read to me when I was little," Mickey announced. "Mickey thinks it was called *The Giant and the Tailor*. Or it could have been *The Selfish Giant* or maybe *Jack the Giant Killer*. I am not sure. My mama read me lots of stories."

Lester chuckled and shook his head.

"That ain't no giant, Mick," Lester said. "He ain't no more of a giant than you are. He's just a mascot, cheering on his team."

Mickey showed no signs of comprehending Lester's explanation.

"I ain't ever seen no mascots," he answered, his eyes glued to the animated man's uproarious gesticulations and antics. "But I sure seen plenty of giants. In books. I also seen some wolves, trolls, and witches. Witches scare me a little. Not cause they are real or anything. Mickey knows that they are not real. But because of how they look. Unless they are good witches, but that don't happen all that much. My mama used to tell me that you can't always tell what's on the inside of a person by looking at the outside, but I reckon that most times I can see—"

"Okay, okay, Mick," Lester said, stopping the young man before he slipped even further into his digression. "I'm just saying that mascots is common in the big leagues. There's lots of things up here that's different from where we come from. Mascots is one. Another would be paying attention to the game on the field. Ya gots to learn here. While you were yammering away, Connie flew out to left and Jet went down looking at a 3-2 hook."

Mickey turned to face Lester with a note of indignation, running his hand over his chin. "I know what's happening out there, Lester," he replied. "Connie hit a 2-2 outside fastball that was caught just before it went foul into the stands and Sammy Jethroe fouled off three pitches before going down on a curveball that looked like it was ball four."

Lester stared at Mickey. He was thinking that the boy's eyes were now deeper than before and was certain there had to be some obscure meaning behind it, but he possessed neither the patience nor the inclination to pursue it.

"Okay, Mick, I get it. Just watch the game, will ya. The way the rest of us do. You never know when Murph's gonna need you. And you's gonna wanna be ready."

Lester would have to wait a while for Mickey's response, for after Willard Marshall grounded out weakly to second base to complete an uneventful 1-2-3 inning, Lester was gearing up and running out on the field to take some warm-up tosses from Braves ace and local legend Warren Spahn. Lester could not help but smirk a bit from behind his mask. Man oh man, if his mama could only see old Lester now, he thought to himself. Playing in the big leagues with all these white boys. He was still having trouble believing it was actually happening.

It became even more surreal when Eddie Stanky stepped up to the plate to lead things off for the Giants. The gritty second baseman they all called "The Brat" had been a baseball fixture for years. He was not known for his skill and baseball prowess as much as he was for his inimitable way of surviving and surviving well. "He can't hit, can't run, can't field. He's no nice guy . . . heck, all the little SOB can do is win" was what they all said about Stanky. Lester had read all about him and so many others for years, and now there he was, "The Brat," digging in the batter's box just inches from the starstruck catcher.

Spahn was not nearly as impressed and disposed of the Giants' pesky leadoff man in quick fashion. The next batter, Whitey Lockman, also fell victim to three very live fastballs, giving the Braves' ace two easy outs to begin the inning.

"Atta boy, Spahny," Murph called from the dugout. "Atta boy. Go get 'em." Spahn rolled his eyes, then pounded the ball in his glove three times as he prepared for his next challenge. Bobby Thompson was the third batter to face Spahn. He strode to the plate, wielding his bat like a samurai sword. His presence further ignited Lester's awe; the wide-eyed backstop shook his head, excited at the sight of yet another baseball legend yet appropriately fearful should he get caught staring at the Giants' all-star center fielder.

Spahn started Thompson off with a curveball that broke out of the zone for ball one. The next offering was a fastball, quick and true, that shaved the outside corner for a called strike. With the count even at 1–1, Lester went to work. He knew that Thompson was a very good breaking ball hitter and would probably be looking for something off speed. Hard fastball inside was the way to go for sure. With the stratagem in place, Lester flexed his glove, pounded it with his fist a few times, and proceeded to put down one finger. Spahn's face became a twisted mask. He stepped off the rubber, removed his cap, and ran his forearm over the sweaty strands of hair that hung just above his furrowed brow. He exhaled loudly and resumed his position on top of the hill. Lester, oblivious to the pointed histrionics, placed one finger between his legs again. This time, Spahn remained where he was, shaking his head vehemently. Lester repeated the request, and once again, Spahn shook him off. Lester removed his mask and turned his head over his left shoulder.

"Time," he called. Then he trotted out to the mound to chat with his pitcher.

"What are you doing out here?" the surly hurler asked. "Just go back where you belong."

"Ain't working out so well that way," Lester replied.

Spahn huffed and narrowed his eyes. "Listen, I don't need some cotton-picking country boy from the Negro Leagues telling me how to pitch to Thompson. I know what I'm doing."

Lester shook his head.

"Ain't saying you don't, Warren, but I do think that Mr. Thompson is looking for a curveball and he's mighty good at hitting 'em. What's say we lock the boy up with a fastball inside then junk him away. That's the way to go here. I can tell by the way he's holding his body what he's looking for."

Spahn's temples began to throb. "Really? Ten minutes into your career and you can tell what he's looking for? Man oh man. You must have really done some serious voodoo magic with all those other boys you played with. I mean I know you can catch. But I didn't realize you could read minds and bodies too."

Lester looked down for a moment before answering. "Listen, Mr. Spahn, I ain't no fortune teller. And yeah, I'm new. But I've played before. Baseball is baseball, black or white. Just like people is people. I'm just saying that sometimes you got to trust your catcher. That's all. Let's do it my way this time, then you can go after him any way you want next time."

The arrival of the umpire at the mound gave Lester the perfect opportunity for an exit. He jogged back to home plate, pulled down his mask, and squatted once again. Spahn peered in, and Lester put down one finger. Without either protest or confirmation, Spahn wound up, kicked his leg, and let the pitch fly. Fastball, in tight. The ball's trajectory was true. It split the air deftly and was just about to come to rest neatly in the yawning leather pocket that awaited when Thompson threw the barrel of his bat out, catching the ball square and launching it high and deep into the crisp spring air. The little white sphere climbed higher and higher as if being pulled by some invisible string, scraping a cloud or two before finally coming to rest well beyond the left field fence.

As Thompson circled the bases, the partisan crowd erupted in a wild celebration, drowning out the litany of expletives that were spilling out of Spahn's mouth. Murph called out some words of encouragement from the bench, and Ozmore and Torgeson made a brief visit to the mound to try and corral their pitcher's untamed emotions. Lester just sank beneath his mask. It took Spahn just a few seconds to regroup. Cleanup hitter Don Mueller took his turn looking to make it back-to-back jacks but proved no match for the incensed Spahn, who channeled his anger into three straight curve-balls that looked as if they had been dropped from some invisible ledge in front of the plate. Side retired.

Spahn's walk to the dugout was slow and deliberate, his gait a clear harbinger of the storm brewing inside of him. He negotiated the dugout steps with little trouble and then fired his glove against the wall before sitting on the edge of the bench, arms folded close to his heaving chest. Lester saw the tirade and despite pangs of angst and uncertainty knew what had to be done.

"Uh, listen, Warren, about that pitch. I just want to say that—"

"Drop dead, rookie-boy," Spahn fired back. "Let that be a lesson to you. You're playing with men now. So let's let the men make the important decisions from now on. Fastball my ass."

Everyone on the bench heard the exchange and cringed. It was as if time had stood still just long enough for Spahn's mini harangue. Then, little by little, each player began to stir again, milling about the dugout with trepidation. Lester was left standing still, inanimate, until the sting of embarrassment dulled enough to allow life again. Then he turned away and let his shoulders fall, drawing long, deep breaths and looking about with forlorn eyes, searching helplessly in the circle of fractured faces all around him for some semblance of hope.

Murph saw the whole thing. His anxiety stirred, rolled around inside of him like a marble that managed to bump into every nerve possible. He cringed with every "touch," fidgeting several times in defiant response. Then, without notice, it morphed into something much larger and surged through him like an ocean swell.

"Murph, you okay?" Mickey asked, mindful of the man's altered state.

"Not now, Mick," he answered, pushing past the boy so as not to lose any momentum. "We'll talk later."

Lester had only managed to get a few steps away from Spahn when Murph made it clear that he was next in line for some verbal sparring with the disgruntled pitcher.

"You know, Spahny, shit like that happens all the time. It does. Ain't nothing to do with experience or color or nothing like that. If that same pitch is just a little more right or even a little left we might not even be having this discussion. It's part of the game."

Spahn's fever abated. He did not address Murph; he barely even looked at him. He simply walked away.

Ozmore, who had been watching, could not resist the opportunity to weigh in. "Man, Murph, you really don't have any idea what you're doing, do you?" Then he pulled out a four-leaf clover that he had been carrying with him and laid it gently on Murph's shoulder. "Here. You could use this a lot more than I can."

The game moved on at a rigorous clip. Both teams' offenses sputtered, resulting in a quick exchange of zeroes for several frames until Boston erupted in the top of the fifth inning for five runs, highlighted by a long three-run homer off the bat of Buddy Ozmore. The prodigious blast gave Spahn and the Braves a comfortable 5–1 lead.

The four-run cushion seemed as though it would be enough for the Braves' ace, who cruised through the sixth and the seventh innings with no trouble at all. However, a leadoff walk in the bottom of the eighth, followed by another walk, an error, and back-to-back doubles plated three runs for the resurgent Giants, who seemed poised for an opening-day comeback.

"Hey, Coops, you and Burris take Antonelli and Mickey down to the pen and get 'em both loose right away," Murph barked. "Ain't no time to waste here. Let's go, on the hop!"

The catcher's face briefly clouded. "If you say so," he replied. "Antonelli, Haefner, let's go. Down to the pen. Now."

Murph's face flushed. "Cooper, didn't you hear what I said?"

"Yeah, I heard you. You said get Antonelli and Haefner down to the pen. What the hell do you think I'm doing?"

"Antonelli and Mickey *Tussler*," Murph fired back. "Mickey *Tussler*. Not Mickey Haefner."

Cooper's irritation was replaced by wild disbelief. "You're kidding, right?"

"Do I look like I'm kidding?" Murph said, his face now a contorted mess.

Cooper laughed and shook his head. Several of the players, including Spahn, heard the commotion and peered into the dugout before resuming play.

"Hey, I don't know what to think anymore," Cooper answered shaking his head. "But if I were you, I would—"

"Just do as you're told, Coops, okay? And do it now."

Spahn battled for the remainder of the inning. Despite the audible excitement of the crowd and gloves popping in the bullpen, the crafty southpaw regrouped and wriggled his way out of trouble. After walking the sixth place hitter, he fanned the next one on a slider in the dirt and then induced a 5-4-3 twin killing to escape with the lead.

The air in the stadium grew thicker as the game wore on and odd, unsettled feelings swirled through the late afternoon shadows. While the Braves prepared to take their swings in the top of the ninth, intent on padding their one-run lead, tempers flared in the corner of the visitors dugout.

"Murph, did I hear right?" Spahn asked. "I'm not going out for the ninth?"

"Just put on your jacket and watch the rest of the game, Warren. You did fine, but you're done." Murph turned to face the field, only to find Spahn back in his face moments later.

"Well if this ain't bush league, I don't know what is," Spahn complained. "There's a little something here in the big leagues called professional courtesy. What that means, Triple-A, is that when you're thinking of taking out your ace, you come ask him how he feels and what he thinks."

"You've thrown a lot of pitches, Warren, and, honestly, you look like you're just about out of gas."

The sound of Sam Jethroe's leadoff single and the response from the bench halted the pitcher's advance momentarily.

"Is that what you think?" he asked. "That I'm out of gas?"

"That's what I said."

"And did it occur to you to come out and check on me — just to see how the hell I was feeling?"

Murph muttered a word or two under his breath and looked into Spahn's eyes. "Look, Warren, do you really want to do this? Really? All I did was get a couple of arms up. That's all. A manager is allowed to do that. I think that's one of the rules that's the same in the majors as it is in Triple-A. And I would have been thrilled to pay you a visit but as luck would have it, you got yourself out of that jam. So there was really no need. So, why don't you zip up, plant it on the bench, and watch the rest of the game. Nice job today."

Spahn banged the fleshy part of his left palm against his thigh. "So that's it," he thundered. "Huh? Just like that? Go sit down? Bullshit. Absolute bullshit!"

Silence settled into the dugout until the Braves' bats, seemingly inspired by the eruption of emotion, caught fire. They sent nine men to the plate and scored a half dozen runs, highlighted by Lester's three-run shot over the center field wall, to grab a commanding 11–4 lead in the ninth. The unexpected success had everyone feeling good, especially Murph, whose last inning pitching decision suddenly seemed much easier now. Bullpen coach, Bob Keely, knew what Murph was going to say long before the rejuvenated manager sidled up next to him to bend his ear.

"Listen, Bobby," he began. "I would go with Antonelli if we were still up by only one, but now that we've cracked it open, it seems like the perfect time to get the kid's feet wet. You know, give Mickey the ball and see what he can do."

Keely said nothing. He just stood still, feet crossed, hands folded over the top railing of the dugout, watching as the bottom half of the eighth frame drew to a close.

"I mean that's the smart thing to do, right, Bobby?" Murph persisted. "'Cause I mean if you think—"

"Murph, you don't owe me or anyone else here an explanation," Keely said flatly. "Your door is the one that says 'Manager,' remember? It's your call."

It did not take Mickey long to get used to the idea of closing out the game. Just a few words from Murph and he was adjusting his cap, pounding his glove, and bounding out onto the big field for his major league debut. He arrived on the mound under a fickle April sun that struggled to heat the chilly afternoon air. Mickey breathed in deeply and arched his head back so that he could see errant wisps of white drifting across the great blue canvas that stretched on for eternity. It reminded him of the silky designs he often saw in the corners of the barn back home in Indiana. The reminiscence was not all that soothing, so he turned his attention to more pressing matters. The dirt beneath his feet troubled him, so he spent a little time with his back to the plate, head down, feet busy, as he made some last-second adjustments to the loose earth in front of the rubber. Then he turned to face Lester.

"Okay now, Mick," Lester called out. "Here we go now. Just like you can."

Mickey executed his warm-up tosses in fine fashion and stood awaiting his first challenge. He felt a bit odd, as if he were outside himself, watching the scene unfold from a distance. He was uncomfortably aware of his heartbeat as it hammered away at the walls of his chest, and the sound of the air whooshing in and out of his nose made him wonder about things like the speed at which his blood now flowed and whether or not it was observable to all who were watching. He was also homesick. This was nothing like Borchert Field. Yes, fresh green grass, three bases and home plate, foul lines, scoreboard, outfield wall, and umpires. But it all felt different somehow—especially the crowd. They were loud and restless, and there were so many of them. The kaleidoscope of faces before him was daunting and he fought momentarily against the impulse to duck from sight. Then he heard Murph calling from the bench and he was almost certain he could make it through okay.

"Go get 'em, Mick," he prodded reassuringly. "Toss that apple right to the glove now."

Whitey Lockman was Mickey's first challenge. The Giants' left fielder was already 2–4 on the day and was looking to get on base and ignite some offense for his deflated club. Lester recognized this and knew Mickey would have no trouble getting ahead of Lockman instantly.

"Here we go now, Mick," Lester called from behind his mask. Then he pounded his glove and put down one finger between his legs. Mickey took the sign, licked his lips, and, with eyes now narrowed, reared back and fired a four-seam fastball that exploded through the strike zone.

"Ball one!" was the call.

Although the pitch missed its target, the crowd—instantly captivated by the velocity of the pitch and the thunderous report of the ball once it hit Lester's glove—fell silent, struck by the sheer wonder of what everyone had just witnessed. The sudden stillness ignited in Mickey a resolve that fueled his next few moments. Mickey missed again, up and away, but then three straight flaming fastballs sealed Lockman's fate. Next for the Giants was Bobby Thompson, who had managed three hits in the first four at bats. The Giants' matinee idol looked foolish this time around, however, offering at two curveballs in the dirt before grounding out weakly to second base.

The Giants' final hope came in the form of Sam Jasper, who stepped to the plate in a silence so deafening that he could hear his own blood pumping, strong and erratic, in his ears. Mickey watched as the Giants' fifth-place hitter smoothed the dirt in the batter's box with two quick passes of his left cleat, only to dig out a small narrow divot toward the back of the box in which his rear foot could rest. He settled in, ready to take his shot at the young hurler. Any feelings of apprehension Mickey had prior to his debut departed, though his fascination with the size of the Polo Grounds and its now silent inhabitants remained. He stood sixty feet, six inches from his last batter, his eyes darting back and forth between the countless rows of seats and Jasper, who was only now ready to face Mickey and what everyone in the ballpark was calling his "electric stuff."

Mickey toed the rubber, placed his hands together at his waist, and looked in at Lester. Armed with his instructions, he rolled his arms, kicked his leg, and let fly a two-seam fastball that twisted through the air like a lightning bolt, vaporizing everything in its path before slicing Jasper's bat in two. The stunned hitter just stood at home plate, dumbfounded—the knob of his Louisville Slugger in one hand and a look of utter bewilderment on his face as the ball rolled harmlessly out toward the mound. Before Jasper could get his wits about him, Mickey scooped up the squib and fired it to first baseman, Earl Torgeson, for the final out of the game.

The impressive victory became great fodder for the press. The coterie of sports writers assigned to the Braves from season to season had spent the majority of their time in typical fashion, camped out at the lockers of Spahn, Jethroe, and Cooper. The bigger names always drew the lion's share of the attention. Although on this day, with the stragglers from the sellout crowd still buzzing about this unknown whiz kid who had lit up the radar gun in his one inning of work, a few reporters found their way to Mickey's locker as well.

The guys all noticed.

"Mickey, were you intimidated out there today?" one reporter asked. "How'd you feel?" The boy said nothing, just gazed vacantly at a point in the distance, as wisps of awareness drifted across his consciousness.

"Come on," another member of the press prodded. "Don't be shy, kid. We know you were called the Baby Bazooka in Milwaukee. Are ya for real or just some flash in the pan? Give us something here. Anything."

"Flash? Pan?" he repeated.

"Come on, kid. Spill it. Tell us about yourself."

Mickey stood now, face pale, mind polluted, rocking back and forth. He resembled a crumbling statue.

"Slowly, silently, now the moon, walks the night in her silver shoon."

The muscles in his stomach and in his legs began to ache. His face burned too. His discomfort continued to escalate as the frustration of those asking questions swelled.

"Hey, what is this?" a third man asked. He was tapping his pencil against a small pad of paper. "Kid, are you all right? What's all that mumbo jumbo about the moon? All we want to know is how you feel about today's performance."

Mickey's agitation grew worse as several beads of sweat ran from his forehead into his eyes.

"I-I-I don't know," he finally said. "Fastball up and in. Breaking stuff away. Nothing too good on 0–2. Ignore the crowd. It's okay, it will be okay. Mickey is—"

Murph and Lester, who had been seated at the opposite end of the room, heard the commotion and rushed to Mickey's defense.

"I think that's enough for one day, fellas," Murph said, stepping in between Mickey and the predatory cluster. "Mickey's had enough excitement for one day. We'll have to catch up with you guys next time."

The group of reporters just looked at each other, frustrated and dumbfounded.

"Come on, Murph." They called after him as he ushered the boy away to safety. "We're just getting started here. Are we gonna see the kid again? What's your plan for him?" Murph walked a few more steps, pushed Mickey gently in the direction in which he wanted the boy to go, then turned to face the ravenous bunch.

"I said enough is enough. No more today. And I mean it."

Now, many minutes later, after the intrusive threat of outsiders had been quelled, a bunch of the guys were all focused on picking up the rattled boy's spirits. For the most part, all the early banter about Mickey's idiosyncrasies and peculiar way of talking was gone. There seemed to be less room for hasty criticism.

"Hey, kid," Spahn said, placing his left hand on Mickey's shoulder. "Not too shabby. I have to admit, I had my doubts. We all did. But that was some real cheddar you were dealing out there. You made some folks sit up and take notice. Hell, it ain't every day that a rookie gets Bob Holbrook and C. Roger Barry to stop by after the game to chat. Even if you did freak out a little. Nice going. Just don't go thinking it's as easy as that every time. This is the bigs, son. Ain't always this easy."

Celebratory laughter filled every corner of the room. It was always good to begin the year with a win.

"Yeah," Tommy Holmes added. "This ain't for the faint of heart. No, sir. But I have to say. Ain't many guys able to silence a packed house at Ebbets Field." Holmes's comment was punctuated by a barrage of supportive slaps on Mickey's back, all of which elicited only a simple, diffident response from the astounded young hurler.

"Thanks, uh, thanks a lot," Mickey said, shrugging his shoulders awkwardly. "Mickey had fun today. Pitching. Pitching was fun."

The entire locker room erupted, once again—this time in waves of laughter.

"Did you hear that, Ozzy?" Connie Ryan screamed from across the room. Ryan noticed, with more than a little confusion, that Buddy Ozmore seemed to be hovering above all the merriment, detached from the feel-good moment in which the rest were basking. "Fun. He said he had fun today. That's priceless. Fun."

Ozmore winced as if some errant specks of dirt had flown into his eyes, then continued placing his gear in his locker. It was only after the last article was in its proper place that he finally spoke.

"Don't see what all the fuss is about," he said, closing the metal door and turning toward the exit. "Shit, he only got three outs."

It was late in the afternoon, and there was just enough light outside for Molly to see the look on Murph's face as he got out of his car and made his way toward her. The strained, severe look on his face puzzled her but then troubled her even more once he was inside.

"Hey, nice win today, Mr. Murphy," she said, winking before her face erupted into an ear-to-ear smile. "Now that's the way to make a debut."

He could barely see her through his fog of worry.

"Yeah, well. Sometimes a win ain't really a win at all."

Molly looked at him with narrow eyes lit by a flash of incredulity. "Are you for real, Arthur?" she asked. "Honestly, you win the first game of your professional career, Mickey pitches a wonderful inning, even the crowd eats it up to some extent, and you come home with that long face on, complaining? I just don't get you sometimes."

Molly folded her arms and shook her head slightly from side to side. "It's not that simple, Molly," he explained. "This is not Milwaukee and some minor league operation. The stakes are much higher here, and the personalities far more complex. Nobody sees that. There's a lot of pressure here. I've got a lot of other issues besides runs, hits, and errors." She stood listening while he rubbed his temples.

"Well?" she asked. "I'm all ears, Arthur. Let's hear it. What's bothering you? Tell me. Please. We always talk about everything. Maybe I can help."

She was right. He had fallen into the habit in the last couple of years of leaning on her when his life as he saw it veered off its intended path. Despite all of her own hardship and turmoil, she was always there to listen, and more often than not, to offer insights that not only allayed his concerns but actually brought an end to whatever was plaguing him. But somehow, this was different. He felt outside of her—removed—as if he were standing on one side of a creek and she on the other. He looked on helplessly as the watery barrier twisted its way for miles and miles, its frothy white gums menacing and unrelenting. Sure, she could see him, and he could perceive the warmth in her outstretched arms, but the disconnect was palpable and uncompromising; she could not see the line of sweat above his lip or hear the hammering of his trepid heart. She could not feel the suffocating fear. The creek just surged on.

"Thank you, Molly," he sputtered, trying desperately to find a way to express his present condition. "But I think this one has to be mine to figure out. At least for now."

# HOME STAND—MAY 1950

A tempest of thoughts swirled in Murph's head, rendering the fledgling skipper ill equipped to weigh the crumbling difference between success and impending misfortune. A couple of weeks had passed and the dissension on the team—a rift that was supposed to be fleeting—was actually gaining momentum. Even a .500 road trip, which saw Mickey earn victories in each of his first two starts, was not enough to mend the splintering clubhouse.

He sat by himself, in the cool shadows of his office, ruminating over his predicament. He had known that life in the big leagues would be challenging given the level of talent here and the brilliant baseball minds he'd be sparring with. Matheson made sure he knew that before they said their final good-byes.

"Ain't no walk in the park or some two-bit rodeo up there, Murph," the old man had prattled. "No, siree. Up there, the shine is on the ball, but it's you who's gots to keep it there." He knew what Matheson had meant, and had no problem putting his baseball acumen up against anyone else's. He was certain he could handle the baseball part. But he never imagined having to play schoolmaster to a bunch of self-indulgent adolescents. Wasn't he past all of that?

In the silence of the small office, he could hear the distant hum of the lawn mowers preparing the field for the day's practice. The sound, while at first soothing, now spawned a restlessness that could not wait. He got up from his desk, looked left, then right, before walking to the other side of the room where he stood for quite some time, hands shoved deep into his back pockets, eyes affixed to the 1948 Milwaukee Brewers team photo that hung above a rusty three-drawer filing cabinet. He mused silently about how far that team had come from those first few weeks and the rash of mean-spirited pranks designed to discourage Mickey. Murph ran his finger over each row of players, reminiscing about each one and what they all meant to him, before stopping on Lefty Rogers. He shook his head and frowned. Boy, did Lefty sure feel the heat once Mickey had arrived with his blazing fastball and pinpoint accuracy. All the sorry south-paw could do was find ways to get the kid off his game and try to infect the others with his venom. Nailing Mickey's cleats to the floor with the help of Woody Danvers. The incessant name-calling and insults. And then there was the heinous abduction at The Bucket, something that could have turned out much worse had Sheriff Rosco not found Mickey when he did.

Cripes, those sure were tough days. Murph continued to move his finger across the picture, as if each intermittent stop were a "Hello, nice to see you." Clem Finster. Arkie Fries. Jimmy Llamas. Boxcar. They were quite a cast of characters. None, however, were more instrumental in the team's success than Elliot McGinty, the shortstop they all called Pee Wee. Pee Wee stood a mere five foot, five inches tall and weighed a staggering 127 pounds soaking wet. He had red, cherubic cheeks and a head full of corkscrew curls. With his uniform on and his cap pulled neatly across his brow, he looked as if he should be studying for an algebra exam or shooting marbles in the schoolyard. Nobody would have ever guessed that his soft hands and lightning-fast feet made him the premier shortstop in the league.

But it wasn't Pee Wee's fielding prowess that Murph was remembering. The troubled manager certainly appreciated McGinty's talent, but it was the shortstop's cabin in Baker's Woods—a small, dilapidated shanty with weathered wood shingles and a rusty tin roof, that had suddenly captured Murph's imagination. He recalled how the team was struggling to come together and how the fishing trip that McGinty hosted had united them and really helped the other fellas get to know and understand Mickey. Murph lifted the dusty frame off the wall, shook his head, and smiled. Maybe that was it. It worked once before. Why not now?

With a renewed sense of hope and purpose, Murph began considering, with more and more certainty, the idea of getting the team together for some sort of team bonding event. This wasn't Milwaukee though, and these were major league ballplayers who were used to more fast-paced, exciting endeavors. Fishing at some tiny lake was not going to cut it. Murph's first thought was a restaurant or saloon, a place where the team could eat and drink and really cut loose. It was the perfect venue. It's what most of the guys did anyway. Murph was certain he had found the answer and had already begun thinking of just the right place when he remembered Molly. All at once his spirit sagged. She would never allow Mickey to attend—not after the last two incidents that occurred while her son was at such a place. And Mickey was the most vital cog in this wheel. There was no point in putting this all together without him. There had to be another way.

These were the times when Murph missed Matheson the most. The garrulous old-timer was certainly a handful, and his incessant babbling and generous use of clichés could really fray one's nerves, but he always seemed to know just what to do in situations like these. "More than one way to skin a cat," he would probably say, or something like that. Yes, there had to be a way—something he was not thinking of. He could hear Matheson's voice, loud and clear, as he considered his options. "There's none so deaf, Murph, as those who will not hear."

Murph spent the next half hour trying to come up with an idea. It had to be just right, right enough to satisfy Molly but also his most unforgiving critics, especially Ozmore. Murph knew that if Ozmore was not on board, the whole thing would tumble like a house of cards. *Why was this guy such a hump? How does someone get to be so self-important, so full of himself?* That was it! What better way to get Ozmore on board than to make it all about him? It was sheer genius. The vainglorious hothead would never be able to resist. Murph laughed out loud as he rubbed his hands together. Why hadn't he seen it before?

Later that day, after practice, Murph stood before his team and began unfurling his plan. His confidence and resolve gained more and more momentum with each word he spoke. It was, perhaps, his most calculated moment.

"So you see, fellas, I think it's important that we come together, both on and off the field. And what better time to do so than during our ten-game home stand." Murph paused, crossed the floor over to the locker room door, and rested his shoulder against the jamb. He had everyone's attention.

"I was thinking that we should get together tomorrow afternoon before our series against the Reds begins," he continued. "You know, maybe a little barbeque, some beer and cigars." He paused briefly, walked back toward the center of the room, then settled right in front of Ozmore.

"And I think that it's only right that we do it all at the home of the team's heart and soul." He smiled, nodded confidently, and put his hand on Ozmore's shoulder. "What do you say, Ozzy? Will you have us to your place if I take care of all the rest?"

Ozmore wrinkled his nose. His mouth contorted as if something sour had just passed his lips. He was just about to speak when the entire room erupted in a mixture of cheers and applause.

"Ozzy! Ozzy! Ozzy!

The walls of the locker room reverberated with raucous adulation for the newly elected host.

Murph laughed heartily as he watched Ozmore's reluctance soften.

"Hey, uh, sure, sure," Ozmore said, slowly embracing the sudden limelight. "I'll have you guys at my place. Why not? It's a little short notice, and I've got some things to take care of, but I can make it work." He paused momentarily before continuing. "And after I do, it will be the best damn time you guys have ever had."

The next morning, under a brilliant, cloudless sky that had just given birth to an early May sun, Murph and the team arrived at Ozmore's with all the accessories needed for a really killer get-together. They divided up the labor, shared the responsibility for laying things out, and within a hour's time, the party was in full swing.

In one corner of the yard, in a perfectly rectangular space between pristine rows of tomato plants and a two-tier birdbath fountain, Tommy Holmes and Johnny Sain were embroiled in a horseshoe match for the ages. Laughter spilled from the half circle of lawn chairs just across the way as a cigar-smoking trio, Lester, Bob Elliot, and Walter Cooper, reacted to Holmes's theatrics after he rattled one of the silver shoes around the metal peg.

"Don't even mess with me, Johnny boy," Holmes boasted. "I'll hit it every time. I am the horseshoe master."

Warren Spahn was watching and laughing too. "I'll school you later on, master," he mocked as he handed out frosty bottles of Pabst Blue Ribbon from a metal washtub overflowing with ice. "Just as soon as I finish watering the troops, I'll show you how a real man tosses them things."

There were other games as well, including cards, croquet, and even an impromptu contest of bocce ball engineered by none other than Ozmore himself. A dirty sack of old baseballs and an errant stick wedged strategically in the ground was all the host needed to get things rolling.

"The cleaner balls belong to one side and the dirty ones the other," he proclaimed proudly as he divided up the contents of the bag. "Who's game?" Only Murph and Mickey, who had assumed the cooking duties at the grill, were exempt from the contest. Their focus remained on the sizzling meats. "You see, Mick, you have to be careful with the ribs," Murph explained. "Don't want to cook 'em too much."

Mickey said nothing at first; he just looked down at his shoes until the silence became too uncomfortable.

"Well how much *do* you have to cook them?" he finally asked.

"Huh?"

"The ribs. If you can't cook them too much, how do you know what's too little and what's just right?"

Murph stared blankly into the white smoke billowing from the grill. "Well, Mick, if you just turn 'em and—"

"Because my mama bakes pies all the time, and she always sets the timer for between forty-five and fifty-five minutes. Apple pie takes forty-five minutes, but sweet potato, pecan, cherry, and peach all cook for fifty. That's the longest, except for rhubarb, which usually takes fifty-five or sixty. And lemon meringue, that's the shortest—sometimes forty or even thirty-five. But if you don't know how—"

"Mick, it's like pitching, ya know? You just have to read what's happening. If you look at how it's cooking, you know when it's time."

Mickey's concern had departed, but his curiosity surged. He was scanning the grill feverishly. "What about the hamburgers and hot dogs?"

Murph shrugged his shoulders and smiled. "Same thing. Just have to look."

"But how can you have ribs, hamburgers, hot dogs, and chicken, too, all on the grill all at once and cook them for different amounts of time?"

"Mickey, it really doesn't—"

"Mickey thinks that the hamburgers and hot dogs should go first because they would take the longest, then maybe the chicken next and then the ribs. They shouldn't really touch each other either, Murph. You don't want barbeque sauce from the chicken getting on the hot dogs or that stuff on the ribs getting on the hamburgers. Unless you put barbeque sauce on your hamburgers, then it's okay, but only if you do it after they come off the grill. But you can't put too much on account of the bun getting too wet. Then it starts to fall apart, gets messy, and sticks to the hamburger. One time my mama put so much sauce on my hamburger bun it fell apart right in my hands."

Murph filled his lungs and exhaled slowly. A swift return of more ordered thoughts helped him to extricate himself from Mickey's whirling mania.

"Say, Mick, how about we talk about something else, huh? Like the team. How ya liking life as a big leaguer? Everything okay?"

Mickey reached for the steel tongs in front of him and began moving the hot dogs so that they were now all perfectly aligned and occupied their own space—a safe distance from the hamburgers and chicken.

"Yeah, I like being a big leaguer," he answered. His eyes were still fixed on the hot dogs. "It's fun. I sort of miss the old guys, like Pee Wee and Woody, but it's okay."

The sun, in its present location, caused Murph and Mickey to look almost silhouetted, as though they were positioned on stage. Mickey continued to fiddle with the arrangement of items cooking on the grill while Murph rubbed his eyes; the white, viscous smoke was irritating.

"Yeah, being a big leaguer *is* fun," Murph commented. "Every little boy's dream for sure. But I have to confess, Mick, it's a lot harder than I ever imagined, you know."

"Why is it hard, Murph?" Mickey asked. "Baseball ain't hard. Baseball is fun. It's the same game you know—three strikes, four balls, nine innings. Same game, Mr. Murphy."

He didn't expect Mickey to understand, but the kid was his only outlet at the moment. Murph couldn't help but recall his long, circuitous route to the bigs—and how on many occasions he had resurrected his dream. It wasn't the sort of idyllic image that faded with waking, acquiescing to the early dawn. This dream was imbued with a colossal vitality, insinuating itself into everything he saw or heard—everything he smelled. He couldn't look at a score-card or put a bat in his hands without hearing the calls from the crowd. Everything was haunted: the smell of freshly cut grass—the sound of flags dancing in a stiff breeze. He couldn't even eat sweet potato pie—even Molly's—without reminiscing about Rosie's, the little truck stop he used to frequent with the guys when he was just a rookie. The images of glory days past spilled out of his head, always most intensely during those minor league moments when he had thought he was going to fall short for sure. It was almost crippling. Now that he had made it, the uncertainty somehow seemed even worse.

"The same game, Mick?" he replied. "Yes, yes, I suppose so." He was looking past the barbeque grill into the yard. "But with a lot more to lose."

The afternoon went on in glorious fashion, and Murph was pleased with the tenor of things. There was plenty of eating and drinking and good-natured fun, all of which seemed to belie the concern that Murph had previously harbored. Even Ozmore, whom Murph deemed his greatest challenge, had embraced the group and his role as the ambassador of camaraderie. The typically irascible athlete had spent the entire day reveling in his assignment as host, tending to the needs of his guests with great alacrity, and in doing so, facilitating a sense of unity and togetherness. Murph couldn't help but smile as the feeling continued to gain momentum.

"Hey, if anyone needs anything, anything at all, I will be inside for a bit with Spahny," Ozmore announced. "Seems as though there's a game of eight-ball that needs to be decided and it just can't wait." He flexed his bicep and growled. "Just let me know when my sister gets here."

The air cooled considerably as the day lengthened, but the festivities held their initial intensity. Even Mickey, who was usually guarded around those whom he viewed as strangers, got swept up in all the hoopla. He had found his way to the makeshift horseshoe pit and together with Lester and Sid Gordon held a couple of the steel shoes in his right hand and was eyeballing the spike some forty feet away.

"Now take it easy there, Mick," Lester joked. "That there ain't no baseball to be thrown like no rocket. Could kill someone with that arm of yours."

Gordon chuckled and then nodded with a modicum of genuine concern. "He's right, Mickey. Be real careful. Maybe you should sit it out for a while and just watch how we do this. You really should know a little about horseshoes before playing."

"Nah, Mickey knows a lot about horseshoes. I can try now."

A light behind the boy's eyes seemed to shine as he made his first toss.

"Mickey reckons he knows everything about horseshoes, Sid," he said.

"It's okay, Mick, I didn't mean to—"

"Horseshoes is made from steel or iron. You nail 'em to the palmar surface of the hoof, but sometimes my daddy used to glue 'em if that was too hard to do, like with Agatha. She were this pretty horse we had on our farm. She had a long, brown mane and pretty eyes. But we could never really get them shoes on her right. She and Oscar got along real well. Oscar were my pig. He didn't have no shoes, but he had a—"

"No, no, Mick," Gordon interrupted. "I didn't mean that. I just meant that it helps to know a little something about the game of horseshoes before you start *throwing* them. That's all."

Mickey heard nothing being said—no footsteps, no voices, not even the loud clanking of each shoe as it hooked around the metal spike.

"Looks like he knows all he has to Gordy," Lester said laughing. "The kid is unreal. Freaky good at some things. And if I know him like I thinks I do, he going to be here a while."

Having heeded Lester's warning, Gordon slipped away with the catcher and moved to the other side of the yard while Mickey continued to throw one shoe after another, pausing only to retrieve the shoes once he had tossed the last one. On his walks to and from the spike, he thought more about Agatha. And his father, Clarence. There were so many moments he wished he could forget, like the time Clarence took apart the horse's bridle in a fit of rage and began whipping her with the throatlatch, all because she wouldn't stand still while he washed her.

"You good fer nothin' nag," he had barked as he slashed at her hind quarters and back. "I'll learn ya to mess around while I'm working here."

Mickey was horrified; his throat closed and tears filled his eyes. His roiling terror and panic and helplessness supplanted his submissiveness.

"Let her alone—stop it, stop it!" he pleaded. "You're hurting her. Stop it! Stop!"

His enraged father had halted his attack abruptly, as if some invisible force had suddenly seized his arm. He stared blankly for a moment, as if he were reading his next move from a random point off in the distance. Then he turned from the horse to face his son, the leather strap dangling lifelessly at his side. His eyes moved slowly at first, up and down the boy's body in measuring fashion. Then, without much warning, the ferocity with which his eyeballs shifted accelerated exponentially, spinning riotously back and forth as if the beady gray dots were about to detach themselves from their sockets.

"So you feel something for this no good, flea-bitten nag, do ya?" he thundered, raising the strap behind his ear. "Well, maybe when you feel this, you'll learn to keep yer big, fat mouth shut and keep yer nose out of my business."

Mickey had not thought about Clarence in some time. He let the horseshoes fall to the ground before wandering over to a wooden bench where he proceeded to sit uneasily, rocking back and forth as if trying to rid himself of the awful memory. These were the moments that, for him, seemed to rage on with an indefatigable vitality and no clear remedy. Sure, the recitation of "Silver" helped calm the tremors, but only after someone else, someone safe, interceded at some point. He had just begun rocking more deliberately and forming the words "Slowly, silently, now the moon" when it happened.

Squinting into the late afternoon sunshine, Mickey saw her. She appeared through the golden haze like an angel. He recognized those soft sandy curls instantly, and was calmed by the familiarity. She saw him as well, and soon the distance between the two had been erased by eager steps from both directions.

"Mickey, right?" she said enthusiastically the second he was close enough to her to hear. "From the bar? What are you doing here?"

Mickey closed his eyes. The scent of lilac was strong and his heartbeat was loud in his ears. "Where is your rabbit's foot, Miss Jolene? I hope you did not lose it again."

Her face softened in remembrance. She studied him, her collard green eyes twinkling in the late afternoon sunlight. "No, no," she said, reaching into her pocket to retrieve her key ring. "It's still right where it needs to be. See?"

Mickey smiled and ran his finger over the soft white fur. "That's good. Good luck too. Just like horseshoes. I was just playing them, over there." He pointed in the direction of the game. She began to comment but before she could pass a word across her lips Mickey was off.

"But I reckon I don't get why horseshoes is good luck neither. Ain't nothing lucky about them for Agatha or any other horse that's got to stay still for the nailing of them on their hooves. And I ain't so sure how them things are lucky for people neither. Can't wear them none and they is too heavy to put around your neck. Four-leaf clover is lucky, cause you can't ever hardly find one. So you's lucky just to get one. Now ladybugs is lucky, I suppose. One time one landed on my shoulder and after that Mickey won three games at a carnival. That was lucky but not as lucky as when I saw a shooting star and—"

"Well I think my little white friend here is pretty lucky too, wouldn't you say?" She smiled and her cheeks turned pink. "I mean, who would have thought I would have ever run into you again—and here, of all places, at my brother's house."

Mickey shrugged. "I don't reckon that is lucky, Miss Jolene. Mickey was invited here."

"No, no, I just mean that—"

As Mickey rambled on about the team and Ozmore and playing in Boston for the first time, Jolene recalled their first conversation, and her mind was lit by the sudden realization that Mickey and her brother were teammates.

"This is too much," she said, shaking her head. "When you said you played baseball that day I met you, I never even thought of that. Don't know why Buddy never said anything."

For many minutes, the two sat together, listening to the song of the sparrows and warblers, marveling at the way some seemed to soar higher and higher while others parachuted gently to earth and came to rest on the lawn all around them.

"Don't take this the wrong way, Mickey, but you seem so different from the rest of these guys. I don't know. There's just something about you. Most of my brother's friends are loud and always talking about themselves. But you, you're just a regular guy. It's not bad. It's actually nice. I never would have guessed that you were a ballplayer."

Mickey frowned.

"Oh, I didn't mean that you couldn't be a ballplayer," she explained, aware now of his discomfort. "I just mean that you are not like these other guys. You know, always bragging and boasting. I rarely spend any time with them. I'm only here today to give something to my brother."

The tinderbox of memories that Mickey's mind housed seemed to unlock, releasing a series of moments that called into question his "different" nature. On so many occasions, Clarence had been all too eager to throw a spotlight of the boy's condition.

"Don't really know what the heck to make of you, boy," he used to complain. "Ain't no explaining you. That's fer sure."

Even Molly, whose tender, watchful eye never strayed too far from her boy, made it clear that he was not like the other kids. "It's okay, honey," she would say when Mickey could not understand why he wasn't able to do some of the things the other children were doing. "You're special, that's all. A little different. You're not like the others. But it's okay, really. Someday you will understand."

"Mickey does not know why I am so different, Jolene," he explained. "It is not so nice. Folks is always telling me that. Even on the field. Sometimes, it feels like—"

She grabbed his hands and held them in between hers. "I didn't mean anything bad, Mickey," she said. "Honest. Actually, it was a compliment. But, listen, I know all too well what it feels like to be the outsider. You know, the one who just does not fit in. I can tell you a whole bunch of stories like that."

They viewed their histories like a fleet of ships, with each reminiscence following closely behind the one that preceded it. Mickey unraveled a few of his most vivid recollections of Clarence and his abusive antics and Jolene shared some of the more regrettable moments from her past.

"I'll never forget that spring when I was a senior in high school," she began. Tears were already forming behind her eyes but she would not let herself cry. Instead, she went on to describe in great detail what she was recalling: It was a warm afternoon in May. The sky above was empty and pale blue and just a hint of hyacinth floated on a gentle breeze. All around her, the world was bursting with life, from the kaleidoscope of painted lady butterflies flitting around a patch of thistle to the melodious song of the pair of northern cardinals foraging in the tall grass just beyond the split-rail fence that defined her parents front yard. Hope and promise abounded, especially since she had just come from St. Anthony's and could not wait to ask her mother about the annual dance.

"Now, Jolene, are we going to do this again?" her mother admonished. "What did we say about this last year?"

"But, Mama, I just want to—" The girl's resolve began to leak from her eyes.

"Jolene, I have told you before. You are not the sort of girl who goes to dances and does that sort of thing. It's not a big deal. Just is what it is. You're different, you know, from the other girls. You're not like them. It's not a bad thing, really. But it is something that you best learn now."

"But I don't understand why—"

"I told you, Jolene, many times, that your time is best spent around here, doing the wash and ironing and things like that. Those are things that maybe one day could help you get yourself a fella."

The words were just as painful now, years later. Her lip quivered as she completed the story.

"Did you ever get to dance, Miss Jolene?" Mickey asked. "My mama dances all the time. She loves music. Plays the clarinet all the time, especially now that she's married to Mr. Murphy." He was noticeably bothered by her labored breathing and could not stop staring at her lower lip.

"No, no, Mickey," she replied, wiping her eyes with the back of her hand. "Figured my mama knew what she was talking about. You know, your parents always know best, right? Besides, I don't know all that much about dancing."

"Are you crying because you wanted to dance? If you are, that's okay. You can dance now. Or maybe later."

"No, Mickey, it's okay. I'm okay. Really. Thank you."

The two sat together for a while longer, listening to the wheezy mewing of a flock of northern pintails circling overhead while sharing the ghosts that rattled around the corners in each of their minds. They tiptoed through most of the memories, mindful of the pain and shame attached to each, but managed to blink away the tears that had formed here and there and eventually arrived at a place that was somehow peaceful and safe. They had even managed to share a chuckle or two, and Mickey was just about to tell Jolene a joke that Matheson had told him, when Ozzy's voice, shrill and reproachful, split the air.

"Why the hell didn't anyone tell me my sister was here?" he thundered. Standing on the back steps, hands dug firmly into his hips, his face twisted and hard, Ozzy resembled the Minotaurs Mickey had read about with Molly when he was just a child. Their host, who only hours before had welcomed Mickey and the team to his home, had morphed into something sinister and menacing.

"Sure, all of you can drink my beer and eat my food, but you're all too damned busy to do the one thing I asked," he ranted as he stomped over to Mickey and Jolene. His face grew darker as he drew closer to them.

"Jolene, that's enough!" he admonished. "Enough, do you hear? Get away from him, right now." His sudden tirade halted all activity. The entire yard went silent, as if someone had run suddenly from a crowded dance floor and accidentally kicked the plug from a jukebox machine, rendering all dancers lost in the awkward silence.

"Don't you ever, ever, let me catch you rubbing elbows with any of these guys, especially *him*," he continued. "Enough of this horseshit. I turn my back for just a few minutes and look what I have to deal with."

The girl's face flushed uncontrollably.

"Never again, Jolene!" he screamed again. "You hear me? Never. Have I made myself clear? Never again."

# HOME FIRES BURNING

The Braves found the friendly confines of the Bee Hive to be just the right remedy for whatever ailed them. They began a twelve-game home stand with a 3–0 victory over the Pirates. Warren Spahn was his usual brilliant self, scattering five hits over nine innings to secure the complete game shutout. Murph's crew didn't exactly light up the scoreboard, managing just six hits themselves. But an eighth-inning surge, including back-to-back singles by Sid Gordon and Willard Marshall, followed by a long pinch-hit home run off the bat of Lester, was all they would need. Sure, it was only mid-May, and it was way too early to declare the game a must win, but it was just the sort of thing on which Murph and the Braves could build.

The victory proved to be a harbinger of good fortune indeed, as the Braves went on to win eight of the next ten games they played, stealing a single game from the Cardinals and taking series victories from the Cubs, Reds, and Dodgers before beating the Giants in the first two contests of a three-game set. Everything was clicking for Murph's Braves. The pitching was superb, fielding stellar, and the bats were providing just the right combination of table setting and power. They were poised to close out the series and conclude one of the most successful home stands in team history; it seemed like a done deal until Johnny Sain came up with a stiff shoulder and could not take the ball.

"So what now, Murph?" Spahn asked when he heard his buddy had pulled up lame.

Murph had already pulled the pencil off his ear and made the necessary adjustment.

"Well, Warren, let's just say all of you are in for a real treat tonight."

Spahn, together with Buddy Ozmore, took one look at Mickey—who was busy running his finger over the laces of a brand new baseball—and exploded.

"Are you shittin' me, Murph?" Spahn asked. "Him? You're *starting* him?"

Murph looked over at Bob Keely, the bullpen coach; Keely turned his head and looked away.

"What kind of harebrained nonsense is this?" Ozmore added. "Relief is one thing. But we are finally on a roll here and you're going to send out an overgrown ankle biter who still don't know his ass from his elbow? This is your great idea?"

Outside, the sun began spilling its light across the ballpark, lighting up everything in its wake, including Murph's fractured expression.

"Really, guys? The season's almost two months old and he's only had three appearances. None at home. What did you think? That the kid was going to go an entire calendar with just doing bullpen sessions? And an occasional relief appearance—really? Did you think that all of this was some sort of publicity stunt?"

Murph's response was curt and continued on with varying shades of intensity.

"You know, you guys are something else. All full of piss and vinegar and a whole damn wheelbarrow full of complaints—nothing but complaints. Just once, one time, I'd like to hear maybe a suggestion, an idea. You know, something helpful, for the good of the order."

Ozmore glared at Murph with beady eyes. "You want a suggestion?" he said through clenched teeth. "Okay, you got it. Here's a suggestion. Put your blockhead friend on the back burner today and give the ball to Chipman. He's the better choice. That is, if you're interested in winning the game."

"He's right, Murph," Spahn interjected. "Chippy hasn't pitched in a while. He's fresh. And he knows the Giants' lineup. Give him the ball. The kid can pitch another time."

"Seems to me Mickey handled the Giants pretty good last time, no?"

"That was relief, Murph. He barely faced anyone. Starting a game at home is a whole other ball game."

Murph closed his eyes and massaged his lids with an open hand. This was way more difficult than he expected. "You guys want Bobby Chipman to start today? Is that it?"

The two malcontents nodded in unison.

"Yeah, and while you're at it, you might want to give Coops the nod behind the dish. What's right is right."

The lines on Murph's forehead grew more pronounced.

"So Mickey and Lester both sit?" Murph asked. "Is that what you want? Okay, you got it. No problem. Chipman gets the ball, just like you asked. And Coops will catch him. Mickey will go out there some other time."

Bobby Chipman began the game in reasonable fashion while Murph tried to convince Mickey that nothing was amiss. The lanky lefty retired the leadoff batter on a sharp single to short, and then after falling behind 3–0 to the next batter, induced a weak pop out that Earl Torgeson caught in foul ground. Then things began to go awry. Don Mueller, the Giants' three-hitter, laced Chipman's next delivery into center field for a single. Roy Weatherly followed with a clean single of his own, and both runners crossed home plate after Bobby Thompson's line drive found the left center field gap and rolled all the way to the wall. The third and final out of the opening frame came by way of a long fly ball that Tommy Holmes managed to run down just before running out of room on the warning track. But the damage was done.

"Chippy ain't exactly fooling anyone out there," Murph whispered to Keely. "Why did I listen to those two?"

"It's still early, Murph," Keely said, shaking his head. "Give him some time to find it."

The Braves went down quietly in their half of the first, including a three-pitch strikeout of Ozmore. Chipman, who barely had had a minute to get some water and collect himself, was visibly rattled and back out for another shot. The lefty's demeanor only worsened after he walked the first two Giants to face him and surrendered back-to-back singles to the next two hitters. He looked like a wilting flower. Murph slammed his fist on the bench and then motioned to his catcher Walker Cooper to take a walk out to the mound and check Chipman's temperature.

"Maybe people will start listening to me around here," Murph grumbled under his breath. He was wild with anger. His blood felt like lava flowing faster and faster beneath his skin. This would not do; it was completely unacceptable. He had to grab on to something, grip with his mind, and find an answer that would allow him to feel whole again and not like some A-ball patsy who was playing bog league manager.

"Enough of this horseshit," he said to Keely. "Take Mickey down to the pen and get him ready."

The struggling southpaw lasted only two more batters. By the time he was through, he had allowed six hits, surrendered four runs, and failed to retire a single batter in the second inning, leaving Mickey with a second and third jam to navigate.

"Okay, Mick," Murph said, as the two of them watched Keely go out to get Chipman. "Nice and easy now. Like you can. That's all. Just be yourself."

Lester, who had been watching from the other side of the dugout, joined the exchange. "Murph's right, Mick," he said, patting the boy on his back. "Just like you did with me all those times. Okay? Just like tossing them apples. You get me? Just do it, kid. Ain't nobody better."

Mickey looked at Lester. "You coming out, too, Lester Sledge — to catch Mickey?" he asked.

A difficult silence stole the moment.

"No, Mick, no," Murph said. "Not this time. Cooper will catch you today. But don't worry, son. Lester will get you next time."

Mickey's entrance was uneventful, like a careless whisper passed between two strangers. He bounded out of the bullpen and ran with purpose across the lush outfield grass toward the hill of dirt that awaited his arrival. He moved awkwardly but with speed, his head raised just enough so that his eyes got caught in the web of indifferent faces packed in the stands. It was nothing like the welcomed frenzy he had grown to love back in Milwaukee. The cold reality was unsettling and worked against his effort to push on, but it paled in comparison to the patchwork of images filtering through his fevered mind. Every step he took rattled another painful recollection. He could see Clarence and smell his rancid breath. He could hear him too. "Ain't no retard gonna ever amount to nothing special. No, siree, Bob. Won't be long before those baseball boys see what I seen yer whole life." The words made him wince. What if Clarence was right? Mickey was a long way from Borchert Field. Who would care about him here?

He was thinking of Lefty Rogers too—and his boots, the right one in particular—the same one that crashed into Oscar's side and sent the porker crashing to his tragic demise. He also could see Lefty's black eyes and was remembering The Bucket that night and Lefty's defection to the archrival Rangers. He could still remember how he awoke in a crumpled heap the next morning. His stomach was beginning to hurt that same way and his mouth was just as dry, as if he had stuffed inside his cheeks too many forkfuls of his Aunt Marcy's homemade sponge cake. And of course, he could still feel the burning pain in his right hand. That was the worst thing of all— that and the weeks he missed afterward healing from the vicious attack. Panic seemed to find him now and was slipping its sticky tentacles around his neck. Only a quick glimpse at Jolene, who was waving from her brother's seats, and the sound of Murph's voice prodding him to just do his thing enabled him to stand tall on the rubber and begin his warm-up.

Mickey's first tosses were easy and true but nothing special. There was no popping of the catcher's glove. It was strange throwing to somebody other than Lester. It bothered Mickey less than he would have imagined. He always felt like the practice throws were less about him getting loose and more about getting accustomed to his new backstop. He understood that. Each ball he delivered ushered in more and more of the remarkable pitching power and precision that had brought him to Boston. But he was still finding himself in front of a strange crowd that was largely unimpressed.

But all that would change minutes later. With the stars winking their collective approval, the umpire put the ball in play and the boy threw his first pitch, a blistering fastball that roared past his first batter like a meteor. It was one of those moments in time when everything else just seemed to fade away. Mickey was front and center now, exposed in all his glory as if the universe had adjusted the glow of every light in the stadium directly over him, illuminating his figure in a brilliance reserved only for the likes of angels and saints.

"Strike one!"

The batter shook his head. So did everyone in the stadium who had been watching.

Murph just smiled. He had seen this unfold before.

Mickey received the return toss from Cooper and set himself again. He took his sign, wound, and fired. The delivery was as true as the first and split the plate right down the middle.

"Strike two!"

The pop of the glove and the buzz that followed filtered through the stands like a ground fog, seeping into every corner of the stadium. By the time Mickey had set himself for his next delivery, everyone was standing, intoxicated by the anticipation of what was fast becoming an epic moment straight from the annals of Greek mythology.

Mickey did not disappoint. The next pitch was equally powerful and precise, but was made even more awe inspiring by the feckless flailing that occurred, courtesy of a batter who was completely over-matched.

"Strike three!"

The crowd, still stunned by what it had just witnessed, only managed a smattering of applause. It was as if the rush of the moment had temporarily paralyzed the limbs of most of the spectators; they could not move. But Mickey's quick disposal of the next two Giants to face him was enough to awaken the Boston faithful and send them into a riotous chant of "Mickey! Mickey! Mickey!" The incantation rained down as Mickey jogged off the field.

When he arrived back at the dugout, he was greeted by a chain of incredulous smiles and just as many celebratory pats on the back. And of course, there was Murph, right there in the middle of it all.

"That's the old pepper, Mick," he said, throwing his arms around the boy. "Whoa baby!" Mickey sat down next to Lester and wiped his face with a towel that he proceeded to fold and place neatly next to him.

"You didn't say nothin' about no pepper, Mr. Murphy," he said quizzically. "Apples. Mickey was thinking about apples out there. Not peppers. Peppers are green. Maybe yellow or orange. Sometimes they are red. But those are always too hot. Mama sometimes uses them when—"

"Hey, it's okay, Mick," Murph said, laughing. "Just an expression. Apples are fine. Just fine."

Lester laughed and shook his head. "Same old Mickey, through and through. Gotta love him."

The Braves managed only two hits over the next seven innings, squandering a brilliant performance by Mickey. Murph spoke briefly after the game about the anemic offense, but the most telling comments came when Murph ran into Ozmore on the way out of the clubhouse.

"Tough one today," he said. Ozmore smirked. Murph knew he should have just left it at that but could not help himself. "You know, Ozzy, maybe you should spend a little more time worrying about who's pitching for the other team instead of us." The loss was of little consequence it seemed. Nobody who was at the game was talking about the Braves being shutout 4–0. The subject on the lips of those who exited through the turnstiles was young Mickey Tussler and his eight-inning gem that included ten strikeouts and only four hits allowed. The press was equally captivated, devoting the entire back pages of both the Boston Globe and Boston Herald to the young man. The headlines told the whole story. BRAVES' BATS SILENT, BUT MICKEY ROARS. TUSSLER TAMES GIANTS IN LOSING EFFORT.

News was spreading fast. Every barber chair, bar stool, and coffee shop housed some Bostonian bantering about the Braves and their fireballing phenom who had emerged out of nowhere. Even Red Sox fans, who rarely gave the other Bean Town club the time of day, could not help but entertain the rousing discourse.

Days later, Mickey and the Braves were still riding the swell of popularity. But Molly's feelings were conflicted. The early morning song of the European starlings mirrored Molly's joy over Mickey's success. She was so pleased that her boy had once again silenced his critics—had overcome his inner demons and the cynics who projected failure for the young phenom—and had emerged a real force to be reckoned with on the professional diamond. She couldn't help but smile, especially when she recalled the excitement in his voice as he told her all about his recent exploits.

"Mickey is just like one of the guys, Mama," he said. "Just like them. And the newspaper men sit by my locker, too, after the game, just like they do for the others. I told them all about Oscar and that there are 108 stitches on a baseball."

She had never seen him so connected to anything before. "Mickey even has a new friend," he said with what Molly swore was a tinge of embarrassment. "Her name is Jolene. She goes to all the games. She's Ozzy's sister. But she likes Mickey. Not like Laney. Jolene is a good girl."

"You have a *what*?" she asked. Her brow furrowed.

Murph swore he could hear the commentary raging inside her head. "Hey, let's not talk about that now, okay?" he interjected in timely fashion. "It's not like that, Molly. It's okay. Look at the boy. He's doing great."

Mickey *was* great. He was much calmer now and having the time of his life. Molly was thrilled for him and smiled when she spoke of the recent turn of events, but the outward bliss belied the lengthening shadows in her heart. Boston was becoming more and more foreign to her, and her patience and resiliency were waning. The promise of getting accustomed to and eventually growing to love this new city had seemed to come and go with the passing of early spring. She felt a little guilty saying anything to Murph, for he had never appeared happier and she did not want to dampen his spirits, but she could not remain silent any longer.

"Arthur, this whole Boston thing is just not working out," she said when she finally got him alone. The two had just finished their dinner at Frank's Chop House and were sitting quietly now in the glow of the dimmed lights, sipping coffee.

"Not working out?" he asked. "Molly, are you kidding me? Things have never been better. How can you say that?"

"Never been better for *you*," she said. "For *you*, yes, life is great. But if you—"

"And Mickey? What about Mickey, Molly? You've seen him. The kid is delirious."

She was at a loss for the proper words to express how she missed him and the way things used to be. They had always been on the same page, even at the very incipient stages of their relationship when she was still with Clarence. But now it all seemed different. Boston and the call to the major leagues had altered all of it. She was sad, frustrated, and very aware of this vague dissatisfaction over having grown to need him more than he needed her.

"Arthur, look at me," she said. "I don't belong here. I just don't. This is *your* world, not mine. You have everything that you need, everything that you have ever wanted. I have no place anymore."

"Come on, Molly, how can you say that? Can't you see that—"

"What I see and what I know is that things have changed, Arthur. Look, I'm not blaming you. I knew who you were when we decided to do this. But you have to understand—I lived a long time as a shadow. But you already know that. It was you who helped me see it. So while I love you, Arthur, and appreciate everything that you have done for both me and Mickey, I just can't go back to being a nobody. I can't."

He reached across the table and grabbed her hand. "But why does being the wife of a major league baseball manager make you a nothing? I don't understand."

"It's not only about the baseball, Arthur," she replied. "Sure, things now are a little more intense, and we do have less time to ourselves than we used to, but you're missing the bigger picture here. Life back in Indiana was not life in Milwaukee. That didn't matter, though. I got used to Milwaukee and all the changes that came with that. It wasn't so easy but I did it. But Boston? Boston is a whole other place, Arthur. It's not for me—at least not on my own it's not."

"So what are you saying, Molly?' he asked. "You're just gonna quit? Give up? Just like that? What about us? And Mickey? You really don't want to be a part of what's happening with him here?"

She entertained flashes of her boy and his unexpected success and how she had seen him evolve into this remarkable young man who somehow, despite his limitations and an upbringing that would have crushed even the strongest of wills, had become successful. She had loved watching it and experiencing it firsthand, but all she could think about now was the unending concrete sidewalks and streets and the vast emptiness created by the clusters of towering buildings all around.

"Of course I do," she said. "But Mickey, just like you, Arthur, is only in town half the time. The other half you guys are traveling with the team. It gets lonely here, especially in a city that does not really care for those who are not equipped to survive."

He leaned back and sighed. His hands were sweaty and fastened behind his head. He stayed in that position for a while, listening to Molly plead her case, until his wrists began to ache from the strain. When the discomfort became too much to handle, he unclasped his hands and rested them on the table.

"So what is this, Molly? Are you telling me you're leaving me? You're just going to pick up and leave Boston, just like that? Is it really that bad?"

Molly shook her head. "No, I am not leaving you, Arthur," she replied. "And I did not say that I am definitely leaving Boston either—not yet anyway. But I have to be honest. If I don't feel any better in the next few weeks, and by better I mean more like I am home, I may have to figure something out. You know, you did say that—"

"Figure something out? That doesn't sound so good, Molly. Here I am, trying to—"

"Relax, Arthur; this is not about you. Understand? It's not always only about you. This is about me. *Me* continuing to find *me*. I know you cannot argue with that. Besides, we both said that someone should be looking after things on Diamond Drive. After all, it is still our home, right? How bad would it be if one of us were there, making sure everything was right?"

"Yeah, but still, Molly. The thought of me here and you—"

She had to think for a moment. She didn't like the idea of being separated from him either. It hurt her deep inside, stabbed at her very core. But in another place deep inside her resided another fear, just as painful and perhaps more terrifying. It was the fear of her disappearing again—vanishing like a shadow at day's end. Losing herself after all she had accomplished was not something she could endure. So she stumbled a bit.

"Just give me some time to sort it all, Arthur. Just a little time. I need to think about all of this, okay? That's not too much to ask, now is it?"

# JUNE MOON

The Braves only managed to play .500 baseball over the next month, a stretch punctuated by lackluster hitting, inconsistent pitching, and a defense that, for some inexplicable reason, was leaking like a sieve. But Mickey was spectacular; there was nothing mediocre about anything he was doing on the field. Three impressive starts, highlighted by one in which he began the game throwing twenty-six consecutive strikes before finishing with a pitch count under ninety, had everyone talking.

"You know, Murph," Keely said, scratching his head. "I like to think of myself as a pretty savvy, knowledgeable baseball guy, but I don't think I have ever seen anything like this. It's like a damn event when the kid does *not* throw a strike."

Murph just laughed. "I know, Bobby. The kid is a baseball oddity for sure. But, he is something special. It's what I've been trying to tell all of you ever since we got here."

The fans saw the same phenomenon unfolding and were not shy about expressing their ardor for their newest baseball idol. They were no longer invoking the *Spahn and Sain and pray for rain* mantra that had helped them deal with the yearly disappointment attached to the Braves' lack of pitching depth. Instead, what was on the lips of Braves supporters and local media was a pronouncement that captured the depth of feeling for Mickey and what he had come to mean to Boston baseball.

*Spahn and Sain and then the rain, but when things get sticky, send us Mickey.*

Mickey was also finding that life outside the ballpark could be just as wonderful. The first inkling of this came unexpectedly when, after one of his stellar pitching performances, he found himself in another conversation with Jolene. The two were standing by the turnstiles, just outside the tunnel. The crowd had exited some time ago, and most of the other players had left as well, including Ozmore. Now, in the waning sunlight that struggled to light the dreary concrete corners of the aging edifice, Mickey and Jolene stood and talked.

"You sure do know how to pitch, Mickey," she said, shaking her head and smiling. "Not sure I ever seen anything like it."

"You've seen lots of baseball games, Jolene," Mickey said. "Remember, you told me that."

"No, what I mean is—"

"I reckon it's on account of your brother, right? You must watch baseball all the time. Must have seen hundreds of games—thousands of pitches."

She stepped a little closer so that he might hear her more distinctly.

"I just mean I ain't ever seen anyone pitch the way *you* do."

"Mr. Murphy taught me to pitch," he said. "He came to my farm. Oscar was there. I always . . . I always . . ."

He was having trouble getting the words to come.

"Are you okay, Mickey?" she asked, putting her hand on his arm.

"Oscar were my pig. My favorite. Every day I would collect apples, lots of 'em, and then throw 'em into a barrel—to make the slop for him and the others. Mr. Murphy saw us." Mickey was remembering and relaying to Jolene with startling clarity the first exchange he and Murph experienced. Murph had just turned the corner past the stable to discover Mickey standing next to a curious pattern of crab apples resting in the dirt—six rows across, five apples deep—firing one at a time from one hundred feet away into a wine barrel turned on its side. What followed was the exchange that changed both of their lives forever. "You've got quite an arm there, Mickey, really.

Ever play baseball?" Then Murph had smiled, handed him a brand new pearl he retrieved from his car, and the covenant was forged.

"Apples?" Jolene questioned. "Are you serious? You went from throwing apples in a barrel to pitching for the major leagues?"

Mickey scrunched his nose and shook his head.

"No, Miss Jolene," he explained. "I went from the apples and my farm into Mr. Murphy's car. We drove to Milwaukee, to his house, where I stayed a bit. Met the guys. There was Pee Wee, my friend, and Boxcar. Boxcar were my catcher. He died because the doctors could not fix him. I cried a lot. Just like when Oscar died. 'Cause of Lefty Rogers. I don't want to talk about that." A heart-sickening silence seized him and held him in its grip.

"Hey, it's okay, Mickey," she said. "It's okay."

"I can still tell you about the others like Woody Danvers, Clem Finster, Farley, there was—"

"It's okay, Mickey, really," she said. Her eyes were a bit wet and glassy, and her face revealed a softness that even she had not antici-pated. "I'm just so impressed with how you pitch. You are wonderful. Unlike anyone I have ever seen. That's all. And I know I said once that you don't look like a baseball player, but after watching you today, that sure doesn't matter a whole lot."

They stood for some time, two shadows whose silhouetted out-lines seemed joined in a celestial dance. Mickey told her more about the farm, and Clarence, and how even though he loved most of the people he had met in baseball he still trusted animals more. She listened and shared with solemn gravity some of her own stories of hardship and disappointment. Mickey had a lot of questions, all of which appeared troubling to her, but she answered with a hint of sadness that seemed to drain from her more and more as they spoke.

"You know what, Mickey Tussler," she said after the conversation had slipped into a comfortable silence. "You and I are a lot alike."

They walked a while from the stadium, down Commonwealth Avenue, talking and even laughing. She found it easy to share things with him, even if he didn't always understand exactly what she meant. She was just happy to have someone to talk to, and even though Mickey seemed a bit wearied by the afternoon, he was still very much engaged.

All around them floated the sounds of a busy city—car horns, street vendors, and inconsequential chatter. The streets and side-walks were clicking and grinding like the gears in some massive machine that was about to overheat. But as the sun went down in a brilliant swirl of orange and varying shades of scarlet, all of it seemed to bounce off the two souls, now hand in hand, who were floating down the street.

When the day finally gave way to night's veil, they said good-bye. By now the crickets had begun their moonlight serenade, and Jolene found herself standing at the kitchen counter, thinking about the events of the previous few hours. Buddy was still not home, so the house was quiet and afforded her the opportunity to reflect.

One thing in particular was still making her blush. Mickey had walked her all the way home. When they arrived, she asked him in, just so he could use her telephone. After removing his cap and announcing that his mama always said wearing hats in the house was impolite, he made his phone call to Murph, then waited with her by the door to be picked up. The two just stood rather quietly, looking at each other, a little lost in the unexpressed feelings that had bub-bled to the surface.

"Mickey thinks you sure are pretty, Jolene," he said unexpectedly. She was instantly uncomfortable. It was not the emotion attached to the sentiment that troubled her but the unfamiliarity of such an expression.

"Thank you, Mickey," she said, slightly lowering her head. "You know, nobody has ever said that to me before." She could feel all of her insecurities burst into flaming fragments beneath her skin.

"Why?" he asked.

"Why?" she repeated. "I don't know. I guess most folks don't see me that way."

He looked at her intently now, as if observing her from an immeasurable distance. "I like your hair, Jolene," he said. "It's the same color as the wheat field next to my farm, back home. I used to hide there, a lot, when my daddy got to yelling at me."

His eyes were distant as he continued to explain about all the times he had run from Clarence, but his hands were right there. He reached suddenly, unconcerned with how she would react to his advance. His fingers found the sandy ringlets that fell gently over her shoulders and he began to talk some more about Indiana. "Yup, it's the same color as that wheat field," he explained while continuing to touch her hair. "But a lot softer. It's very soft, Miss Jolene. Like rose petals, or Duncan and Daphney's fur. More like Daphney's. Duncan is soft, too, but not like Daphney."

"Thank you, Mickey," she said, only half conscious of herself as she felt his kind words and gentle touch lift her away from the unpleasant memories still vying for position. "You know, when you are away on the road, we can talk on the telephone. I mean, just to say hello and all."

"Looks like the water in Williston's Creek too," he went on. "I mean not the color but the curly circles—especially the ones on the end here, by your shoulders. Mickey loves them circles. From the creek. I could pick a leaf off a tree and drop it in that water and sometimes it would spin forever. Round and round, round and round. Never change none."

He could see the sparkling succession of watery hoops and smell the damp leaves and the musky scent of the poplars that flanked the rotting log on which he always sat. From his perch, the world always seemed to make much more sense.

"Sounds pretty," she said, inching a little closer to him so that she could feel his breath against her face. "A lot different from the city streets of Boston. And those other cities. Which is why, if you get sort of lonely and want to talk, you can call me. We could chat, just like we are now, and I can wish you good luck and all. In your games."

He was aware of her altered proximity and smiled. She was lit from behind by moonlight that spilled through a front window and attached itself to her, making her appear even more angelic than he had previously thought. He was wondering how her hair had managed to catch every sliver of light that had passed through the casement glass; she was thinking about how soft his face must be, especially his lips. The honesty of the moment made her feel somewhat shaky and exposed but she leaned in closer anyway.

"You know what," he said, rushing past her suddenly, his eyes now fixated on a bronze bobcat figurine he noticed on a shelf. "We had one of these little guys running around the farm once. Made my daddy real mad on account of the chickens it were chasing all the time. I tried to catch him so I could feed him and tell him not to chase them chickens and make my daddy so mad. But he was too fast. Could never catch him none. Then daddy took out his shotgun one night and shot him. I told him not to but he did so anyway. Yup, he looked a lot like this here statue."

The foolishness she still felt over having misread the moment gave way to a soft, gentle calm. She was still feeling it now, after Mickey had gone home and when Buddy blasted through the door, half in the bag from his postgame celebration at Otto's Tavern.

"Jo Jo, I'm home. Where the heck are you?"

"In the kitchen," she called back.

There was an unusual silence that followed. She could hear him banging around in the living room. Then, without warning, he stormed into the small space she occupied. His face was red and sweaty.

"What the hell is this?" he said, flipping a large Braves cap on the table.

She turned her back to him and busied herself with some dishes in the sink. Her heart was rioting and her breath erratic and labored. She had half a mind to just tell him it was none of his business and that she could keep the company of anyone whom she wished. But the longer she stood there, the more she could feel the dissolution of her resolve.

"Did you hear what I said?" he repeated. "What the hell is going on?"

"It's just a hat," she said, turning to face him. "That's all."

Buddy exploded. "Oh really now. It's just a hat, huh? Is that what you said? What did I tell you about—"

"It's no big deal, Buddy. It's Mickey's. We just walked home together and he came inside to use the phone. That's all."

His eyebrows shot up as if being pulled by some invisible thread. He said nothing to her initially, and she was unable to gauge what exactly was running through his brain. But then without warning, the words came. And they wouldn't stop.

"I told you weeks ago that I don't want you rubbing elbows with any of the guys—especially that freako, Tussler. I am responsible for you. Have you forgotten what—"

"He's not a freak, Buddy," she protested. "You don't understand. If you would just sit and talk to him you would see that."

"That boy is a retard, Jolene," he said. "He ain't right. Do you know what happens to girls who get mixed up with that? I told you, when Mama and Daddy passed, that I would take care of you. That I was looking out for you, remember? All you have to do is take care of the house, cooking, and cleaning, and I would handle the rest. Well I'm reminding you, again. I make the rules here, and that boy is off limits. That's it. No more talk."

"But, Buddy, I—"

"It's the perfect time anyway to make the break. We're leaving for Philly tomorrow so you don't even have to deal with it at all. By the time we get back, it should be done."

He walked away, leaving her heartbroken and helpless. The tears began slowly; they dripped one at a time, sliding down each side of her face, despite her best efforts to stem the tide. Before long these same tears multiplied, drowning her eyes like a swollen river rushing across a levee. They fell more steadily and with greater urgency, soaking her fingers as she tried desperately to wipe them away. All she wanted to do was to feel the way she had earlier that night. And Mickey—she wanted him too. Instead, all she felt was a hollowing of her center, as if all the air she was swallowing could never fill the empty chamber deep within. The tears kept coming and probably would have continued for some time had she not looked up and noticed—that Buddy was staring at her.

# ROAD TRIP

The Braves arrived in Philadelphia with a record that had them stuck right in the middle of the division. They had been playing better of late, and Murph was feeling like they had turned the proverbial corner and were poised for a run, but he was still questioning his ability to navigate these uncharted waters.

"Okay, fellas," he said before the opener against the Phillies. "We got Spahny on the hill tonight, Johnny tomorrow, Bickford for game three, and Mickey to finish it out. Sounds like a clean sweep to me. Let's just get the bats going gentlemen, shall we? Some of you need to do a little less talking and a lot more hitting."

Ten minutes later, after everyone had gone off to tend to their individual pregame rituals, Murph received a visit.

"I certainly hope you were not looking at me when you made that hitting crack. 'Cause if you were, I think we may have a problem here."

It was quiet in the office, with the exception of some muffled exterior sounds that seeped through the walls. Murph wondered if it was worth responding—getting into it. Ozmore's misery was always going to be there, so why bother? Still, he couldn't help but think that his silence would be mistaken for weakness.

"You know, Ozmore, it's a wonder you can hit anything at all, with that giant chip you carry around on your shoulder. Seems like it would get in the way, don't you think?"

Ozmore's face contorted into an angry mask. "You know what, Murph, you really bother me—have from the very first day. All your bullshit talk about teamwork and how special it is to be a major leaguer . . . nobody's buying it, okay? What does a broken-down has been who had nothing more than a cup of coffee in the majors know about pro ball anyway? And I'll tell you something else. If you want to pal around with some freak of nature you call a pitcher, that's fine. It's your funeral once the rest of the league catches up with him. But I'm telling you this, and you better hear me good. Keep him away from my sister. I mean it."

Murph shook his head and laughed. "Is that what all this is really about? Mickey, and your sister?"

"Just keep him away from her. That's all."

"Mickey's a sweet kid, Ozzy," Murph explained. "Doesn't have a mean bone in that huge body of his. Take it from one who knows. Your sister would be mighty lucky to have a friend like him watching out for her."

"I'm warning you, Murphy, if I even hear—"

"Relax there, will ya, and focus on matters at hand here. You talk about being professional and a big leaguer. Please . . . look at you. Get your shit together—now. We've got a game to play in a little while, and I'm sort of hoping that we can start this trip off on the right foot."

Not long after, Murph's hopes were realized. Spahn gave him seven shutout innings, and the bullpen made the four runs the boys from Boston managed to score stand up as the Braves cruised to a very convincing 4–0 victory. It wasn't the sort of performance that had the rest of the league trembling with fear, but many of the guys who had been struggling at the plate got off the schneid, resulting in a season high of thirteen hits and smiles all around after the game. Nobody was happier than Tommy Holmes, who snapped a 0–13 drought with three knocks of his own.

"It was raining hits tonight in Philly," Holmes boasted. "Better warn the locals round here that the forecast for tomorrow looks about the same."

Roy Hartsfield laughed. "Yes, sir, it sure was," he said, lifting a mug full of beer in celebratory fashion. "A regular hit parade. Cripes, even Torgy and Elliot got in on it."

Earl Torgeson and Bobby Elliot, who were busy drinking and rabble-rousing at the piano bar, heard the call to arms and took playful offense, rolling up their sleeves and waving their fists in the direction of Hartsfield and the others who were still laughing.

"You'll pay for that, Roy, you little shit," Elliot shouted. "Just as soon as we finish our beers and maybe one more song."

While most of the guys continued to drink and regale each other with tales of their baseball exploits, Mickey sat with Murph on the other side of the lobby, eating at a small table pushed up against a picture window.

"How's your burger, Mick?" Murph asked.

Mickey had taken just two bites and was presently busy creating a railroad track pattern around the periphery of his plate with his french fries.

"Hey, Mickey, everything all right?"

The boy continued to lay both track and rails in hypnotic fashion.

"Yeah, Mr. Murphy," he answered without looking up. "All right."

Murph frowned. The wind had picked up outside, creating a cyclone of swirling papers and leaves that blew across the sidewalk. He followed the curious pattern with both eyes until he could no longer focus. He turned his attention to Mickey once again, cleared his throat, and spoke.

"Mick," he began, grabbing the boy's hand so that he had no choice but to listen. "Talk to me. I know you, son. Remember? And you know me too—well enough to also know that you can tell me anything that's bothering you. Come on now. Talk."

Mickey looked up at Murph, blinked a few times and frowned. He started to speak, then stopped, unable to convey accurately what was troubling him. He made several more attempts, but each time the words got stuck. So he sat there, hands folded tightly in front of him, staring across at Murph.

"Is it the guys?" Murph asked. "Are they giving you trouble, Mick? Because if they are, all you have to do is—"

"Jolene," Mickey said, followed by a rush of breath that suggested the difficulty with which it was said.

"Jolene?" Murph repeated. "Is that what you said?" He was at once concerned. "What about her, Mick?"

Mickey looked down at his plate. He was imagining what it would be like to be hit by a train—how it would feel just before the locomotive collided with his skin. He thought of Clarence and how it felt all those times to be hit by that two-by-four or the assortment of other objects his father had turned on him. Those all hurt. A lot. So a train, he imagined, would be decidedly worse.

"Mickey called her, like she said. Let it ring eight times. Did that three more times. But Jolene was not there to answer it. She told me to telephone her. I only called her because—"

"Is that it?' Murph asked. "Because if it is, then it's okay, Mickey, really. I'm sure it's okay. She's probably just busy, that's all. You can try again tomorrow."

Tomorrow also brought another opportunity for the Braves to continue their winning ways. Game two of the series against the Phillies saw Johnny Sain pitch into the eighth inning, having allowed just two unearned runs while scattering nine hits. Supported by some stellar play in the field and solo shots off the bats of Lester, Ozmore, Holmes, and Jethroe, the Braves coasted again to an easy victory, disposing of the Phillies by a score of 7–3. The additional news that they had gained some valuable ground in the standings had them all feeling particularly good afterward.

"Nice job, fellas," Murph announced while the team showered and got changed. "Good all-around effort today. It was really fun to watch."

"That's it, Murph?" Torgeson challenged. "Nice job? Come on now. I think you just happen to be sharing this locker room with the hottest team in the National League. I'd say that is a little more than just nice, don't you think?"

Murph shook his head and tapped his finger against his temple.

"When you're right, you're right, Torgy. And are you right." Murph didn't want to get too high about their modest winning streak. He knew all too well how fickle the baseball gods could be. But something about Torgeson's emotional proclamation and all the hooting and hollering in the room got to him. It was too delicious to resist.

"We are on fire, boys!" he shouted. "Fire. And you know what's so goddamned great about fire? It spreads. And once it gets going, it's hard to control. Spreads out of control. Wildfire they call it. That's us, fellas. Right now. Wildfire. And I ain't too proud to say I'm feeling mighty lucky just to be a part of it."

He watched with satisfaction as the room erupted even further.

"Well yeehaw, look at you, Murph," Spahn gushed, clapping his hands and smiling a toothy smile. "I have to say, I like this side of you. I sure do. Getting in right behind us like that and all. It's good— good stuff. So maybe you'll meet up with us at the hotel and we can continue this brotherly love at one of the taverns downtown."

Murph was pleased by the gesture, as it marked the very first sign of progress since he had arrived, but he was content to revel in the moment in a more conservative fashion.

"No, I think I'm gonna just head back to the hotel, get some dinner, and enjoy all of this quietly," he said. "I'm a little tired. But thank you all the same. You guys go, enjoy, but remember we still have work to do tomorrow."

"Oh, come on, Murph," Sain added. "I just threw eight innings and I'm good to go. Come on, one beer. What's the harm?"

"I'll get you guys the next time," he said, holding three fingers up in the air. "Scout's honor."

"Okay, okay," Sain rumbled. "We're gonna hold you to that. Won't be the same without you tonight. But help us out some. How about giving us Mickey then? I'm sure he's not too tired."

Murph looked at Mickey, who was staring off at a point in the distance, oblivious to the revelry unfolding all around him. He knew what the boy had on his mind and what he had planned for the night. Still, Murph had to ask.

"How 'bout it, Mick?" he said, disentangling the boy from his secret weavings. "You want to go out with the fellas tonight?"

The room grew quieter as they waited for Mickey to register what Murph had asked.

"No, no, Mr. Murphy," Mickey finally said. "Mickey wants a hamburger and fries. At the hotel. Just like last night. No beer."

Murph shrugged his shoulders and tilted his head slightly to one side. "You heard him, guys. Maybe another time."

The night was quiet and gray, with the city lights burning in a sleepy haze. Murph and Mickey walked back to their rooms, showered, and got dressed. They agreed to meet at Mickey's room in an hour after they had each had some time to take care of a few things before heading downstairs for dinner.

The hotel lobby was decidedly quieter than it was the previous night after Ozmore rounded up what he called his "party posse" and turned them loose on the city. Murph and Mickey sat at the same table as before, at Mickey's request, and chatted while they waited for their food.

"So I spoke to your mom," Murph said.

Mickey nodded and continued to fix his silverware so that his fork, knife, and spoon were all properly aligned.

"Said she'd like you to give her a call later . . . or tomorrow. She misses you, Mick. I think hearing your voice may help her a little. She's having a tough time you know."

This time the boy wasted no time articulating his troubles.

"Jolene did not answer her phone again," he said, staring out the window at the people rushing by. "Let it ring eight times. Then I hung it up, called again, and let it ring eight more times. Then I put it down again, picked it up, and let it ring eight more times. Nobody was there. Mickey will try again later."

A lump settled in Murph's throat.

"Maybe you should wait on that, Mick," he said. "You know, sounds like she's just busy and all. Don't worry. Why don't you give your mom a call instead and then try Jolene again tomorrow. I'm sure it . . . uh . . . will all work out."

"But she said to call her—and that she had to wish Mickey good luck. I-I don't—"

"Mick, it's okay. Don't worry. Everything is fine. Just call your mom. Have a nice talk with her, the way you always did, and you'll feel a little better about everything."

Mickey's conversation with Molly was good for her, but it did little to quell the boy's unfurling anxiety. He loved Molly just the same, but something had happened to him the day he met Jolene at the bar. It was as if a small part of him that had been hiding somewhere deep inside had been released and revealed itself to him with a breathless wonder and rhythm that could no longer be denied. It had changed him — or at least the way he saw things. Jolene had stirred something, and the boy was in a state of disorder. And now it was only Jolene who could make him right again.

Murph suspected as much and felt compelled to try and set things back in place. He caught Ozmore the minute he came in the next morning, before he made it to his locker.

"Hey, Ozzy, you say something to your sister?" Murph asked. "You know, about Mickey?" Ozmore's eyes narrowed and his mouth flattened into a thin, straight line.

Ozzy was thinking about the last time someone questioned him about something he had done. It was another rookie, two seasons ago, during the final week of spring training. Ozmore was sitting in front of his locker, untying his cleats. A wide-eyed rookie sauntered over to him, stood by his side, and started a conversation.

"Hey, Mr. Ozmore, you know you were one of my favorite players when I was a kid."

Ozmore rolled his eyes up and glanced quickly at the boy's smooth face. "Is that right?" he replied.

"Sure. Met you at a Braves game. You tossed me a ball. I didn't have a pen, and the game was about to start, so you yelled to me that I could send you the ball and you would sign it for me. Remember that?"

"Kid, you know how many letters and balls I get?" Ozmore explained.

The rookie shook his head and blew some air out of his mouth. "No, but what I do know is that I waited for weeks for that ball.

My mom kept telling me that it wasn't coming, but I said 'Buddy Ozmore said so. He's my hero.' Yup, you sure were. I had pictures of you in my room. Had your baseball cards pinned to my bicycle spokes. Stood like you when I played stickball. Yup, you were my idol."

Ozmore stopped what he was doing and took a closer look at the kid. "Man, you must be mistaken rook," he said, laughing. "Jesus, I ain't that much older than you."

The rookie paused for a moment, then brought his hand down hard on Ozmore's shoulder.

"No, I ain't mistaken, Pops," he said. "You broke a little boy's heart. That ain't something anyone ever forgets."

"Well, greenhorn," Ozmore explained. "That may be true, but you best get your hand off me right now—or a broken heart ain't the only thing you'll be crying about."

"Yes, sir. I always said that if I ever had the chance to ask you why you did that, I would. So, I'm asking. Why the hell would you do something like that? Huh?"

Ozmore exhaled loudly and looked up at the kid. "You gonna get your hand off me, newbie?"

"You gonna tell me why, Mr. Baseball Hero?"

The end result was a fistfight that took three other players to break up. Ozmore took some blows, came away with a shiner and some scratches, but not before he knocked out the kid's two front teeth and broke his jaw.

Ozmore was remembering all the towels it took to stop the bleeding as Murph stood there, questioning him.

"Are you serious, Murph?" he asked. "You're really asking me this?"

"Yeah, I'm asking you. Seems like you said something to Jolene and it's a bit of a problem."

"I don't like to be questioned, Murph," Ozmore said. "Haven't the boys told you that?"

What existed in Murph's mind now was the sudden horror that he had just, with one question, eradicated all of the goodwill and energy he had only just begun to enjoy. Still, he knew all too well

that Mickey was unsettled, and with Molly's discontent already prey-
ing upon him, he was facing a far more formidable threat than
Buddy Ozmore.

"Look, I don't want to make any trouble for you, Ozzy," Murph
said. "I don't. All I know is that Mickey is upset because all of a sudden your sister won't talk to him. Just like that. I really don't see why
it's a big deal if the two of them are friends."

"You don't listen so well, do you, Murph?" Ozmore asked. "I told
you how I feel about this."

"So you poisoned her mind? Told her that she shouldn't talk to
him anymore?"

"I did nothing of the sort. She's a big girl and probably realized
that she needed some space and that she was uncomfortable around
Mickey. That's all. We all are. He's a little weird, Murph. I mean —
come on."

"So you didn't —"

"I didn't tell her anything, but I have to say, I sure as shit ain't
upset about it. Regular folks and other kinds should not mix. It ain't
natural. So save your breath here. Ain't nothing I — or you, for that
matter — can do about it. Besides, shouldn't you be worried about
baseball anyway?"

Murph thought about his new life as a big league manager and
how he had become the focus of, even scapegoat for, everyone else's
woes and insecurities. It was always he who was trying to mitigate
some issue or problem or concern of someone else's. Molly. Ozmore.
Mickey. Now it was Jolene. All of them needed something from him.
And he could not help but feel that although none of it was of his
doing, somehow if he did not do the right thing on all accounts, he
would end up paying the price.

"That's exactly what I'm worried about," Murph said.

Game three against the Phillies was a struggle from the start. Shoddy
defense by Bobby Elliot and Roy Hartsfield in the first inning,
coupled with three walks from starter Vern Bickford, put the Braves
in a 4–0 hole from the get-go.

The next five innings provided more of the same lackluster play by the Braves' defense, resulting in three more runs for the Phillies. The Braves' offense, however, did manage to chip away at the deficit, capitalizing on some station-to-station small ball and some questionable defense by the Phillies so that come the last half of the seventh, the game was somehow knotted at 7–7.

Murph had let Bickford start the seventh frame, but after a leadoff single and a hit batsman, Murph was motioning to the bullpen for another hurler and on his way to the mound for a brief meeting with his enervated pitcher and Lester.

"Okay, Bicks," he said, holding his hand out for the ball. "You did fine. Not much help out here today. Next start will be better."

Johnny Antonelli took over for Bickford and was able to dance through the raindrops en route to an escape routine rivaled only by the great Harry Houdini himself. It gave the rest of the guys a real shot in the arm.

"Atta boy, Johnny," Murph yelled from his perch on the bench. Everyone else was also swept up in the unexpected heroics—all except Mickey, who sat quietly by himself at the end of the dugout, arranging a group of pebbles he had unearthed during the game. Murph's bunch parlayed that momentum into a modest rally that began when Sam Jethroe led off the eighth inning with a Baltimore chop to third base that he beat out for an infield single. Two pitches later, he had advanced ninety feet with his league-leading twenty-first stolen base. Next up was Tommy Holmes, who crushed a 2-2 fastball to the deepest part of the ballpark. When it left the bat, everyone was certain it had enough behind it to leave the yard, but the Phillies center fielder ran it down just in front of the wall. Holmes cursed his misfortune and kicked at the dirt as he rounded the first base bag; but Jethroe, who had tagged up despite what appeared initially to be a long home run, trotted into third base easily. There he stood representing the go-ahead run with just one out and the heart of the Braves order coming up.

Bobby Elliot wasted no time cashing in Jethroe's savvy base running, lacing a single to left field that scored the speedster. Next was Lester, who Murph had moved into the fifth slot after the catcher began showing signs of coming out of a minor funk. With the Braves up by one and looking to pad their lead with an insurance run or two, Lester strode to the plate with one thing in mind—just hit it hard somewhere.

The first offering from Phillies right-hander Blix Donnelly was a fastball off the plate. Lester stepped out of the box and exhaled loudly. He surveyed the outfield configuration with a quick glance, then banged his cleats with the barrel of his bat and stepped back in. Donnelley came back with a fifty-five-foot curveball that bounced in the dirt, putting Lester in a perfect hitter's count. He was ready, sitting dead red all the way.

The ball was delivered with great force and left the batter's box as quickly as it had come in. With one mighty swing, Lester scorched the cripple pitch into the right-center field gap. It touched down some 330 feet and rolled all the way to the wall. Elliot coasted home with the second run of the inning, and Lester, who was not known for his speed around the bases, pulled up at third with a stand up triple. The bench erupted with cheers and playful taunts.

"Woo hoo! Look at that boy run!" they screamed, all the while laughing and slapping each other.

"Whoa, Lester, you like lightning! Lightning, Lester!" The group became even more unhinged when Gordon and Torgeson hit back-to-back jacks, staking the resurgent Braves to a five-run lead.

The visitors dugout was now in a state of complete pandemonium. "We can't lose, boys!" they screamed. "Nobody's hotter. Nobody! Fire, fire, we're on fire!"

The postgame celebration followed the pattern of the previous two. Ozmore's group assembled once again for what was to be a third consecutive night of drunken debauchery while Mickey stayed back at the hotel with Murph, rattled by his inability to reach Jolene.

"Come on, Mick, you've got to snap out of this," Murph prodded. "It's okay."

"But she said it. She told Mickey. She told me. She did."

"Don't worry so much. I'm sure you'll catch up with her soon. You've got a big game to pitch tomorrow anyway so it's for the best.

We need this game, Mick. Do you know how long it's been since the Braves swept a four-game road series from the Phillies?"

A sudden break in Mickey's mania struck Murph as odd.

"Yes," the boy said.

Murph shook his head. "What?"

"Yes," Mickey repeated.

"Yes, what?" Murph inquired, growing a little more impatient with the exchange.

"In 1914, the Boston Braves swept the Philadelphia As in the World Series. But that don't count none since it weren't the Phillies. Then in 1925, the Braves were swept two times by the Phillies, once at home and once on the road. The next year, 1926, the season began with the Phillies sweeping the Braves again. Then in 1928, the Braves finally swept the Phillies four games, including a double-header on May 30th. But it weren't until 1945 that the Braves swept four games again from the Phillies. That was two doubleheaders that they won. June 6th and June 7th. That were the last time it happened. Last year, in September, the Phillies swept the Braves four straight. But no sweep for the Braves. So it has been five years, sixty months, one thousand, eight hundred twenty-five days, or—"

Murph stood, shaking his head and muttering to himself. "Mickey, I don't know how the hell you can possibly know all that. But it doesn't matter. I'm just trying to tell you how important tomorrow is, that's all. No need for—"

"Mickey needs to call Jolene."

"What?" Murph asked. "You're not listening to what—"

"Jolene," Mickey repeated. "She has to wish me good luck."

Despite Murph's best efforts to divert Mickey's attention away from what he knew would be more disappointment, Mickey spent the better part of the night dialing the phone with no luck. Then, when his fingers tired, he laid his head on his pillow, the only light in the room coming from a streetlamp just outside the window. His eyes were heavy, but hollow, and remained fixed on the ceiling shadows for some time. He traced every inch of the unusual patterns with great precision until he found that these random shapes had somehow morphed into a montage of images with which he was very familiar—Indiana cornfields, Oscar's pigpen, Lefty's twisted smile, and the dank prison cell in Sheriff Rosco's station. He could see with alarming clarity men with hoods and torches, Pee Wee's cabin in Baker's Woods, and somewhere in the whirling fusion of the myriad of configurations was the long, sandy curls that flowed over Jolene's shoulders. It was enough to keep him from sleep the entire night.

So when morning came, and the boy got dressed and made his way with Murph and the other guys over to Connie Mack Stadium, he was not himself at all. It showed. Instantly.

He struggled the minute he took the field. His warm-up tosses to Lester were flat and off the mark. The buzzing of a crowd that had never seen him throw seemed to bore its way into his brain. The laboring only grew worse once the game began. Phillies leadoff man Richie Ashburn walked on four straight balls. Granny Hamner was issued a free pass in the same manner. It was ugly—fast. Eight straight balls to begin the game. Murph saw the young man unraveling out there and knew he had to do something.

"Time," he called. Then he motioned to Lester and the two of them walked deliberately to the mound. When they arrived, Mickey was distant and unapproachable. His back was turned to them, as if he were attempting to fend off some terrible gusts of wind—winds of the world that swirled all around him like horrible twisters, cyclones, and hurricanes. He was also engaged in the crippling recitation that Murph had not heard in quite some time.

"Slowly, silently, now the moon, walks the night in her silver shoon."

Mickey turned around slowly once he knew he was no longer alone.

"Oh no, Mick, you're not doing this now," Murph said, putting his hand on the boy's shoulder. "No way. We've come too far. *You've* come too far. Come on now. What's bothering you?"

"Yeah, Mick," Lester said. "What gives, kid? This ain't like you no more."

Mickey expression was vacant. He stared right past them into the kaleidoscope of faces in the stands. "Mickey don't feel right," he said. "No good. No good."

"You sick or something, Mick?" Lester asked.

"Don't feel right," Mickey repeated.

"What do ya think, Murph?" Lester asked.

Murph lowered his head and filled his lungs, as if preparing to lift some heavy load. Then with a renewed sense of purpose, if nothing else, he plowed forward. "Let's go, Mick. You can do this. Just like always. Just hit the glove. That's all. Hit the glove."

"But Mickey—"

"No buts, Mick," Murph insisted. He was much more stern than he usually was when handling the young man. "There's no time for this. This is the show. Ain't no hiding or monkey business. You hear me? Just throw it like you can. Apples in a barrel, remember? That's all. That simple. We need this game, and we need you. Now."

Mickey appeared to be processing the command. His face softened some and his eyes were still. He had even just settled on something he wanted to say when over Murph's shoulder he caught a glimpse of the umpire on his way to join the meeting. The words never left their tomb.

"Okay, fellas, let's move things along. Make a move here. Let's play ball."

Mickey's shoulders tensed. Murph frowned.

"You heard the man, Mick," he said, patting the boy on the back. "Time to play ball. Go get 'em." With those final words of encouragement, he and Lester walked back to their respective positions. Somehow, the walk seemed longer than usual.

"He gonna be okay?" Lester asked.

"Not sure, Les," Murph said. "I'm just not sure."

"Sure wish I knew what was wrong with him," Lester continued. "Damndest thing I ever saw."

Murph lowered his head and kicked at the grass. "Don't worry about it too much," he said. "I know what's wrong."

The visit to the mound had only an immediate impact. Mickey's first two deliveries to Phillies first baseman Eddie Waitkus were called strikes. And although Mickey eventually ran the count full, struggling to find his rhythm, he retired Waitkus on a towering foul out up the first baseline that was corralled by Torgeson.

Cleanup hitter Del Ennis stepped to the plate amid all sorts of encouragement for Mickey coming from the Braves bench. Murph had all the guys on the top step of the dugout, chattering and cheering for Mickey's continued success. It seemed to be working, for the first pitch Ennis saw was a blistering fastball that was by him before he could even move the bat off his shoulder. But the next pitch was high and way outside. So was the next. The two that followed were in the dirt, producing yet another walk and a bases-loaded jam for the Braves.

"Come on, Mick." Lester prodded as he threw the ball back. "Nice and easy. Just toss it to me, nice and easy."

Something about Lester's request caught Mickey's attention. He was suddenly recalling a summer day back in Indiana. He was eight years old, maybe nine, and standing with Molly by the pond behind their farm. It was early morning, and the sun had just crept over the distant tree line, lighting the flotsam that drifted slowly on the sleepy body of water. Molly had taken him away from the house to talk to him about Clarence and how to best control his emotions when he got frustrated and things were not going his way.

"So you see, Mickey," she said, picking up a smooth flat stone that she proceeded to skillfully skip across the water. "Sometimes it's better to be less angry and forceful, not as strong. Do you understand?"

The metaphor was lost on the boy, who was fixated on what he had just seen. "That rock bounced," he said smiling. "On the water. It bounced."

Molly smiled back and handed Mickey a rock of his own. "Yes, I'm trying to show you that—"

"How did it bounce?" he asked. "Rocks don't bounce none. Water ain't hard neither."

"Here, sweetheart," she said, opening his hand. "See for yourself. You try now."

He took the rock from her; it disappeared behind his massive fingers. He rolled it around and back and forth for a while as he surveyed the water, looking for the perfect spot. Then he cocked his arm, aimed, and fired. The rock traveled a great distance in a mere second, then entered the water with a loud plop and sunk straight to the bottom.

"Mickey broke it," he said, beginning to rock back and forth.

"No, no," Molly said, putting her arm around his waist. "You didn't break anything honey. You just threw it too hard. Remember what I said. Nice and easy. That's the way to do things sometimes. Slow down. Don't be so strong and too forceful. Just let it come."

Mickey thought about how the next few rocks he tossed were more and more like the one Molly threw. It made him smile, a small, modest grin that paled in comparison to the ear-to-ear radiance he flashed when he finally managed to skip a stone from one side of the pond clear across to the other.

"See," Molly said, rubbing his back. "Sometimes nice and easy is all you need. Remember that, sweetheart."

Lester's words had unlocked a precious memory for sure and had Mickey standing on the mound, feeling like he knew exactly what to do.

"Nice and easy." He kept hearing in his head. "Slow down. Don't be so strong or too forceful."

So when Willie Jones stepped in to take his hacks, Mickey delivered a fastball that was straight and true but less than its normal speed. Jones's eyes lit up as the ball floated across the plate like some swollen piñata. Jones did not miss. He sent the offering screaming down the left field line, where it rolled around in the corner before finally being scooped up and thrown in, but not before two runs had crossed the plate.

Dick Sisler was next. The chiseled left-hander jumped on the first pitch as well, one hopping the wall out in left center field. That scored two more runs and put Sisler on third with still only one out.

"What the hell is he doing out there?" The guys on the bench complained. "He's not even pitching. What the hell, Murph?"

Murph pulled his cap down over his brow and cringed. There was nothing he could say.

The next two batters, Mike Goliat and Stan Lopata, both had similar success against Mickey's halfhearted effort, registering back-to-back doubles that plated two more runs. The carousel was in full motion. And the natives were restless.

"Come on, Murph, are you kidding us here?" the bench carped. "Get him out of there. He's killing us—absolutely killing us. We've barely broken a sweat and are down six runs already." It pained Murph to have to go and get him. But letting it go on was brutal, and he had to save some face in front of the guys. As it was, he feared he had now lost what little credibility he had gained.

The walk to the mound seemed unending, as was the removal of Mickey, but not nearly as painful as what was to follow once the final out had been recorded. Many of the players were sullen and quiet, but their silence spoke volumes.

Some, however, were not inclined to let their displeasure go unheard. They spoke freely about things like bush-league play, failure to execute, and colossal stupidity. And it was loud and pointed. Warren Spahn fired the first salvo.

"Murph, what the hell was that today?" he asked. "Are you shittin' me?"

"Just back off, Spahny, all right?" Murph shot back. "The kid had a rough outing. That's all. Happens to all of you."

"Really? That's your assessment of this? Rough outing? Not that we pissed away a golden opportunity to gain more ground and to keep the train rolling—or that it was the most embarrassing moment of all of our lives as ballplayers? You don't see that? Only that it was a rough outing?"

"You know what? I am so tired of your 'look at me' candy-ass prima donna attitude. Maybe once, just once, you can look at things beyond what they mean to you. Try it some time. That's what guys on a team do."

Bickford, who came over once the yelling began, joined the fracas. "That is what we're saying, Murph. This team just suffered because you think the whiz kid has the right stuff. Maybe he was good on the farm. And yeah, he throws okay and even fooled some guys up here. But he's not on the farm anymore. And he's nuttier than a fruitcake besides. That ain't gonna work here."

Murph's rage soared. He began screaming about teammates and loyalty and watching backs. Then he stopped—as if he had an epiphany—and motioned an imaginary line down the center of the locker room with his outstretched arm.

"Okay, fellas, everyone who is so damned perfect and has never screwed up in a game or had a really awful performance can stay on this side of the locker room from now on. The rest of us neophytes who are not worthy to share that hallowed space with you will stay on this side. Better?"

A few guys snickered and mumbled under their breath.

"What the hell are you getting all crazy for, Murph?" Torgeson asked. "The guys are just upset."

"Upset? Upset? No, *I'm* upset. Me! I'm the one who should be upset here. One bad outing and you're all ready to lynch the kid, is that it? Huh? Pathetic. Nobody else wants to take any responsibility here. Or behave like a professional. Or act like you're part of a team. No? Okay then. Be upset. But that's just tough shit. I'm in charge here. And I make the rules. So you can bellyache all you want. Mickey Tussler is on this team. He's part of our staff and he will be getting the ball again in five days. I told you all from day one my door says 'Manager.' Mine. Nobody else's."

"Yeah, well I told you that the kid was trouble," Ozmore said, slipping out of the shadows like a serpent. "Nothing but trouble."

Now it was on.

"You're gonna say something?" Murph mocked. "Really? Please. You? You're the last one who should talk about what happened today."

"Oh yeah, Mr. Big League Manager, and why is that?"

"You really want to do this now, in front of everyone?"

"I don't know what you're talking about, Murph."

"You really are a piece of work, Ozmore, you know that? All Mickey wanted was to talk to her. Because *she* asked him to. That's all. Because they're friends. But I guess you're a little intimidated by that. So you couldn't keep your big, stupid mouth shut. And by golly, look what happened. Was it worth it? Huh?"

The room grew noticeably quieter as those who were listening either sat or stood, processing what was just said.

"I didn't say nothing to her," Ozmore protested. "I don't know what he's talking about. Why do I care who my sister talks to. Honest, guys, she must have changed her mind. On her own."

The silence that had filled the room now gave way to a steady murmur that had Ozmore in a sheer panic.

"He's got no proof I said anything," he rambled. "None at all. Like I just said. Why would I care if the kid talks to my sister? Right? Come on. It's crazy talk. Besides, what the hell does my sister have to do with the kid pitching anyway? He couldn't find the strike zone today because the kid just don't got it. Ain't nothing to do with me or my sister."

Murph stood now, frustrated and uneasy.

"All of you, especially you, Ozzy, know about Mickey," Murph said in a desperate voice. He was not looking at Ozmore as he spoke but at the others who had gathered around the commotion. "He's not like the rest of us—in a lot of ways. Things bother him. And he has trouble at times dealing with those things. But he's also incredibly talented on that mound. You guys have only gotten a glimpse of that so far. So what I'm asking is that you cut the kid a little slack. You know, do what you can to make him feel comfortable and okay—not because I love the kid or because I asked you to. But because his arm can help all of us win a championship here."

Murph's impassioned plea was not his best speech ever, but it had enough power to change the tenor of the room. Players were nodding and a couple even emitted an audible "okay" under their breath once Murph was finished speaking. The only one who was completely still was Ozmore, who was slowly discovering that the tide had somehow changed.

"Hey, whatever it takes," he finally said, appealing to the prevailing sentiment in the room. "You know me. I just want to win. Whatever it takes. If that's what everyone wants, then I . . . uh . . . want that too."

Murph smiled and wrinkled his nose. "So let me see if I understand you now. Then it's okay if Mickey talks to your sister? *You're* okay with that?"

Ozmore surveyed the room. The tacit judgment was more than enough to influence his response. "Well, yeah, of course I am. I'm a team player. And they're just talking. Just friends. That's all."

"And you're willing to get off the kid's back, about everything, so we can really make a run at this thing?"

"You heard what I said, Murph," Ozmore announced. He swallowed with some difficulty. "Yes, I will help him out. Of course. We'll all watch out for him. Hell, why wouldn't I?"

# ALL-STAR BREAK

With just three games left to play before the midsummer classic, Murph was feeling pretty good about things. The three days off would give tempers a chance to cool. The break would also provide him with the opportunity to get away with his family—back to Milwaukee—where he could counsel Mickey and also begin to set things right with Molly.

The first half of the season concluded for the Braves by Murph's crew taking two of three in Cincinnati from a struggling Reds team. It wasn't exactly what Murph had hoped for, but he was happy to get away at the half with a third-place finish, trailing the league-leading Phillies by just two games. If people had told him before the season began that he'd be just two games out of first place midway through his rookie season at helm of a major league club, he would have said they were crazy. It was more than he could have hoped for. He was also pleased that he had successfully managed to avoid Mickey's spot in the rotation, thinking that it would be best if he had his next outing in front of the home crowd after the break.

Molly had already left Boston after the last home stand and was awaiting the arrival of Murph, along with Mickey of course, and Lester, who had no place special to be for the next few days. Diamond Drive was like a tonic for her; Milwaukee was where she had begun her new life with Murph.

The place was a far cry from what it was when she first saw it—a small, modest gray dwelling that looked as though it had been dropped indiscriminately in the middle of a pale grass field flanked by clusters of big dead trees and restless tumbleweeds. The windows, clouded casements that winced uncomfortably at the barren acreage just outside, allowed only glints of light to pass through. Molly remembered commenting on how she had never seen a place so dark inside. So when they had married and the place became hers as well, she had gone to work immediately.

Her touch was everywhere, from the carefully sculpted flower beds in front to the white lace doilies and warm, bright country curtains in every room. It even smelled like her—like lilacs. Now she was as much a part of that house as he was. And now that she was back, she wondered how she would ever be able to leave again.

It had taken her so long to arrive, to be able to live in a dwelling that was not just a house but a home. For so many years prior to Murph, she had lived as a prisoner, her soul fettered to something dark and sinister. Her heart had been incarcerated as well, beating timorously as though it were resting between two stone walls drawing closer and closer, inches away from pressing together. She survived the only way she knew how, by immersing herself in the chores germane to life on a farm. She could lose herself in the mixing of animal feed or the husking of corn. She knew how to milk the cows and could spend a whole afternoon bottle-feeding the lambs. And of course Clarence needed his clothes washed and his meals prepared. She could do all that.

But there was never any time for *her*—time to read about distant places and the romances unfolding there. There was no opportunity to ride horses or to walk in the morning when the sun had just begun to tickle the dewdrops on the sleepy grass, lighting them up like a blanket of diamonds. And there was no occasion to sit and play her clarinet, something she loved more than anything else. She had simply trudged forward, day after day, certain that her tortured life would conclude one day on that farm.

Then she met Murph, and all that changed. She realized that those things that made her who she was were forgotten but not gone.

She was alive again and doing all the things she had long since relin-quished. And there were so many other wonderful things she discov-ered, too, like what it felt like to be loved and cared for—what it felt like to be a woman. Sure, the demands of living a baseball life posed some challenges, but they were making it work. Somehow it just worked. They were totally in sync and she had at long last conquered her demons. And then Murph got the call to the show, and like a dandelion seed caught in a stiff breeze, her new life was gone—just like that. The feeling of just how much she missed it all was never as strong as when Murph, Mickey, and Lester arrived.

"Hey, just in time," she said, smiling behind a tray of warm choc-olate chip cookies. "You boys must be starving."

Mickey was the first to greet her. He grabbed a cookie, put the whole thing in his mouth, then struggled to say how much he missed her as he draped his arms over her shoulders.

"Whoa, Mick," Lester said, coming up quickly behind him. "Mrs. Murphy, lemme grab that tray before all these beautiful cookies hit the floor."

"Why thank you, Lester," she said from underneath Mickey's enveloping hug.

"My pleasure, ma'am," he replied. "It's the least I can do."

With the cookies now secure, Molly was able to return her boy's embrace. "Oh, I missed you too," she whispered in his ear. "I know it hasn't been that long, but still."

Murph's heart filled as he observed the heartfelt reunion. It was good to see her, especially here, where she had blossomed before his eyes from a hopeless shadow into this radiant being. It had been far too long since he had seen her smile the way she was smiling now.

"Hey, you know I haven't seen you in a few days too," he teased. "What about me?"

Molly squeezed Mickey one more time, kissed his cheek softly, then reached for the tray that Lester had set on the table just inside the door. "Here, sweetheart," she said to Mickey. "Why don't you take these into the kitchen and you and Lester can grab some milk, maybe sit down at the table."

The boy took the tray and bounded through the foyer and into the kitchen with an amused Lester trailing close behind, leaving Molly and Murph to themselves. She took a deep breath and smiled, stretching out her arms as if to say *Well, here I am.* What else could he do but smile back—and of course move in closer so that both of them were now locked in an embrace.

It was warm and familiar and just what she had been missing. It was right. She closed her eyes like a little girl and wished with every fiber of her being that this feeling would last beyond the three days they had planned. She kept them shut tight, mindful that the minute she opened them again, the light of a world she still refused to accept would eradicate the sweet vision.

"Hey," he said, pulling away from her just far enough so that he could see her face. "Place looks great."

"Thank you," she said, opening her eyes reluctantly. "Just like we never left, right?"

"Yup, this place sure is a sight for sore eyes."

They talked for a while, first about the team and how he felt about the first half of the season. He spoke with modest enthusiasm but was clearly pleased with what he had accomplished in a fairly short time under less than ideal circumstances. She listened and was even happy that he was so encouraged and feeling good about himself and the way things were going. She knew how much it meant to him. But she was still troubled by where she fit in the equation and what she was to do with *her* feelings. Despite her attempt to be nothing less than excited and supportive, her eyes told the true story. He read her concern with relative ease.

"Hey, what's bothering you?" he asked, stroking her hair. "Why the long face?"

"It's nothing," she said. "I'm okay. Just overwhelmed a little I guess."

"Are you sure, Molly? You don't look right."

"Yeah, yeah, it's nothing, Arthur. Really. It'll pass."

She looked away and moved the conversation to Mickey, looking for insight into the boy's present condition, a midyear report of sorts.

Part of her was hoping that the promotion was not working out so well and that he would be back down with Brewers again. She had secretly hoped the same thing for Murph as well.

Murph had told her all about the difficulties he was having with some of the players and the pressures of managing a big league club. It was more than he had expected. But he was also careful to share with her the recent success that both he and Mickey had experienced, and how he felt that both of them were doing better than most had initially thought. He also revealed that Mickey was making friends off the field, but left the whole Jolene situation for another time.

"Well, that's great," she said. "I guess you are getting everything that you wanted." Her last few words were spoken with a slight, yet discernible, tremor.

"Molly, talk to me," he said. "What is going on? Are you still—"

She felt as though she might cry. "Later, not now," she said.

"Listen if you are—"

"Come on," she interrupted, taking his hand. "Let me show you what I did in the other rooms."

Out back, the sun bathed the yard in a brilliant gold that highlighted all of Molly's recent efforts. She had removed a good deal of the dead underbrush and had begun replacing it with flowers and a few stone sculptures she had found at an antique store. She had even found a new cover for the rabbit cages, which Mickey noticed instantly. It was there he and Lester stood, poking celery stalks through the holes in the cages while having a conversation of their own.

"Happy to be home, Mick?" Lester asked.

"Mickey loves Duncan and Daphney," he said. "My mama takes good care of them. And when she can't, on account of Boston, Mr. Bailey just up the road comes over and checks up on them. But they love me best. See? They're smiling at me."

"I know, Mick," Lester said laughing. "They sure do."

"Animals is the best sort of friend, Lester," Mickey continued. "Best sort. They are never mean to you. Never hurt you. I just told—"

"Yeah, Mick, but you can't only survive with just animals you know. A person needs other people too. You know that, Mick, right?"

Mickey didn't answer. Instead he leaned down a bit and pushed his face up against the cage so that his nose was now touching the tiny twitching black one just across from his.

"You know, there's some good folks that you've met before." Lester went on. "Remember Pee Wee? He's a swell fella. And what about Farley? Remember old man Matheson? The way he used to help you out whenever you needed something? And of course Murph? Ain't nobody better than Murph, right? And hey. Ole Lester likes you too. So you see, ain't all people bad news, Mick."

"Don't see much of Pee Wee no more," Mickey said, his face still pressed up against the wire mesh grid. "Nope I don't. Don't see Farley neither. Murph I see a lot. But he's like a pa, so he don't count none."

"Well, you can always still see those guys," Lester explained. "And besides, you've met some new people this year. Just like I have. What about Torgy, and Jethroe, and Crandall? They nice guys. What about them, Mick?"

Mickey pulled his face away from the cage so that he could grab another celery stalk. "Those guys ain't Mickey's friends. They just laugh. And say things. Duncan and Daphney don't say nothing."

"Ah, those guys ain't so bad," Lester said. "That's just how major leaguers are. They rode me something fierce when I got here. All of us. Only stopped once I started hitting."

Mickey said nothing. His focus remained on the rabbit cages.

"And Ozzy and even Spahny," Lester continued. "They were downright brutal to me. But now, I got nine home runs; they know who I am, and all is forgiven. It's time Mick. Sometimes, all you need to do is give people some time."

After some hesitation, which saw Mickey open one cage door and adjust the bed of hay inside before doing the same with the other, he spoke purposefully. "Mickey's got time," the boy said. "Lots of time."

"There you go, Mick, see? That's what I'm saying. Things change with time. Look at you and Ozzy's sister for instance. Just a few months ago, you didn't even know her. And now you have yourself a real friend. That's how it works. In fact, maybe you should give her a call while we are away. You know, just to say hi. That might make you feel better."

Mickey face grew severe. "Mickey can't talk to Jolene until we get back," he explained. "That's what Murph said. Said I would see her at the ballpark, when I pitch, and then everything would be just the way it was before. Three days. That's all. Three days. Mickey's got time."

The rest of the day went fast, with the weather changing in dramatic fashion. The skies turned dark early, followed by winds that bent the tall grass and treetops and a flurry of drops that fell with unrelenting vigor, all of which put an end to the outdoor activities until finally, after having finished dinner, Murph and Molly retired to the porch to watch the storm. They sat in silence for a while, both marveling at the flashes of lightning that illuminated the distant tree line and rooftops with intermittent splashes of brilliant purple and blue. Then, above the claps of thunder and steady drumming of rain against the roof, Murph finally spoke.

"Some storm, huh?" he said, placing his hand on hers. "Sure glad it held out until we got here."

"Yeah, it's really coming down. I hope we don't lose power. Mickey and Lester just started listening to *The Green Hornet*. I'd hate to have them miss out."

"Yup, that would not be good," Murph chuckled. "Mickey's been talking about it all day."

"Oh, I know. Believe me. He's a funny kid." She stopped herself and shook her head. "Listen to me," she continued. "I guess I should stop saying that word. *Kid*. He's a man. I just think I will always see him as a little boy. And not because of who he is or anything. It's just all the things that make him happy are so simple and pure—childlike, you know? But childlike or not, as long as those things continue to make him happy, how can I complain, right?"

Her eyes, which had been following the distant flashes of light to the sparkle of a couple of fireflies willing to brave the storm, lowered under the gravity of her last statement.

"And what about you, Molly?" he asked. "Talk to me now. What are you thinking about?"

"What about me?"

"Come on now. You know what I mean. What's going to make you happy again?"

That was a good question, one that she had been wrestling with for months. She had spent a lot of time tracing the path of her life and how she had arrived at the place she now occupied. It began with a petulant, cold father who had little interest in her desires and dreams and even less patience for those times when she expressed them.

"That there's yer problem, little lady," he had always said. "You think yer better than everyone else. Always fooling around with that clarinet and reading all the time. Poetry? What's the use in that? Nobody, nobody worth a damn, wants to talk about that."

She learned at an early age to bury her soul, and that to show it would almost certainly cause her shame and disappointment.

"You ain't getting no younger, and you ain't exactly turning too many heads neither," her father had told her when Clarence had expressed interest. "Now I know that there boy ain't no movie star, but by cracky he's got his own farm. His own farm, Molly. I reckon you best think twice, missy."

But truth be told, she did not think at all. She never really stopped and considered what her life would be like living beside a man who was a brutish, cantankerous simpleton who viewed both her and Mickey with nothing but unadulterated scorn. That was a realization that took many years to cultivate. She really had Arthur Murphy to thank for making her finally see her situation for what it was.

It was Arthur Murphy who awakened her and gave her the resolve to start her life anew. And it was Arthur Murphy who held her future in his hands once again. She didn't want to tarnish his happiness regarding his promotion to the big leagues or his success in his new position, and she loved him dearly and appreciated all he had done for both her and Mickey, but her voice had taken many years to come out of hiding, and she found, even to her own amazement, that it would not be silenced ever again.

"You want to know what's going to make me happy?" she asked.

"Yes, Molly. Yes. I can't stand to see you this way. It's not like you."

"I don't know, Arthur," she said. "It's not that easy. I have a lot on my mind lately."

Her thoughts zigzagged all over the place. Outside, it was dark and silent now, the storm clouds having given way to a partial moon whose light was infirm but strong enough to offer some shape to the shadowy, noiseless forms that moved through the night.

"Well, this is where we always used to talk," he said, rubbing her leg gently. "Now's as good a time as any to share what's troubling you."

"That's sort of my point, Arthur."

His entire face wrinkled with confusion. "Did I miss something?" he asked. "*What's* your point?"

"All that used to be, Arthur," she answered. "It's Boston. I told you. And I have been trying to tell you. It's just not me."

The smell of fresh rain dripping from the tree boughs was strong in his nose. It should have been invigorating, life-affirming, but instead all he could feel was exaustion.

"Is it really that bad, Molly?" he asked, rubbing his eyes.

"How can you ask me that, Arthur? Have you not been listening to me—paying attention to me?"

"I have. I mean, I've heard what you've said. I just don't know why you can't—"

"When I left Clarence, you promised me that my life would be different. And it was. But now, it all seems like—"

"Hold on here," he said, his temples throbbing. "Don't you dare compare me to Clarence. Are you kidding me, Molly? Is that what you really think?"

She closed her eyes and cringed. She had been waiting so long to broach this subject with him, and despite all of her careful planning, somehow she had still said the wrong thing.

"Wait a minute, Arthur, wait. Let's start over here. I'm sorry. I am not suggesting that you are *anything* like him. I'm not. I'm just upset and I don't know what I'm saying anymore."

He exhaled loudly and let his head fall into his hands. He remained that way for some time before finally directing his frustration back to her. "I just don't understand why it's so bad. I mean, I'm there, so is Mickey. Things with him are going well. Is it really so awful?"

A nervous chill ran up her back. She couldn't speak at first for fear of saying the wrong thing yet again. So she sat silent, picking nervously at the skin around her fingernails. Her reticence irked him even more than the thoughts she had previously shared—bothered him in some vague, gnawing way that had him balancing on the edge of his chair.

"Why is it so bad?" he asked her. "Can you please explain that to me?"

"Yes, you are with me there, and so is Mickey. But not really, Arthur. I'm by myself a lot. Like when you guys are at the ballpark or with the team. So I only get what little time is left over. And when you're on the road—well, then I am really on my own. It gets lonely, Arthur. And I am not the sort of girl who can just take off into a city I neither know nor like. So then I ask you . . . Where does that leave me? Where does that leave *me*?"

"Look, Molly, we've been through this before. Boston isn't Milwaukee. It's not. I know that. But just because it's different doesn't mean it's bad. I just think you need to give it—"

"More time? Is that what you were going to say? Because I have to tell you, Arthur—I love you, I really do, and I am happy for you that this dream of yours is finally coming true. But I made a promise to myself that I would matter from now on—that what *I* wanted would matter. And I just cannot break that promise."

"It does matter," he said desperately. "It does. It totally does. Why would you say it doesn't?"

"Because you obviously are in Boston, Arthur, at least for now. That's not going to change. And I do not want to be in Boston. You know that. So I have no real choice here. Either I stay and suffer like I have been—or I live without you and Mickey for the next three or four months. So I don't really see how what I want matters."

Murph sighed and shook his head without taking his eyes from hers. "How about making friends with the other wives?" he asked. "You know, just to give you a way of passing the time."

"Really? Are you serious, Arthur? Those women don't want any more to do with me than I do with them. Be serious now. Besides, I keep telling you, fast city life is not for me. It's just not. It's not who I am."

Murph's face flushed and his eyes grew large and gray, revolting against the implications of her protests. "So what are you saying, Molly? What's the bottom line here? Are you asking me to leave Boston? Am I quitting?"

"No, no, of course not. I would never ask you to do that."

He looked away, his breath heavy as though he'd just run a race. "So are you . . . you know, quitting?"

An involuntary rush of air escaped her lips. Quitting?" she repeated incredulously. "You? Us? Of course not. Don't be silly."

"Well, then what are we supposed to do now, Molly? I don't know what you want."

There was no easy way that Molly could think to say what she really wanted—the life they shared before Boston—she could not have, and could never ask for, anyway. So she steeled herself like one about to leap from a great height and said the one thing that finally came to her lips.

"I want to stay here, in Milwaukee."

"I don't understand," Arthur replied. "You mean all of us?"

"No, Arthur. I told you that wouldn't be fair."

"So you're telling me that you're not coming back with us when we leave in two days?"

A trace of anger stole across his face as she quietly nodded.

"You can't stay here in Milwaukee all by yourself," he protested. "It's not safe. Or right. Come on, Molly. That is crazy talk. We are your family. And Boston—Boston is your home."

She took a deep breath. "No, Arthur, Milwaukee is my home. It's really the only one I have ever had. Being back here, especially now that you are here, too, has made me realize just how much I've missed it."

He braced himself.

"So we are splitting up?" he asked, his face awash with despair. "That's it?"

"No, no," she said, taking his hand and bringing it to her cheek. "Listen to me. I know Boston and this job mean the world to you. So go; do your job. It's only another few months. It will go fast. And when it's all over, I will be here, waiting for you."

They both stopped talking. A long silence settled between them. She was out of things to say. He wondered what he would do without her, how he would get by knowing she was so far away. He also worried for Mickey, and how yet another emotional issue would affect him. The gravity of both uncertainties rendered him desperate.

"And maybe you will realize that you miss Boston—and me and Mickey—and decide to come back? Maybe?"

She lowered her head for a moment, looked into his eyes, and nodded. "Sure, that's possible. But I have an idea of my own, Arthur."

"You mean there's more?"

She put her arms around his neck and placed her lips gently against his ear. "Maybe, just maybe, *you* will discover that you miss it *here*—and that after all of this talk about Boston and the major leagues, you might see that this place you have been running from for so long is where you truly belong."

# SECOND HALF

Murph and the Braves began the second half of the season at the Bee Hive with a three-game set against the Pittsburgh Pirates. Murph's decision to forgo the usual pitching rotation and start with Mickey had him wondering about all the second-guessing that he'd probably be doing, but that concern paled in comparison to the tearful good-bye he had shared with Molly the night before. He was having more trouble than he had thought he would at shaking the emptiness.

"So you promise to call me if you change your mind?" he asked her. She was clutching him with both hands, and her face was buried in his shoulder.

"Yes," she replied, her voice barely audible through her gentle crying.

Now he was back in the saddle, facing another half of the season that would be even more challenging than the first. And he was beginning with Mickey, a decision that he knew was the right one but fraught with potential disaster should things not go the way he envisioned. Spahn was the first one to voice the collective trepidation.

"I sure hope you know what you're doing, Murph," he said when he saw Mickey's name penciled in as the starter for game one. "Ain't where the smart money is."

Spahn's commentary proved to be more of a prophetic declaration than a malicious jab when Mickey trotted out to the mound to take his warm-up tosses. The young man appeared skittish, just as he was in his prior start, and his first few throws to Lester were forced and erratic.

"Uh, Murph, you watching this?" Keely said. "Look, I'm just the bullpen guy, but looks to me like—"

Murph felt his insides burning. "Yeah, yeah, I see it, Bobby," Murph snapped back. "Let's just let it play out, okay? I got it."

"I mean, he's not even looking at home plate," Keely continued. "Seems like he's looking clear past Lester, into the stands. Not sure how that's gonna do us any good."

Murph considered going back at Keely but thought better of it. He knew exactly what was going on with Mickey and could have run right out onto the field and wrapped his hands around Ozmore's neck. He resisted the urge, opting for a conversation once the bottom half of the opening inning was complete—but would have had a much more difficult time doing so had he known about the conversation that took place just prior to the game.

"So do we understand each other, Jolene?" Ozmore had asked, his finger waving wildly in the girl's face. "Do we?"

"He's just a nice guy," she replied. "And all we did was talk—until you said no more. And now you're telling me that I can't even go to the games? Or wave to him?"

"That's exactly what I'm saying. And if anyone asks you about it, remember what I said—it was your idea. I had nothing to do with it. Ya hear?"

She lowered her head so that he wouldn't see her crying. Then he left for the ballpark.

Murph's insides mirrored the advance of twilight and the riotous swirls of pink and orange that were staining a darkening sky. He was only now beginning to realize just how much more onerous Ozmore had made his decision to start Mickey. Mickey remembered what Murph had said about everything being just like it was before they went on the road. That included Jolene being at the ballpark—in the stands—where she always sat.

Now Mickey was about to deliver the first pitch of the game, but his eyes, like his thoughts, were fixed on the empty seat behind home plate. He stood on the mound, waiting for the umpire's call to begin play, distracted. *Oscar's gone. Cleats are broken. Doctors can't fix Boxcar. Where is Jolene? Duncan doesn't like the new lettuce Mama's giving him. Curveball spins from your hand. Where is Jolene? Head hurts. Lefty still doesn't like Mickey.* He could not free himself from the juggernaut of worry. *Miss Mama. Gotta throw strikes, like I can. Can't miss. Papa's screaming and hitting me. Lefty is too. Jolene, where's Jolene?* The progression was swift and crippling and would have completely destroyed him had the call of "play ball" not torn him from his mania.

Leadoff hitter Pete Castiglione stepped in, tapped each of his cleats two times with the barrel of his bat, and dug in with his back foot. He exhaled briskly, blinked three times, and stared at Mickey. At first the look was nothing more than just the final part of the methodical routine Castiglione followed each time he got ready to hit. But the longer he stared, windmilling his bat, waiting for Mickey's first delivery, the more disturbed he became by the wildly vacant eyes looking back at him. Then the first pitch came, and the concern for everyone grew exponentially.

It was a high fastball that exploded out of Mickey's hand and shot through the air, off course like a heat-seeking missile that buzzed by the batter's chin, sending him to the dirt in a crumpled heap. The errant toss had the entire Pirates bench on the top step of the dugout, screaming at Mickey and pointing fingers at the handful of Braves players who were also watching the events unfold from a similar vantage point on their side.

"Tell your boys to have a seat and dummy up," Murph yelled over to his counterpart, Billy Meyer. "If we wanted to hit him, we would have."

"We can miss too, Murphy," Meyer yelled back. "Remember that. We can too."

Murph muttered something under his breath, adjusted his cap, then focused his attention on Mickey.

"Let's go, Mick. Enough of this. Hit the glove. Hit Lester's glove. Let's go."

Mickey heard Murph's encouraging words, but somehow the other voices, the ones hurling invectives in his direction, seemed louder. It hurt his ears. His eyes were burning, too, still preoccupied by that empty seat. He walked around the perimeter of the mound, breathing deeply, repeating Murph's command in his mind before stepping back on the rubber. His eyes vacillated between the signs Lester was flashing to the area behind home plate and that empty seat. If it wasn't for Lester pounding his glove and calling to Mickey to bring the heat, he may never have reared back and fired the next pitch—which was another fastball equally wild to the opposite side of the plate. Murph shook his head and silently cursed Ozmore, especially when the crowd started buzzing. It was hard enough to appease the clubhouse critics, but once the fans started voicing their displeasure he was really going to have an issue.

"I hear 'em, I hear 'em," he said to Keely before he had a chance to say anything. "I won't let him go too long."

Mickey's third delivery missed its mark, too, something that had Murph on the top step considering doing the unthinkable. He had never before pulled a pitcher after just one batter and certainly didn't want to start now with Mickey. Besides, he had nobody else warm yet. But the kid was crumbling and the crowd growing more restless by the second. His only hope, if he had to go get him this early, was to have the boy feign an injury so that whomever he brought out of his bullpen would have plenty of time to get ready. He had just about hatched the entire plan and was about to put it all in place when a sound rang out that stopped him as if he had run into an invisible wall.

"Strike one!"

Murph turned to look at Mickey, who was toeing the rubber now with a look of quiet conviction. His motion was smooth and effortless, almost poetic in its execution.

"Strike two!"

There seemed to be, all at once, a force at work that now belied the desperation of the situation.

*What the hell?* Murph asked himself.

He scanned the field for a clue but only saw the same incredulous look he had on his own face on the faces of the other eight out there. He looked into the Pirates' dugout next, where he noticed that every man wearing black and yellow was standing, watching open-mouthed as if they had just seen a ghost or some other supernatural entity. They were befuddled.

Murph shrugged. It made no sense to him, none in the least, until he caught a glimpse of a young lady with soft eyes and long sandy curls sitting in her seat watching the game. She had just arrived at the park, and as she made her way to her seat, she held up her hand to Mickey and mouthed the words *good luck* before sitting down. Murph never saw that. But the sight of Jolene in her seat and Mickey smiling was enough to have him back on the bench, legs crossed, fears vanquished.

"Strike three!"

It was from that position that he watched the remainder of the game. When it was all said and done, Mickey had fanned fourteen Pirates in all and allowed just three hits en route to one of the most dominating performances of the season. The Bee Hive was vibrating all night with thunderous applause and cheers for the young man that Braves' fans were only just now getting to appreciate. Naturally, the festivities that had accompanied all of Mickey's starts at Borchert Field paled in comparison, but there were indicators everywhere that it was about to begin all over again.

Midway through the game, one of the more creative of the thirty-seven thousand faithful fans who was sitting in the center field stands began a homage to Mickey's mound domination, celebrating each strikeout by pasting on the cement overhang a series of Ks that he made from hot dog wrappers, a charcoal briquette, and chewing gum. Others who were less creative chose to honor their new-found hero in a much more traditional manner, chanting in unison "Mickey! Mickey! Mickey!" each time the young man came on and off the field. And there was a swarm of reporters by Mickey's locker following the boy's brilliant performance, all clamoring for a little time with the young phenom they were all calling "The Bean Town Burner." Even the Braves players who ordinarily were the object of the media's attention had to smile at the storm of interest in Mickey. The only one who was not swept away by all the hoopla was Ozmore, who showered, got changed, and left the ballpark all within a half hour. But not before Murph got a chance to say something to him, something he'd been crafting throughout the game.

"Hey, Ozzy, I sure am glad you don't have any problem with those two kids being friends," he said, winking. "Sure is something special, huh?"

Murph expressed a similar, albeit far more sincere, sentiment to Jolene, who he was fortunate to catch just as she and Mickey were leaving together.

"Boy, am I sure thankful you showed up today," he said, smiling. "And just in the nick of time."

Jolene appreciated Murph's gesture, but it made her sad as she recalled the awful exchange that she had with her brother just hours before the game.

"Well, thank you," she said. "Sorry I was so late. I had a little trouble getting to the ballpark. Wasn't sure if I was going to make it at all actually, but sometimes you have to go with what you know is right. Know what I mean, Mr. Murphy?"

Her response seemed to free some encumbered spirit deep inside. All at once, everything was imbued with sharper focus and vitality. The air was sweeter and the lights outside the stadium burned with limitless splendor.

"I sure do, young lady," he said. "I sure do."

A short time later, Mickey and Jolene walked for a while, a careless jaunt that took them down Commonwealth Avenue and across some smaller streets, the last of which narrowed into a long, winding path comprised of dry earth and cracked concrete that broke apart beneath their feet as they strolled. The crumbling road twisted and turned interminably before giving way to an open area flanked by towering sycamores and a vast expanse of grass that lay sleepily beneath the muted glow of yellow light wafting from the iron street lamps. Here and there, figures glided in the soft shadows, disappearing now and again until the only real indicator of their presence were the whispers and soft laughter they emitted. Mickey and Jolene followed the sounds to a wooden bench, where they sat for a while.

"You sure did make a lot of Braves fans happy today, Mickey," Jolene said while they stared up at a brilliant gathering of stars that appeared to be pressed against a canvas of black velvet. "That was really incredible."

"I like baseball," Mickey said. "Pitching is fun most of the time."

She laughed and shifted her eyes over to him. "Yeah, I imagine anyone who can do what you can would find it fun."

He was still looking up at the sky as she spoke.

"That over there is the Great Bear, Jolene," he said, pointing to a group of stars. "You see him? If you look at the Big Dipper over there, and those two stars that make the outside part of the bowl, and follow them a ways, you can see him."

"Yeah, yeah, I think I can see him," she said smiling. "I mean I think I do. The only constellation I could spot when I was a kid was Orion, on account of his belt. Those three stars right there. Never was much into the others when I was a little girl. I would mostly just stare at them and pretend they were diamonds that I could reach up and grab and hold in my hand."

"Oh there are lots of them to see," he continued. "Over there, that's Aries, the Ram, and there is the flying horse, Pegasus, and over there are the Gemini Twins, and there is—"

"How do you know so much about the stars, Mickey?" she asked, pushing the hair away from her face so that she could see him better.

"There is Leo the Lion. You can see his head and mane right there."

"I see it, I do," she said. "But come on. Tell me. How do you know all this?"

He tilted his head down and turned to her, caught momentarily by the way the starlight gleamed off her hair.

"My mama taught me," he said. "She taught Mickey everything. From a book first, then just by sitting with me and looking up."

Her mind swirled as she thought about what he had just told her. "And you're sure nobody taught you how to play baseball?" she asked. "Not even how to throw the ball?"

"Lots of folks helped Mickey learn baseball," he said. "Mr. Murphy, Pee Wee, Boxcar, and Farley. There was Woody, and Arky, and Jimmy Llamas. They all helped Mickey learn baseball. Lester and—"

"No, no, silly," she said laughing. "I know that. I mean did anyone teach you about baseball. You know, when you were a little boy?"

He grew quiet, completely unprepared for the flood of memories her words unleashed. He sat for some time, his gentle rocking the only visible sign that he was still with her.

"Mickey, is everything okay?" she asked, placing her hand on his.

"Papa said that there were no use for games on a farm," he said, breaking the silence almost tearfully. "Especially for a water head like Mickey. Only thing I was good for was baling the hay and making the slop for Oscar and the other pigs. I was real good at that. Oscar loved them apples. Mama taught me poems and about music and skipping stones and how to make a house out of cards, but never told Papa. If he found out he'd just get mad and start yelling and throwing things and hitting us."

Instantly she was lost in a succession of memories. The horrible yellow wallpaper in her bedroom. Her father's voice, cold and abusive, and the smell of whiskey when his breath found her nose. The long nights spent by herself, staring out the window at a world moving swiftly by. The message that both her parents managed to convey with ruthless regularity—the message that made her think and believe that she was less than ordinary and had no business pursuing anything that others could.

"It's funny, you and me," she said. "Looking at us, nobody would ever guess how much alike we really are."

Mickey took time to examine her entire face, feature by feature, before moving his eyes in a more cursory fashion across her entire body. "You and me ain't alike none, Miss Jolene," Mickey said. "I have brown eyes and yours are green. I am tall and you're a little shorter. My hair is dark and short and yours is—"

"Okay, okay," she said. She stroked his hair, slowly so that she could feel the thick wisps of brown in between her fingers, and kissed him on the cheek. "You are really cute, Mickey Tussler, you know that? Really cute."

They walked back to her house, hand in hand, under a magnificent moon that splashed a silky sheen across the sidewalks. The air was cool and fresh and carried on it the distant song of crickets and some other night dwellers. They talked some more about growing up and the things that bothered each of them and those things that made them smile. It was free and easy. Jolene had never laughed so much in one night. She found that Mickey was the most refreshing person she had ever met. She was certainly not in the habit of hanging onto every word a person spoke, but she found herself doing just that as they strolled along. Mickey had just finished talking about the way he always ate his mashed potatoes and was about to tell her all about the owls back in Indiana when a car pulled up next to them.

"Do you know how late it is, Jolene?" the driver asked. "Do you?"

Her face lost its softness and twisted into an ugly mask. "Go away, Buddy. We are heading home. It's fine. Murph is picking Mickey up at our house. We were just walking and talking."

"That's right, you *were*. No more. Now get in this car right now. I'm taking you home."

"I am not a little—"

"Listen, Jolene, don't make me get out of this car and—"

"Stop it! Stop it right now, Buddy! Just leave us alone. Drive yourself home and I will meet you there shortly. You're making a scene."

"Jolene, are you going to get in this car or not?"

She did not answer him. She just kept walking with Mickey slightly behind and Buddy rolling alongside her.

"Jolene, get in this car or I'm—"

"Jolene does not want to get in the car, Buddy," Mickey said without warning. He had caught up to her and was standing right beside her now. "Didn't you hear her say that?"

Buddy threw the car in park, turned his body to the side, and leaned toward the opposite window so that he could face both of them squarely.

"What did you just say, buckshot?"

"Buddy, stop it. Right now. Don't you start with him now."

"No, no. If Romeo here wants to say something, I'm ready to listen. Come on, Romeo. You got something to say?"

"Mickey's not Romeo," the young man replied flatly. "Mickey is Mickey. From the team, Buddy. Remember? Mr. Murphy says we are like family. You know Mickey."

Frustration flowed through Buddy. "You're kidding me, right?" he said. "Really, Jolene? This is what you're willing to fuss over?"

The whole scene began to dissolve in front of her—slowly—as if merely watching from a safe distance. It might have played out a dozen different ways, each preferable to this. The thought was paralyzing at first, then served to ignite inside her a rebellion whose seeds had been sown years before.

"You listen to me, Buddy Ozmore," she said as she thrust her head through the open window opposite her attacker. "I am walking home with Mickey now. I will be walking with him tomorrow too. And the day after that. We may even eat together or see a movie. And I am telling you right now, stay out of it. I am not a child, and you are not my father. So leave me the hell alone and just worry about yourself."

Her words were loud and pointed and reverberated in the dark spaces between the buildings and houses. Her outburst was so explosive that even she did not know what to do afterward. So she took Mickey's hand and started to quietly walk, her eyes fixed directly in front of her.

Buddy was far more animated. He slammed his open hand on the steering wheel and began rolling after her. "That's fine, little lady," he screamed before speeding off into the night. "But you listen and listen good. You've done it now. For real. So you have your little walks and talks and whatever else it is you think you want to do with this weirdo. But when it all turns to shit, and you see I'm right—like I always am—don't come crying to me."

# CAN OF CORN

Despite Ozmore's protests and threats, Mickey and Jolene continued to see each other. Jolene found in Mickey someone who would allow her to be herself, free from judgment and expectation. And Mickey looked at Jolene with eyes of wonder. There was something familiar and warm and safe about her, even though he hadn't known her for all that long. But there was also a rising undercurrent of new feelings attached to her, ones he had never felt before.

Being with Jolene was easy, even with Buddy's objections. These were unchartered waters for Mickey, whose entire life had been spent in the throes of struggle. When he was very young, the signs of this struggle were frequent and disturbing. The inability to perform even the most rudimentary tasks, like reading or completing puzzles, resulted in him kicking walls and slamming his fists against his forehead. It enraged Clarence, who tried to remedy the issue with his own fists. All it did for Molly was break her heart.

As Mickey grew older, Molly employed other strategies to help Mickey cope with his inability to execute certain tasks and the frustration that always followed. She would often take his hands and rub them until the fit had run its course or divert his attention away from what was plaguing him by singing or playing the clarinet when Clarence was not around. When those activities became impractical and ceased to work, she moved to more calculated measures, like loosening his collar and rubbing the back of his neck or simply removing him from the situation at hand. These stratagems were all effective for a while, but the grim reality that she would not always be around to help him haunted her. That's when she decided to teach Mickey her favorite poem, "Silver," by Walter de la Mare.

At first she would sit him on her lap when he was in the midst of one of his episodes and softly, gently recite the words in his ear. The words had a soothingly hypnotic effect on the boy. "Slowly, silently, now the moon, walks the night in her silver shoon." It wasn't long before Mickey learned the words himself and would recite the lines with her as she spoke. "This way and that, she peers and sees, silver fruit upon silver trees." It became their special thing—and always worked when he was feeling threatened or just out of sorts. When he grew older still, and she was not around to recite the words for him, she discovered much to her relief that he had adopted the practice and could execute it all by himself. "Couched in his kennel, like a log, with paws of silver sleeps the dog."

Mickey had not had to rely on this crutch as much lately, although he still invoked the words now and again when his world began tilting in ways he could not negotiate. But Jolene had seemed to balance him and everything around him so that when he finally spoke the words again, it was only to share them with her during one of their conversations.

"Your mother taught you that?" she asked. "That is so sweet, and the words—they're beautiful."

She held his hand as the two of them sat on her front porch, gazing up at a moon that revealed itself in a starless sky almost on cue.

"My mama taught me lots of things," Mickey said. "She's real smart."

"Sure sounds like it," Jolene said. "Sounds like she really loves you too. That must be a nice feeling."

She could not help but think of her own mother and how the woman she called Mom was absent from her life in so many vital ways long before she had passed away. She could recall as a young girl trying everything to get her mother's attention and maybe, just maybe, a warm embrace. She saw how her parents, especially her mother, had fawned over Buddy and his extraordinary athletic ability. So she had tried everything she could get her hands on—croquet mallet, basketball, roller skates, tennis racquet—anything to turn her mother's head her way. But her lack of physical dexterity and coordination and her mother's indifference rendered each endeavor a colossal failure.

When she couldn't replicate her brother's talents, she decided to discover one of her own. She tried painting, the violin, and writing poetry. She dabbled in needlework, baking, and pottery. But no matter what she did, it always resulted in the same response from her mother. "You're just not good at anything, Jolene," she would say. "It's okay. Ain't your fault none. Just pray real hard that one day someone will love you anyway."

She would have liked to have shared it all with Mickey, to unburden her heavy heart, but knew it would be too much to ask. So she swallowed her pain and continued their conversation as if nothing were wrong.

"Yup, your mama sure sounds like one terrific lady. I cannot wait to meet her."

"You can't meet her today, Jolene, or even tomorrow," Mickey said. "On account of she's not here in Boston. She's in Milwaukee, taking care of Duncan and Daphney. You can meet them too. But not today or tomorrow neither, cause they ain't here either."

"It's okay, Mickey," she said smiling. "I'm not going anywhere. I can wait."

It was the day before the Braves were to head out on a quick three-game trip to Cincinnati. Mickey and Jolene had just finished eating a late afternoon picnic lunch that she had packed and were sitting in an elementary school playground, on painted wooden railroad ties that framed a giant sandbox.

"Did you like the chicken and everything else, Mickey?" she asked. "I'm afraid I'm not a very good cook."

Mickey's feet were busy, making tiny hills in the sand. It had rained the night before, so the sand was perfect for building. When she looked down, Jolene noticed that he had gotten some of the drier grains on her shoes.

"Mickey, did you hear what I said? Did you like the food?"

She was thinking about how he had separated, with painstaking precision, the tiny pieces of celery and carrots she had put in the potato salad.

"Yes, Jolene. Mickey liked it. A lot. I ate five pieces of chicken, three rolls, one scoop of potato salad, and two hunks of cherry pie. I like lemonade too. Three cups. Yes, Jolene. It was good. I liked it. A lot."

She smiled. "That's good. I'm happy you liked it."

They sat for a while longer, listening to the rumble of cars and trucks coming from the road just beyond the tiny brick building, and set their eyes upon a group of sparrows that were busy building a nest in a small birch at the far corner of the school yard. They also talked some more—about the team, and Boston, and what he was going to do once the season was over. It was something she had been thinking about for a while.

"So what do you think you'll do when the season ends, Mickey?" she asked.

"Well I reckon that me and Mr. Murphy will go back to his house, with my mama, in Milwaukee. It's a nice house. Duncan and Daphney will be there too."

A future for which she cared very little began forming in her imagination.

"And what about us? You know, when the season ends?"

"Well we both won't be at Mr. Murphy's house, Jolene. Just me."

"No, I know that, silly. I mean, what is going to happen to us when you are gone? You know, when will I see you or talk to you?"

The thought had never occurred to him until that moment. The dizzying mix of fear and confusion that came across his face surprised her a little.

"I will call you, Jolene, on the telephone," he said in a desperate voice. "And you can call me too. On the phone. But you have to answer. Answer, Jolene. And maybe you can visit Milwaukee. It's nice. I think that'd be all right. I think. Unless my—"

"It's okay, Mickey. I didn't mean to get you upset. I'm sorry. It's just that the time is going fast, and I really—well, I sort of—I kind of—"

She was having great difficulty saying the words she wanted him to hear. So she sat there for some time, listening to him roll one idea into the next. He continued with all the possible ways they could still talk to or see each other, then quickly moved to the number of miles that lay between Boston and Milwaukee, which led to a litany of distinctions between the two cities and a five-minute dissertation on the differences between Boston baked beans and the famous Milwaukee real chili.

"So you got to see, Jolene, the beans baked in Boston are navy beans. They are smaller than the kidney beans in the Milwaukee chili. Taste a little better too, but the chili has meat, and I like hamburgers so I kinda like the chili better. Oh and it has cheese, too, instead of molasses, which my mama always—"

Her focus shifted from Mickey's ramblings to the square in front of her. She was still searching for the right way to tell Mickey how she felt, and nothing was good enough. She found her words were often misconstrued or ill timed. She couldn't bear the thought of screwing this up. Then, in the midst of her staring, while Mickey continued to drone on, an idea swept across her.

Mickey was so engrossed in what he was saying that he never saw her reach down, index finger extended, and begin scrawling a message in the sand. Her entire arm moved artfully, in passionate, graceful bursts that produced what she had been trying to say all afternoon. *I like you, Mickey.*

When he stopped rambling, she took his chin in her hand and gently guided his eyes in the direction of her message. He looked with noticeable interest and read. She waited breathlessly for his reaction. He said nothing. Did nothing. When she saw this, she looked down and then away, embarrassed by what she had written. She wasn't sure why she had done it. Perhaps it was because the words were too hard to say out loud—for both of them. Or maybe it was that writing it in the sand just seemed safer than saying it. Once it was said, it was out. But the sand could be erased, along with the embarrassment of unrequited affection—and it would be as if it were never said at all. This realization spurred her to action. She turned back with the intention of dragging her foot across her message when she noticed something else was now written below.

*Mickey likes Joleen*

The *c* in *Mickey* and the *e* in *likes* were backward, and of course her name was spelled incorrectly, but she couldn't help but smile nonetheless. She felt happy and protected all at once and wanted to capitalize on this newfound method of communication. So before the splendor of the moment had any time to dim, her foot had cleared the makeshift slate and her finger was back in the sand.

*I am very happy.*

Mickey read this message, too. It did not take him long to respond this time.

*Me also.*

They both sat quietly, dreamily, as the sunset rolled pale tints of yellow and orange across the playground. Jolene felt her heart beating stronger than before, and though she tried to control the swell of emotion rolling inside of her, she couldn't stop the pounding. Mickey's receptiveness to her was soothing, almost calming, and made her entire body feel as though it were submerged in warm, pulsating water. She thought about how at that moment she had never been happier. But each time that thought gave way to the consideration of what she wanted to write next, her heart was jolted and she was caught in a torrent of desire and fear and helplessness. It was all so much more than she had anticipated. And it left her wondering what Mickey was thinking—until, without any warning, he took her hand in his.

It was warm, and she could feel the moisture in his palm. Her heart beat even faster as he stroked the back of her hand with his thumb. Maybe she wouldn't have to write anything else. Maybe, if she could get the words to come, she could just whisper what she wanted to ask, gently in his ear.

"Mickey, is it okay if I kiss you?" she asked with far greater ease than she could have ever anticipated. She also did not expect what happened next.

The second the words left her lips, Mickey began spiraling out of control. In the short time it took for him to process what she was asking, he was back there again—at The Bucket, with Laney. He could still feel her warm breath against his neck and could smell her perfume. The ugly recollection rocked him slowly first, then with more aggression. Jolene was beside herself with worry and self-loathing.

"I'm sorry, Mickey, I'm sorry," she pleaded desperately. "Please, it's okay. It's okay. I shouldn't have said that. It's okay."

The rocking continued, accompanied by a steady but inaudible mumbling. The only words she could make out were "Mickey fooled—Rosco," and "head hurts." At first it seemed like a random flurry of thoughts, spawned by her moving too quickly for him. But then a switch clicked in her brain. She remembered what he had told her about that night at The Bucket, and she felt even worse. But at least she knew what was happening and why.

"No, no, sweetie, it's okay," she said, stroking his hair. "I know that was a bad night for you. And that girl was bad too. But you're okay here. You're okay with me. It's Jolene. Jolene and Mickey. *I like you*. Remember?" She pointed to the sand.

His breathing eased and the severity of his spasmodic movements began to lessen. She could see in his eyes, which were dark and distant, that the stroking of his hair was bringing him back.

"It's okay, Mickey," she kept whispering. "It's okay."

Eventually, his anxiety flattened. Gone were the thoughts of Laney and Lefty and that horrible night, replaced by new thoughts that were far more pressing. He had taught himself about all of the relationship rules and social cues germane to the locker room and baseball field. He slipped up now and again, of course, but his vigilance in reviewing these guidelines regularly had allowed him entrance, and now finally acceptance, into that world. But this thing with Jolene, and the feelings that accompanied it, was a whole different story. He had no idea what he was feeling, or why, or how to handle it. He had even less understanding of her and what it was she was feeling and wanted him to do. The maelstrom of insecurity and confusion was overwhelming.

Then he felt Jolene's hand on his shoulder. The ticking of his watch seemed to slow to almost nothing. So did the rocking. She was whispering beautiful things in his ear now. Her voice was soft and warm. He wanted to answer her but couldn't say anything, as his words were blocked by the lump in his throat.

"Is this okay?" she finally asked him. He nodded without speaking. She massaged the top of his shoulder, then moved her hand up and down his bicep, squeezing gently from time to time. He liked that. It felt good.

He let her soothe him while he continued to try to put in order all of the thoughts that were bouncing off the walls of his mind. On more than one occasion, he opened his mouth as if to speak, then discovered he did not know what he would say. He wanted to tell her that her hands were soft, just like her curls—and that the way she smelled made him think of spring on the farm when everything was bursting with new life. He would have also liked to explain the rush he was feeling all over his body, how it seemed as though he could feel each drop of blood gushing through his veins. But again, he had no words. So instead, he decided to follow her, to use her as a guide. He touched her gently, with fingertips that tingled, the same way she was touching him.

At first it was just her shoulder. He made tiny circles with his fingers, up and down the entire length of her arm, the same way he did when petting Duncan and Daphney. Her skin was smooth. It was soft too. So soft.

When he saw that it was okay and that she liked what he was doing, he moved his hand to the back of her neck where he lingered for a while, his fingers engaged in the same circular motion. He spun each one tighter now, so that in time, the loops began to overlap. He was thinking about the rings that formed in the pond back home when he dropped a pebble in the center. The more he thought about it, the faster his fingers worked, until his excitement created a tangle in the fine hair at the nape of her neck and she lurched forward and cried out in pain.

"No, it's all right," she said when he abruptly halted what he was doing. "It's fine, Mickey. You just pulled my hair a little. That's all."

He was inconsolable. All he could see was her face when she pulled away. All he could hear was the sound of Clarence's voice berating him for the couple of times he mishandled the chicks.

"You damned lunk-head. Ain't right to put those paws on them chicks like that. Don't you know nothin? Ya's got to be gentle with 'em, see? Not rush in there like a confounded grizzly bear, all full of happy and stupid. Never let me catch you near 'em again."

He was rocking again, and his eyes were beginning to fill with water. Jolene panicked. She was angry with herself, not so much for her reaction but because she feared that she had lost him, destroyed the magic of the moment. She sat dumbly, listening to herself breathe, trying to divert her attention away from what had just happened and help her focus on what to do next. Each breath she took was like the ticking of a clock and for a moment; it was too much for her. Then she forgot the incident as if it had never occurred and took his face in her hands while she sang softly to him.

*"Sentimental me, guess I'll always be, so in love with you, don't know what to do, sentimental me."*

Her voice was enchanting, each word she sang a beautiful, melodious bubble that, if pierced, would flood the earth with a warm, magic glow, illuminating everything in its path. She continued to sing, looking into him and he into her. Then there were no more words, just a soothing silence that gave way to the gentle pressing of her lips against his.

At first his whole body stiffened, as if his limbs and extremities were cast in cement. He could not move, and she could feel his rigidity and the shame and fear and confusion washing over him. Her lips remained pressed on his, moving slowly, softly, like a tiny heartbeat. There was no response at first, and she began to feel that same shame and fear and confusion as if it has been passed from his body to hers. Then it happened. He stirred.

It began with his eyes, which rolled into focus to reveal her face, beautiful and safe and close to his. Then came the sleepy awakening of his hands and fingers and other places, too. The wonderful rioting of energy and emotion surged, igniting something deep inside him that triggered a current that coursed through his entire body before finally finding his lips. And at that moment, two separate souls that were equally lost became one.

# GOOD OLD-FASHIONED HARDBALL

Early August brought with it thick air and oppressive temperatures that flirted with triple digits for several days. It also ushered in an unexpected stretch of spirited play that became the hallmark of a Braves team that was already entertaining dreams of the postseason.

Murph's crew was winning games in every imaginable way—pitcher's duels, barn burners—and coming from behind, late-inning dramas. They could do no wrong. They even eeked out a victory one night on a Sid Gordon squeeze bunt that scored not one run but two when Sam Jethroe caught the opposing infield napping and came around to score all the way from second base.

Mickey was also in the midst of his best stretch of the season. He had won his last three starts, compiling a staggering 1.27 ERA over that stretch to go along with twenty-six strikeouts and only six walks. He had surrendered just twelve hits in those twenty-seven innings and opposing batters were batting a paltry .108 against him. It was perhaps the most dominating exhibition of pitching prowess ever recorded.

But the numbers only told a small portion of the story. All around the city of Boston, signs of this infectious excitement were cropping up everywhere. Naturally, the Bee Hive became the epicenter of this idol worship, with legions of fans sporting Braves jerseys with the number eight on the back, while packs of others brought placards with messages such as WE LOVE YOU MICKEY, TUSSLER TIME, and MICKEY FOR PRESIDENT.

The media was also captivated by the young man's sudden rise to stardom. After every game, even the ones in which he did not pitch, a legion of reporters camped out around his locker with a list of questions for Boston's most popular celebrity. They wanted to know everything, ranging from what cereal he ate for breakfast and his shoe size to who taught him to throw and how he was enjoying his time as a big league pitcher. And they all got a hearty laugh after his last outing, when one reporter asked him why nobody had heard anything about him before.

"Cause Mickey was not here yet," he said in typical matter-of-fact form.

The stir he had created cast a spotlight on the entire team. Murph and his boys were the toast of the town. Everyone was talking about the Boston Braves. They were the hottest team in the league and appeared unbeatable. The string of victories had catapulted them almost to the top of the division, so when the Dodgers came to town on August 10, the Braves found themselves with an opportunity to leap into first place.

Vern Bickford got the call for the hometown crew and cruised through the first three innings. Dodgers hurler Don Newcombe matched Bickford pitch for pitch for two innings but found himself in some trouble in the home half of the third after a leadoff walk to Ozmore and a hard ground ball off the bat of Marshall that appeared to be a tailor-made twin killing until shortstop Pee Wee Reese mishandled the ball on the exchange and all hands were safe. The miscue left Newcombe in a jam, but that wasn't the real story unfolding. In his eagerness to beat the throw to second, Ozmore came in hard at the bag, spikes flying, and took out Reese. The Dodgers did not take kindly to Ozmore's aggressiveness and in the bottom of the fifth, when he came to bat, made their displeasure known.

The first pitch Ozmore saw was a high fastball that rode up under his chin, sending him to the dirt. Ozmore went down in a heap, but got right back up, dusted himself off, and nodded at Newcombe. He had been expecting retaliation and was okay with that. It was good old country hardball and everyone knew the rules. But when Newcombe came back with another heater that buzzed right by his head, Ozmore glared out at the mound and bared his teeth.

When the tension-filled inning came to a close, Murph found Ozmore and asked if he was all right. The outfielder was visibly agitated.

"Yeah, yeah, I'm fine," he said. "Whatever. Gonna take more than that to get to me."

"Hey," Murph said, grabbing Ozmore by the arm, preventing him from walking away. "Nobody screws with my players—nobody." Then he went to Bickford and with cool deliberation gave him an edict about which there would be no discussion. "First Dodger you face, first pitch, stick it in his ear."

Bickford heard Murph's command as a call to arms and did not want to disappoint. The second Carl Furillo stepped in the batter's box, Bickford sized him up, crafting in his mind's eye the exact spot he would plant the baseball. He reared back and fired a dart that nailed Furillo square in the upper arm. The Dodger batter was not expecting it but took the shot in stride, tossing his bat aside and trotting to first, but not before shooting Bickford a warning look. The score had been settled—much to the delight of Murph and the rest of his team.

The game continued on, with only subtle hints of the previous aggression punctuating a close contest. The lead changed hands four different times before the Dodgers pulled ahead by one in the top half of the eighth on a bloop and a blast, the latter coming off the bat of Furillo who took just a little extra time circling the bases. It did not go unnoticed.

The bottom half of the eighth frame opened up with Roy Hartsfield grounding out weakly to second base. Sam Jethroe followed with a squib up the first baseline that Newcombe scooped up and fired to first for the second out of the inning.

Ozmore was next. He stepped in, looking for something he could drive the other way in order to get on base. The first pitch he saw was a slider, low and away, that had him leaning out over the plate. The realization that Newcombe seemed to want to work him away was perfect, given Ozmore's intention of going to the opposite field anyway. It would make it that much easier, especially after he cheated a little closer to the plate before the next pitch was delivered.

The next offering was not what anyone expected. When the ball left Newcombe's hand, Ozmore could see instantly that the trajectory was off. Although he tried to pull away, there just wasn't enough time. In the blink of an eye, Ozmore had been drilled in the back, right between the numbers.

There was a collective silence after the thud, as if a giant glass dome had been placed over the stadium. The momentary quiet that fell over everyone was shattered when Ozmore fired his bat in Newcombe's direction and charged the mound. The Dodgers' catcher, Bruce Edwards, had anticipated Ozmore's reaction and tackled him almost instantly, something that ignited a bench clearing melee whose chaos and disorder resembled something straight out of a Jackson Pollock painting. Arms flailed and legs kicked as the crush of players swarmed around the pitcher's mound, engulfing the original combatants. Random blows rained all around, most missing their intended targets, and it was virtually impossible for anyone to distinguish Newcombe or Edwards or Ozmore from the motley mess.

One by one, players were tossed here and there, to the left and to the right, until all that remained in the center, flanked by opposing players who had paired off, was Mickey, eyes wild with fury, and Ozmore and Edwards, who both were still rolling around on the ground. Then even Edwards disappeared after Mickey grabbed him by his chest protector straps and flung him to the side. The boy was somewhere else and continued to move like a whirling dervish, swept away by the mania of the moment until Murph was able to get close enough to him to get in his ear.

"Mick, it's okay, it's over now," he kept saying. "It's over."

Mickey was still absent and his breath continued to come in short, violent bursts.

"Yeah, what the hell is wrong with you, Tussler?" Ozmore said, struggling to adjust his uniform top. "I had it. It was under control. I don't need no jughead fighting my battles."

"Hey, easy, Ozzy," Murph chided. "You don't know what you're saying. Go cool off. This jughead just saved your ass."

"Saved my ass?" he repeated. "Really, Murph? Is that what you think?"

Ozmore's eyes narrowed and burned a straight path to Murph. He looked ready to fight again, like at any second he would lunge at his manager. All of the muscles in Murph's body tightened in preparation for the assault, but the umpires, who had proved to be largely ineffectual during the fracas, stepped in and broke up what remained of the skirmish. Murph was feeling lucky to have escaped the debacle with no further incident but found himself in the owner's office after the game, embroiled in more conflict and controversy.

"Would you mind telling me, Mr. Murphy, what happened out there today?" The Braves' owner, Louis Perini, was puffing away on a fat cigar while he awaited Murph's response.

"What do you mean, sir?" Murph replied. "You know baseball. Things happen. And sometimes it gets a little heated."

Perini leaned back in his chair, the shift in weight revealing the crisply laundered sleeves beneath his navy suit jacket. Murph could also see a gold Rolex strapped to the man's wrist. His eyes were briefly fixed on the man's massive hands and the four great rings that sparkled under the bright lights of the office.

"Mr. Murphy, I haven't been around as long as you have, but I'm old enough to know that in life—and in baseball—very few things *just happen*," he said, releasing a dense cloud of smoke into the air between them. "So I'm going to ask you again—what happened out there today?"

"I don't know," Murph replied, shaking his head. "Ozzy went in hard at second, and I guess Reese and some of the other guys got all bent out of shape. So they threw at Ozzy in his next at bat, we hit one of their guys, then they came back and drilled Ozzy. It all sort of exploded after that."

"And why wasn't it all square after they threw at Ozmore the first time? They didn't hit him initially, correct?"

"Well, no, they didn't, but—"

"And did you give the order for the beanball that hit Furillo?"

Murph's shoulders buckled a little under the weight of the owner's stare. "Yes, I told Ozzy and Bickford that I will not have my players thrown at without retaliation. I just don't think it's right."

Perini scrutinized Murph from behind a veil of white smoke. "I don't pay you to think, Mr. Murphy," he said, tapping the end of his cigar against the beveled edge of a crystal ashtray. "You are here to manage this club until Southworth is well again. That's all. Nothing else. Remember that. Your little stunt not only cost us the game but also the services of four of our players who were injured in the scrum. That doesn't make me happy."

"Well, with all due respect, sir," Murph said, "that seems a little harsh—and unfair. I mean, the team is playing well, real well, and—"

"Fair is not a priority for me, Mr. Murphy. This is major league baseball. The highest level of professional baseball. We play hardball here. That means you do as you're told or you don't do anything at all. Do I make myself clear?"

"Yes, sir, I understand, but I just thought that since—"

"Have I made myself clear, Mr. Murphy?" he repeated.

The room was rife with resentment. *Why was every owner he had ever dealt with such a horse's ass?* Real baseball wasn't about tailored suits and imported Scotch. It was about spikes on your shins and dirt in your jock and fiery, hard-nosed competition that demanded that justice be served on the field of play—the field of battle.

"Yes, Mr. Perini," Murph said, his thoughts spiraling in a thousand different directions. "Yes, I understand. Everything you said is now perfectly clear."

# TELEPHONE LINES

Molly missed Murph and Mickey, but it was good to be back. She had spent the entire morning baking and rearranging the living room furniture that she and Murph had picked out together just the way she had always envisioned.

When she finally had every last piece exactly as she wanted, she turned her eye to the knickknacks and the bric-a-brac that filled the empty spaces in the room. Nothing was safe from her restless organizing. Vases, candle lanterns, and her collection of crystal animal figurines all found new resting places. Other items, like her cherub curio tray and Alice in Wonderland snow globe, occupied new places in the room only to end up right back where they started. Books were reordered and photo frames reconfigured. Some of Murph's baseball mementos also drew her attention. Her clarinet, however, would remain where it always had been, right on the end table next to the chair where she loved to sit and read or crochet. It was a little dusty, though, so she spent some time cleaning it up, which ultimately led to her bringing it to her lips and playing.

She played longer than she had intended. One piece spilled into the next, and before she realized it she had been playing for over an hour. When she looked outside and saw that the sun had ascended to its highest point and that she still had not touched the laundry, she placed the clarinet back where it belonged.

She hung some sheets and blankets she had washed on the line out back, then stood before a gathering of whispering sycamores. She still recalled with difficulty Murph's reaction to what she had shared, and perhaps had she thought about it much longer she may have begun to doubt herself. But a stiff wind blew through the grassy ravine and across her face and all she could see now was sunshine—alive with hope—and that gathering of sycamores, nodding their heads together in approval.

When she walked back inside and observed her handiwork from earlier in the day, she thought she might have to make a few more adjustments. She had just begun formulating an idea for the five mini golden barrel cactus plants she purchased the day before when the phone rang.

"Arthur, is that you?" she said. His voice was weak and distant. "I can barely hear you. Are you okay?"

He wasn't sure how to answer her.

"I don't know, Molly. I guess so."

"What's wrong? Is it Mickey? Is he okay?"

He laughed. "Is he okay?" Murph repeated. "Okay? He's better than okay. Never seen the boy better."

"Then what's the matter? Is it you? Do you not feel well?"

He was still at a loss. The shit with Perini had him feeling used and foolish—powerless—like he had only been pretending to be a big league manager the last few months. And if that wasn't bad enough, Ozmore was at it again, and it was worse. His discovery of Mickey and Jolene's budding romance had him ornery and looking for a fight.

"I told you, Murphy, I didn't want your boy anywhere near my sister," he ranted the day one of the other guys teased him about it. "You should have listened to me."

"What are you getting all bent out of shape for Ozzy?" Murph said. "Jesus, they're friends. Friends. And I told you Mickey is true blue. Salt of the earth. You couldn't have a better friend. I should think you'd know that after he pulled *you, you* of all people, out of that scrum."

"First of all, your definition of friends ain't mine. So don't you go preaching to me, damn you. Just don't. You try listening to these jackals in the locker room talking about my sister and wonder boy. It ain't right. And I told you once, and I ain't about to say it again after this. I didn't need Mickey's help that day. I can handle myself. You best remember that. Especially now."

"Why does it bother you so much that they like to spend time together?" Murph asked. "You don't know him, Ozzy. He's simple, good. If you would just get to know him, I think—"

"Stop your thinking and start listening, you hear? I do not want that boy with my sister. And nothing you say is gonna change that. And if you can't understand that, then I am going to have to help you."

Ozmore's words were fresh in his mind, but how could he even begin to tell Molly about all that without alarming her. Besides, his real concern remained Perini and this nagging sense that he had perhaps been duped.

"It's probably nothing, Molly," he said, taking a stab at expressing his feelings. "The owner, Lou Perini, called me in the other day and I guess it's still bothering me. That's all."

"Called you in? For what? You guys are playing so well. What's going on?"

He sighed loudly "I don't know. The other day we got into a brawl with the Dodgers and—"

"Brawl?" she asked sharply. "Is everyone okay? Is Mickey—"

"Everyone is fine," he said. "It really was no big deal. I don't know why everyone is getting so freaked out about it. It's part of the game. But it seems Perini didn't like the way I handled it, that's all."

"And that's it, Arthur? You're upset just because he didn't approve of what you did during the brawl? I think I know you a little better than that."

He tried to fortify himself with another shot of whiskey. The enormity of his concern, however, proved far too formidable.

"Well, he did say something else that is sort of bothering me." He went on to tell her all about how Perini more or less said that he was only there for a little while—temporarily. And how it had really hit him hard. He had known when he accepted the position there were no guarantees, and perhaps he was worrying for nothing. But after the job he had done, he expected a little more appreciation and loyalty.

"So I sort of feel like what I'm doing here is going unnoticed, you know what I mean, Molly?"

"I do, Arthur, but—" She stopped herself prematurely.

"But what?" he asked. "What were you going to say?"

Now it was her turn to measure what it was she would say. There was so much right at the edge of her tongue, but she did not want to make the moment worse for him. "Well, I can't say that I'm surprised," she finally said. "That's all."

"What's that supposed to mean?"

The brief hesitation became the new focus between them.

"You're too good for them, Arthur. It's a business up there. There's no heart, no feeling. It's as cold as the streets of that city."

"Molly, this isn't about Boston. Not everything is about Boston. It's not even about being here, in the majors. I'm just saying that this snot nose Perini really pissed me off. I'm just looking for a little support here."

"And that's what I'm giving you," she snapped back. "I just told you. You're too good for this, Arthur. For all of it. It's not all bright lights and fancy hotels—rubbing elbows with politicians and celebrities. And I didn't want to say this but I feel like I have to now. I told you this when you were given the offer."

"How is saying 'I told you so' supporting me? Don't you think I know all of that? I do; believe me. But what you don't know, or perhaps have forgotten, is that politicians and bright lights are not reasons for me being here, Molly. I love the game. And when you love the game, you go with her as long and as far as you can."

Her courage faltered. It was not a complete malfunction, but enough of a glitch so that she could not release what she had been harboring for so many months. What she really wanted to tell him was that this dream of his was becoming a nightmare. She settled for something less inflammatory.

"And what happens when the game stops loving you back, huh? Then what?"

"Is that what you think? That I'm washed up. Done?"

"I'm only reacting to what you've told me, Arthur. Don't get angry at me."

"That's not what's happening here, Molly," he answered back. "It's not. And I'll tell you something. If you were here with me, you'd know that. And maybe—"

"And maybe what, Arthur? This wouldn't be happening to you? Is that what you were going to say? Because if it is, stop right there. Don't you dare blame me for this. I never—"

"I'm not blaming you, Molly, for anything. I'm just saying that it might be a little easier for me if you were here—and if there was more connecting us than these damn telephone lines. That's all."

She paused. "That might be true, Arthur," she said in time. "But consider this. It's quite possible that it might be *a lot* easier for you— all of it—if *you* were *here.*"

# ROOKIE RUMBLINGS

With more than two-thirds of the season in the books, news of Mickey's exploits on the field was no longer news. In fact, most people involved in the league—players, coaches, upper-office brass, and news media—had grown so accustomed to reports of Mickey's incredible feats that they only found it noteworthy when something superhuman *didn't* happen.

Mickey's last game was a case in point. The Braves entered play that day in third place, trailing the Dodgers by five games and the first-place Phillies by eight. They had been playing subpar baseball for a while and now found themselves in a dogfight with these two teams as well as a more daunting battle with an hourglass whose sands were quickly falling.

They were hosting the first-place Phillies on that day, and by all logical estimations put forth by baseball pundits everywhere, a Braves loss would have just about sealed their fate. It was a classic case of "do or die." Everyone knew it, especially the guys sitting in the home dugout. Nobody said anything, but there was a tacit, albeit palpable, angst in the air.

Mickey took the ball in front of a sellout crowd that was there as much for him as it was to witness what could have been the last game of the season with any meaning. He saw the banners and heard the cheers, but in typical fashion went to work without giving any of it a second thought.

There wasn't anything electric about his performance that day, at least by his standards. He got through the first two innings in uneventful fashion, retiring all six batters on routine plays in the field. The Braves scratched out a run in their half of the third and Mickey made it stand up until the top of the seventh, when a walk, a seeing-eye single, and a miscue in the outfield knotted the contest at 1–1. The sudden turn of events had Murph a little concerned and got him off his perch and out to the mound for a visit with Mickey and Lester.

"Hey, Mick," Murph said. He struck the classic managerial pose—hands on hips, head tilted slightly to one side, eyes wide and full of speculation. "How do you feel?"

"Mickey's okay," he answered. "My ear is a little itchy and I'm hungry. I also want to—"

"No, Mick," Lester interrupted, propping his mask up on top of his head. "How do you feel about the game? About finishing pitching the game?"

"Yeah, yeah," he said, tugging at his left lobe. "I'd like to finish."

"Is your arm okay?" Murph asked. "Lester, how's he coming in?"

"Yes," Mickey replied. "My arm is okay."

Lester nodded in agreement. "He's coming in fine, Murph. He ain't lighting it up like usual, but he's fine."

Murph removed his cap and scratched his head. He felt a sick uncertainty rising inside him, like everything in his immediate world was riding on this one decision.

"Well okay then," he said, lingering until the home plate umpire broke things up. "Let's get out of this mess and get back to hacking. And you let me know, Mick, if anything changes and you need to come out."

A weak comebacker and a timely punch out got Mickey and the Braves out of the jam with no further damage. The game seemed to slow almost to a halt from that point on. Both teams exchanged threats in their respective halves of the next two innings, but at the end of nine, the score remained 1–1. It was going to take extra innings to decide the winner of the contest.

Murph sat with both Mickey and Lester before the start of the first extra frame.

"Can you go one more, Mick?" Murph asked him. "I got Ernie warm and ready in the pen, but you seem to be rolling along okay. Tired yet?"

"Not yet, Mr. Murphy," he said. "My ear is better too." Murph's eyes shot skyward and he shook his head as the Braves spilled out of the dugout for the extended play.

"Watch him, Les, please?" Murph whispered in Lester's ear. "I mean it."

Mickey had been dancing through raindrops for the majority of the game, recording just two 1-2-3 innings out of the nine he had completed. His line score was respectable for sure but not punctuated by the eye-popping statistics that had come to define one of his starts. He had surrendered eight hits and walked four while only fanning five Phillies. It was not the sexy performance that fans had envisioned as they came through the turnstiles, yet somehow he had held the first-place Phillies to just one run and had his team poised for a much-needed victory.

Mickey ran deep counts on the first two Phillies batters but retired each on a routine grounder to Roy Hartsfield at second base. The next batter dunked a dying quail that landed in between short and left field; the one after that got jammed with a running two-seamer but somehow managed to inside out the ball over the first base bag and into the right field corner, where it rattled around as the runners dashed around the bases. By the time Tommy Holmes had thrown the ball in, there were Phillies standing on second and third, and the Braves bullpen, which had already been on standby, prepared now with urgency.

Murph's next decision was easy. With the go-ahead runs on second and third and an open base at first, it didn't take long for him to call Lester's name and hold up four fingers. The intentional pass would set up a force at any base and move Mickey one step closer to getting out of the inning unscathed.

The young man would need all the help he could get. He was running on fumes. He had thrown well over his usual number of pitches and was laboring with everything he did. The ring of sweat around his cap and the slumping shoulders told the whole story. Murph saw what everyone else was noticing but grit his teeth and offered up a prayer to anyone who would listen. *Just one more batter. Come on, please. One more batter.*

Play resumed with Mickey firing a fastball that sailed high and wide for ball one. He exhaled and took the return throw from Lester, squinting into the stadium lights that, together with the bright, merciless moon, cast the entire event in blurred, gleaming white. Mickey's next delivery was somehow perfect, a four-seam heater that split the plate right down the center. The crowd roared its approval.

With the count now even at 1–1, Mickey peered in at Lester for his next sign. He stared long and hard, and saw the two fingers Lester was dangling between his knees. But his thoughts were prickly and varied. Sure, he was considering how he was to get this final out, and the sight of Jolene behind home plate certainly aided him in his cause. But the heat had fevered his mind so that every thought, fear, or concern that was housed inside his brain was released from its cell simultaneously.

It started with him remembering how when he was a boy and got overheated, Molly would dip a rag in cold water and wrap it around the back of his neck. He remembered how her hands felt as she held the cool cloth in place and could still hear her soft voice as she spoke to him. But Mickey's present fever also brought back images of Clarence and how he would explode every time he caught Molly with that rag and basin of cold water.

"Confound you, woman!" he would thunder. "Ain't I told you a million times to stop babying that boy. What in tarnation you trying to do, make a damned sissy outa him? Bad enough he's a retard." That harsh reminiscence led to other disturbing snapshots in his mind's album, like Oscar's lifeless body crumbled in a bloody heap, Boxcar's funeral, the men in white hoods who had issue with Lester, and of course Lefty—there was always Lefty. Ozmore bothered him too—not so much him, but the way he spoke to Jolene. It all came rushing at once, so the signs Lester continued to flash were met with glazed eyes with the film of a tumultuous past. Only the impatience of the man standing at home plate waiting to hit had the power to shatter the paralysis.

"Time!" the umpire yelled as the Phillies batter stepped out of the box to regroup. The interruption was enough to free Mickey from his stupor so that he could hear Lester's encouragement and really see the two fingers the catcher was putting down.

The 1-1 curveball was flat, a helicopter that spun over the middle of the plate but too high to be called a strike. Lester figured the batter would be sitting on a heater for sure now, so he doubled up and put down two fingers again. This time Mickey found the zone, dropping in a 12-6 hook that looked as though it parachuted straight into Lester's glove. All of a sudden, things for Murph and the Braves were looking good.

"Atta boy, Mick," they yelled from the bench. "One more now. One more."

Mickey breathed deeply and licked his lips. The sweat dripping from his forehead was bothersome, especially when a few drops snaked their way down the side of his nose and into his eyes, causing him to blink wildly until the stinging subsided. It made focusing on Lester difficult at first, but after another deep breath and a quick glance at Jolene, who was watching him with hands folded and pressed nervously to her lips, he acknowledged Lester's request for a fastball on the outside corner.

The ball left his hand as if it had been launched from a howitzer. It sped through the thick August air, its path straight and true, and entered Lester's glove with a thunderous thud after shaving the black on the outer portion of the plate.

"Ball, outside!" was the call.

Lester held his glove in place momentarily, a tacit protest of the blown call. Murph was not nearly as reserved.

"Are you shittin' me back there?" he screamed. "That plate's got corners!" He paced back and forth for a moment before continuing. "You've been giving it all game, goddammit. Now you're gonna start squeezing him? Now?"

The umpire, incited by Lester's showmanship and Murph's ongoing diatribe, called time, removed his mask, and from his position behind home plate, fired back at Murph.

"The ball was outside. That's it. Now shut your mouth in there. Enough. I've heard enough. One more word and I'll run ya. Now let's play ball."

Murph mumbled a few choice words under his breath before nervously resuming his place on the dugout's top step. Bases juiced and a 3-2 count to the batter in a tie game was more than enough to twist his insides and make his mouth dry—and all of it with Mickey out there.

"Come on, Mick," he yelled in the most optimistic tone he could muster. "Go get 'em."

Mickey heard the encouragement despite a raucous crowd that was trying to will the home team to victory. He composed himself as best he could after Murph's argument with the umpire and leaned forward to take his sign. Then, with fifty thousand of the Braves' faithful holding their collective breath, he fired. It was a fastball that ran in on the batter's hands. It beat him, but he managed to catch a little of the ball and foul it into the ground. He fouled the next three pitches off as well, each time spoiling Mickey's stellar effort at the last second.

The nine pitch at bat began to vex Murph. Mickey was out of gas and he was not sure how much longer the kid could go—how many more strikes he could throw. If he only knew what the next pitch or two held in store, he would have gone the unconventional route and pulled him now, instead of doing so after a disaster had occurred. He also thought, with a tinge of sardonic humor, how useful glimpsing the future would be in the rest of his life as well. But those sort of ruminations died a quick death once he remembered Matheson and what the timeless baseball sage would have to say about that.

"Baseball, Murph, like life, my friend, can only be understood backward," he'd always said. "You feeling me? It can only be understood backward, but it must be lived forward."

So forward he went, calling to Mickey with any words he could think of to cajole the young man into one more strike. Whatever he was saying was somehow working, because Mickey continued to battle, pumping in four more fastballs that the batter fouled off straight back. Murph was pleased that the boy was up for the challenge, but knew, as any good baseball man does, that the more pitches the batter saw, the more likely it was he was going to get a pitch he could finally handle. The at bat was becoming interminable. Eight foul balls in a row and thirteen pitches in all. And with each one, the advantage swung closer and closer to the batter.

But Mickey kept firing. Inside. Outside. Inside. Outside again. Four more fastballs that found the zone, only to be spoiled once again by the intractable bat of the man standing sixty feet, six inches away from him. The strategic dance went on for three more pitches until finally Murph had seen enough. The collective heartbeat of an anxious crowd whose murmuring had escalated like the distant rumbling of thunder had become his own. He could no longer stand by as just an observer.

"Hey, Les," he called from the dugout. The catcher turned his head to discover Murph, his eyes wide and expressive, his right hand holding up three fingers. The catcher nodded and then turned his attention to Mickey, who was looking more and more like a wilting flower.

"Okay now, Mick," Lester prodded. "Here we go. Hit the glove now. Nice and easy."

Lester set up on the outer half of the plate. He pounded his glove three times, nodded his head, and let three fingers hang down between his knees. Mickey accepted the request with little consideration. Then he came set, lifted his leg, cocked his arm, and released the payoff pitch.

The ball zipped through the air seemingly with the same velocity and vigor as the previous dozen pitches. But as it moved closer to its target, it slacked and sputtered before dying entirely just as it approached home plate. The batter, who thought he had finally received the fat fastball he had been waiting for, swung wildly, missing the ball by a good six inches, thereby ending the marathon inning and setting up an opportunity for the Braves to win the contest in their last at bat.

Murph wasted no time putting his plan into action. Jethroe led off the inning with a beautiful bunt that he pushed past the pitcher. By the time the second baseman had time to corral the ball, Jethroe was standing on first base. Murph continued his small ball strategy by calling for a sacrifice bunt from Hartsfield. It was executed to perfection, moving Jethroe to second base, which gave Murph and his boys two shots to drive home the game-winning run.

Lester was the first to get a shot at playing hero. He worked the count in his favor to 2-0, but given the recent success he was having at the plate and with an open base at first, the Phillies issued an intentional pass, eliminating the threat while setting up a double-play situation.

Tommy Holmes was next. He jumped on the first pitch he saw, hitting it right on the screws. The ball jumped off the sweet part of the bat and seemed destined for a date with the left field corner when Phillies third baseman Willie Jones dove with his backhand fully extended and snared the rocket in his webbing for a game-saving out. Now the momentum swung to the other dugout, where the whiz kids from Philly were hooting and hollering and suddenly feeling good about their chances. The only one standing in their way now was Buddy Ozmore, who was hitless on the day with three strikeouts.

Ozmore had cooled off considerably since the brawl with the Dodgers. He was hitting just .186 since, with a wheelbarrow full of strikeouts. The advanced scouting that the Phillies had done made the present predicament that much more palatable for them. They were so sure Ozmore represented little or no threat that they wasted no time going right after him. The first pitch he saw was a four-seam fastball right down Broadway for a called strike. That was followed by another fastball that just missed high for ball one. There appeared to be very little strategy being employed by the Phillies' battery. It was a good old-fashioned challenge: Here's my fastball. See if you can hit it.

After falling behind 2–1 on another heater that missed upstairs, the Phillies hurler took a little walk around the mound, trying to regroup. Ozmore went nowhere. He dug in deeper, so that when the next pitch was finally delivered, his whole body was still and ready. And in one deft slice of his bat, he sent the ball high and far. At first it appeared to have just enough to elude the sprinting outfielders. But then it kept carrying, as if being guided to its intended destination on the wings of an angel. When the celestial journey was complete, the ball had easily cleared the left center field wall and touched down some 390 feet from home plate. The walk-off heroics delighted an already frenzied crowd that roared and cheered and stomped its feet as the hometown boys lost themselves in a delirious celebration that began at home plate and spread across the entire infield.

When the merriment made its way into the locker room, they were still feeling good. It was just one victory, but it kept them alive and had provided a newfound energy that had them all believing in the impossible. At every locker, talk of the upcoming run down the stretch was rampant, as was praise for those who had carried the load on this particular day. Naturally, Mickey received the lion's share of attention.

"Hey, Mick, you were really something out there today," Murph said. "You didn't have your usual stuff but you gutted it out. Hell of a job."

The boy sat in front of his locker, one cleat and sock off, the others still intact. He was trying to figure out what Murph meant by "stuff," but the traffic around his area didn't allow for much contemplation.

"Hey, uh, Mickey," called out Spahn. "I just want to tell you something. You're all right, kid. Not sure if you remember the first time we met. It was back in Milwaukee, two years ago. I visited the Brewer clubhouse as a favor and you were there—just a scared little rookie. Makes today all that much more incredible. Just thought I should tell you."

Mickey reached out his hand to meet the one coming toward him. "Yes, Spahny, I remember," he said. "They called you The Invincible One. Only I didn't know why or what that was. Mr. Murphy told me. Only I don't know still."

Spahn laughed and slapped Mickey on the back. "That's okay, pal. No sweat. Everyone else knows."

Others heard the exchange and laughed too. Everyone except Ozmore, who, despite receiving a few pats on the back, was feeling a little underappreciated for his late-inning heroics. "Sure," he mumbled under his breath. "Give the kid all the attention and thanks. All I did was win the game for us. But everyone can't stop talking about Mickey. Rotten, no good—"

People *couldn't* stop talking about Mickey. September arrived quickly, bringing with it cool air, pennant races, and heightened speculation about end-of-the-year honors. Mickey's domination on the mound and tremendous fan appeal made him the topic of just about every conversation, including the obvious realization that he was the odds-on favorite for Rookie of the Year. Lester, who was making a pretty compelling case for his own candidacy, often joked with Mickey about their competition for the hardware.

"You're killing ole Lester, Mick," he'd say. "Man alive. Eighteen round trippers, fifty eight RBI and a .273 batting average would be more than enough any year to win that there trophy. Ain't too many rookies putting up numbers like them."

Mickey never knew what to say.

"But no, siree. Not this year. You's have to go and light the whole world on fire. Seventeen wins. All those strikeouts. Damn, boy, how's 'bout giving a black man a break."

Lester would carry on for a while and really kick it up a notch when he knew the other guys were listening. It was all harmless fun and would go on until Mickey always responded the same way.

"Mickey sure is sorry, Lester," he would say. "I am not trying to kill ole Lester. You can have some of my strikeouts, Lester. We can share."

Mickey's heartfelt confusion always broke up the entire room. The guys laughed so hard every time Mickey said something like that they nearly starting crying. And Lester's half of the repartee made them roar even louder.

"Oh, so you's gonna share with Lester, huh? Of all the things he wants to share, he gives me strikeouts. Like I don't have enough of them blasted things already. What a guy."

Everyone wanted to talk to Mickey, especially as the season wore on. He was like a lightning rod. Opposing players stopped over before each game. Umpires couldn't help themselves either. The fans embraced him as one would expect—with the affection only afforded to one who had captured their hearts and imagination like nobody had ever done before. And of course the media saw in Mickey a different story every day.

The Braves remained in mathematical contention, and it was indeed newsworthy, but the real story that had reporters scrambling day after day still belonged to Mickey. They still could not get enough. Before and after every game, they spilled across the Braves locker room like ants at a picnic and settled in front of his locker, bombarding the young man with question after question.

*Hey, Mickey, can you tell us about what it's like to be in a pennant race?*

*Mickey, how are you handling all of this attention you're getting?*

*Talk to us a little bit, Mick, about all the buzz circulating about you being named Rookie of the Year. What can you share with us?*

The barrage went on and on. They were relentless and not dissuaded the least bit by Mickey's oftentimes circuitous and nonsensical responses. In fact, for some it made the game that much more appealing.

One of these reporters was Caspar Doyle, a sports writer for the *Boston Globe*. He was on hand months before for Mickey's debut and had seen him pitch every time since. But it wasn't Mickey's blistering fastball or pinpoint control upon which he was fixated. He was impressed by all of that for sure, but it was Mickey himself that intrigued him. He saw the young man as the ultimate human interest story and was in constant search of the elusive tidbit that would help him break the ultimate story. His questions reflected this lofty goal. He was always probing, inquiring about things like Mickey's life before baseball, his hobbies, eating habits, and outside interests—

anything to unlock the incredible enigma before anyone else did. Most often Mickey would simply sit and answer as best he could, in his own way, and Doyle would chuckle over Mickey's response while formulating his next question. He had actually developed a good rapport with the young man, something that had him thinking that there were no limits to what he could ask.

"So, uh, Mickey, rumor has it you've been keeping company with a young lady," he asked one night after a home game. "Can you tell me who your friend is? You know, like her name? Where she's from?"

Mickey said nothing. His face showed the signs of something turbulent brewing inside his head.

"Come on, Mickey," Doyle persisted. "Your fans want to know all about you. No secrets now. Who is this girl?"

Only a trace of emotion showed in Mickey's blank eyes—a mere glimmer of the storm that was raging inside his mind. All he could hear now were the words exchanged between him and Jolene, not so long ago. They had just finished having lunch at a local diner on a day when Ozzy was occupied on the golf course with Spahn, Bickford, and three of the other guys.

"You know how I feel about you, Mickey, right?" she asked him.

He was occupied with arranging the sugar packets on the table but heard what she said. It was only after she repeated it that he answered her. "You like Mickey, Jolene," he replied.

She smiled. "Yes. I do. I like Mickey very much."

"I like you too, Jolene. Very much, too."

Her eyes were wide and inviting, but soon a shadow of concern darkened their glow just enough to alter the tenderness of the moment. "That's really good," she went on. "I'm happy about that. I am. But we have to be careful, at least for a while. You know, about telling people about how much we like each other."

Mickey stared intently at her. "Why Jolene? When you know something is true, you should always say it. My mama always told me that telling the truth is like watering the flowers. Ain't nothin' gonna grow without water."

"No, no, I know that, Mickey. But it's not that easy sometimes. You know what I'm saying?"

His brain sputtered, weaving in and out of the shadowy thoughts that were stretched across his mind.

"It's Buddy," she said, aware of his struggle. "He's just worried and protective and doesn't understand. Not yet anyway. But he will. He's just always watching out for me since my mama and daddy passed. I think he still sees me as a little girl."

"But I like you, Jolene," he said. "Mickey likes Buddy too. I like Lester and Spahny and—"

"I know you do, sweetie, I do. But it's just—" She paused to regroup and perhaps alter her approach. He was ever so simple and trusting and pure.

"Maybe this will make more sense to you. Let's keep you and me a special secret. Just until Buddy and everyone else has time to get used to the idea. So we won't tell anyone anything more than we are friends. Okay? Can you do that for me?"

He nodded as if he understood what she was saying, but his face was tattooed with worry.

"Buddy just doesn't want anyone talking about me, that's all, Mickey. Do you understand?"

"Yes, Mickey understands."

"So friends with a special secret?" she asked again.

"Yes," he repeated. "Yes, Jolene."

The whole exchange with her swirled in his mind. But as he sat there, trying to organize it while caught in the crosshairs of Caspar Doyle, one thing stood out from all the rest. *He just doesn't want anyone talking about me.* It's what echoed loudest in his ears as he finally addressed the question posed to him.

"Mickey's not talking about that, Mr. Doyle."

"Not talking about it?" the obdurate reporter repeated. "Come on now, Mickey. Your fans want to know all about you."

Mickey sat in front of his locker, trying to free himself from the confusion.

"So come on, Mick. Tell me. Is she just a friend or maybe a groupie—or has she stolen the heart of our young Bean Town Blazer? Tell me. What's the story?"

"Mickey's not talking about that," he repeated a little louder. His face was a shade darker and his hands were opening and closing in a frenzied rhythm.

"Don't be bashful now, Mickey," Doyle persisted. "We're all friends here. Just give me something—anything. You know, is she the kind of girl you take out in the alley when the sun goes down or the sort you bring home to Mom? People just want to know if—"

Before Doyle could even complete his thought, Mickey had succumbed to his nervous misgivings, grabbing the startled man by the shirt collar in what had quickly become a fit of unbridled rage. He was shaking the man and hollering uncontrollably. His eyes were wild with anger and escalating confusion.

"Jolene's a good girl!" he shrieked. "She said no talking about it. No talking. No groupie. No alley. Friends. Special friends. Mickey likes her. No talking about it. No talking."

Others heard the commotion and ran to intercede, pulling Mickey off his muted victim.

"Come on, Mick, it's okay, it's okay," they offered, patting him on the back and guiding him gently away. He resisted at first, twisting and flailing his arms. He was still shrieking.

"No talking about it! No talking! Mickey said no talking!"

A group of them just held onto him, listening as he worked out his rage and frustration. He ranted for a while, but it wasn't long before his face showed signs of melting—changing slowly from harboring fiery rage to a more sorrowful emotion—regret, uncertainty, or perhaps shame. Then the young man grew silent, as did the entire room, and it was over.

Afterward, all anyone could talk about was Mickey's violent, erratic behavior—how he was just plain crazy and a threat to both himself and everyone around him. Murph tried his best to mitigate the damage, explaining to both the media and his own players that the boy was a gentle soul who posed no danger to anyone unless provoked. But it was of little use, as they all had seen way too much and had drawn conclusions that could not be altered. So Mickey now faced the judgment of everyone around him—a group that suddenly saw him not as the quirky but talented darling that had stolen the hearts of everyone even remotely affiliated with baseball but as a disturbing, enigmatic, alien presence who could no longer be trusted.

Everyone on the team was filled with questions and doubts about what the future could hold for Mickey. Everyone, that is, except one—someone with a quick temper and a sister who he had to protect, someone who had witnessed the entire fiasco and was left speechless as he struggled now to lift the weight of the truth, the uncompromising reality that maybe, just maybe, he had been wrong about the kid all along.

# GHOSTS OF INDIANA

The last thing Murph needed was any more controversy. He was still smarting from the last lashing he took from Perini and he was not about to put himself in that position again. He needed to mitigate the dissension and the gossip as quickly as possible, so he decided to call a closed-door meeting with just him and the team. He had barely formulated the idea in his head, and had just sat down to map it all out, when he heard a knock at his door.

"Ozzy, listen, this is not a good time," he said, waving at the air. "I'm in the middle of something here."

Ozzy had barely stepped into Murph's office before sensing the manager's angst. "This won't take long, Murph," he said, pushing his way inside.

"I said I don't have time, Ozzy," Murph complained, this time with a voice laced with bitterness. "I've got a team to take care of here—one that is moving in the wrong direction—and a mountain of bullshit. So whatever it is you have to say is going to have to wait."

"I know all about it," Ozmore said. He closed the door behind him and eased himself into one of the chairs across from Murph's desk. "That's why I'm here."

Ozmore's face was a blend of altruism and self-loathing. His mouth was twitching oddly from side to side and his eyelids sagged and were heavy, like a late-summer sky that promised plenty of rain but could not deliver. He appeared to be mustering the strength just to breathe, and thus sat dumbly for some time—silent and blank. Murph stared at him with a swelling curiosity that soon turned to agitation.

"Well Ozzy? I'm waiting."

Ozmore leaned forward in his chair as if to shorten the distance his words would have to travel. "This isn't easy for me, Murph," he offered in hushed tones.

"What isn't easy, Ozzy?" Murph complained. "Good God, are you trying to kill me? I told you. I'm busy. I don't have time to be—"

"It's about Mickey," he blurted out, collapsing back into the chair as if the force of the announcement pushed him there.

Murph set down the paper he was holding. His eyes were wide. "Yeah?" he asked. "What about him?"

"I saw everything the other day. You know, with the reporter, Doyle. When Mickey freaked out and nearly killed him."

"So," Murph said. "Big deal. All of us did. So what do you want, Ozzy? You want to gloat—rub my nose in it? Tell me you saw it coming all along?"

"I don't think you're understanding me here, Murph," Ozmore said. "It's not like that."

There was indeed no indication that Murph understood Ozmore's intent. The manager just sat behind his desk, his insides twisted, staring at the guy who was responsible for a good deal of the knots.

"I mean I saw why Mickey did it," Ozmore explained. "And I want to tell everyone today that he was not wrong for doing it. And that if anyone was wrong then . . . well, uh, that person is me."

"Come again?" Murph asked.

"Look, you have to understand, Murph. I know what people say about me. I do. And I'll tell you something else. I can't say I blame 'em. I've got a way about me, I know."

Murph raised his eyebrows, nodded, and laughed out loud.

"Yeah, yeah, I get it, smart guy," Ozmore said. "But what folks don't realize is that my sister is my only family. All I got, ya know? And she ain't totally right herself. So I'm protective of her. I gotta watch out, especially for others who might take advantage or hurt her. So that's why—"

"That's why you had a problem with Mickey."

"Yes, that's why I had a problem with Mickey. But what I know now—I think—is that the kid has his heart in the right place. Seems like it anyhow. Head's still a little screwed up for sure, but the heart is good. So, if you don't mind, after I let him know he's all right by me, I'd like to tell the fellas too. Sort of clear the air and get us back on track. Would that be all right?"

Murph had to laugh. He couldn't believe the sudden turn of events. "Yeah, Ozzy. Sure. I think that would be all right."

Less than an hour later, Murph called the team together for a meeting. But it was Ozmore who had the floor right from the beginning. He postured for a bit with a peremptory air and insisted that everyone stand or at least sit at attention, but his voice was low and faltering, far less certain than it had been with Murph in his office.

"So, uh, I thought I should talk to all of you about the other day. You know, with what happened with Mickey."

The mention of the boy's name spurred everyone's eyes in his direction, something that caused Mickey to call out unexpectedly. "But, Buddy, I thought you said that it was okay that—"

"Yeah, yeah, I did Mick," Ozmore answered. "I did pal. It's all good. I'm just trying to explain everything to the rest of the guys."

The room seemed to lapse into a silent state of suspended animation as Ozmore unburdened his soul. He described in passionate detail how he had watched Mickey attempt to defend Jolene's honor by refusing to answer Doyle's questions. And how it was only after the merciless newsman pushed the issue that Mickey got agitated and had to use physical force to end the assault. The minutes passed slowly, with most of the guys still struggling to understand. It was not so much the words that befuddled them but the mouth from which those words came.

"So what I'm trying to say here is that I was wrong about Mickey," Ozmore concluded. "And also wrong to give him a hard time about some things. Murph was right. The kid has our backs. I know that now—just took me a while." The raw sentimentality of his expression was powerful and effective but made him balk once he remembered who he was.

"So if any of you sons a bitches want to mess with Mickey, you're gonna be messing with me too. Now let's do what Murph said and be a team—a family—and win this damned thing."

When Ozmore completed his oration, there was a long silence. Everyone was still stunned, trying to reconcile the sensitive, thoughtful sentiments just expressed with the cantankerous SOB who had just spoken them. For Murph, the silence was more of a pause for relief and celebration than for confusion, but he understood why the others were having trouble. So rather than risk squandering the goodwill that Ozmore had just laid at their feet, he decided to ensure that the moment would not slip away in vain.

"Okay, fellas," Murph said, clapping his hands a few times as he surveyed the room. "You heard what Ozzy said. It's official. We're all on the same page. Finally. Now there's but one thing left for us to do. So let's get it done."

Murph spent the rest of that day basking in the glow of this most recent turn of events. He was feeling as though something celestial had occurred, something in the most remote sector of the galaxy, like the cosmic alignment of the stars or some other ethereal event. Whatever it was, it had rendered him poised to achieve what had seemed impossible just a few days ago.

Hours later, he still found himself wonderfully happy, like what had happened was too good to be true. The implications of Ozmore's radical departure from his previous mien were too much for Murph. He could not wrap his brain around it with all the fuss and buzzing in the clubhouse. It was only after he had broken away for a spell and had time to digest it alone, did it finally become real. Then, there was only one thing he wanted to do.

"Molly? It's so good to hear your voice. Listen, honey—I have the greatest news to share. Really. I just could not hold on to it any longer."

The phone line held some static but he could hear her breathing.

"Hi, Arthur," she said in a hushed tone. "It's, uh, funny you called. I was actually just getting ready to—"

"Molly, you cannot believe what happened to me. And Mickey. I still feel like I'm dreaming."

Absorbed completely in her own thoughts, she hardly heard him as he chronicled Ozmore's impassioned speech supporting Mickey and the subsequent goodwill and camaraderie. He was rambling on, his breathless excitement fueling all sorts of gilded images of the future. She said nothing until he mentioned something that jostled her from her overwrought state.

"Arthur, I can't come there to be with you," she said. "Not now."

"What is wrong with you, Molly?" he asked. "Don't you know what this means? I mean I know you've been unhappy, but can you at least—"

"I can't come see you, Arthur," she said. "It's not a good time."

All of Murph's ebullience left him, like air exiting an opened balloon. He was instantly on guard, battling the surging suspicion that Molly was attempting to renew their fight.

"Really, Molly? Not a good time? Why, because you're still angry about Boston? You know, I really think you are being—"

"Clarence passed, Arthur," she said, thwarting any further attack on her. "I got the call last night."

Only the sound of Arthur's labored breathing was audible.

"Passed? Really? But how? Why? What happened?" His words came slowly and in short, intermittent bursts.

"Jonathan Krupsky found him on the ground, out behind the barn. Heart just gave out most figure."

Silence stole the moment once more. At first he was just numb, frozen by the inability to process the news. Then slowly, his mind thawed, giving rise to a rapid montage of images of the surly farmer and his abusive exploits. It was difficult for him to feel any real sorrow for the man, knowing all he knew. But somewhere in the blurred succession of scenes still filtering through his brain, he imagined Clarence's final breath, the struggle for life, and the inevitable end, one that was met all alone. That made him a little sad.

"So now what, Molly?" he asked.

"Well, that's the other part of why I needed to call you, Arthur," she replied. "It seems that Clarence left the farm to me. I'm not sure if—"

"What? He left you the farm? Well, I'll be. How did you find out?"

"Chester Grove was the one who called me, after they found him and all of that was taken care of. He's the attorney up in town. Apparently, Clarence had a last will and testament. I sure didn't know nothing about it. But he did, and I am named."

"So you need to go to Indiana. Is that what you're saying?"

"Yeah, I do," she said. "The funeral is in two days, and there are some things that I need to sign and some other things that need looking into."

"Funeral?" he asked. "Look, Molly, I'm not one to tell you what to do, but after everything that has happened, everything that he did to you, is it really a good idea to haul yourself down there and pay respects to him? Really? I just don't see why."

All of her memories of Clarence and her time in Indiana held a nightmarish edge, and most were downright terrifying, but that feeling paled now in comparison to her need to conclude this part of her life in a way that she could be comfortable with. It bothered her some that Arthur was not recognizing that need.

"This is not about respecting Clarence or his memory, Arthur," she explained. "This is about me. Me, Arthur. I need to do this so that I can finally close the book on all of what I have lived through, and so that I can continue to move on now. I need you to understand."

"I understand, Molly," he said. "I do. "I just think it's asking a lot. It's not like Indiana is around the corner."

"I know that, but it's what I have to do." She paused just long enough to steady her nerves. "And it's what Mickey has to do too."

"Mickey? Molly. No way. You cannot be serious. We are gearing up for the home stretch here. And you heard me. I finally got everyone on board. I can't lose him now. No way."

"He's not even scheduled to pitch for three days," she said. "You forget that I've learned a few things since we've been together. He'll be back in plenty of time. Won't miss a thing. The only issue you may have is seeing if Bob Keely is okay managing the team while you're gone."

He felt another ripple of irritation rolling up inside of him. "Huh? Come again?"

"I need you, Arthur. You're coming with Mickey—to help the both of us through all this. Don't even tell me that you weren't planning on being with me for this. Not every important moment in life occurs on a baseball field. What has happened to you?"

The weight of the conversation started weakening his knees. "Don't do that, Molly, okay? I'm getting tired of having to apologize for taking this job. We talked about this. All of it. We knew what it meant from the beginning. But all I have done, it seems, is defend myself for being lucky enough to have this chance. How is that fair?"

"*Fair?*" she asked. "You said *fair*? I don't think that's something you want to say, Arthur."

"It sure is. I know this is hard on you, Molly. I have said that. I do. But you have no idea how many other stressful issues I've had to deal with here. It's not easy. So fighting with you about it all the time just makes it worse."

The sting of his words worked against her attempt to maintain her composure. She tried to respond to him, to reclaim her footing in this push and pull she was in, but her tears were already falling, and what she wanted to say was now stuck in her throat. She formulated a different approach in her head, then another. But she could not seem to push any words past her lips. All Murph could hear now was the low, steady hum in the phone interrupted now and again by sniffling and short, erratic breaths.

"Molly, are you okay?" he asked. "Come on. I don't want to do this with you."

"I just wanted you to be with me," she muttered brokenly. "I'm scared, and I need you, Arthur—to lean on. That's all."

It hadn't occurred to him that this was not about baseball or him being in Boston. He had been so blinded by their previous exchanges that he never even considered that all Molly really wanted was a little love, understanding, and support. The sudden realization made all the muscles in Murph's face tense up so that his eyes were now just two thin slits.

"I'm sorry, Molly," he said. "Come on now. No more crying. I know what you're saying. Look, no promises, okay? This could be tricky, but I understand. Really. I'm not sure exactly how this is going to work, but I will see what I can do."

Once Murph hung up the phone, his thoughts zigzagged all over the place. He was in and out, here and there—a living testament to the truly conflicted. He did not want to leave Boston, not even for a minute, but he knew that Molly would never forgive him if he did not stand beside her while she exorcised her demons once and for all. So with the weight of his helplessness rounding his shoulders, he found Keely and passed the torch for the next two days.

The Indiana morning sky was cloudless and wide, like a giant canvas awaiting the brushstrokes that would determine its direction. Molly stood in between Murph and Mickey, her head bowed, as the preacher delivered his graveside benediction. It was just the three of them and Reverend Larson, standing alongside a yawning hole in the earth.

*I am the resurrection and the life, saith the Lord.*

Molly listened, eyes closed and heart oddly heavy, as the most difficult part of her life was about to be buried. She had a wild mixture of thoughts traipsing through her mind. So much had happened to her, all at the hands of this man whom nobody else thought worthy to say good-bye.

*Remember not the sins and offences of my youth, but according to thy mercy think thou upon me.*

Much of what ran through her mind's eye involved Mickey— with that eye she observed the painful memories. Mickey was staring blankly at the hole in the ground, wondering how deep it was, and why one side seemed flatter than the other, all the while marveling at the way the sun slanting through the tree limbs had created a curious pattern at the very bottom. He imagined Clarence opening the lid of the casket, rising from the wooden box in a fiery rage, demanding to know why the hole was not even on all sides, and insisting that the pattern on which he would ultimately rest was not uniform. The words *numbskull* and *water head* were clear in the boy's mind. For a moment, he felt a little sick in his stomach. Then he heard the priest ask each of them to close their eyes and bow their heads, and his focus shifted.

Mickey squinted but did not shut his eyes. Through the thin space between his lids he watched the final scene unfold. A dandelion seed that the wind had picked up blew across the proceedings. A gray squirrel darted back and forth between two giant oak trees. The reverend's massive hands dwarfed the Bible he was holding. And Molly—she had one hand in his, the other in Murph's, and he could see her cheeks, streaked by a steady progression of tears.

*Earth to earth, ashes to ashes, dust to dust.*

He watched the tears fall, one after the other, increasing in frequency and speed as the reverend commanded the lowering of the casket into the grave. The holy man spoke about resurrection and life, redemption and faith, while emptying a handful of dirt on the wooden box. Unforeseen sadness seized Mickey's soul. All at once he was sick with it. His body stiffened and his mouth went dry. There was also a steady hammering at the base of his skull. He felt like he wanted to say something, like something very important was inside of him and needed to come out. He wanted to tell Clarence how sorry he was for failing to understand so much of what he had asked of him. And how bad he felt for making him so angry all the time. He wanted to tell him a lot of things. But he was bereft of words, infirm of purpose. So he simply watched, with great attention, as the attendants made quick work with their shovels. Little by little, the wooden box disappeared. Then the hole vanished too, so that all that was left was a rectangle of fresh earth sporting the same pattern of light he had seen before. He stared at it longer than he should have.

"Come on, baby," Molly said, grabbing his hand. "It's okay." Murph placed his hand on her back, steadying her as she gave one last look herself. Then through a late-summer breeze that had turned decidedly cooler, the three of them walked, eyes cloudy with memories, up the gravel path that led back to Murph's car.

# LATE SEPTEMBER

With just ten days left in September, the Braves found themselves sitting in third place with only fifteen games left to play. They would need to climb over the Dodgers first, who they trailed by three, in order to have a shot at making up the six games that separated them from the surging Phillies and the National League pennant.

Despite the seemingly insurmountable odds, Murph felt okay about where they sat. Keely had guided them to two straight wins in his absence, and the schedule was favorable in that it had his Braves going head-to-head with both teams eight out of the final fifteen contests. Fate was in their own hands. He was sure they could get it done and wanted nothing more than to begin formulating his plan, but much to his anger and frustration, all he could think about was the exchange he and Molly had at the farm before he left with Mickey for Boston.

"So you'll finish things up here and be back in Milwaukee in a day or two?' he asked. "Maybe even Boston?"

They were both staring at the outside of the place, which had fallen into an alarming state of disrepair.

"I can't leave the place like this, Arthur," she said. "Not like this. You see what's happened here. Fences need fixing, the silo looks like it's seeping. And the animals don't take care of themselves. Plus you saw what the inside looks like, with all the bottles and papers every-where. There's a lot of work to do here."

"But you *are* leaving, right? I mean the plan is to sell the place and get on with your life. Isn't that what we said?"

A rush of wind brought with it the smell of wildflowers and feelings of longing and uncertainty.

"Yes, Arthur, that was the plan," she said softly. "But I need some time to think through some things."

He frowned. He had heard those words before and was afraid what they meant. "Look, Molly, I didn't want to have to bring this up, but you know, I really think that Mickey could use some help. You know, now that he has this girl Jolene he's been seeing. I mean . . . I am talking to him and watching out, but I know how you feel about this sort of thing." The second the words left his mouth he was hating himself. He knew he shouldn't have done it. It was low and manipulative, but he was desperate and just wanted all the angst and uncertainty to go away.

"Now why should that matter any, Arthur?" she asked, raising her eyebrows. "It wasn't so long ago that you insisted that there was nothing to worry about, that this girl and Mickey were just friends. Remember?"

He frowned and turned his head away. "Yeah, well, I just think that it would be good if you were around, that's all."

"Good for who, Arthur, huh? Good for who?"

Despite a myriad of misgivings about Molly and that last exchange, Murph trudged forward with his game plan for the stretch run. They had two more games with the Giants in order to complete the series, then it was on to back-to-back, head-to-head showdowns with the Dodgers and Phillies. It was Mickey's turn in the rotation, but the boy seemed a little tired from the trip and out of sorts, so Murph gave the ball to Bickford and penciled Mickey in for the final contest of the four-game set.

Bickford was really good for the first five innings, scattering just four hits over that span. And the six runs that the Braves managed to plate in the same time had everyone on the Bean Town side feeling pretty good. The swell of optimism ballooned even further when they all caught a glimpse of the scoreboard and saw that both the Dodgers and Phillies were trailing in their respective games.

"Well would you look at that," Keely said to Murph, patting him on the back and smiling from ear to ear. "Seems like everything's going our way these days."

"Yeah, well, we've still got a lot of work to do," Murph said, unwilling to allow himself to be swept away in the hope of the moment. "As a good friend of mine used to say, hasty climbers have sudden falls. So you'll forgive me if I don't go popping any champagne corks yet."

Murph's point was proven only moments later when Hartsfield booted an easy ground ball and the next two Giants singled sharply. Murph glared at Keely, who was cowering in the corner of the dugout, as though his assistant had somehow jinxed their good fortune.

The Giants went on to plate three runs in their half on the inning and seemed poised to parlay the momentum they had just generated into something far greater than just cutting the Braves' lead in half. But some of Boston's big sticks had something to say about that. It began with Lester, who launched a 1-1 fastball over the center field fence. Ozmore followed with a solo blast of his own, an opposite field shot that left the yard on a line. Sid Gordon was next. He doubled on a 3-0 pitch after being given the green light by Murph and scored in front of a towering home run off the bat of Tommy Holmes. Murph's crew was hitting everything, and when it was all said and done, they had batted around twice, and in doing so they chased two pitchers from the game en route to an eleven-run barrage. They coasted the rest of the way.

After the game, Murph spent a little time with some of the guys, including Mickey, just feeling good about what had transpired. Just about all of the guys were feeling confident and loose, but Mickey seemed a little off, even for him. Murph had tried to talk to him on three different occasions, but the boy was unresponsive. Murph figured Mickey was still fatigued from the trip, so he decided to leave well enough alone but not before reminding Mickey of what was expected of him in less than twenty-four hours.

"The ball is yours tomorrow, Mick," he said. "I want you ready, understand? Not too late talking to Jolene. Can't be burning up the phone lines tonight, kid. We've got to keep this thing rolling in the right direction."

Mickey heard what Murph said, but his attention was elsewhere. And after everyone had finished changing and headed back to the hotel for the night, he sat on the end of his bed, staring blankly out the window at the blazing lights of the New York City skyline as they burned like a raging forest fire. He marveled at the way the orange and red and blue and green all seemed to swirl together—a brilliant burst of sky-glow that resembled paint splashes against a black satin sheet. He spent a little time trying to figure out where each color began and met the next, and thought on several occasions that he had discovered the answer, but his eyes began to hurt and he grew tired quickly. So when he could no longer entertain the colorful riot unfolding outside his window, he leaned over to the nightstand, picked up the phone, and dialed.

"Jolene?" he said with impatience when the ringing gave way to a click and pause.

"Hi, Mickey," she said, laughing like a little girl. "Of course it's me. Who else would it be?"

He thought about her playful query more than he should have.

"I reckon it could have been Ozzy, only he's here, with us, in New York. Maybe it could have been someone visiting the house and all, like your aunt or someone like that. My aunt Lucy loves to talk on the phone. My mama's always saying that—"

"Mickey, hello there? Come on, it's me. Just talk to me."

"Could have been a stranger, too, on account of Mickey phoning the wrong house and all. Happens a lot 'cause of my fingers being so big. Sometimes get stuck in the wrong number hole and all."

"Well, it's not my aunt or some stranger, silly," she said. "It's me. Just me. So talk to me, Mickey. I'm all yours."

He continued to stare out at the wild swirl of colors just outside his window, a relentless glittering that burned with such wild vitality that it glazed his eyes a bit. He noticed that when he squinted, every color in the electric rainbow seemed to thin and run together, morphing into a myriad of shapes and objects, most of which he had seen before. Each time he altered how close his eyelids were together, the image changed. First, all he could see were a cluster of triangles and circles, interlocked and floating from side to side.

A slight adjustment of the space through which he looked turned those shapes into more recognizable images. He could make out a horse and Pee Wee's cabin down at Baker's Woods. Not too far from those he saw a pirate ship, a church steeple, and what appeared to be a lumberjack holding a candy cane. That made him smile a little and prompted him to try and hold the unusual picture in place as long as he could—something he did successfully until an unexpected sneeze wiped the makeshift screen clean once again. He narrowed his lids once again, trying to retrieve the comical image, but all that remained were shapes again—triangles, circles, squares, and one rectangle that at first looked like the pig trough from which Oscar would eat but then, to his horror, revealed itself to be a colorful casket—Clarence's casket. He felt something knocking inside his chest, and his limbs grew weak, as if the blood that sustained each was now leaking from some unknown place. His voice was absent too.

"Mickey, are you still there?" Jolene asked. "Come on now. I said I'm all yours. Tell me how you're doing and what's happening there."

The panic grew worse—and grew to include thoughts of Clarence and the steady stream of invectives that he constantly hurled at Mickey. He could hear once again the merciless mocking that stripped him to the bone—words like *nitwit*, *bonehead*, and *retard*. Each had the effect of a fist slamming into his face, and he winced as each recollection presented itself. It was only another voice, one warm and inviting, that was able to arrest the fitful flight and extricate him from the momentary fit.

"Mickey, uh . . . is, well, okay," he answered.

"Are you sure?" she asked. "You don't sound like it. Whatcha doing?"

"Talking to you, Jolene," he said. "On the telephone."

She laughed out loud. "I know that, silly. I mean what is happening there? How was today's game?"

"It was okay," he said. "We won. We scored seventeen runs. That's thirteen more than we usually score."

"Wow, that's really—"

"Not exactly though," he rambled on. "We usually score 4.62 runs per game. So today we were able to score 12.38 more runs. Not thirteen."

"Hey, that's still amazing," she said. "Sounds like it was a great game."

"Yes. Great." His curt answers and labored breathing aroused her concern.

"So if it's so great, why do you seem upset, Mickey? Is it because you didn't pitch?"

"No. no. Mickey is pitching tomorrow. Tomorrow, Jolene."

"Then what's bothering you?" she asked.

His mania returned again suddenly, but not like the overt assault that has previously rendered him helpless. This time the panic and anxiety set in stealthily, like an ambush.

"Well, it's uh—I am sort of—I mean Mickey is kind of—"

"Mickey, I'm sorry that I couldn't be there with you—you know, at the funeral and all. I really wanted to be there to help you. But you know what we said. It was probably too soon for that. And I wasn't sure how I would get there and all that. I hope you're not angry with me."

He didn't say anything at first, making her think she had discovered something she did not want to know.

"Mickey is not angry with you, Jolene," he finally explained. "I am happy talking to you. I am always happy talking on the telephone, or when we sit together at your house, or the park."

"So what is it then?" she persisted. "I'm worried about you. Is it Buddy again? Because I thought that—"

"My pa yelled at me, Jolene," he blurted out. "Not now, I mean. He's gone. Buried under the dirt. He called me names and hit me sometimes. Mickey made him mad." His words were filled with pain.

"I'm so sorry, Mickey," Jolene said. "That's awful. I know what it's like to feel that way—about parents. You are probably upset with him, maybe even angry about what he did to you. I understand. It's okay to be angry with him, Mickey. It's okay."

"Mickey is not angry with him," he said. "I am scared, when I think about it sometimes. And I am sad. I am sad that I did not tell him that I was sorry for making him so upset with me. I wanted to say that I was sorry."

Tears formed in the corners of her eyes. She was thinking about how for years the same words were on her lips when she thought about her mother and father. She also thought about all those times she struggled with what was handed to her. Sometimes at night, when the sky was its darkest and the stars were at their highest point, she would lie in bed and imagine who she could have been had God chosen to hand her to different people. The possibilities unfurled before her like the beautiful pink ribbons she always wanted for her hair. She could have been so many people—had only she been given the chance.

"Sorry?" she said. "You shouldn't be sorry, Mickey, for anything. You didn't do anything to be sorry for. What happened with your father was his problem, his fault, not yours. You can't do this to your-self. Believe me. You will understand that in time."

"But I couldn't get the water from the well, or hammer the nails straight, or understand what he was saying to me. Mickey just kept making mistakes. It made him angry, so angry. It were my fault, see?"

Jolene tried to convince him that what he was saying was wrong, but her efforts to mollify Mickey's uneasiness were no match for the guilt and helplessness he was harboring. She wished him luck in his game the following day and told him it would all be all right, but he lay in his bed that night, eyes wide to the ceiling, with thoughts of the farm and Clarence and the great distance between heaven and earth that had now made a reconciliation impossible.

The sun's light the next morning slipped through the uneven spaces between the shops and skyscrapers outside Mickey's room, bursting onto the streets and sidewalks into a million tiny flecks of yellow. Mickey rubbed his eyes as he recalled the multicolored images that only hours before had occupied the darkness with such startling vitality. He was at the ballpark in unusual fashion some hours later, running through his typical pregame practice. He had done the same thing exactly the same way before every one of his starts with the big club, although on this particular day it was taking him longer.

The ritual always began at his locker, where he would remove his shirt first, then proceed to fold it in half vertically, with the arms together. Then he would fold the arms back onto the shirt, followed by another fold horizontally, so that the hem of the shirt just touched the neck. After a few passes with his hand over the fabric so that no wrinkles were visible, he would place it gently on the shelf of his locker.

His shoes were next. First the right, along with the sock, followed by the left, then that sock. These were placed in the bottom right corner of the locker. He always sat for a brief time, bare feet on the cool tile floor, staring into the empty space before him as if searching for instructions on how to proceed. The momentary break would last a minute or two, sometimes longer, but it always gave way to the next phase in the routine—the removal of his pants. This was a process that always took longer than the others, for it required that much more attention.

The right leg always came out first—always. The left followed immediately afterward, at which point he would get up from the bench, turn around, and lay the trousers flat on the wooden surface on which he had previously sat. The intricate process of preparing the garment for temporary storage began with Mickey smoothing out the pockets. He would insert his hand into each one, pushing them to their furthest extent. Then with a flat palm, he would press down and pass his hand over each three times. When he was satisfied with the outcome, he would hold the trousers upright and with a definitive purpose shake them three times. His fingers then found either end of the waistband, where he was sure to keep the seams of each leg straight and visible along the outer side. This was followed by more shaking, two short, emphatic flaps to remove any of the obvious wrinkles. Then he would fold one leg of the trousers over the other, lining up each so that the seams remained on the outside—the final step before folding the trousers in thirds, so as to make them the perfect size for placement next to his shirt.

The next facet of his ritualistic preparation involved the nine baseballs that he kept on the lower left side of his locker. Clothed now only in a T-shirt and boxer shorts, Mickey removed each pearly white ball, one by one, creating a straight line on the floor just below him. Once each of the nine had assumed its place in the procession, he would begin the process of selecting one at a time, holding each in his hand as he closed his eyes and visualized his approach on the mound—one inning at a time.

He labored more than usual, his mind's eye clouded by thoughts and images that had him feeling as though two different people were occupying the space inside of him. The feeling was so palpable that he could barely get through the next part of his preparatory observance. He had only managed to put on one stirrup stocking when Lester, who Murph had sent to gauge the boy's mood, walked in.

"Hey, Mick," he said, dropping his bag to the floor. "Getting ready?"

"Yes, yes, Lester," Mickey answered. "Getting ready."

Lester took a few steps in the boy's direction and plopped down on the bench next to him. "Man, old Lester sure is sore today," he groaned, trying to position himself comfortably on the unforgiving slab of wood.

Mickey said nothing.

"What's eating at you, Mick?" he asked. "You're usually out on the field by this time, stretching and doing your running. Not like you to break any routine."

Mickey was still silent and remained motionless as well. Even his expression, which was largely flat and stone-like, had not changed.

The only discernible sign that the young man was indeed still in this world was his breathing, which by this time had begun coming faster and faster.

"Ain't no use swallowing worries, Mick," Lester went on. "They just sit in your stomach." He paused and shook his head. "My mama use to say that to me. I think about that a lot. And some of the other things she's say too. Yup, I reckon all of us think about those people close to us who ain't no longer here. Ya know, Mick?"

Somehow, the sound of Lester's words forced its way into Mickey's brain over the anguished shouting from the past.

"My pa never said nothing like that to me," he said. "Not never. Only Mama talks to Mickey like that."

"'Cause you got yourself a good one, Mick," Lester explained. "You and me is lucky that way. Ain't always like that. You know, you can't pick yer folks, Mick. No, sir. Someone else decides that for us."

Lester's eyes shifted skyward, as if in search of validation. Then he returned to matters at hand, reaching into Mickey's locker and handing him his other stirrup.

"It all works out in the end," he said. "All of it. The good, the bad, and all of it in between. Just gots to give it time, Mick. That's all."

Time, however, was in short supply. Mickey was on the mound before he knew it, facing a Giants team that was still licking its wounds from the previous day's drubbing. If anything that Lester had said to him had any meaning for Mickey, it was lost in the immediacy of the moment unfolding before him.

After Giants' pitcher Jimmy Hearn retired Murph's boys one, two, three in their half of the first, Leo Durocher's crew went right to hacking. Eddie Stanky saw just one pitch from Mickey, a fastball he left over the plate that Stanky laced to center field for a clean single. Whitey Lockman stepped in next. Mickey stared at him, then Lester's signs, struggling to focus amid the images emerging from the long stretches of shadowy memory.

Murph, recognizing the look on Mickey's face as one he had seen before, called to him from the bench, trying to push him past the struggle. Lester did as well, pounding his glove while urging Mickey to bear down and fill up the target. Mickey heard them, but he could not extricate himself from all things Clarence—the man's voice, his face, and the wicked combination of whiskey and tobacco that always lingered in the air after he walked past.

Lockman watched Mickey's first offering miss wide outside. The next pitch was low and missed its mark as well. So did the next. Mickey's control and command of the strike zone was as erratic as the cyclone of thoughts that swirled inside his mind. A few deep breaths and some desperate cajoling got him through the next two deliveries, running the count full. Mickey managed to locate the strike zone again with a pretty good hook that Lockman spoiled at the last second with a desperate flick of his wrists that sent the ball out of play. The rhythm and sequence of the last few pitches had Murph feeling a little more hopeful, but any twinge of optimism was cast off with Mickey's next delivery—a fifty-five-foot fastball that took everything Lester had to keep the errant toss in front of him.

Bobby Thompson was next. With runners on first and second, the Giants' center fielder made his way from the on-deck circle into the batter's box with thoughts of drawing first blood. Mickey watched as New York's most popular player dug in, spinning his foot back and forth until it was securely planted. Thompson continued his pre-at-bat routine in classic style, loosening his arms with a few practice swings before finally bringing his hands to rest over the hitting zone. He stared out at the pitcher's mound as Mickey took his sign, came set, checked the runners, and fired.

In the blink of an eye, the ball left Mickey's hand, was in front of Thompson, then on its flight—a high, arcing voyage that took the ball closer and closer to the promised land that lay just beyond the left field fence. Everyone at the Polo Grounds watched as the ball spun hypnotically toward its appointed destiny—only to exhale in disappointment as a last-second turn took the blast to the wrong side of the foul pole and transformed what looked to be a home run for sure into just a very long strike. The frustrated crowd barely had time to reconcile their disappointment before Thompson sent another towering drive the opposite way—an equally impressive blast that wrapped itself around the wrong side of the *other* foul pole. The unbelievable spectacle had everyone out of their seats and the entire Braves' bench marveling at Mickey's luck.

"Now that's living right," Keely commented to Murph, who was still trying to remember a time when he had seen anything like it before. "That boy sure is lucky."

"Lucky?" Murph asked. "You look at what's going on out there and you see lucky?"

"Come on, Murph," Keely explained. "*Two* foul home runs? Back-to-back? And not a crooked number to be seen on that scoreboard? I'd say that is pretty lucky."

"Well it's the luckiest 0-2 count I've ever seen, I'll give you that, Bobby," Murph said. "But I ain't so sure that's the kind of luck that's gonna bring home any prizes." Murph's commentary proved to be more of a premonition than mere conjecture. After missing up and in with his third pitch to Thompson, then low and away with a curveball that spun harmlessly out of the strike zone, Mickey fired a 2-2 fastball that cut in on the hands of the Giants' slugger. It appeared at first as if the placement of the pitch would be enough to tie him up, but somehow Thompson was able to drag the barrel of the bat through the zone and drop a parachute that landed just inside of the right field line before skipping up against the side wall. In the process, Stanky scampered home with the game's first run, and the Giants had runners on second and third with nobody out.

"Where are your leprechauns now, Bobby?" Murph griped.

A sacrifice fly, walk, and a timely double play had Mickey out of the inning with just two runs having crossed the plate, but the damage seemed far worse. Murph's panic was no longer contained, departing from his body like bees from a hive.

"Hey, Les, I thought you said you talked to him? What the hell is going on?"

"I did, Murph," Lester replied. "But he wasn't giving me that much. Damn if I know how to get to him."

"But you said he was good to go. You said that—"

"Hey, I ain't wearing no white coat, Murph. I said I thought he would be okay. Still might. Damned if I know. I'll keep talking to him out there, but if you want to get inside that head of his, you need to do it yourself."

Mickey stumbled through the next three innings, pitching well enough to hang around. Midway through the game, he had been tagged for seven hits and had surrendered four walks, all of which resulted in six runs for the home team. But he was battling and had showed signs now and again of coming out of it. The clock, however, was ticking and already down four runs. Murph did not have the luxury of rolling the dice and risking falling further behind. It killed him to do it, but Murph pulled the kid after the fourth inning and handed the ball off to Bobby Chipman. The move, which was born strictly out of the need for damage control, acted like an ember blown in just the right direction, sparking a deflated Braves crew who just saw their rookie sensation falter. Chipman didn't have his best stuff either, but he got the bats back in his team's hands with much-needed dispatch, retiring the Giants in order in the home half of the fifth inning.

Sam Jethroe got things started by working out a walk. He stole second on the very next pitch and scored easily on Ozmore's ringing double to left field. Lester singled sharply to right, plating Ozmore, and when Tommy Holmes ripped a 2-2 changeup over the third-base bag, Holmes came around to score, carrying with him the third run of the inning. The assault was on, and even though the inning concluded with the Braves still trailing by a run, the groundswell of optimism had risen to the surface.

Chipman further fueled the momentum by fanning the first two batters he faced in the bottom of the sixth and recording the third out on a weak comebacker. The Giants looked ill, flailing against a tide that was poised to wash over them with fury. It appeared that the home team had made some progress in stemming the swell when Sam Jethroe grounded out weakly to begin the Braves' half of the seventh. But consecutive doubles by Willard Marshall and Bobby Elliot followed by a towering home run off the bat of Sid Gordon opened the floodgates for good.

The Braves went on a rampage, banging out thirteen hits over the final three innings, resulting in their most prolific offensive demonstration of the season. The carousel of base runners kept spinning, depositing player after player at home plate. It looked as though it would never stop. Many New York fans left the ballpark—it was more than they could stomach. Those who chose to stay booed loudly. And all Durocher and the Giants could do was play out the rest of the contest, hoping for an expedient, merciful end. When the final out was recorded, the scoreboard told the tale: Braves 21, Giants 8.

Even though the Braves were feeling pretty good, there wasn't much time to hang around and shoot the shit in the locker room; they were all due on a bus heading to Philadelphia in less than two hours for a quick two-game set with the league leaders. Mindful of their abbreviated postgame stay, most of the guys showered quickly, packed a bag, and grabbed some food that the clubhouse manager had arranged for them. The few who moved at a much less urgent pace, including Mickey and Lester, hung around at their lockers chatting before going through the necessary preparations most of the others had already completed. Murph could hear through the clubhouse office door some of the good-natured ribbing going on between both groups and smiled, even though it was distracting him from completing the next day's lineup card. His thoughts came to a complete standstill when Ozmore walked in and sat down.

"Hey, listen, Murph," he began. "I know you're busy and all, and I guess we can do this on the bus if you want, but we really need to talk about Mickey."

Murph nodded as if he was receptive to the request, but his face was hard and stiff and told another story.

"So you want to talk about Mickey, now do ya?" he said, folding his arms before leaning back in his chair. "You know, Ozmore, you are really some piece of work. It's never enough with you, is it? We're winning, you're hitting, and still you have to continue to—"

"Whoa, hold on there, Murph. Easy. I think you have the wrong idea here. I just want to ask if you know what's bothering him. And, uh, if I can help in any way."

Murph shifted his eyebrows and leaned forward so that he was almost entirely off his chair. "Let me make sure I heard you right. First a public declaration? And now you, you want to help Mickey? Really?"

"Yeah, yeah, I know," Ozmore said. "I get it. And I guess that's fair. But listen. The kid is loyal. He's got my back and everyone else's on this team. And most important to me is that he does right by Jolene. He does. I see it now—totally. So I feel like I sorta owe him. You know?"

Ozmore was thinking about his sister. And not just the way Mickey defended her name when that reporter tried to sully it. His vision was of a girl who was once nothing more than a shadow—a tiny boat with feather oars, trying to pass through currents that always pushed her back to the place from where she started. He had seen it her whole life and had always been equally helpless to initiate any change of direction for her.

Then Mickey came along, and somehow it had changed. It was slow, but he recognized that now. All at once he could see how her heart leaped at the mere mention of Mickey's name or at the sight of him. Ozmore understood that the cloud of anger and suspicion and uncertainty had lifted, that her hand was much steadier since it had found Mickey's—and that her voice, all too often small and fading, was now full of song. He was never more thankful to anyone for anything in his life.

"Are you for real, Ozzy?" he asked. "You sure there's not some other reason why you're saying this?"

"Come on, Murph, this ain't easy for me," Ozmore said. "I told you. I want to make things right. Why else would I be here?"

Murph glanced up at the clock on the wall.

"Not sure I guess," he answered. "And I don't have a helluva lot of time to figure it out either. I'm just hoping that it's not because you finally realize we need Mick if we are going to make a run at this. Or worse yet, something sneaky or underhanded. That would be a serious mistake."

Ozmore's face flushed."Look, I'm just saying the kid ain't been right since he left, that's all. And I'm asking if you know what's wrong and if I can help. That's all, Murph. Really."

Murph shook his head. He didn't want to think about any of it. It was complicated and full of entanglements. All he wanted to do was sit there and do his lineup card—and focus on baseball.

"I think I know what's wrong. I'm pretty sure anyway. But I also know that there ain't nothing for us to do. No way to help."

"What about Jolene?" Ozmore asked. "I can have her here by tomorrow, or at least on the phone. I'll take care of that right now."

"No, don't do that," Murph said, sighing. "Won't do no good."

"How do you figure, Murph? The two of them are as thick as thieves. She's gotta be able to do something."

Murph looked around the tiny office through a fog of doubt. He was thinking of the phone call he'd have to make and the conversation that would perhaps ignite a brushfire of other issues he had no desire to tackle. But he was out of options.

"There's only one person who can help the kid now," Murph said. "Our only hope. And what's worse is that while there is a chance it will do something, I'm afraid to say that there are no guarantees there either."

# TUSSLER FARM

The ghosts of pain, loss, hardship, and regret rattled in every corner of the old farmhouse. Molly knew it would be difficult being back there, but never anticipated—even as she conquered her impulse to run as she stood in the doorway—that the quiet inside could be so loud and unnerving. She thought initially that it was the cool breeze and the sound of the leaves that had already begun to fall that had whispered in her ear and brought her back in time to a place she reviled so deeply. But she was wrong. It was the house and its slumbering contents that had her struggling for air.

Clarence was everywhere. And it wasn't just the beer bottles, papers, and empty cartons strewn all over the floor. Every object that embodied his grizzly, unrestrained presence had risen up to greet her the second she opened the front door. His rifle, propped up against one of the chairs in the living room, was the first thing she saw. It was never too far from his reach—neither was his pipe, which she noticed still had a fair amount of tobacco stuffed inside. She wondered if he had been planning on smoking it before he collapsed to the floor. Or if the pie crust he left on the kitchen table was all that remained of the last thing he ate. Everything she saw held its own question, and the insidious power to transport her back in time to a life marked by silent subjugation, fear, and longing.

There were still some of her things there as well, abandoned in various parts of the house. She made her way through each room, as if touring a museum. Only traces of her remained—just those things she could not grab the day she had finally packed and left. She remembered looking at her sewing machine that day, just as she was now, and thinking how big and clumsy it was. She had wanted to take it but knew that there'd be no room for it in Arthur's house. There were other things that remained, simply because she had missed them in her haste to leave. She ran her finger over the ceramic pie plate that had somehow acquired a series of chips during her absence. Her music stand also bore the signs of ill treatment, as did the hand carved wall clock her mother had given them as a wedding gift. She could barely look at it.

But it wasn't just the objects. The whole idea of being back again haunted her. So many years of her life were entangled in all the debris. It was like some twisted patchwork of crime and punishment. And all of it came with tears—plenty of tears. So when she had had enough, she found a broom and a big old empty barrel and began erasing the memories. She had only been at it a short time when the phone rang.

"Now how did you know that I was needing to talk to you?" she said the second she heard his voice. He just laughed.

"Just lucky, I suppose," he said. "Turns out I could really use your ears too."

"Uh oh, that doesn't sound good, Arthur. Is everything all right?"

"Well, things here are a little out of sorts, that's for sure. But you first. What's going on with you? You think you might be coming home soon?"

She surveyed the mess in front of her, and in some distant unknown, imagined herself one day free from all of it.

"I've got some things here to tie up," she said. "There's more here than I thought. And it's been harder than I expected. A lot of ghosts here, you know? That's why I was so happy to hear your voice."

"It doesn't have to be this way, Molly," he reminded her. "You could be here, with me."

"Don't, Arthur, please. We've been through this. And where is *here* anyway? You're not even *in* Boston. And from the sounds of things you've got your hands full anyway."

"Molly, I just don't know why you would—"

"Tell me what's going on. Why did you call?"

He held the receiver in his sweaty hand, listening to her while trying to shake off the weight of disappointment. He felt as though he was no longer equipped to handle the sting of *almost* where his baseball life was concerned. There was only so much satisfaction to be derived from pats on the back and the deluge of gratuitous "good season, get 'em next year" sentiments that followed each of the previous seasons. They stuck in his craw the entire winter. He was tired of *almost* winning, of *almost* making it all the way. It was the one thing that burned in his mind most as he considered how Molly was his only hope in saving Mickey—and ultimately him as well.

"I was hoping that maybe you could talk to Mickey," he said.

"What's wrong?" she asked. "Did someone do something to him, Arthur? Tell me—please."

"No, it's not that, Molly. He's fine. There's no trouble like that."

"Then what's the problem?"

"I think he's having some difficulty dealing with the whole Clarence thing," Murph explained.

She sighed. Murph sensed that she wanted to drop the whole subject but at the same time had to know more.

"What do you mean?" she asked. "What has he said?"

"Well, he hasn't said anything to me," Murph replied. "But I know he's talking to Jolene. And Lester too. But it's not helping much. I mean he's still real distracted and all, and he's just not himself."

"So what can I do? The wounds are deep and the scars don't go away. Trust me, I know." The silence that followed verged on a kind of helplessness.

"Look, Molly, there's no magic potion here. I know that. But I think if you talk to him, you might be able to find a way to get him to put it all behind him. Sorta what you're trying to do now for yourself."

"Well, of course I'll try," she said. "But I don't know. I just don't know."

Murph sat by himself during the entire bus ride, thinking about Molly and Mickey and how it would all turn out, until the demands of the first game against the Phillies took over his mind. The fever of game preparation spiked all through the night and into the next day, right up until the first pitch. It was only then that Murph could breathe a little easier as he watched his methodical maneuverings roll out.

The results came immediately. His decision to move Jethroe into the leadoff spot and bat Hartsfield second paid instant dividends. After working the count full, Jethroe drew a walk to begin the game. Murph's wheels were turning. He knew the Phillies were expecting him to run and that Hartsfield would be seeing a steady diet of fastballs from Phillies hurler Curt Simmons in order to give them a fair shot of gunning Jethroe down at second. He also knew how adept Hartsfield had become at hitting behind the runner and exposing the hole on the right side of the infield. So on the second pitch of the at bat, Murph flashed a hit-and-run. Jethroe took off the minute the ball left Simmons's hand, and Hartsfield slapped a single through the vacated spot at second base, giving the Braves first and third with nobody out to begin the game.

Things continued to go swimmingly for Murph when Earl Torgeson lined a sharp single to left field, plating Jethroe with the first run of the game. The Braves were off and running.

"Atta boy, Torgy," Murph yelled from the bench. "Looking good today, boys. I like what I see."

"Seems like the boys came to play today, huh, skipper," Ozmore yelled from the on-deck circle. "Now you watch the brotherly love old Buddy's about to share."

Ozmore slipped into the batter's box like a cheetah stalking its prey. He was smiling, the sort of toothy expression that children sport after having gotten away with something. Once inside, he puffed his chest—as if the appearance of more of him would make him more dangerous—and cut the air a few times with his bat before settling in.

Simmons did not appreciate Ozmore's display; he felt a spasm in his gut, as if he had just been kicked. He was already smarting from the damage done by the first three Braves batters. He did not need any of Ozmore's bullshit besides. So he began the confrontation with an inside fastball that rode up just under Ozmore's chin, sending the most brazen of the Boston club crashing to the dirt. The Braves' bench erupted in a maelstrom of obscenities directed at both Simmons and the entire Phillies team. But Ozmore was cool. He stood back up, dusted himself off, and got right back in the box. His face was blank, but his eyes burned with a wild determination. Simmons was equally upset; he was still seething over Ozmore's disrespectful antics and would have loved to actually stick one in his ear, but he had a game to pitch. And a real jam to navigate.

Confident now that he had sufficiently rattled Ozmore and placed enough doubt in his mind as to what was coming next, Simmons came set and fired again. The intended destination of the pitch was the outside corner, about knee-high. The ball, however, got away from the Phillies hurler and drifted out across the plate unexpectedly, where it slammed into the eager barrel of Ozmore's Louisville slugger. The collision was violent and produced a crack so thunderous that the reverberation could be felt throughout the entire ballpark for the duration of the ball's flight. Only when the ball touched down in the second deck just beyond the center field fence did the noise abate, replaced by an eerie silence that suggested to the Philadelphia faithful that something ominous had just transpired. Connie Mack Stadium was suddenly a morgue, all except the visitors dugout, which continued to erupt with smiles and laughter and gloating.

Ozmore's three-run blast powered the Braves' Johnny Sain, who went out to the hill in the bottom of the first inning and set down the Phillies in order with no issue. The same pattern followed throughout the entire game. The Braves kept putting up runs on the board, and Sain went about his business of dismantling the Phillies attack with an assortment of fastballs and off-speed stuff that had the home team bats baffled. And when Sain recorded the final out of the game by way of a weak comebacker that he scooped up and fired to first, the papers in Boston were already printing the headline for the next day: BRAVES SCALP PHILS TO CLIMB CLOSER. Every barbershop, diner, and watering hole in Boston was bristling with talk of the surging Braves and what looked to be a certain date with postseason glory.

Murph was pleased. But more remarkable than the victory over the first-place Phils and the sudden bump in the standings was Mickey. The young man had been noticeably more at ease, much more like himself. He had spent the entire game watching from the top step of the dugout while chatting up anyone who would listen. He discussed with Sid Gordon the number of pecan nuts that typically appear on the top of a pecan pie, rambled on with Bucky Walters about the shape of the leaves of the red oaks that lined Somerset Street, and analyzed with Vern Bickford, who was trying to prepare himself for the next game's start, how much steel it took to lay the train tracks that ran through the city. He even spent as much time as Warren Spahn would allow prattling on about the difference between spiders and bugs.

"Spiders ain't bugs, Warren Spahn," Mickey explained to the Boston ace. "Spiders are arachnids. They have eight legs and maybe sometimes fangs and also many eyes. Bugs have six legs and antennae. And spiders can't be bugs 'cause spiders eat bugs, Warren. One time, I saw this spider in our barn, and he was just about to—"

"Hey, cut the gas, kid. Cool it. All I asked was how you feel about bugs and that big old spider in the corner there. Geez."

Murph also noticed that Mickey called Jolene after the game and was chattering away with no visible sign of distress. Murph wasn't sure what it was that Molly had said to him, but whatever it was, it sure looked as though it had done the trick. The boy had come back to himself just the way Murph had hoped.

"Yes, Jolene, we beat the Phillies today," Mickey said to her. "It was a lot of fun."

"So you're feeling better?' she asked. "You know, from the other day?"

He had not really thought about the way he was feeling at all. But now, in his slow, ruminating way, he was instantly aware of a change.

"Mickey feels better," he said. "Yes. Yes. Happy. And not worried no more."

"That's great. Really great." She paused a minute to weigh her next thought. "Do you know why?" she asked. "You know, why you're so happy again?"

He huffed a little into the telephone receiver.

"Because we won, Jolene," he said. "Mickey likes it when we win."

"I know that, silly. Of course you do. I just thought that maybe there was something else. You know, like maybe you talked to someone. Or someone helped you. Something like that."

"Mickey talks to a lot of people. I talked to Gus today. He is the security guard at the stadium here. Mickey met him before. He helps me when we are here. And I talked to Vern, and Warren, and Murph, and then—"

"Wow, that sure is a lot of people," she said. "How about on the telephone. Did you talk to anyone on the phone?"

He had to think a moment.

"Not today I didn't, Jolene," he explained. "I am talking to you now, but that don't count none. Oh and I talked to my mama, too, but that wasn't today neither. So I guess—"

"How is your mama?"

"Mama is good. Real good. She's at the farm still. It's messy there. Very messy."

"I bet it is, Mickey," Jolene said. "So, uh, what did you guys talk about?"

"Oh my mama told me lots of things," Mickey said. "Like how Bumper and Juno still love sugar cubes. Bumper and Juno are the only two horses left on the farm. Where I used to live. They sure love sugar cubes. Carrots, too."

"That's good, Mick, but what about—"

"There are a bunch of new chicks, too, running all around the ground," Mickey continued. "Mama says she ain't never seen a brood run around so fast. She can hardly keep up with them."

Mickey went on to tell Jolene all about the overgrown cornfield and the birds' nest Molly found ten feet above the ground, built right into the ceiling of the front porch. He also laughed about the family of field mice that had taken up residence in the barn and began telling her all about the dozens of crab apples that needed to be collected before she interrupted his fevered flow of thoughts.

"What about your daddy, Mick?" she asked. "Did your mama talk about that?"

He had one eye on the door of his room as he listened to her, as if he expected at any minute some troubling interruption. He did not answer her at first. He felt disoriented, like he used to as a kid trying to walk immediately after Molly had playfully swung him around in the open field next to the barn. The room spun for a moment. He held on to the arm of the chair to steady himself. Then he took one loud, desperate breath and stumbled clumsily through the next few words.

"My pa, he passed away, Jolene," he said. "On the farm. He passed."

"I know, I know, Mickey. I know that it was upsetting for you. Remember how we talked?"

He did not answer.

"That's why I was wondering if your mama also talked to you about it. You know, how you are feeling and all? About everything?"

"Mama said Mickey doesn't have to worry no more. Or be sad."

"That's good."

"On account of my pa saying he loves me. And that he weren't mad no more about all those things I done to make him holler and scream."

All sorts of vague imaginings filled her head.

"Your mama told you that?" she asked.

"Sure, my pa said it about Mickey," he went on. "He told Mama. Before he passed away."

"Well then, if that's what she said, then that's wonderful, Mickey. Now you can be yourself again and think about pitching and the team and well, of course, me, too."

"I always think about pitching, Jolene," he said. "Can't be a ball-player if you ain't always thinking about it. Mr. Murphy told me that. A long time ago."

She laughed.

"Well, just save some room up there for other things too. You know, like our walks and talks and all that. I've missed you, Mickey. I can't wait to see you. As soon as I do, I'm going to give you a big hug."

"As soon as you see me?" he repeated. "You will see me at the ballpark, Jolene. During the game. You can't hug Mickey while the game is going on. Maybe you can wait until it's over and we are walking from the stadium to your house. Because I will be on the field, and you will be—"

"That sounds perfect, Mickey," she said. "Exactly like you said. Good night. Good luck with the Phillies tomorrow. Have a safe trip home and I will see you when you get back to Boston."

"Well, you won't see me right away," Mickey said. "First I have to—"

She shook her head. She couldn't help but smile when he rambled on. It was a feeling she had never known before. Like all of her vital functions—her blood flow, breathing, and heartbeat—were somehow, after all this time, operating at full capacity. She sat for quite a while, long after they had said good night, staring out an open window into the darkness that no longer seemed so dark. The cool air was sweet too. She wasn't certain, but she thought she could hear the night singing—a gentle, rhythmic whispering of beautiful things in her ear.

# THE RACE IS ON

A bright orange sun rose in Boston and burned with the fire and intensity that matched the headline in the Boston Globe that morning. Murph had just sat down to have his coffee when his eye caught the back page of the morning paper. His face exploded into a toothy smile.

SURGING BRAVES POISED FOR PLAYOFF PUSH

It was everything that he had ever dreamed of. He still could not believe it was actually happening. He could still feel the poison of a life that was slowly disintegrating right before his eyes. It wasn't that long ago. He had thought he would never feel anything else, ever again. And now here he was, on the precipice of something even *he* could never have imagined. His mind flooded with thoughts of more headlines, interviews, and applause. His eyes, which had sagged from the weight of a painful past, were bright and wide and hopeful. He was a new man.

Yet somehow, he could not shake the feeling that it was not complete. After years of searching, of dreaming of the climb to the top, the sacred chalice was well within his grasp, but somehow it was not polished. He had it in sight, only to discover that the luster he had envisioned was dulled. It gnawed at him a little, but he wasn't foolish enough to linger there too long. The momentary spasm of doubt yielded to the realization that they were riding a seven-game winning streak after a brilliant performance against the Phillies and had eleven games left. Eleven games to catch those same Phillies, secure the National League pennant, and punch their ticket to the Fall Classic.

So when the Dodgers rolled into town for a four-game set, everyone had just one thing on his mind — each victory would bring them that much closer to baseball's promised land. They had three games to make up on the Phillies in the eleven that remained. And with the schedule holding exactly three more head-to-head contests, even with no help from other teams, if they could just keep winning and keep pace with the Phils, they would have a shot for sure.

The Boston faithful arrived that night at the Bee Hive with the same excitement and expectations. They poured through the turnstiles with insatiable yearning, wedded to the vision of what awaited them in a little more than an hour's time. Then, soon enough, under a late September sky from which emerged the fullest, brightest moon anyone had ever seen, Warren Spahn delivered the game's first pitch.

The action moved along at an extraordinarily rapid clip, with Spahn and Dodgers' ace Don Newcombe stifling batters in what quickly had become a good old-fashioned pitcher's duel. They traded zeroes for the first six innings, with neither team's offense mounting anything even close to a threat. In fact, both hurlers were so effective that no runner on either team had even reached second base until at last, in the home half of the seventh inning, Lester scorched a double off the left field wall, instantly infusing life back into the crowd that had been almost lulled to sleep. All at once the Bee Hive was buzzing, alive with the sounds of clapping hands and stamping feet. The reenergized crowd had found its voice as well, chanting with dizzying enthusiasm the words *Let's Go Braves! Let's Go Braves!* over and over. It was pandemonium inside the Bee Hive, a tumultuous outpouring of enthusiasm that only waned after the next two batters struck out, stranding Lester at second base.

Spahn did his part to keep the crowd poised for another outburst by disposing of the heart of the Dodgers order in easy fashion. A dribbler to second, a pop up to shortstop, and a routine fly out to center field ended the top half of the eighth inning and had the hometown heroes ready again to draw first blood. This time, the crowd would not be disappointed.

The inning began innocently enough, with Earl Torgeson and Tommy Holmes each flying out harmlessly to right field. Newcombe was still bringing his fastball, and the smattering of off-speed deliveries he had been using was still proving quite effective in keeping the Braves' hitters off balance. Both Torgeson and Holmes returned to the dugout muttering and scratching their heads.

"What's he throwing, Torgy?" Ozmore asked.

Torgeson and Holmes both just shook their heads.

"Shit that we can't hit," Torgeson said. "We better start praying for some walks or something. 'Cause we sure as hell ain't touchin' anything anytime soon."

It was almost as if Torgeson's words ascended into the heavens and altered the grand design the minute they left his mouth. Sam Jethroe leaned into an inside curveball that did not break and ended up plunking the speedster on the elbow. Jethroe then swiped second on the very next pitch and came racing around with the game's first run when Willard Marshall blooped a single over the second baseman's head. The ball fell like a wounded pigeon, but once it touched down on the outfield grass, it seemed to take on the properties of a grenade. The explosion in the crowd that followed the landing rocked the stands and shook the entire building. There was hooting and hollering and cheers as the legion of Braves' followers sensed another victory.

"Sure does get loud in here," Mickey said, covering his ears.

"You ain't seen nothin' yet, kid," Johnny Sain said, laughing. "These folks love to win."

Spahn gave them just that—a 1–0 shutout that allowed them to keep pace with the Phillies, who also happened to win that night. The excitement was infectious; everyone, even the most reserved players on the team, could not help but gush with unfettered optimism and predictions of future glory.

Mickey, who loved to win but was ordinarily unfazed by the emotion of any game, also could not help but join in. "Mickey hopes we win again, and again, and again," he announced to the entire locker room.

They all laughed.

"So, looks like our boy has caught pennant fever," Holmes joked.

"Yeah, guess so," Lester said, putting his arm around Mickey and pulling him in close. "That right, Mick? You caught the bug now, did ya?"

Mickey scanned the room, his eyes flat and clouded with their usual obscurity, and shrugged.

"I don't know nothing about no bug, Lester," he said. "No, sir. No bugs. But Mickey wants to hear how loud the Bee Hive's gonna get next time."

Mickey exited the room to a full chorus of laughter. He smiled—uncertain as to exactly why—but carried his good feeling with him nonetheless and shared it immediately with Jolene, who was waiting for him in her usual spot just outside the tunnel.

"Jolene, did you hear all the cheering and clapping and yelling?" he asked as soon as he caught sight of her.

"I sure did," she said, opening up her arms as he walked toward her. "Now come over here right away. I owe you a big hug and it cannot wait any longer."

He bounded toward her, but once within her reach, he sputtered awkwardly. She sensed his apprehension, but threw her arms around him anyway.

"Oh my god, it's so good to see you," she said, kissing his cheek while squeezing him tightly. "I really missed you."

"We won the game, Jolene," he said, his arms still stiff within her embrace. "Spahny pitched."

"I know, I know, silly," she said. "I was here, remember?"

"Mickey pitches tomorrow," he continued.

"That's great, Mickey. So you're feeling good?"

"Yeah. Feeling good."

"That is so great. I'm so happy to hear you say that."

She did not spend too much time thinking about his recovery as she was occupied with thoughts of a different nature.

"So, Mickey. Can I, uh, ask you a question?"

He nodded.

"Did you miss me too? You know, while you were away?"

The mere mention of the emotion sparked something deep inside him—like a reigniting of some old, familiar flame. He felt the same rush of blood, the same happiness of their first encounter—all the same comfort and joy filled his insides and lit his memory before traveling to his lips.

"Mickey likes your hair, Jolene," he said. "Looks pretty. Smells nice too."

"So did you—"

"Your face is soft too. I like the way it feels on my face. Where's your rabbit's foot, Jolene?"

She laughed. "Oh, I don't need that anymore," she said, laying her hand softly against his cheek. "I have all the luck I need."

Mickey seemed to be enjoying his share of good luck as well. He rode the swell of happiness he was experiencing all the way to the ballpark the next night. The emotion coursing through his veins was strong and swift and found its way to his arm. Then, in the light of a full moon that had attached itself to the young man, casting him in a celestial glow, Mickey went to work.

It did not take long for everyone to see that he was the sharpest he had been all year. He struck out the side in the first inning on just ten pitches, and in doing so, produced a rush of thunderous applause that resonated throughout the entire ballpark. The game had only been underway a few minutes, but it was bedlam in Boston.

"Shit," Holmes said after trotting in from the outfield. "These people are jazzed up tonight."

They would have a lot to cheer about the entire night. Mickey and his pitching prowess seemed to take center stage. It began with the chants. First it was *Let's Go Mickey! Let's Go Mickey!*—a rhythmic recitation that was followed each time by a feverish clapping of hands and stomping of feet. Then, as Mickey blazed through the Dodger lineup, ringing up strikeouts at a dizzying pace, the declarations of love and affection became truncated and far more passionate. *Mickey! Mickey! Mickey!* rained down from the rafters as the hometown hero continued to fill the scorebook with Ks—eleven in just the first five innings.

"He is scary tonight, Bobby, huh?" Murph whispered to Keely.

Keely just shook his head. "I ain't never seen anything like it. Ever."

By the time the seventh inning rolled around, the Braves had shifted into cruise control. They had plated seven runs and Mickey still had a stranglehold on the Dodger offense. With victory no longer a question, the crowd began amusing itself with other ways to pay homage to their rookie phenom. A group of younger, opportunistic Tussler fans made good use of a paint can the maintenance crew had left out and drew Mickey's number eight in dark green on each other's backs. Another group went around collecting all the hotdog wrappers they could find, which they then tore into tiny pieces and cast into the air every time Mickey fanned another batter. Others who were less resourceful, but equally inspired, simply held or waved the placards and banners they had brought with them, creating a sea of heartfelt sentiments such as MICKEY MANIA, IN MICK WE TRUST, and MICKEY FOR PRESIDENT. And of course Jolene was there too, smiling from her seat the way she always did.

All Mickey did was continue his domination, delighting an already delirious crowd with his assault on the record books. They savored every last second of it, and when it was all said and done, the young farm boy from Indiana, who the city of Boston was still just getting to know, had punched out a record twenty batters en route to the 9–0 shutout victory. An infield single and a walk in the last inning were the only blemishes on an otherwise perfect performance and the entire team wasted no time in celebrating baseball history after the final out was recorded. An eager swarm of Braves players, led by Lester, who was still holding the ball from the final pitch, charged the mound and proceeded to jump on a stunned Mickey,

who knew all the numbers but not what they meant. Then the boisterous mob hoisted onto its shoulders the brightest star that night
and carried him off the field to the fevered chant of *Mickey! Mickey!
Mickey!*

A few hours later, Mickey and Jolene walked hand in hand from the
stadium, marveling at how the brilliant moon spilled its luster over
the trees that lined Commonwealth Avenue, making electric light-
bulbs out of the leaves that had yet to fall.

"Just like in that poem of yours, huh, Mick?" Jolene said. "You
know. 'Silver fruit upon silver trees?'"

"My mama taught me that," he said.

"I know. I remember you telling me."

"But 'Silver' is only for trouble, Jolene, or when Mickey feels bad.
That's what Mama told me."

She squeezed his hand a little tighter when she felt him beginning to detach himself. "Well then, that's not what we should be
talking about now, is it?" she said. She paused for a while, as the
two of them measured their steps on the sidewalk. "I got it, Mickey.
How's this? Those leaves look like tiny stars that fell from the sky.
All here to say hello to you and tell you how wonderful you were
tonight."

Mickey smiled. "Phillies lost to the Pirates. Murph told us."

"That's wonderful," she said. "Wow. You guys are even closer
now."

"Two games behind, Jolene. And we have just a few left to play."

"Well, it looks like you guys are going to do it. It's so exciting.
Really. Tonight was just so great."

They walked some more, their thoughts colliding with the trees
and sky and shadows all around them. Mickey went on some more
about the games and how Murph and the others were certain that
they were destined for the World Series. His mind took him to
other topics as well, ranging from the shape of the carrots in Molly's
chicken potpie to the number of spokes in a bicycle wheel. His mind
was racing.

Jolene just listened. She was thinking too, but her thoughts were far more focused. All she could think about was the two of them—how they met, the improbability of such a union actually working out, and the undeniable truth that her life was markedly better since Mickey had entered her life. She was fairly certain she loved him and was remembering all the times that she had almost told him. And of course she was imagining his response—and hoping that she would know when the time was right to share her feelings with him. The uncertainty remained suspended in the artificial haze created by the red lights burning atop the Skyliner Diner.

"Hey, Mickey, do you think we could stop for a minute before we go inside to eat?" she asked. She was lost suddenly in the soft, chilly night air; the spectacular moon that seemed set in a sky more blue than black; and the shadowy banks of New England asters that lined the sidewalks on either side of the street.

"Mickey is real hungry, Jolene," he said rubbing his stomach.

"Oh, I know," she replied. "It will only take a minute or two."

For a split moment the weight of what she was about to say was too much for her. She even let it go momentarily, certain that it would not unfold the way she wanted it to, but recovered in time so that Mickey was still with her.

"Remember when I asked you before if you missed me?" she asked.

"I remember that," he said, his attention diverted slightly by the smell of french fries and onion rings.

"Well, the reason I was asking is—"

"Mickey smells something good, Jolene. Real good. Do you smell it too?"

She sighed, grabbed him by the arm, and held him still. She was so enveloped in the moment and what was about to happen, so possessed by it that she suddenly had nothing apart from it.

"Mickey, stop for a minute," she said. "Come on now. I'm trying to tell you something here."

"I know, Jolene, but I was just thinking that—"

"What I meant by saying that I missed you is that—well, you see . . . I love you, Mickey. I'm happy when we're together and sad when we're not. I think about you all the time and when I do I get this funny feeling like maybe—"

"Mickey loves you too, Jolene," he said without warning.

"What did you just say?" she asked him. Her eyes were wide and wet with growing emotion.

"Mickey said I love you too," he repeated. "You know. Your hair, the way you smell, and the squeaky sound you make when you laugh. Sounds like a chipmunk, I reckon."

"Yeah? You love those things about me? You do?" Her face glistened from the procession of tears that had begun to fall.

"Sure, Jolene," he said. "Heck, Mickey reckons nobody's ever been like you before. I mean my animals and all, but that don't count none cause they is just animals. *People* is what Mickey means. *No* people is what Mickey means. Well not always I guess. There's my mama, and Mr. Murphy, and Lester, and when Mickey was with the Brewers, Pee Wee—"

Before he could say another word she had both of her hands on his face and was staring into his eyes. He blinked a moment, then stared deeply into hers as well—suddenly thoughts were flashing like heat lightning. Spellbound, the two of them melted into each other, their lips locked in the perfect embrace. They were really together now.

# THE FINAL COUNTDOWN

Murph sat at his desk and stared at the walls of his office. They were more like pages of a history book than walls. Each was adorned with photographs of Braves' past and all who had been there before him. He sipped his whiskey as his eyes went frame by frame. John Montgomery Ward, the man who was the first to call the national league team from Boston the Braves. Dick Rudolph and Bill James, the dynamic one-two pitching punch that carried the club all the way to its only World Series crown in 1914. Of course the photo next to that one interested him more. It was a faded shot of manager George Stallings, holding the World Series trophy. The words MIRACLE MAN had been inscribed on the bottom of the photo. Murph lingered over that one for a while.

There were so many others to look at, like Johnny Evers, Burleigh Grimes, Rabbit Maranville, and George Sisler—all Boston baseball icons. Then there were the framed still lifes of other watershed moments in Braves' history—the opening of Braves Field in 1915, Tom Hughes's brilliant no-hitter, and the 1948 National League pennant. Murph could have sat there for hours, trolling through the pictorial annals of Braves' history, but knew if he had any shot at taking his place on those walls alongside the other greats, he had to focus on what was before him.

The first things he examined were the standings. After completing a sweep of the Dodgers, then going on to win three of the next four games, he found himself still trailing the league-leading Phillies by two games. That was the bad news. The good news, however, was that his final three contests of the season were to be played against those same Phillies, at home in front of a crowd that had grown more vocal in its support of the team as it crept closer to the ultimate prize.

Murph spent a good two hours working out his pitching rotation and lineups for the three-game showdown. His head hurt, but there was still a lot of work to be done. He had just opened a folder filled with game stats and player profiles, intent on double-checking everything he had already done, when the phone rang.

"Oh, Arthur, I'm so happy I finally got you," Molly said. "I've been trying and trying to reach you at home but the phone just keeps ringing."

"Yeah, I haven't spent too much time at home lately," he said, sighing. "I've pretty much moved into my office here at the ballpark."

"I know, I know. Mickey told me all about what's going on. Of course I have been following from here, but when he called the other night to tell me that you guys have a real chance to make it to the World Series, I couldn't believe it. I am so happy for you. For both of you."

He shut his eyes and shook his head. "You know, Molly, you would have known that, and a whole lot more, if you were here where you belong. I really could use the support."

She said nothing. The silence irked him.

"So what—I could be playing on the biggest stage in the world in a few days, and you're not going to be here—because it's Boston?"

She fought valiantly to keep his words from marring the moment. "That's why I'm calling. I told Mickey that I would not miss both of you playing in the World Series for anything. I have plans already to be there if—I mean *when*—it happens. How could I miss that? Don't be foolish, Arthur. We're having a little disagreement about some things, but I love you. And I know how much this means to you, how long you have waited."

Ambivalence stabbed at him.

"I love you too, Molly," he said. "I told you before, I spent many years in baseball as a bachelor. It got lonely. Very lonely. I was really happy the way things changed after we were together—felt right. And now this. I'm okay. And I'm happy you'll be here if we manage to pull this thing off. I just wish things were different. That's all."

Murph carried that feeling with him to the opening game against the Phillies. He was worried, too, that he had taken his team this far and had accomplished so much but could still come up short. The anxiety made his head heavy, like the viscous clouds hanging low in the darkening sky that threatened to spoil the night's activity. He had Spahn on the hill, and their bats had never been hotter all season, but still, he could not help but feel that it was all about to crumble beneath storm clouds and wild winds.

But the clouds never opened up, the winds moved on, and Spahn took the ball in front of forty thousand screaming fans and instantly set the tone—kicking his right foot high in the air before fanning leadoff man Eddie Waitkus on a 2-2 curveball that spun artfully over the inside half of the plate. It was a good sign for sure.

"Spahny only threw nine curveballs last game," Mickey whispered to Murph as the two sat on the bench watching the events unfold. "Just two for strikes. Rest were fastballs mostly. Seventy-eight exactly. The other fourteen were screwballs and changeups. Not sure how many of each. If you want I can—"

"Mick, it's okay," Murph said, still wrestling with anxiety simmering deep inside his stomach. "As long as he can drop that hook in the zone tonight, like he just did, and can do the same with everything else, I don't give a rat's ass how many he throws of anything."

Spahn's sharpness carried over to the rest of the team. The Braves batted around in their half of the first, sending ten men to the plate in one of their most productive innings of the season. They banged out seven hits and scored six times, a relentless barrage that sent Phillies' ace Robin Roberts for an early shower.

The rest of the game followed a similar pattern. Spahn dazzled Phillies hitters with an assortment of pitches, rendering their bats ineffective, and the Braves' offense continued to pump and grind like a massive machine, producing eight more runs en route to a resounding 14–1 trouncing of a stunned Phillies squad. Murph's stomach was still tight, but he was able to smile afterward as he addressed his team.

"Okay, that was a pretty good start, fellas," he said. The entire room erupted in laughter. Murph laughed too, but only until the circumstance in which he toiled again slid across his consciousness, altering his attitude and the rest of what he chose to share with his team.

"I want all of you to feel good, at least for a little while, but remember that we have not won anything yet. We are still one loss away from the end. Trailing by one game with two left is not cause for celebration. All it does is give us a chance—a chance that we need to take advantage of. Some of us may never get this close again." He paused for a moment, as if he had never really thought about what he said until just now.

"When you walk out of here today, leave all the hoopla behind, men. We have a lot of work to do still. Tomorrow night is round two. Come back here ready for a fight."

Murph's words were powerful but also prophetic. The Phillies came into the Bee Hive wearing the wounds of the previous night's beating, but they stood tall, suggesting they were not yet ready to just roll over and die.

They parlayed that attitude into an instant assault on the field. An angry Eddie Waitkus lined Johnny Sain's first pitch right past the pitcher's head for a leadoff single. The well-struck blow did more than just set the table for the visiting Phillies, who scored two runs in their first at bat—it delivered a clear message to the upstart Braves that they were not going to go down quietly, if at all.

The first fastball buzzed under the chin of Lester in the Braves' half of the first inning. The purpose pitch sent Lester to the dirt. The normally even-tempered Lester emerged from the dust cloud a changed man, glaring out at the mound. He brushed off the evidence from his plunge to earth, cocked his bat, grit his teeth, and proceeded to deposit the next pitch over the center field wall, answering the challenge with a thunderous reply that had the home crowd cheering just as loudly as they had booed only moments before. It was the only run the Braves scored that inning, but it was enough to make everyone in the ballpark understand that they were for real and were not going anywhere.

Johnny Sain had his own answer to the Phillies' calculated efforts. He knocked down two of their batters during the next inning, the second of which cleared the benches. Both teams spilled out of the dugouts and onto the field, morphing into a riotous swirl that washed across the infield grass with fury and fire. They eventually paired off, with fists full of flannel. The umpires were quick to disperse the mob and restore order before any punches were thrown, but not before Murph and Phillies skipper Eddie Sawyer had an opportunity to exchange pleasantries.

"This ain't rookie ball, Murphy," Sawyer jawed. "You play with fire up here, you get burned."

Murph appeared unaffected by his counterpart's warning.

"I like it hot, Eddie. I'm from the South, so don't you worry about me."

When play resumed, Sain showed no ill effects from being at the center of the scrum, retiring the side in order with very little difficulty. The next few innings were tension-filled but just as uneventful, with both teams mounting little or no offense. The few runners on each side who managed to reach base safely wound up stranded as both squads traded zeroes for the better part of the game. Both sides were feeling the pressure, but it was Murph and the Braves that really felt the noose tightening as they still trailed 2–1 heading into their final at bat.

The suffocation grew worse after Sam Jethroe flew out to left field on the first pitch he saw. The massive ballpark, which was once bristling with hope and anticipation, now resembled a balloon that had lost most of its air. Everyone felt it—a nagging, impending doom that became even more real after Willard Marshall grounded out to shortstop. The entire Braves' dugout seemed to wilt. An eerie silence rolled across the stands like a thick fog. They had come so far, and now they stood on the precipice of elimination. Murph couldn't even watch as Earl Torgeson, their final hope, stepped into the batter's box.

Torgeson took the first pitch he saw for a ball. He stepped out of the box, exhaled loudly, then got back in to continue his at bat. The next pitch also missed, high and tight. The classic hitter's count made Torgeson breathe a little easier, but did little to assuage the angst of his teammates and the crowd that was watching the proceedings through fanned fingers. Even when the third and fourth balls were thrown, and Torgeson was granted first base, all that remained in the stadium was a somber silence, interrupted by the impassioned cries of some of the Phillies players who were now urging their pitcher for one last out.

It was only after Lester lined a 2-2 curveball into left field that the collective heartbeat of the crowd resurfaced and became alive once more. Hands that had previously been used as a shield against heart wrenching catastrophe were now creating thunderous clapping that reverberated for miles. In a matter of seconds, despair had been converted to hope. There was—all at once—a chance. It was possible. Everyone knew it.

All eyes were on Buddy Ozmore as he carried with him to home plate an opportunity for salvation. Murph was watching too. He couldn't help but be swept away by the reality that they were just one hit away from tying this thing.

"Come on, Ozzy," he yelled. "All you, now. This is you. Take us home."

Ozmore had never expected to be in this position. After Marshall made the second out, Ozmore had already untied his cleats and pulled off his jersey. His thoughts had left the field and traveled to his cabin in the woods, to his off-season hunting and fishing trips. But a turn of events had him right back, front and center, with an opportunity to rescue his team and the city that so desperately wanted something to cheer about.

It took him some time to get ready once he walked up to the plate. He placed one foot in the batter's box, moved around some dirt, then pulled it back out, like someone testing the temperature of bath water. He breathed in the excitement that was riding on the crisp night air, moved his head back and forth in an effort to loosen the muscles in his neck, and stepped back into the box with both feet this time.

The first pitch he saw was a called strike. He made no attempt at it—let it go by as if it were tossed to him in a dream. He was awake now and uncomfortably aware of the disadvantage his momentary paralysis had created. The hammering of his heart matched the pulsating excitement of the stadium. His blood rushed quickly now, filling his muscles with renewed purpose and strength. The sudden surge of vigor served him well, flowing through his arms and hands and into his bat. The next pitch he saw would be the last. His eye caught sight of it the second it left the pitcher's hand, as if released in slow motion. It moved toward him, laces spinning, on a path that was straight and true. The closer it came, the larger it grew, until finally it sat before him, a great white pearl whose value rose exponentially when Ozmore struck it clean, sending it through the middle of the diamond into center field. Torgeson, who took flight the instant he heard the crack of the bat, scored easily, bringing with him the tying run and immediate cause for a wild celebration that ripped through the entire ballpark.

"We're alive again, Murph!" Keely yelled, jumping up and down like a little boy. "Shit, I can't believe this. Do you hear this place? We're back! We are back! Whoa! I just hope the building holds up long enough so that we can finish the damn thing."

Murph smiled. All of a sudden the weight of the dark sky above them was endurable. "We're gonna finish it," Murph replied. "We've got to."

The crowd continued to stand, roar, and stamp its feet. It was complete bedlam inside the Bee Hive. Phillies' pitcher Blix Donnelly was eager to get back to work, but had to step off the rubber more than once just to gather his thoughts. Sid Gordon waited as well, just outside the batter's box, as the legion of Boston Braves fans continued to bask in the splendor of their sudden good fortune. It took a full four or five minutes before order was restored so the players could resume their business.

Gordon jumped right in the second the umpire put on his mask and pointed to the pitcher's mound. He felt only a fraction of the trepidation that those before him wrestled with, for the worst that could happen now—even if he failed—was extra innings. And, of course, there was that chance that the baseball gods would smile on him at just the right moment, branding him the creator of some late-inning heroics.

Gordon's peace of mind was evident in his approach, as he offered at Donnelly's first delivery, fouling it straight back. The crowd, which was still on its feet, let go a collective *oooh* that washed across the field from one foul line to the next. He had just missed it. Donnelly knew it too and altered his plan accordingly, serving up back-to-back breaking balls that both missed low and away.

With the count again back in Gordon's favor, he dug in deeper and focused on getting something out over the plate that he could drive somewhere. Donnelly knew that was what Gordon was probably thinking, so he ran his next fastball in on Gordon's hands, resulting in an awkward check swing that produced a harmless foul tip that rolled quietly to the side of home plate. Donnelly's next pitch was in tight as well, but missed its mark by two inches. The 3-2 count escalated the crowd's impatience and engendered once again a cacophonous outpouring of emotion. Donnelly stepped off the rubber, waiting for the surge to subside, but when it became evident that the only end to the storm would come by way of a third and final out, he resumed his position on top of the mound, took his sign, and fired. The payoff pitch was yet another two-seam fastball designed to bore in on Gordon's fists. When it left Donnelly's hand, the beleaguered hurler was satisfied that he had executed the delivery successfully; the ball would slice the air and slash across the inner half of the plate, ending up in Gordon's kitchen. It was the perfect 3-2 pitch.

But somewhere between its takeoff and appointed destination, the ball veered off course, altering its trajectory just enough to allow Gordon an opportunity to pull his hands through the hitting zone in an inside out motion, lofting a weak fly ball—the proverbial dying quail—that spun and fell in between the second baseman and right fielder. Under normal circumstances, such a weak effort would not have been enough to allow Lester to come around with the game winning run. But the wily catcher's two out jump from second base, coupled with a crazy English that had the ball spinning all over the place, made Lester's jaunt home more like a leisurely jog than a mad dash to victory. By the time the Phillies' right fielder had the ball, Lester was home safely and the celebration was unfolding.

The mania of the moment spilled over into the next night, fueled even further by the various headlines emblazoned on every newspaper in town. The sentiments varied, but the city had just one thing on its mind.

BRAVES ALMOST THERE

ONE WIN AWAY

BRAVES SHOOT FOR SERIES

It had been on Murph's mind too, so much that he could barely close his eyes the previous night when his head had hit the pillow. It was no better now, as he sat in his office, scratching out the lineup card for the most important game of his career.

His stomach burned, and his breathing was labored as if he just had the wind knocked out of him. His ears were ringing with the sound of Molly's voice wishing him good luck. It made him feel better on some level, but he could not help but think that he could have used her there with him. The phone call actually had made him feel worse.

But he was riding a serious wave of momentum, and he had Mickey, who by now was the odds-on favorite for Rookie of the Year honors, taking the ball. It all seemed perfectly lined up. Even the weather was right. The morning sun, which had been blinding and unusually warm for this time of year, slipped quietly into the night. Now what remained was a brilliant twilight sky, a cobalt blue mat that was diffused artfully with pinkish hues. Murph wanted to believe it was a harbinger of good things to come.

227

As game time approached, the sky faded to black, lit now only by a three-quarter moon and a collection of stars that were scattered about. The crowd was sparkling too, intoxicated with excitement and expectation and nourished by the thought that maybe, just maybe, they were about to witness another chapter in baseball history.

That fervor only swelled when the Braves took the field, led by one Mickey Tussler, who ran directly to the mound where he began his usual groundskeeping routine. First it was the area directly in front of the rubber, where his right foot would eventually pivot each time he fired a pitch. He used his cleat like a gardening tool, moving it back and forth until he had created a divot that was both wide and deep enough. After wiping away the dirt that had landed accidentally on the rubber and restoring the shiny white rectangle to its original condition, he moved to the area toward the front of the mound, where he proceeded to drop to his knees in an attempt to flatten any bumps or irregularities on the earth that spoiled the perfect symmetry in his landing area. Each pass of each palm eradicated any imperfections, so that all that remained was a smooth slope that resembled a scoop of cocoa—the kind Molly always used when baking her chocolate drops or marble pound cake. Then all that was left were the finishing touches—three claps of his hands to rid himself of any remnants of dirt, followed by some spit in the middle of each, and a quick pass down the sides of his pants. Once his hands were clean, he climbed back on top of the mound, toed the rubber, and began his warm-up tosses.

Murph was not in the habit of watching Mickey warm up; he learned early that the number of idiosyncrasies, especially pregame, were enough to drive him crazy. But tonight was different. Tonight, he could not help but watch everything that was going on, trying desperately to glean some meaning behind the peculiar face of things— or any sign that things were going to be okay.

"Hey, Spahny, does he always do that—you know, the whole mound thing, with the hands and all of that?"

Spahn laughed. "No, not always," he said, winking. "Sometimes he takes off his cleats and socks and runs in circles around the mound."

Murph leaned against the dugout wall and shook his head. "Well, after what I just saw, I guess anything's possible."

The two of them chatted some more while watching Mickey complete his warm-ups. The young man seemed ready to go but was calling to Murph and pointing to the stands.

"What the hell is he doing?" Murph asked. "I swear I—"

"He's saying something about 'her' being here," Spahn said. "He's telling you."

"So what," Murph grumbled. "Jolene is here *every* game. Why is tonight any different?"

A sick feeling grew inside of Murph as he continued to watch Mickey carry on. It only got worse as both Mickey's antics and voice became more and more pronounced.

"Look, Mr. Murphy! Look, over there!" he screamed. "Look! Look!" He exhaled in frustration.

"I know, Mick, I know," Murph called back. "Come on now, pitch the game. I know. Jolene is here to watch. I know. Just focus on what you're doing out there."

Murph's response did nothing to alter the boy's hysteria. His fevered cries drifted on the wind, all around the park. Everyone was staring now.

"Murph, just look over there and shut him up," Spahn said. "It's getting a little embarrassing now."

Feeling guilty that he had mishandled the situation, Murph took two steps out of the dugout and looked over to the area behind home plate. He saw her instantly, her familiar eyes and warm smile. He waved to her, as if he were seeing her for the first time in his life. She waved back. Then before he returned to the dugout, she smiled again and mouthed the words "Surprise! I love you, Arthur." Surprised he was. It was Molly.

He could not believe Molly had kept it from him and laughed now as he recalled some of the more obvious comments she had made regarding why she could not make the trip. He felt foolish that he had doubted her but was still a little annoyed that she hadn't told him her intentions. Knowing she was coming would certainly have taken the edge off. Still, he was happy she was there. So was Mickey, who finally managed to settle down once he knew that Murph had seen Molly.

With his eyes still engaged in a dance between those two seats behind home plate and the Phillies leadoff man Richie Ashburn, who was just making his way to the batter's box from the on-deck circle, Mickey stood atop the rubber, readying himself for the game's first confrontation. It was a matchup that favored Mickey and the Braves. Ashburn was enjoying a good season at the plate, sporting a .303 batting average to go along with his team-leading 180 hits, but he had struggled the few times he had faced Mickey before. Lester recalled the approach that had neutralized Ashburn before—hard stuff in tight to get ahead and off speed away to finish him—and went to work immediately with the same plan. Mickey was his usual agreeable self, nodding each time Lester called for a particular pitch in a certain location.

The two of them could not have scripted it any better. Ashburn saw just five pitches. The first fastball Mickey fired was a dart that painted the inside corner for a called strike one. He followed that with another heater that Ashburn fouled off, placing the game's first batter in an 0-2 hole. The crowd, which was just itching for an excuse to get up and cheer, rose to its feet and roared in anticipation of the first of twenty-seven outs they needed to keep their date with the mighty New York Yankees on the biggest stage in sports. They'd have to wait, at least a little longer.

Mickey's 0-2 curveball was sharp, but Ashburn did not bite. He also passed on the next offering, a letter high purpose pitch that buzzed by off the inner part of the plate. Ashburn removed one foot from the box, collected himself, and stepped back in. Mickey, who had remained on the rubber while Ashburn caught his breath, took Lester's sign, wound up, and fired. Ashburn, finally aware of the strategy that was being employed, was looking at the curveball all the way. He was not going to get beaten the same way again. He would lay off the breaking stuff until he got something hard out over the plate. He had all but settled the thought in his head when he saw that the ball was not tumbling toward him the way all of the previous breaking balls had. This was a straight, flat trajectory, indicative of a fastball. Even better. He wouldn't have to wait. He would spoil the change in plans, the stratagem intended to take him by surprise. This was the last thought in his head before he loaded his hands, grit his teeth, and swung mightily.

The bat, which whipped through the hitting zone, caught nothing but air as the ball took an unexpected dive into Lester's glove, which had been hovering patiently just above the dirt. Once the ball was past him, Ashburn's shoulders sagged, his head hung, and his legs bowed some. He dragged himself back to the dugout, muttering something about changeups and loaded balls. He was livid, but nobody could hear him because, following the umpire's call of "strike three," the crowd erupted in thunderous applause and the collective recitation of *Mickey! Mickey! Mickey!* It was the perfect start to the game.

As the innings wore on, the contest resembled more of a tennis match than a baseball game. Mickey and Phillies' starter Bob Miller traded zeroes for the first three innings, each of them cruising through the opposing lineup in perfect fashion. It made for a quick start and had inadvertently subdued the once boisterous legion of Braves worshippers who, despite their vocal support and appreciation of Mickey's efforts, seemed now to be waiting patiently for their team to break out on top.

"Not much happening so far, huh?" Molly said. "Seems sort of strange."

"Yes, I know what you mean," Jolene said. "I've seen every game, and this isn't usually how it goes."

They both labored a bit beneath the veil of awkwardness that hung over them.

"Well, at least Mickey is doing really well," Jolene finally said. She was fiddling nervously with the keys in her pocket as she spoke. "He really is something."

"He *is* something," Molly said. "Something very special. It's important you know and understand that, Jolene."

Both of Jolene's hands grew still. A wave of anxiety washed over her. "Look, Mrs. Tussler, I understand completely where you're coming from. I do. But you have to believe that I care about Mickey. I do. I know all about some of what's happened to him and I would never do anything like that. Or hurt him. You don't know me very well yet, but the truth is that Mickey and me are a lot alike."

Molly smiled and placed her hand on Jolene's knee.

"I know, dear. Arthur has told me all about you," she said. "Thank you for being his friend and for looking out for him. It's just that— well, he's not easy, Jolene. It has been a struggle with him. I know you understand that Mickey is not like the other guys you might know. I just think you should know what you're getting into here."

Jolene hesitated, considering the implications of such a statement. "That's just it, Mrs. Tussler. That's *why* I feel the way I do about Mickey. *Because* he's not like those other guys. I knew it the second I met him."

Molly was pleased. She felt that Jolene was sincere. It eased her mind considerably and made her comfortable to the point of almost sharing some stories of her son's life, when Lester, leading off the bottom of the fourth inning, drove a 1–2 slider over the left field wall to put the Braves on top 1–0. The eruption in the stands made it impossible to do anything except revel in the comfort of a Braves' lead.

But the jubilation did not last long. The Phillies answered right back with a tally of their own, manufactured by a walk, a single, and two sacrifice fly balls. The seesaw battle continued for the rest of the game, with the teams changing leads on four different occasions. The last one came when the Braves tied the score at 6–6 in the home half of the eighth after Sam Jethroe's suicide squeeze bunt scored Earl Torgeson, just when it was beginning to look like the hometown heroes were going to fall just a little short.

The euphoria created by the turn of events spilled into the ninth and final frame and then into extra innings as well, where the mirth and merriment that had flowed suddenly converted into heart-pounding anxiety at the thought of just how tenuous the future really was.

Fortune could be decided by one bad bounce or a few inches one way or another. They all knew how fickle the game could be. All of it could disappear in a heartbeat. All of it, just like that. Hopes, dreams, and this incredible run they had all been enjoying. Up in smoke. It gave pause for thought. All forty-five thousand minds were joined by this one horrible thought—the end of the season would bring with it not only the usual emptiness that accompanies the season's end but the death of the vision to which they were all wedded—a date with the mighty New York Yankees in the Fall Classic.

The anxiety-riddled spectators breathed a little easier when Murph sent Mickey out for the top of the tenth. Even though the Phillies had managed to scratch out five runs against Boston's rookie sensation, all but one were of the unearned variety. Mickey had been sharp all night, still had good stuff, and appeared to be just as strong—if not stronger—as he was at game's start.

Murph had struggled a little over sending Mickey out again, simply because the young man had never pitched this far into a game before and certainly not one of this magnitude, but the concern left his manner instantly when Mickey disposed of Del Ennis with easy fashion, fanning him on a 1-2 fastball that exploded in Lester's glove. The crowd was delighted, roaring its approval with an impassioned homage to its favorite player.

*Mickey! Mickey! Mickey!*

The energy inside the Bee Hive increased more and more with every pitch Mickey threw. Every strike recorded was like a magic carpet, transporting everyone in the building closer and closer to baseball's promised land. It was pandemonium. When the final strike of the inning was thrown, and the Braves hustled off the field and prepared to take what everyone hoped was their final at bat, all in Braves nation were on their feet, chanting and screaming in a frenetic attempt to will the team to victory.

Bob Miller began the bottom of the tenth inning for the Phillies. He had not been as sharp as Mickey, but had been helped out by some stellar defense behind him and a couple of fortuitous bounces and calls by the umpiring crew. He had also been largely unaffected by the raucous atmosphere that seemed to deepen as the night wore on. He was still okay as he prepared to face Buddy Ozmore to begin the first extra frame, but after he bounced the first pitch in front of home plate and missed again in the dirt with his second delivery, Miller began to unravel. All at once he felt sick and swallowed. The despair was palpable. Everyone in the Braves dugout saw it. Every fan saw it. Everyone—even the two pigeons that had come to rest atop the screen behind home plate—saw it. Eddie Sawyer was watching too. And he had seen enough.

"Time," he called. Then he began that long walk out to the mound, his eyes fixed to the ground the entire time. It was only when he reached the mound that he picked up his head.

"Did a good job, Bobby," he said flatly. "Really. Pitched your heart out." Miller slumped. Then Sawyer held out his open palm, and the hurler dropped the ball and limped off the field.

After a motion to the outfield, summoning reliever Kenny Johnson from the bullpen, Sawyer sighed. He stood with his hands on his hips, his feet busy moving some loose dirt around with his feet while he waited for Johnson to arrive. When he finally got there, the exchange was brief.

"Throw strikes, Kenny," he said handing him the ball. "Just throw strikes." Sawyer raised his eyebrows and tilted his head slightly to one side. Then he patted his catcher on the back and followed the same path back to the dugout.

Johnson, who had only just begun to get loose when Sawyer made the call and thus was visibly annoyed by the premature request, was equally unhappy about the 2-0 count he had inherited. His irritation was evident by his uncharacteristic lack of control—both of his first two offerings missed high, sending Ozmore to first base and an inconsolable Eddie Sawyer to the water cooler.

Sid Gordon was next for Boston. Johnson regrouped once Gordon stepped in, his wide, gleaming eyes stared at the catcher, who was hard at work flashing signs. Common sense dictated that Sid Gordon would be squaring around to bunt in order to advance Ozmore into scoring position. So with the most rudimentary of baseball logic as their guide, the new Phillies battery opted for a curveball to start off Gordon, knowing full well that a breaking pitch was a lot harder to lay down than a fastball.

With the crowd now fully immersed in a fit of delirium, Johnson came set. He checked Ozmore at first, refocused his ambition on Gordon and the catcher's glove, then broke off a beautiful curveball that initiated its flight at shoulder level but began a sharp descent as it entered the hitting zone. Gordon, who had squared around early and had both eyes fixed on the spinning ball, followed its path dutifully, determined to offer himself up as part of Murph's plan to build the winning run. He watched it all the way in, and just as it was about to cross the plate and touch down softly in the catcher's glove, he dropped the bat head and caught it on point, deadening the pitch so that it rolled quietly and with purpose up the third baseline. Johnson, the catcher, and the third baseman all converged on the ball, but it was Johnson who fielded it, turned, and fired to first base, nipping Gordon by an eyelash. The athletic play resulted in the inning's first out, but it was of small consequence; the mission had been accomplished—Ozmore was standing on second base clapping his hands and calling to the bench for someone to drive him home.

Connie Ryan would be the first one to take a shot at fulfilling Ozmore's request. He came to the plate, serenaded by thunderous applause and the rhythmic chant of *Connie! Connie! Connie!* His adrenaline surged with each blast of his name. He had been given an opportunity of a lifetime, the kind of moment that every little boy dreams of while playing pick-up games with his friends. One hit— just one hit could send the Braves and their fans to the World Series. And now there he was, determined to do just that.

Johnson, however, seemed unfazed by the implication of the moment. He felt only a tiny pinprick of anxiety—not enough to make any real difference in his performance—and even that subsided when he considered that he had an open base to work with. He was a seasoned veteran, one who had managed to extricate himself from similar jams many times before. This was no different. He had the upper hand for sure. Ryan would have to hit his pitch.

To the casual observer, Ryan appeared to be sporting the same equanimity. Perhaps it was because he, too, knew that Johnson was not obligated to throw him anything good to hit. So he dug in the way he always did, loaded his hands in the hitting position, and waited patiently for Johnson to initiate the dance.

But Ryan's icy veneer belied the storm raging inside of him. His heart was rioting, pounding against the walls of his chest so violently that he could no longer hear the hoots and hollers from the crowd. His blood bubbled and burned, passing under his skin like a rush of lava. The sudden change in temperature made him sweat beneath his flannels. It cooked his thoughts as well. What if Johnson did challenge him? Crossed him up and decided to go right after him. Would he be up to the task? Would he be ready? The uncertainty was killing him. He thought about calling time, about stepping out to regroup, but he felt paralyzed and before the words could pass his lips, Johnson had reared back and fired.

The ball approached him as if it had been thrown in a wind tunnel. It was a fastball but he saw it as if it were traveling at half its speed. Somehow it appeared larger, too. His eyes widened as it came closer and closer, and for a split second disbelief sullied the vision. It had to be a mistake. How could Johnson leave such a fat pitch over the center of the plate? He had to be dreaming. But illusion or not, Ryan was there to play. He started his hands, swung with great power and precision, and slammed the sweet spot of the ball with the barrel of his bat. The collision jolted him back into the game and had him entertaining visions of postgame adulation and glory.

The contact was perfect and sent the miscue screaming toward the left center field gap. Phillies' center fielder Richie Ashburn, who had been playing more shallow than normal in order to shorten any potential throw home, got on his horse instantly—turned and hightailed it toward the cavernous area for which the blast seemed destined. His cleats tore through the grass, leaving behind him a mini-cyclone of severed green blades.

Meanwhile, Ryan trotted up the first baseline, admiring his handiwork, waiting for the ball to touch down somewhere in the outfield and for the subsequent celebration. Ozmore was watching, too, suspended somewhere between second and third base, just waiting for his cue to jog the one hundred eighty feet, carrying with him the game-winning run and Boston's ticket of admission to the greatest show on Earth.

Ashburn, however, had other ideas. His legs pumped like two pistons, carrying him closer and closer to Ryan's blast until he was at last close enough to leap, glove extended, and snare what should have been the final blow in what many were already calling a game for the ages. The improbable catch deflated the forty-five thousand strong that had already begun celebrating and sent Ryan into an unhinged fit that included throwing his hat and cursing the heavens and all that lay beneath. The only person in the stadium who managed to parlay something positive from the disappointment was Ozmore, who, despite the unforeseen turn of events, had gone back to the second base bag and tagged up so that he stood ninety feet closer to home plate.

When the dust had finally settled and the reality of what had just transpired had sunk in, there was a discernible change in the Bee Hive. It was more than just the momentum shift that occurred the instant Ashburn snatched his team from a crushing defeat. There was something ominous in the air now—noxious, invisible fumes that floated on the winds that had suddenly shifted course. The Braves were still in a position to steal a victory, but with two outs and their best opportunity now just a painful memory, all anyone who bled for Boston could muster was a strained optimism when Sam Jethroe stepped in to hit.

Jethroe had only one thing on his mind—put the ball in play. Ozmore was just ninety feet away. Ninety feet. All that was needed was contact. That winning run could score on a hit or a bad bounce or a miscue by one of the Phillies' fielders. "Put it in play," Murph always said, "and good things will happen." It was Murph's mantra that had now become Jethroe's sole reason for existence.

Johnson was entertaining his own thoughts. He was just one out away from getting his team off the field and in a position to go back on the offensive. His focus was sharp and pointed and resulted in a fastball that painted the outside corner for a called strike one. Jethroe bristled at the call and stepped out to demonstrate more clearly his protest. The crowd voiced its displeasure as well, raining down torrents of boos over the umpire's poor judgment. Murph, who couldn't really see from his angle, took his cue from the others and joined in the emotional disparagement.

"Don't take the bat out of our hands now!" he called. "Jesus. You missed that one. Come on now! You've been here the whole game. Let's not fall asleep now."

The umpire glanced over at the Braves' dugout, but said nothing. It was so loud inside the stadium that nobody was even sure what he actually heard. But it appeared that the man calling balls and strikes had all at once developed a bad case of rabbit ears, for the next two calls went the Braves' way—something that had Sawyer on the top step of his dugout screaming bloody murder.

"Are you kiddin' me!" he bawled. "*You* call the game, not *them*! Shit, grow a set behind there!"

The umpire turned his head in Sawyer's direction, paused momentarily to let the Phillies' skipper know that he did not appreciate his commentary, then turned back to face front, pointed to the mound, and called for play to resume. Johnson, who felt as though he had been squeezed on the last two pitches, took his time rubbing up the baseball before getting back on the rubber. Then he checked Ozmore at third, took his sign, came set, and fired a four-seam fastball that rode up on Jethroe at the last second so that all he could be was fouled—the ball out of play. He would do the same thing with the next four pitches he saw, fighting to stay alive until he could get something he could handle.

Johnson, feeling frustrated and a bit irritated by the escalating noise that had come about due to Jethroe's at bat at this most critical juncture in the game, decided to alter his approach. Five consecutive fastballs had produced five consecutive foul balls, so it was time to toss in a wrinkle. It was actually the perfect time. He knew that Jethroe would be wondering just how many more fastballs he would throw, but without any real way of knowing, the seed of doubt would be enough to catch him off guard.

So when Phillies' backstop Andy Seminick put down one finger, Johnson shook him off. Seminick repeated the request, this time altering the location, but Johnson shook his head again. Feeling certain that Jethroe would not be expecting another fastball, Seminick tried a third time, showing just one finger, but Johnson would not agree. He shook again, his eyes hardened by the frustration he was battling and only softened when Seminick capitulated reluctantly and flashed an extra finger. Johnson nodded. Curveball it would be.

But the hype was short-lived. The second he released the ball, he knew it was off. His arm lagged behind a bit and his left foot turned to one side when he landed. The ball spun helplessly like a crippled 'copter, destined to crash into the dirt in front of home plate. Jethroe remained still and held his swing, but Seminick was in pure panic mode, lurching forward with arms and legs extended in a desperate attempt to smother the wild pitch. He dropped to both knees, plugged the hole between his legs with his glove, and squared himself to the ball. His back, which had been slightly curved, was now perfectly straight. Then, behaving more like a hockey goalie than a catcher, Seminick leaned into the ball and extended his chest while rolling his shoulders forward. The errant toss struck the dirt first, glanced off his right shoulder, and kicked off to the side. Seminick was like a boxer who had just absorbed a blow to the jaw. He was dazed and confused, and for a second or two could not locate the ball.

Jethroe, who had taken the customary lead with the delivery, kept his eye on the ball the entire time and broke from third base instantly. He put his head down and ran, ran with the urgency of one whose very life depended on the safe completion of his course. He was efficient and swift, eating up the dirt with every step he took. He was moving so deftly that it appeared to most as though he were running on the air just above the ground.

239

Seminick, in his frantic attempt to locate the ball, could not see him coming but could hear the desperate cries of Johnson, who had run to cover the plate, and a few of the others who were pointing at the ball and imploring him to grab and toss it before it was too late. It was only when the harried catcher had actually retrieved the ball and looked up to make the desperate throw to Johnson that he saw Jethroe, now only steps away from safety.

The throw was rushed and executed from his knees, but Seminick managed to deliver a perfect pitch to Johnson, who caught the ball and swung his glove across the plate all in one motion. The sweeping tag clipped the sliding Jethroe on the left cleat, prompting the crowd to gasp in unison as the umpire made a fist and threw it forward in a punching motion. An ominous stillness fell across the entire ballpark, a death-like silence that suffocated everything in its wake until the dust cleared just enough to reveal the aftermath of the development. There was Johnson, head hung, glove empty. Not too far from him lay the ball, whose sudden escape from its leather tomb engendered an emphatic reversal of the umpire's call.

"Safe! Safe! Safe!" he called, arms outstretched on either side.

The stands erupted, the walls overrun by an inexorable flow of fans that spilled out onto the field toward their hometown heroes—heroes who had also been swept away by the reversal of fortune, storming the area around home plate to join Jethroe in the impromptu celebration. The delightful melee went on for several minutes, a fevered intimacy that saw strangers and ballplayers and their fans joined in the perfect ending to an incredible season. And when it was all said and done and everyone who had witnessed the breathless excitement that transpired that evening returned to the practical sensibility of their everyday lives, there was still one thought that remained foremost in all of their minds: Murph and his Braves were going to the World Series.

# FALL CLASSIC

The early October sun shone like a gold coin in a pale blue, cloudless sky. It had only been a few hours since Murph's finest moment, and as he stood by the window gazing out at a city that was just now resting from the previous night's merriment, his own weariness had him briefly wondering with some degree of panic whether he had only dreamed about the events that had his imagination all aglow. But before his anxiety had time to settle in, Molly put her hand on his shoulder and made it all real once again.

"Hey there, manager of the year," she said, slipping her arms around his waist. "Too excited to sleep?"

Murph closed his eyes and filled his lungs with the cool morning air slipping through the window.

"I don't know about manager of the year," he said, turning to face her. "But excited? Yeah, I'd say that covers it. Oh, and maybe throw a little scared to death in there as well."

"Scared? Of what? Isn't this what you've waited for your whole life? Isn't that what you've always said?"

He laughed. "Yes, of course. Of course it is. But that's just it. It's been a lifetime for me, Molly. An entire lifetime. And now? Well, now it's here."

"So?"

"So, now that it *is* here, I'm a little worried. I may never get back. This is my chance. So, I want to do this right. It's a one-shot deal.

And when you have a one-shot deal, that shot had better be a good one."

She glanced down a moment, her eyes caught momentarily in the play of the shadows on the floor.

"Look, Arthur, you're here. It's the World Series. Only two managers can say that. And you're one of them. And in a few hours, you will be sitting at a press conference, and everyone will want to talk to you—to tell you how great the season was and to learn your thoughts about the next few days. Just enjoy it. Be in the moment. It's wonderful. And win or lose, it will always be wonderful."

He nodded, but all Murph understood at the moment was that Molly's words, though heartfelt, expressed a reality that he could only wish were true.

"Yeah, I just hope it all plays out okay," he said. "Not only for me, but for the guys, too. And Mickey. I hadn't even really considered that piece of it until now. Christ, this may be a lot for the kid to handle. I'm glad that you're here. You know, for support and all."

She smiled. "Well, I have to say, I had some misgivings about Mickey's world here. I mean, all of the new people he has met. I think you know what I'm talking about. But I have to be fair. It seems like Mickey has a lot of good people watching out for him. Supporting him and all. I think he'll be fine. But I'm glad, too, that I'm here. Just in case he needs me. Just in case *you* need me."

Murph laughed, put his arms around Molly and kissed her nose. "Well, the boy's sleeping now, but as soon as the circus starts, I think we are *both* going to need you."

Hours later, the media blitz that descended on both teams was not as bad as Murph had imagined, although he did find that his most private thoughts were drowned out by the flash of cameras and overzealous writers jockeying for position. They were all a little overwhelmed.

"So what's it like?" one reporter asked Murph. "You know, rookie manager making it all the way to the series in the very first year."

"It's exactly like you would imagine," he replied shortly, tiring of the same insipid questions.

"Tell us how you feel, Murph!" another shouted.

"How I feel?" he repeated. "It's the World Series. How do you think I feel? I'm happy. Really happy."

Murph stood for several minutes more. He was thrilled to be the object of their attention, but had grown tired and intolerant of what he felt were mindless inquiries and wanted out.

"I mean, did you ever think you'd be here, so soon?" the first reported persisted. "You're new here, and did it with a lot of other rookies and inexperienced players as well. How'd they handle all the pressure?"

Murph folded his arms, stood up, and paced a bit before finally erupting. "Look, I have a lot of work to do here. You want to know about my guys, why don't you ask for yourself?" he said, leaning his head toward Lester's locker. "I'm out."

"But, Murph, I just want to—"

"I'm done here, fellas. I am. Talk directly to the guys who you have questions about. And when you're done over here, you can always talk to some of our more experienced guys too," he continued, raising his eyebrows and pointing his finger in Spahn's direction as the Braves ace stood tall in front of his locker. Murph could tell his suggestions gave the reporter pause. The man lingered a moment, then started toward Lester once Murph was gone. He was several steps but altered his course abruptly when he found Mickey, who had suddenly come into view. This was by far a more compelling story.

"Hey, Mickey, hey, can we talk for a little while?" the zealous newsman asked. "How 'bout it?"

Mickey wrinkled his nose and looked right into the man's eyes. "We *are* talkin' mister, on account of you asking me if we can talk for a little while. Even though Mr. Murphy says that I really oughn't be talking to no more reporters after what happened last time."

The man laughed uncomfortably. "Uh, yeah, I guess so," he said, frowning a bit. "But still, I'd like to ask you some questions. You know, about the season and the series. That sort of stuff. Can I do that?"

Mickey nodded and sat down on the bench in front of his locker. His eyes wandered around the room, stopping here and there before finally settling on the stranger in a sports coat and fedora who was sitting in front of him.

"So," the reporter began. "You had quite a season up here. What has that been like?"

"Mickey had a good time here," he said.

The man smiled and scribbled something on his tiny pad.

"Good time," he repeated out loud. "Yes, I'm sure. Got it. So I guess you are used to all the talk about you being the favorite to win Rookie of the Year honors. That's gotta be nice too, huh?"

"Yes, Mickey thinks it's nice. Lester, he is good, too, mister. He is. Very good."

The man scribbled something else, his growing intrigue visible.

"Hey, that's funny, the way you do that."

"Do what, mister?" Mickey asked.

"You know, the whole 'Mickey' thing, like you're talking about someone else. It's different. Some may even say downright peculiar. But I like it."

Mickey stared at him. His eyes narrowed and focused, as if trying to make out some faint writing scrawled on a wall somewhere off in the distance.

"So, is Mickey excited about pitching in the World Series?"

"It is exciting," he answered. "My mama is here, to watch me play. Jolene, too. Lots of other people will come, too, to watch all of us play the Yankees. It will be loud."

"Loud is not the word son. This is the show of shows. And this city is the ultimate stage. I know you've been here before but not in the fall. How you liking New York this time around? Do any sightseeing?"

"Mickey doesn't really like the city," he said, biting the inside of his cheek. "Too many cars, and horns, and people. Don't like the way it smells neither. Smells like—"

"Hey, hold on there. Are you saying that you don't like New York? Wow. Go on. Do you hate the Yankees too?"

"Mickey didn't say that—"

"Is Boston so much better than New York, Mickey?' he persisted. "Can you tell us why?"

"I, Mickey, well, it's um, not so—"

"Do the other guys hate New York City, too, Mick? You know, Lester and Spahn? What have they said?"

The young man's head began to spin. He was thinking way too many things at once.

"Mickey likes the farm," he managed to say. He was rocking a bit now and looking left to right. "Trees, tall grass, and animals, sir. I reckon that—"

"How do you think the people of New York will feel about your comments on their city?"

Mickey tried to focus on just one thing in the room, but his eyes began darting from one spot to another, one face to another. His legs were starting to hurt and he could feel the blood drumming at his temples. He wanted to explain what a day on the farm was like and how he missed it sometimes, but all that passed over his lips was his tongue.

"New Yorkers don't take too kindly to folks, especially from Boston, knocking on their city. Rookie mistake there, my friend. Ain't smart, no, siree. But I tell you what. Sure makes for a good story. Anything else you want to add? Got my pencil all ready."

A swell of frustration washed over Mickey.

"No more talk!" he exploded. He was standing now and had grabbed the bag of clothes and equipment that was on the bench, holding it over his head. Lester, who had been busy fielding questions of his own, heard the commotion and rushed immediately to his friend's aid.

"No more!" Mickey continued, his eyes wild with fear.

"Hey, hey, it's okay, Mick," Lester said, stepping in between Mickey and his assailant. "What's the problem here?"

The reporter, who had been paralyzed by a true fear of his own, spoke freely now. "I'll tell you what the problem is," he complained. "Your friend here has got a few screws loose. I should have known after that other incident."

The commotion was enough to draw the attention of everyone in the room.

"Look, why don't you move on, mister, okay?" Lester asked. "There's plenty of guys here who will answer whatever question you ask. Just move on. Leave us be."

Murph, who had heard the disruption and rushed out to learn more, jumped in.

"Yeah, Lester's right," he added. "I know what you're doing. It's enough. You're done here. Just move along now." Then he put his arm around Mickey, closed his eyes, and sighed. "My fault, Mick," he said. "I should have known better. Never should have left you here by yourself. Just not thinking, I guess. No worries though. All is good. It's okay. From now on you stay with me."

The pageantry of baseball's ultimate showcase continued to unfold with pride, pomp, and circumstance until, at last, the time to begin play arrived. It was a brilliant fall afternoon in New York, with an October sky that housed a colony of white, fluffy puffs of cotton that appeared to be pressed by hand onto a bright, blue parchment. Crisp jets of air invigorated an already enthusiastic city, slipping though the streets and in between buildings, carrying with them fallen leaves, discarded papers, and a palpable excitement that had everyone bristling over what was about to transpire.

The pitching matchup for game one, which was touted more as a heavyweight prize fight, lived up to its billing, as Warren Spahn and Vic Raschi exchanged powerful blows inning after inning, treating the sold-out crowd to a pitching duel for the ages. Through six innings the score remained knotted at zero, with each pitcher allowing just two runners to reach base safely. The nail-biter had both managers, especially Murph, laboring over every move he made.

"Top seven," he groaned to Keely. "Seven damn innings and we still can't get anything going. Spahny's been dealing all game and we can't get nothing for him. We gotta make something happen here, don't you think?"

Keely shrugged. "Raschi's dealing too Murph. Ain't sure what else we can do."

"Well I've got to try something," Murph insisted, as the game moved into its latter stages. "I can't let this one get away."

With that, he got up on the top step of the dugout and made certain that Connie Ryan, who was due to lead off the inning, received his order to lay one down. Ryan had no difficulty with the sign and proceeded to push out the perfect bunt, steering Raschi's first pitch up the third base side, where it hugged the line until coming to rest at the feet of third baseman Bobby Brown, who quickly abandoned any hope of fielding the gem and instead just stood dumbfounded, praying for it to roll foul. The ball, however, remained true, giving the Braves the leadoff man on with nobody out. Murph's wheels were spinning even faster.

"If I let Marshall swing away, even with a hit-and-run, we run the risk of a double play, or being caught stealing if he fans. But he ain't the best bunter, which is what my gut is telling me to do. You know, build that run. What do you think Keels?"

Keely was just shaking his head. "I don't want to touch that one," the skittish coach admitted. "That's way too important a decision for me to carry around if it don't work out. I don't know. Could go either way. But it's your call. You're the boss, Murph. Just go with your gut."

His gut was killing him, filled with bile of uncertainty and potential failure, but it was also pushing him in the direction of station-to-station run building. So, once again, he ordered a bunt.

Marshall, who had very little experience sacrificing and even less confidence that he could get the job done, sagged a little after receiving the sign from the third base coach's box. Murph read the body language immediately.

"Come on now, Marsh!" he shouted. "Nobody better than you. Help us out here. We need you in there!"

Marshall heard the desperate plea, but it did little to assuage his concern. He stepped in the box, took a few perfunctory practice swings, then readied himself for the pitch. The minute Raschi came set at his belt, Marshall squared around, setting off a frenzy that saw both corner infielders charging while the middle two were busy rotating to cover the necessary bases. Raschi, pleased that the Braves were playing things so conservatively, laid the ball right over the plate, a made-to-order, room-service pitch that could not have been any easier to handle.

But Marshall was still struggling, thinking about how he would have much preferred to be swinging away. His mind was restless and his body followed suit. So when the ball got in on him, he lunged a bit, catching the ball on its lower half and sending it in the air, where it hovered a second or two before landing in the outstretched glove of Bobby Brown. The botched sacrifice was bad enough, but when Brown took the ball and fired it to first base, doubling off Ryan, the entire Braves' bench just hung their heads. Murph was far more animated.

"Damnit!" he boomed, firing his cap to the ground. He paced around, muttering a litany of expletives under his breath. They had squandered the best chance of the game. Gone, just like that. What made it worse was that he could not decide who he was more angry at. He was thinking now that he just should have gone hit-and-run and was torturing himself with second-guessing when Mickey unknowingly made things a little worse.

"It's okay, Murph," he said, putting his arm around the raging manager. "That was a good bunt, if it weren't popped in the air. And if Brown didn't catch it. He almost *didn't* catch it. Did you see how the ball just stuck in the top of his glove? Like a snow cone. Only snow cones aren't white like that, and they taste good. Like cherry or orange. Bunting's hard sometimes. Mickey tried it once or twice, but every time—"

Murph freed himself from the young man's hold and just walked away, leaving him to his scattered thoughts and ramblings.

The next two innings offered nothing for either side in way of offensive chances. Spahn and Raschi were still sharp and neither was showing any sign of faltering. This made the botched opportunity in the seventh even harder for Murph to swallow. He sat up against the dugout wall, shoulders slightly rounded and cap pulled down over his brow, watching as the hometown Yankees played the bottom of the ninth to a frenzied crowd just waiting for a walk-off celebration.

The partisan stands were particularly energized as their beloved Yanks were sending the heart of their order to the plate. Yogi Berra led things off. The Yankee backstop had been held in check all afternoon—no small task given Berra's legendary plate coverage and ability to handle balls out of the strike zone. Spahn and Lester had worked him over pretty well nonetheless, feeding him a steady diet of fastballs up and in and breaking pitches off the plate. They followed the same formula this time around, and while Berra managed to golf a curveball off his shoe tops and send it screaming on a line to the outfield, Tommy Holmes had him played perfectly and corralled the well-struck ball for the first out of the inning.

Murph breathed a little easier, but the next hurdle, which came in the form of Joltin' Joe DiMaggio, was even more daunting. The Yankee Clipper had hit the ball hard each of the first three times at bat with nothing to show for it. Spahn had been getting away with murder all afternoon; it was only a matter of time before his luck ran out. Everyone in the park knew it. It was the reason why the fans were now on their feet and why Murph could barely pick up his head to watch. It was also the cause for DiMaggio's cool demeanor and the flurry of signs that Lester was flashing to Spahn in a desperate attempt to retire the Yankee icon one more time.

The at bat began innocently enough, with Spahn getting a called strike one on a first-pitch slider. The second pitch, a two-seam fastball, missed away, as did the next fastball. The third consecutive heater caught more of the plate, and DiMaggio, who was a little out in front, offered at it, slashing a blistering foul ball into the seats behind third base. Both Spahn and Lester, realizing they had gotten away with a mistake, altered their plan once again. The 2-2 delivery was a slow, roundhouse curveball that had DiMaggio out on his front foot just enough so that all he could do with the pitch was pop it straight up. The second contact was made, Lester threw off his mask, turned around, looked up to the sky, and waited for the ball to fall harmlessly into his open glove. And when it did just that, the Braves were two-thirds of the way toward escaping the most ruthless middle of the order in the entire league. The only challenge left to conquer was Johnny Mize.

Mize wasn't the most prolific of the Yankee sluggers, but his twenty-five-round trippers during the season certainly made him a formidable threat. He was a dead fastball hitter who could handle breaking stuff as well. He didn't command the same gravitas as Berra and DiMaggio, but everyone knew that he was dangerous and approached him accordingly.

Spahn started Mize off with a fastball that just nicked the outside edge of the plate.

"Strike one!" the umpire called.

The crowd, which had grown somewhat frustrated and impatient, booed loudly over what they felt was a clear injustice. Mize was unhappy as well, and demonstrated his displeasure by stepping out of the batter's box and taking an inordinately long time stretching and swinging before getting back in. Spahn, seeing that Mize was perturbed, took the opportunity to quick pitch the slugger. He pumped another fastball, a four-seam dart that seared the other half of the plate. Mize was not ready.

"Strike two!"

The umpire's call was true, but the crowd booed some more. Frustration had also gotten the best of Yankee manager Casey Stengel, who began screaming wildly something about glasses and Seeing Eye dogs. Mize, who was still angry about the first call, mumbled something under his breath as well. The only people in the ballpark who did not share in the Yankee protest were wearing red and navy. Some, like Murph, were even reveling a little in what certainly seemed to be a clear shift in karma.

That emotional shift had Spahn feeling good too. He was up 0–2 now and had Mize right where he wanted him. The catbird seat, he used to always say. Four chances to make the batter hit *his* pitch, not the one he was looking for. He thought at first that he'd play with Mize a little, maybe tempt him into fishing for something low and off the plate. That seemed to be his best bet. But his pitch count was climbing, and he was beginning to tire. As he stood on the mound, staring in at Lester's signs, he also considered that there was certainly no guarantee that this stalemate would end any time soon. And he definitely wanted to go the whole way. So when Lester put down two fingers, Spahn shook him off. Lester tried three fingers next, but Spahn rejected that too. It would have to be good old number one. He'd conserve whatever it was he had left in the tank and go right after Mize with a fastball.

Spahn's reasoning seemed faultless and would have worked out just as he planned had Mize not been thinking the very same thing. He was sitting dead-red all the way. And when Spahn left it out over the plate a hair more than he had intended, Mize took full advantage, crushing the mistake high and far into the lengthening afternoon shadows. The ball sped through the air as if it had been shot from a canon, climbing higher and higher until most who were wedded to its flight could no longer follow its path. It was only when the ball began its return to the earth, a lofty descent that would ultimately result in a crash-landing some fifty-five feet beyond the 399 marker on the left-center field wall, that it became visible once again — igniting a fevered celebration that saw Yankee players and their fans swarm the area around home plate. The reaction from Murph and the Braves was far more stoic. All of them stood around, catatonic, watching in punch-drunk disbelief as game one slipped through their hands.

Still reeling from the previous contest, the Braves came back the next day with one thing in mind — getting things even. Game two was the antithesis of the opening matchup. Johnny Sain and Whitey Ford hooked up for what most baseball pundits thought would be another pitcher's duel, but early offensive explosions on both sides that continued throughout the entire game proved otherwise. It was a classic seesaw battle, with plenty of extra base hits and a parade of runners crossing home plate. The result was a 13–9 Braves victory and a trip back to Boston with the series knotted at 1–1.

Murph and the others were happy to be home again. So was Mickey. There was still a lot of media hoopla surrounding the series, but somehow it all felt a little friendlier. Perhaps it was just being in familiar surroundings and having Molly and Jolene there. Maybe he was just getting used to it.

"Gee, the reporters sure were interested in you today, Mickey, huh?" Molly said. She smoothed his hair with her palm and smiled. "You were clearly their favorite."

"Well, of course he is," Jolene added, smiling. She grabbed his hand and squeezed gently. "He's the man of the hour. Tomorrow he takes the mound for an entire city. They love him and wouldn't want anyone else to have that ball when the game begins."

"Yes, this conference went much better than the one in New York," Murph said. "He did fine."

Mickey stood up a little straighter, as if eager for a better view, and joined the conversation. "Mickey don't have the ball yet, Jolene. Ain't 'til I'm getting ready that I get that."

They all laughed. Amid everything, Mickey was still just Mickey. They marveled at how far he had come since the days of tossing apples on the farm and chatted some more about this and that. Everyone was feeling good and reveling in the splendor of the moment. All except Murph, who was on the hot seat and feeling the flame.

"Okay, enough of the chitchat," he finally ordered. "Mickey and I have a game to prepare for."

The outpouring of love for Mickey was well represented the next day as well, as many of the sold-out crowd came to the Bee Hive as they had each of Mickey's previous starts, sporting placards and banners professing the undying affection for good old number eight. The homage took on a variety of looks, from the basic and simply stated LET'S GO, MICKEY! to declarative expressions of reverence like IN MICK WE TRUST, to one whimsically absurd request that read MARRY ME, MICKEY! The sea of praise was as much awe inspiring as it was fodder for some of the guys who just loved to bust chops.

"Hey, Spahny, how many marriage proposals did *you* get this year?" Ozmore teased. The Braves' ace rolled his eyes and snarled a little before offering the one-finger salute.

"Come on, Ozzy," Holmes said. "You know Spahny ain't the marrying kind. No, sir. That don't make a lick of difference to him. He's pissed off because before tonight he believed in only one god. Now he's having trouble swallowing the discovery that it ain't him."

Some of the other guys laughed and offered a comment or two of their own, but the matters at hand were pressing, and before long they were working the field in front of a packed house full of rabid Bean Town devotees who had been starving for some postseason home cooking.

Mickey's emergence onto the field and subsequent ascension to the mound was steeped in pure enchantment; the entire crowd rose in unison the second they saw him, waving hats and towels and anything else they could grab, all while calling out his name with unconstrained passion as he performed his pregame ritual. Even the sun, which had been fickle all day, seemed complicit in the ardent reverence, emerging in full force to bathe the strapping young man in golden hues. Each warm-up pitch he tossed became reminiscent of some ordained ritual sanctioned by a higher power.

Mickey appeared relatively unfazed by all the hoopla, delivering his warm-up tosses with little trouble. He was focused and ready to help his team grab the series lead. The only break in his concentration came right before the game's first pitch when his eye caught not only Molly and Jolene seated behind home plate but some other familiar faces as well. Pee Wee, Jimmy Llamas, and Woody Danvers all gave Mickey the thumbs-up sign as soon as they knew he had discovered them. He had not seen them in quite some time and was excited that they had made the trip from Milwaukee just to see him. Consequently, the first pitch of game three of the 1950 World Series had a little extra zip on it. So did the second and the third. In fact, all of Mickey's pitches that day possessed a little something extra. He was absolutely brilliant, reducing the potent Yankee attack to nary a whimper while at the same time igniting the hopes and imagination of an entire city that had now officially adopted him as its favorite. And when all the magic and revelry had abated, and the turnstiles at the exits had clicked for the final time that day, the Braves had a 2–1 lead in the best of seven showdown, with game four back at the Bee Hive the following afternoon.

Spahn and Raschi hooked up in game four for another battle that saw the Yankee righty get the better of things this time, moving the series back to New York all even at 2–2. Game five followed suit, with Johnny Sain outdueling Whitey Ford in a nail-biter that sent the Braves back to Boston with a 3–2 lead and a chance to be crowned champs in front of their fans.

Mickey took the ball in game six, and in doing so, had just about made the game's outcome a foregone conclusion in the minds of every Bostonian. But a series of defensive miscues by the Braves early on had the young phenom snakebitten. Sid Gordon let an easy pop up fall right in front of him, Connie Ryan booted a routine grounder, and Sam Jethroe and Tommy Holmes collided in the outfield while attempting to catch the same fly ball. The result was disastrous. All three defensive lapses handcuffed Mickey, who lasted only three innings. The home team never did recover, much to the roiling disappointment of everyone who had already awarded the World Series trophy to the boys in red and navy. It was a bitter pill to swallow, especially for Murph, who knew he still had one game left, but also knew, better than anyone, that one game could turn on a dime. Anything could happen.

# GAME SEVEN

The circus-like atmosphere surrounding game seven was like nothing anyone had ever seen. The Big Apple had never hosted an event quite like this before. From the Bowery to the garment district, and Times Square to the tiniest shops in Little Italy and Chinatown, the entire city was electrified by talk of the New York Yankees and the intoxicating anticipation of one game to decide the championship of the world.

It was Spahn versus Raschi for a third and final time. Both men had pitched extremely well all season, despite the 1–1 record that each of them brought to the deciding contest. Each was on top of his game; all of the baseball pundits were predicting a knock–down, drag-out event that would be the fitting end to one of the most spectacular Fall Classics ever played.

Play began in uneventful fashion, with both pitchers retiring the first six batters they faced on a combination of routine ground outs and lazy pop ups. It wasn't until the top of the third inning that something finally happened. Tommy Holmes worked out a 3–2 walk to become the first player to reach base safely. The two out, base on balls gave the Braves something to work with and the Yankees and their fans minor cause for concern. Both feelings were extinguished when Bob Elliot struck out looking, putting an end to the minor threat.

It took another two innings, but in the bottom of the home half of the fifth, the Yankees finally answered with a base runner of their own. Then another, and another. A single and back-to-back walks had loaded the bases with nobody out and put the home team in an excellent position to draw first blood.

The only thing working in Spahn and the Braves' favor was that the Yankees were at the bottom of their order. So with the bases drunk with the boys in pinstripes, Spahn went to work on Jerry Coleman.

Coleman wasn't in DiMaggio's or Berra's league, but he was no easy out. Spahn and Lester knew that he'd be looking for something to drive into the outfield, so their approach would have to be cautious and calculated—as much as it could be with no place to put him.

What Spahn really needed was a strikeout, or at least a pop up or force out at home. Then a tidy 6-4-3 double play and he'd be out of the jam and back on the bench warming his arm. Lester was thinking the same thing. As such, he began the sequence to Coleman with a curveball away. Coleman, certain that Spahn was going to try and get ahead with a fastball given the dire nature of the situation, waved at the pitch helplessly. Spahn had fooled him so badly that he decided to double up with another hook, this time dropping it in the zone for a called strike two.

Coleman's head was reeling and he began muttering to himself. Spahn smelled blood in the water and went right after him. A brush back fastball that pushed Coleman off the plate came next, setting up yet another breaking ball on the outer half. It was the perfect plan, until Coleman leaned out over the dish and tagged the ball just as it was about to dart out of the hitting zone. The ball zipped across the ground like a heat-seeking missile, burning up the grass and dirt as it streaked toward the hole between short and third. The well-struck blow seemed destined for left field until Buddy Kerr scampered to his right, snaring the ball in his web with a quick flash of his backhand. Then, in one motion, Kerr spun, fired a perfect strike to Elliot at second who caught the throw and pivoted seamlessly before firing it to first in order to nip Coleman and put an exclamation point on a stellar twin killing. It was truly a magnificent play all around and would have had everyone buzzing about the acrobatic exploits of both middle infielders—but the bottom line was sharp and sobering: while Kerr and Elliot were busy performing their magic, a run crossed the plate, giving the Yankees a 1–0 lead.

Raschi and the Bronx Bombers made that one run lead stand up until the top of the eighth, when Lester got a flat slider that he deposited over the center field wall to tie the game. It was only the Braves' third hit of the game, but the timely blast reinvigorated the visiting team and had them back in business.

The sudden surge carried over to the top half of the ninth. With the score still knotted at 1–1, Sam Jethroe led off the inning by topping a soft roller up the first base side that he beat out for an infield single. After Willard Marshall fouled out to Berra, Bob Elliot ripped a 0-1 changeup into right field for a clean single, placing runners on first and second with just one out.

Ozmore was next. He sent Raschi's first two pitches soaring high and far but a good ten feet to the wrong side of the foul pole in left field. Ozmore was all over Raschi. He was locked in and seeing the ball about as well as anyone could. The only thing off was his timing. Raschi knew it. He was getting tired and had lost something off his fastball. He wasn't beating anyone anymore. He knew he'd have to employ a stratagem, pull a string or something, just to get Ozmore out of his rhythm. Berra had the same thought, so when Ozmore got back in the box to take his next hack, Berra put down two fingers, then wiggled them in a tight circle. Raschi nodded. Slow curve. Yes, that was it. The perfect time to show it. If nothing else, it would give Ozmore something to think about. And maybe, just maybe, he would induce a ground ball and escape the mess unscathed.

Raschi got what he had wished for. Ozmore was not looking for a languid, looping bender and ended up rolling over on it, producing a sharp ground ball to third baseman Jerry Coleman. It was a tailor-made double play. Coleman saw it the second it left Ozmore's bat, watched it the whole way with the vision of scooping up the grounder, stepping on third and firing across the diamond to first to end the inning. But in his eagerness to begin the rally ending twin killing, he lifted his glove off the grass a second too early. The ball, which was just about to settle in the palm of Coleman's glove, squirted underneath instead and rolled into the outfield, eliciting a collective groan from the stands that could be heard throughout Manhattan. Coleman's blunder allowed Jethroe to race around from second base with a go-ahead run and set off a carnival of celebration on the Braves' side. The unrestrained jumping, backslaps, and clamorous laughter spilled out of the dugout and into the on-deck area, setting up a spirited welcoming committee for Jethroe, who crossed the plate full tilt before running right into the arms of several delirious teammates.

Spahn took the mound in the last half of the ninth with Jethroe's run in his back pocket; he also took with him a slightly burdensome reality that they were just three outs away from glory. All he had to do was retire Gene Woodling, Phil Rizzuto, and Yogi Berra, and the Braves would be crowned world champions. It was right there for the taking.

The partisan crowd, which was not about to abandon hope, was on its feet cheering as Woodling stepped to the plate. He adjusted his helmet, dug his right foot deep into the back portion of the batter's box, set his chin on his front shoulder, and prepared for Spahn's delivery.

The pitch sequence began with a fastball that missed up and in. Spahn shook his head and pounded his fist in his glove. The frustration continued to grow after the next pitch missed its mark as well. Spahn wasn't the only one feeling the pinch.

"Shit, Bobby," Murph complained to Keely. "He's struggling out there. Looks like he's spent. I don't know if he can finish this."

Keely shrugged. "Just watch him, Murph. But in the meantime, you'd better get someone up and ready. Just in case."

Murph sighed loudly. He did not plan on having to make a decision like this, and for a short time continued to balk at Keely's suggestion. He found himself, however, tapping a couple of his pitchers on the shoulder after Spahn missed two more times and lost Woodling.

The crowd was roaring now—evenly and deeply. Everyone sensed that opportunity was knocking, and they became even more unhinged when Rizzuto also reached safely on a base on balls. Spahn was out of gas.

"Time!" Murph called before emerging from the dugout to take that dreaded walk to the pitcher's mound. It was one of the worst parts of the job. He loathed the walk, but this one seemed longer and more arduous than any other he had taken before. His heart was beating feverishly and he was sweating through his uniform top.

"Okay, Spahny," he said when he arrived, extending his open hand. "You pitched your ass off. You did a great job. Really great."

Spahn's eyes hardened in disbelief. "Are you kidding me?" he growled. "Really? You're pulling me, now? In the damn last inning of game seven?"

"You're tired, Spahny," he said with discomfort, "and they got their big bats coming up. Let's not make this any harder than it has to be. I need the ball."

Spahn stood, hands on his hips, staring at Murph. "You want the ball, Murph?" he finally asked through clenched teeth.

Murph's eyes moved from Spahn's face to his open hand and back to Spahn. The irate pitcher looked to the heavens and shook his head.

"Here's your damned ball," he finally said, slamming it in Murph's palm. "Good luck."

Murph winced. All his blood rushed to his head and beat wildly behind his eyes as he motioned to the bullpen for Spahn's replacement. Here he was, for better or worse, the engineer of a decision that would define the rest of his baseball life. Lester, who had joined him on the mound and had noticed the angst plastered on his manager's face, felt compelled to say something to soften the uncomfortable silence.

"It's the right move, Murph," he offered. "Ain't nobody worth a lick can question it. Spahny was fried. No doubt."

All Murph could do was shake his head. "Yeah, well somebody always has something to say. You can bet on that. And if my decision to use—

"Mickey is the right choice, Murph," Lester interrupted. "He's rested, and he's our best chance. Makes perfect sense. I got him, don't you worry. I got him."

The two watched as Mickey made his way from the outfield to the pitcher's mound. He was jogging at a steady pace, and his hat was pulled down over his brow. His gait was calculated and deliberate, as if he were counting his steps, and his eyes were set dead ahead.

His arrival, which seemed to take forever, raised more than a few eyebrows. There was also a discernible buzzing coming from the stands, as thousands of mouths were simultaneously wrestling with what was unfolding before them. Nobody had expected this. Mickey's appearance also signaled the end of Murph's visit. It was time to return to the dugout and await the outcome of the bold move he had just made. But before the beleaguered manager took his leave, he placed his hand on Mickey's shoulder and shared one final thought.

"You're the best, Mick," he said. "Apples in a barrel. That's all it is."

Then he walked off, leaving his young hurler to navigate a jam of epic proportions with only Lester for guidance.

"Hey, it's you and me, Mick," Lester said, pulling down his mask. "We will get this done. Just listen to me."

Mickey's first test was Berra. The Yankee catcher had faired pretty well against Mickey in previous at bats. The matchup just worked for him. He was a tough one for sure, and in the present circumstance, with no margin for error, his waving of the bat assumed a far more menacing aura.

Lester's approach was taught by that aura. Berra was a free swinger, and there was no doubt he'd be looking to strike early. Lester could sense it, so he put down two fingers and set up on the outer half of the plate, glove hovering just above the dirt. Mickey took the sign, came set, and broke off a tightly wrapped hammer that started at Berra's shoulders before taking a nosedive into Lester's glove. All the Yankee slugger could do was waive feebly at the pitch.

Mickey's next pitch was a four-seam fastball on the inner half of the plate that flat out beat Berra. He swung mightily, but all he got was air. Down 0–2 now, Berra decided to take a more defensive posture, shortening up on the bat in such a way as to allow him to serve the ball somewhere in play. It was the prudent thing to do, and under normal circumstances it would have resulted in the intended results, but on this night, at that moment, Mickey's fastball was just too much for Berra. It was as if the ball were no longer just a ball but a fiery orb that had just blistered its way through the earth's atmosphere en route to the batter, who had only just begun his swing when he heard the loud thump behind him and the umpire's call of "strike three, you're out." The crowd, which had been previously embroiled in frenzied cheering that threatened to bring down the house, fell silent for the moment. Berra just shook his head incredulously and walked back to the dugout.

The stadium stupor lasted for a beat or two, then lifted when Joltin' Joe DiMaggio strode to the plate. With the Yankees down by only a run and their best hitter stepping in, thoughts of a game-tying hit or perhaps even a game-winning blow danced through the heads of everyone who was standing and screaming DiMaggio's name.

Mickey was unmoved by the commotion. Amid the swirling mass of faces in the crowd he found Molly and Jolene, seated with some of the other members of the Braves' family. He didn't smile, but seeing them made him feel safe enough to continue.

The spirits of the Yankee faithful were buoyed by what they felt was a most favorable matchup, but the showdown with DiMaggio did not last long enough to allow for anything more than bitter disappointment when the baseball idol drove Mickey's first pitch high and far, only to see Tommy Holmes track it down and record the put out in front of the wall in right center field.

The second out of the inning was a devastating blow to the Yankee effort, although both runners did manage to move up ninety feet after tagging up. Now the home team stood on the precipice of victory, just one hit away from bringing home the crown in dramatic, walk-off fashion. And they had one of their best hitters, Johnny Mize, ready to play the role of hero.

Murph, however, had other ideas. The savvy base running of Woodling and Rizzuto had placed the Yankees in a position to win, but at the same time left first base open and provided Murph with the ability to bypass Mize and take his chances with Billy Johnson, who had just appeared in the on-deck circle to bat for Coleman. It didn't take long for the decision to be made.

"We're putting him on, right, Murph?" Keely asked.

"Not even a question," Murph replied, holding up four fingers to Lester. "That's an easy one."

The intentional pass to Mize did not sit well with the crowd, who booed loudly as they watched one of their best hitters stand helplessly while Mickey issued four straight balls. The calculated move loaded the bases for the Yankees, but gave Mickey and the Braves a far more favorable matchup; Johnson was not the hitter that Mize was and had several weaknesses that could be exploited.

The obvious advantage did little, however, to assuage Murph's concern. He stood in the corner of the dugout, his hands together like a steeple covering his nose. He could barely watch. The rest of the Braves bench did not share Murph's reservations; they could not take their eyes off the action. They stood together, arm in arm, waiting for the signal to charge the field and join the celebratory dog pile in front of the pitcher's mound.

Mickey and Lester started Johnson off with a fastball that just missed the inside corner. The second fastball missed in exactly the same spot. Murph stood now, eyes fully exposed, watching from his perch while hurling invectives at the man calling balls and strikes. The fading sunlight caught his face and revealed a discernible growth of dark stubble on his jaw and two severe lines on either side that danced wildly while he hollered.

"Those are right there, right there!" he bawled. "Open your damned eyes!"

The implication of loading the bases loomed larger; Murph was inconsolable and paced back and forth muttering about something Matheson had told him once about fortune being a fickle shrew—until Mickey found the zone with his next pitch. Then Murph was back and flirting again with visions of baseball ecstasy. His caved-in expression of concern softened even more when Mickey threw the next pitch right past Johnson. Now they were one strike away. One strike.

The air in Yankee stadium grew noticeably still as Mickey leaned forward to get his sign from Lester. The young man's eyes wandered briefly, moving back and forth between Lester's flashing fingers and the kaleidoscope of faces behind home plate. He was wondering why so many he saw appeared stricken by fear—blinding, paralyzing fear. He recognized the look; he had seen it so many times before. It was Molly's—the one she used to wear whenever Clarence would come home. He had come to understand why that was and often sported the same countenance himself for the same reason. But this was a game—just a game. Nobody was going to get hurt. It didn't matter whether he threw a fastball or a curveball or changeup. It was still just a baseball game. So why all the drama? It was the final thought he had in his head when he released the 2-2 pitch.

The ball left Mickey's hand so effortlessly that it appeared as though it were being pulled by some invisible string toward its intended destination. It was the hardest pitch he had thrown all day. It whizzed through the air like a cruise missile, speeding with great purpose and wonderful urgency. Its flight was awe inspiring, and depending on from where it was being viewed and by whom, invoked glorious anticipation or fearful disappointment. But every eye, regardless of personal investment, was fixed on that ball.

And when it finally came to rest, with a lusty thud that refused to be muffled by the thick padding sealed inside hand-stitched leather, time stood still for a moment. There were no movements, no sounds. Just the silent processing of life and its equivocal meaning, which was ultimately shattered by the shrill cry that brought everyone back.

"Strike three!"

The crowd of spectators was struck dumb and could only watch in suffering silence as their Yankees stood around defeated, while the boys from Boston danced about wildly on the infield grass, celebrating what was undeniably the sweetest of endings to a storybook season. And in the center of it all was Mickey, hoisted above the merriment by Lester, Ozmore, and Gordon. His hands were raised to the heavens and his eyes were affixed to that familiar area behind home plate, where he managed to see through all the craziness two smiles that mirrored the luster of his own. "Champs!" he kept saying."Champs! Champs! Champs!"

Molly viewed the whole scene through watery eyes. Her blood was rushing and every part of her body was on fire. Jolene was swept away by the euphoria as well and struggled to corral her surging emotions. She grabbed Molly's hand, squeezed tightly, and together the two jumped up and down, yelling to Mickey. The boy waved and laughed in the rapture of the moment. It was the first time in his life that he thought of nothing else—not Clarence or the farm or Lefty Rogers. There wasn't even the slightest hint of ruthless snickering behind his back. Not even the loss of Oscar entered his mind. It was all behind him, at least for the time being, as he continued to swim in the moment. Then, like a rolling wave that had finally reached the shore, Mickey and the entire team was gone, off to continue the celebration in more private fashion.

After the champagne showers and postgame interviews were complete, Murph sat in the shadows of the dimly lit visitors office with Molly, trying to process what had just occurred. For Murph, the happiness came with an element of fear, like a dream right before waking.

"Can you believe this, Molly?" he asked, shaking his head. "World Series champions?"

She smiled and took his hand in hers. "It really is something else. Just incredible."

"I know. Who would have ever imagined this? Any of it."

Molly sat there, harboring many thoughts. She decided, though, to confine her comments to only those she knew wouldn't mar the moment for him. He deserved at least this from her.

"It is certainly an accomplishment, Arthur," she said. "A very special one. You said yourself that so many guys go an entire career and never even get to a World Series, let alone win one. It has to feel amazing."

Murph was staring at all of the Yankee history displayed on the office walls. "It feels amazing because of *that*," he said, pointing at the pictures and pennants plastered all about the room. "Baseball is all about history and honoring past accomplishments. The game has a way of immortalizing men, you know? And while we don't have as much of a past as the pinstripes, I made it, Molly. I'm finally legit. I am part of Braves' history and will be remembered forever. There is something really great about that."

She smiled and reached for his other hand.

"Look, Molly, I know we have some talking to do."

"There's time for talking," she said. "But I do have things to do back home, and naturally you have to take care of business here. So at some point—"

"What are you saying?" he asked. "Maybe we should just talk about it now that it's out."

She hung her head and sighed. "Look, Arthur, I'm not going to tell you what to do." Her arms were folded and the smile she had previously worn had melted into a thin straight line. "You've accomplished something that is truly wonderful. It is. I am so proud of you and could not be happier that you have finally achieved what you have been chasing all these years. And I know that I should probably be more vocal about all you've done for Mickey—and for me. You gave me back my life, Arthur. You saved us. But you know where I've been and how far I've come."

"Molly, you cannot be serious here," he pleaded. "All that talk was *before* all this happened. *Before* the World Series. *Before* tonight. Tonight changes everything."

She sighed and tilted her head slightly to the side.

She looked beautiful, and he wanted to get up and rush to her, to throw his arms around her and tell her all the things she wanted to hear. But he couldn't.

So she nodded, brought two fingers to her lips and blew him a kiss, then left him sitting in his chair, hunched in the darkness like a broken branch.

# EPILOGUE

The dirt beneath the wheels of Murph's car rose and swirled like the breath of angry giants, lingering in the heavy morning air even after his blue and white Plymouth Road King had disappeared around the bend like a stealthy apparition. He had been driving all night with nothing for company but endless rows of cornstalks, a diamond-dotted sky, and the static coming from a car radio long past its prime. He rubbed his eyes. Truth was, he had not slept all that much in days and was really feeling it. He just wanted to get where he was going.

He had had a lot of time the past few days to think about things — what his life had become and where it was heading. The accolades and attention that were showered on him in the days following the victory were dreamlike. He had been basking in the glow and enjoying all of it. But he couldn't understand why the shine on that World Series trophy seemed a little duller than he had imagined. And why he was not feeling as satisfied as he had some days ago. It made him stop. It made him scared. What if this victory was just as much a defeat? After all this time, what else in the game could provide the same focus, the same drive? His epiphany was riddled with doubt but he was pretty certain that he knew what he needed to do. And now, having made that decision, he needed to just do it and make it official.

Up ahead, just around a bend in the road, stood the farmhouse and the familiar red silo hovering just above the arching oaks. He could still remember the first time he saw it and all that happened afterward. He shook his head and laughed when he thought about that day and everything he had said and done. And he still could not believe everything that had happened since.

His car rolled up quietly and came to rest right in front of the mailbox that was still weather-beaten and hanging in melancholy silence. It looked exactly the same, except for the faded letters that by this time had all but vanished. He got out of his car and began following the narrow, winding path that led him past a tiny field that still housed a small gathering of slanted gravestones overrun with cucumber vines and crabgrass.

As he walked toward the back of the property, he recalled the last time he had been there, and the way Clarence had carried on when he finally understood that Molly was really leaving him. Murph also remembered her smile as they were pulling away from the farm and how they talked the whole way back to Milwaukee about her new life and about all the things that they both wanted to do. The warm recollection made his visit now all the more emotional.

He paused momentarily. His eyes turned skyward, as if seeking some divine insight into what was about to happen. He could see only streaks of blue peeking through the dense cover of clouds, and a sun that was struggling to release its golden ribbons. He closed his eyes and, filled his lungs with the fresh morning air. He was ready now to do what needed to be done. Then he heard a sound that captivated him the same way it had the very first time he had heard it.

*Thud. Thud. Thud.*

The moment came with all the joy and pleasure of listening to a favorite song he had not heard in some time. The only thing different this time was the pleasant intermingling of voices, which he followed until he had discovered their source.

"Arthur, what are you doing here?" a soft voice asked.

He smiled wryly. "Well right now, I am having a most wonderful déjà vu," he said, pointing at Mickey and the row of apples he had on the ground in front of him.

"Oh yes, Mickey is just showing me his very cool apple trick. Before now, I had only heard about it."

Murph walked over to Mickey and put his arm around the young man. "That's right, Jolene. I forgot you never got the chance to see how all of this began. Pretty remarkable, wouldn't you say?"

"Seven apples so far, Mr. Murphy," Mickey said. "Mickey used to throw twenty-six for Oscar, on account of him eating a lot. But that ain't so now. Now I'm just showing Jolene how it works."

"Well I always enjoyed watching it," he said. "Definitely worth the trip here, that's for sure."

Jolene raised her eyebrows and made a funny face. "Now, are you saying that you drove all the way here from Boston just to watch Mickey throw apples into a barrel? The manager of the World Series Champion Braves, hanging out on a farm in Indiana, when he should be making plans for next season? You expect me to believe that?"

He tried to neutralize the tremor in his voice by looking away from her as he answered. "Well, maybe not *only* to see Mickey toss his apples," he said. "There may be a couple of other things here that pulled me in this direction."

Mickey continued firing the apples into the barrel while Murph and Jolene volleyed comments back and forth.

"Now what on earth would bring a big city, big league manager out to the sticks?" she asked, laughing. "Hell if I ain't even having a little difficulty getting used to all this country living."

"Ex–big city, big league manager," he announced.

Her mouth fell open. "What did you say?" Jolene asked, eyes wide with incredulity. "They fired you after winning the World Series?"

"Not exactly," he said, hurriedly as if it were the only way the words would actually pass his lips. "I resigned."

"You did what!" she said. "Come on, Arthur. You're kidding, right? Why on earth would you—"

"Mr. Murphy ain't gonna manage baseball no more?" Mickey asked, taking a brief break from his exhibition. "Mickey doesn't understand. You love baseball."

He did love baseball. It was all he ever had loved. Maybe it was because he had finally made it to the top of the mountain, or maybe he was just tired, but somehow, all he could think about the last couple of days were the losses—not the games he'd failed to win but those casualties that had come at the hands of one who had wedded himself to one vision. He could still see all three of them—women with whom he had begun relationships, only to see each one go up in flames because his devotion could not be divided. The last one had hurt the most.

He could still remember the cold shadow of doubt that fell over him the last time they had spoken.

"Arthur, I think we need to talk."

He never forgot those words or the year that followed. That incessant hunger he had and all the lonely meals that did little to fill him. He was plagued by the emptiness, his inability to satisfy those relentless pangs no matter how hard he tried. He thought he could short-circuit the longing, cut it off at its source by replacing it with something else. Baseball seemed like the logical choice. It was all he had. But even then he knew it was impossible to wrap his arms around a late-inning loss or an exciting come-from-behind victory. And now he thought he had finally realized something else. Baseball wasn't the answer to his longing—it was the cause, and had been all along. Baseball had brought him some of the most glorious moments of his life, but baseball was the reason why all he ever had was baseball. Now he stood, years later, on a piece of muddy farmland, glancing anxiously at his watch. It was almost nine and he had wanted to tell Molly the news long before then. It made his stomach burn.

"I do love baseball," he explained. "I've loved baseball more than anything my whole life. But not too long ago, a pretty lady who just so happens to live in that farmhouse over there mentioned to me that maybe, uh, it was time to love something else that way. So I've been, uh, thinking about it . . . a lot, and I'm pretty sure she may be right."

Jolene folded her arms and flashed a peculiar smile. "Um, Arthur," she said oddly. "Before you head up to the house, there's something you should know."

He was confused and suddenly alarmed. "What's the matter, Jolene? What's wrong?"

"Molly's not here," she said.

His whole face dropped. "Not here?" he repeated. "What do you mean? I don't understand. Where is she?"

Jolene's smile became more pronounced and gave way to some laughter that had Murph really scratching his head. "She's headed to Boston—probably just got there. Seems like the both of you had the same idea."

He closed his eyes and shook his head. Then he opened them, blinked and smiled. "Well isn't that something? I guess she didn't think I was ready for life on the farm."

Murph was reeling from his discovery. *She went to Boston*, he kept saying to himself. In that moment, he knew he had made the right decision. He was luckier than he realized. Vivid scenes from the past three years flashed through his mind. His life had really changed in such a short time. Mickey's too. He stood looking at the boy, almost unable to process the remarkable transformation.

"Hey, Mick, *you're* not thinking of coming back to the farm *too*, are you?" he asked. "I mean, you've just gotten started and have plenty of work to do still, kid."

Mickey grimaced and fired another apple into the barrel. "Heck no, Mr. Murphy. Mickey's heading back to Boston with Jolene. I'm a ballplayer now. You taught me that."

Murph nodded and smiled hard. "Yes, yes you are. Mickey Tussler is a ballplayer. And a darn good one at that. Maybe one of the best there ever was." Murph turned toward the farmhouse. Thoughts of the call he needed to make drummed inside his head. But before he took his first step in that direction, he bent down, picked up another apple, and placed it in Mickey's hand. "Yes," he repeated. "You are one helluva ballplayer, Mickey Tussler. The kind that legends are made of."

# AUTHOR BIO

Frank Nappi has taught high school English and Creative Writing for more than twenty-five years. His debut novel, *Echoes from the Infantry*, received national attention, including the Miliatry Writers Society of America's silver medal for outstanding fiction. His follow-up novel, *The Legend of Mickey Tussler*, garnered rave reviews as well, including a movie adaptation of the touching story, *A Mile in His Shoes*, starring Dean Cain and Luke Schroder. Frank continues to produce quality work, including *Sophomore Campaign*, the intriguing sequel to the much-heralded original story, and now the much-anticipated third installment of the critically acclaimed series, *Welcome to the Show*. Frank lives on Long Island with his wife, Julia, and their two sons, Nicholas and Anthony. For additional materials, please visit www.franknappi.com.